THE SILVER STRAND

CHARLEMAYNE REEVES

The Chronicles of Caelium Series:

The Timekeeper's Tale
The Silver Strand

Coming Soon:

The Open Door

CAELIUM
GROVE OF EIKS
NORTH FOREST
WEST MOUNTAINS
TIMEKEEPER'S COURT
WALL OF MIST
COURT OF MOUNTAIN FAIRIES
SEIKIE ISLES
COURT OF MERROWS

THE CHASM
HAIMA MOUNTAINS
TRAVELLER'S PASS
E PLAIN
COURT OF WARRIORS
MEALITA
OUTHERN SEA

For those who have loved and lost.
Take heart.
You will meet again.

1 Thessalonians 4:13–18

Hiraeth: (Welsh)
a homesickness tinged with grief and sadness, a deep longing,
especially for one's home.

THE TREATY OF HIRAETH
BY DECREE OF LORD DOLION

❀ *The selkie clan is hereby banished to the islands. Henceforth, the Selkie Isles shall be their residence.*

❀ *Merrows are forbidden to trespass on selkie lands without expressed permission from the councils and court rulers. Likewise, no selkie shall enter the Court of Merrows without the same expressed permission.*

❀ *It is hereby forbidden for a merrow man to look upon a selkie woman. He will avert his eyes in her presence, lest he risk his own skin.*

❀ *Courtship or intermarriage between clans is hereby forbidden, and likewise, no child borne of such a relationship may stand.*

These rules shall be enforced henceforth,
on penalty of death,
From this day,
Until the end.

Chapter 1

The strap of Elysia's shoe was hung in the lattice, again. She glared at it furiously, twisting it left and right. *Why* had she worn these shoes? The gold flats were her favorite, but she made a mental note to burn them as she turned her ankle a little further to the left. The strap slipped free, and she lifted her foot, grinning. But that was when she lost her grip.

Whoosh. She fell from the lattice of climbing vines beneath her high window and smacked the ground hard with her side. She bit her lip, stifling a groan. *Ouch.* She rolled to her belly, silently scanning the palace grounds. She had made a lot of noise with that fall, but luckily, no one was awake. It was just before sunrise, and the grounds were silent.

Quietly, she sat upright. She dusted her palms on her skirt, then held them out to examine them. They were scraped a bit where she had hit the dirt, but the wounds were shallow, and they would heal quickly. She stood slowly to her feet, assessing herself with each movement for further damage. Her side hurt a bit from catching her fall, but otherwise, she was fine.

She took one last look across the grounds, then crept down the left wall of the gardens towards the woods beyond. As she moved to the wall's far edge, she eyed the cluster of sandstone houses marking the edge of the village across the field to her right. The houses were mostly silent, but a candle was lit in the nearest window, and she tucked herself tightly against the wall as a woman passed the frame. She was carrying a large water pot on her hip, and Elysia waited until she stepped out her door and turned away to walk down the lane before she shot from her hiding place.

She only released her breath when she was safe in the cover of the trees. Quietly, she wove down the small path she had worn in the soft dirt, and soon, she was deep in the forest. The calming sounds of rushing water tickled her ears and early sunlight streamed between the dense tree branches, creating dancing patterns on the water as Elysia guided her small raft from its hiding place in the river's reeds. Once more, she scanned the wood for watchmen, then she stepped onto her raft and pushed out with her oar. At once, the river swept her into its current, and Elysia crouched flat on her belly, her head safely hidden below the bank as she allowed the river to guide her swiftly around the bend and out of sight.

It wasn't long until she was tugging her raft to shore. She tossed her shoes onto the rocky beach and scaled barefoot up the highest hill, moving to her favorite perch on her secret island. But the spot didn't bring her peace like it normally did.

Elysia sat down heavily, bracing her back against a tree and staring bleakly out over the water. The morning breeze blew in softly from the sea, feathering lightly across her face and stirring the tall grasses and wildflowers on the hillside below. The shimmering rays of the early sun warmed her bare arms, and she watched as they glittered on the surface of the water, creating a kaleidoscope of dancing light. White-breasted gulls flew low above the surf, calling out to one another. She watched as one swooped into the waves, catching a small fish in its beak. Then, the bird took flight, hounded by the group for a bite of his breakfast. She smiled flatly at the display, then lay her head back against the tree and crossed her arms over her chest, grimacing.

It was a beautiful day, but Elysia's heart was anything but light. She hugged her knees to her chest, burying her face. Usually, secreting herself away to the island soothed her spirit, but today, there was nothing that could soothe her. Nothing.

She sighed heavily, lifting her chin to rest on her knees. Ena would be frantic, once she caught wind of her absence. Soon, she would be visiting Elysia's rooms, ready to start the day. Elysia knew she couldn't stay much longer. There was so much to do before tonight. It wouldn't be fair to keep Ena waiting. She turned to glance up at the sun, creeping higher above her with each moment. She had stayed too long, already. As much as she needed the solitude of her secret island, she would have to go, soon.

Elysia had discovered the secret island two cycles ago, and since, it had become her favorite escape. Elysia was adventurous by nature. She loved exploring, and sneaking out of the palace to do so was not a new habit for her. There wasn't a single stone she hadn't uncovered on the Selkie Isles, but the uninhabited island just south of her home had been her greatest discovery of all.

The first time she had gone there, she had thought she was lost forever. The path through the river was twisting and treacherous, and she had been convinced she could never find her way home. Since then, she had visited so many times that she was certain she could find her way to the secret island and back with her eyes closed.

Fifty weaving steps down her worn path in the wood, the wide river flowed to the right, weaving eighteen oar strokes through the forest floor before passing to a fork. The left arm of the fork continued through the forest, spilling into a clear, smooth loch in the glen beyond. To the right, the river flowed beneath a rocky outcropping, its path hidden by the overhang of twisted vines and low tree branches.

It was Elysia's grandmother, Ríona, who had initially led her to the secret island. Ríona was fond of tales of adventure and misfortune, and as a child, Elysia had often listened to these from her place on the threadbare rug beneath her grandmother's cushioned seat. She had listened in rapture as her grandmother told of a wide river behind the palace woods, whose mouth led to a hidden paradise. As with most of her tales, the story came with a warning. She had insisted that Elysia avoid the river, which she called the Brook, for fear that her granddaughter would drown.

Elysia had nodded obediently, but she had struggled to keep her seat, longing to rush from the small sandstone house and find the Brook for herself. It hadn't been easy, but she had forced herself to be still, picking the edge of the rug as she listened with awe. Her grandmother's brown eyes had danced as she told how the Brook passed through the low opening of rock, where it wound through the base of a high cavern. Once hidden in the rock, the wide river collected itself into a slender, winding stream. "The stream appears gentle—shallow, even," her grandmother warned. "But the water beneath churns and swirls in a deadly series of spins, and its depths are immeasurable."

In the Histories Ríona recounted, many Selkies had attempted its passage, but most had drowned in the Brook's swirling depths. The Brook was particularly dangerous for land-dwelling sea folk, like Elysia's clan. At one time, the Selkies had dwelled beneath the sea, but since the exile, they had been land-locked, and as a result, their sea lungs were shallow and weak. This made survival in the Brook's dark waters almost impossible.

Despite her grandmother's warnings, curiosity got the best of Elysia, and one day, she braved the passage of the Brook on her own. For weeks before, she had fashioned a raft she deemed worthy of the treacherous journey. Excitement swirled in her belly at the thought of passing the Brook, but an equal measure of fear swirled just as strong. She had almost abandoned the idea, but her adventurous nature urged her on.

That first time, she had squeezed her eyes shut and buried her face on the floor of her raft as she passed through the caverns. The dark air inside had pressed heavily against her as she floated onto the narrowing stream. As the rushing waters quieted, she had sat as still as a stone, allowing the churning current to swirl her raft unchecked. It had bounced her left and right, and once, she had thought she would topple overboard, but at last, she made it safely through the cavern to the other side. There, the bright sun shone once again, and the soft sea had carried her the short distance to the secret island's stony shore.

Since that first passage, she had braved the Brook regularly. Often, she visited her secret island several times a week. It had become her place of peace and solitude, a much-needed escape from the pressures of court.

Elysia frowned as she rested her small chin on top of her knees. It was no surprise she needed an escape today. Her mother's expectations, no, the expectations of *everyone*, weighed heavily on her mind. Tonight was the Midsummer Ball. It was usually a favorite of Elysia's, but the schedule of events for this evening were a little different. Tonight, was Elysia's Presentation to the Selkie

Court, and with it, came the choice of her suitor. By the end of this evening, she would be betrothed. Elysia wrinkled her nose. Nothing could have displeased her more.

Her mother's words echoed in her mind: *You're overdue for Presentation, Elysia, by at least a full cycle. You simply must pick a suitor. I picked your father at 17 cycles, and every Selkie ruler before you have done so on the proper schedule. The council and I have been patient, but now, we expect you to make your decision.* Elysia rolled her eyes. At 18 cycles, picking a suitor could not have been further from her wishes.

For the last two cycles, she had been forced to attend each and every court event and council meeting. All this, on top of her lessons, which taught her the Histories and the ins and outs of becoming the court's next ruler. Though she did her best to please her mother and pay attention to the meetings and her lessons, sitting in a stuffy throne room on the Selkie Isles for the rest of her life was the least of her desires. Especially if she was sitting next to a mate that she had been forced to choose.

Elysia narrowed her eyes, peering out over the water. *No.* That just wouldn't do. She would rather live alone forever on her secret island than endure that.

Silently, she watched the sea lapping against the stony shore. The sun danced across the cresting waves, and secretly, *so secretly,* she longed for adventure beneath its depths. She pressed her lips together, looking away. That would never happen. She was land-locked, and soon, her fate would take an even worse turn.

Despite Elysia's best efforts to delay, her mother, Lady Malca, had *insisted* that her Presentation be tonight—at the Midsummer Ball. Traditionally, the Presentation of female selkie rulers and the accompanying selection of their mate occurred on the 17th cycle. By this standard, *and* her mother's, Elysia was already one cycle late. Even so, she didn't understand the rush. What did it matter? So what if it was tradition. Why did it have to happen now?

Elysia frowned. It was probably because the council, or *the Hounds*, as Elysia liked to call them, were biting at Lady Malca's heels for a chance to fling their sons at the next ruler of the Selkie throne, thus ensuring their connection to the power the position afforded. And no councilman had been more insistent than Lord Ciar. He had thrust his son Connor before Lady Malca's eyes on more than one occasion, and he'd recounted the benefits his son could afford the court ad nauseum.

Ciar was the wealthy and powerful owner of several of the island's mines, and his son was thus considered the most eligible suitor in the Selkie Islands. Everyone said so, even Ena. Connor was attractive enough with his dark hair and flashing black eyes, but Elysia bristled at the thought of being close to him. She thought of Connor's smug face and cringed. He thought he was so charming, but he couldn't have been more wrong. Charming he was not. If anything, Elysia thought him extremely arrogant.

Unfortunately, Connor appeared to be the forerunner in the game to woo her with his so-called *charms*. After the councils' complaints at the last meeting that Elysia was overdue to pick her suitor, her mother, whom she was certain had been encouraged by Lord Ciar, had made it clear that Connor was to be her choice. Tonight, when the sun dropped below the horizon, she would endure her Presentation, and she would be *forced* to choose Connor as her mate.

Elysia felt like she could vomit every time she thought about it, but her mother and the council were thrilled with the match. They were making a huge fuss. In fact, despite the talk of the islands' lowering resources, this Midsummer Ball was supposed to be the most opulent they'd had in cycles.

According to her mother, tonight, her life would begin. Elysia squeezed her hands into fists. It was more like tonight; her life would be over.

Connor certainly wouldn't have been her first choice. He wouldn't have even made the list. In fact, if it were left up to her, there wouldn't *be* a list, and she wouldn't be forced into any of this at all. Anger singed the back of her neck, and she stood abruptly. She kicked a small stone, watching as it sailed down the hill and skipped through the waves in a satisfying line. At a far distance, it bounced twice, then sank beneath the surface.

She narrowed her eyes at the spot, then marched down the hill, bending to grab another stone from the shoreline. "Grrraahhhh!" she screamed, hurling it into the water. She glared after the stone, imagining it smashing Connor's perfect nose as it dropped into the surf.

Elysia ground her teeth into a grin.

That felt good.

She scrambled to grab two more small rocks and toss them into the dark waves, grinning. Then she scooped up a handful, and then another. Over and over, she sailed fistfuls of stones into the sea, until her face and dress were spattered with silt and a small patch of wet mud remained on the shore at her feet.

The sun was rising higher. It beamed against the back of her dress. Sweat beaded on her back and brow, and she paused, her chest heaving. She glared at the waves, then brought her trembling hands in front of her face, examining her nails. Dirt caked the ends of her fingers, and two nails were broken. She grinned down at them and bent to scrub them into the dirt. Then she wiped them flat against her face, smudging her cheeks. *Ha.* What would Connor think now of his betrothed?

Her joyous display of defiance only lasted for a moment, then Connor's superior expression crept back into her mind. She grimaced at his smug grin and kicked at the lapping waves, sending a spray of water into the air.

Throwing stones was not enough, even if she had smushed Connor's nose in the process. She needed to let off more steam. Shielding her brow with her muddy hand, she peered up at the sun. It was late. Ena was probably already looking for her. She'd have to hurry.

She flicked her eyes to the sea, gazing at the inviting water.

Her body was itching for a swim. Quickly, she flung her shoes into a heap and peeled off her stockings. Though she knew no one was there, she still gave the shoreline a furtive scan, then she unbuttoned her cream-colored blouse and dropped her emerald skirt and underthings to the stony shore.

As she dove beneath the waves, the familiar tingle blazed from her toes, and her body transformed. Elysia grinned as she glided through the surf, slicing the water easily with her silvery tail. She angled her arms into a point and pumped her lower body powerfully, diving deep below the surface.

She flipped to her back when she reached the sea floor, pausing to stare up towards the sun. The world looked very different from the bottom of the sea, and for a moment, the problems awaiting her above seemed far away. She wished she could stay, hiding beneath the water, but in a moment, she needed air, and she pushed hard for the surface.

A deep inhale slid into her lungs as she broke above the waves, and a loud *whoop* slid off her tongue as she curved her body into a high arc. For a moment, Elysia felt like she was flying, and she soared through the open air before slicing a perfect dive back into the water. She giggled with pure delight, then gasping, she lay flat on the surface, allowing the smooth waves to lap over her skin. A mixture of heady emotions swirled through her chest, and she closed her eyes, smiling. As always, being in her sea form made her feel free. Joy bubbled in her center, and excitement coursed through her at the possibilities of the strange world beneath the waves. It was one she had never known, but even so, it was one she wished to.

But the feeling didn't last. Somewhere, deep within her, there was a niggle of shame. Her mother would have had a fit if she would have seen her. Everyone else would have, too. A Selkie woman was forbidden from showing her sea form outdoors, and though her secret island was nearly as private as her bedroom, Elysia was clearly breaking that rule.

After their exile, the Selkie people had become fearful of stepping into the waves. Over the long cycles, their fear had multiplied, until only the Guard went into the water. And they rarely did.

Even Elysia was hesitant. Though no one could see her here, she rarely allowed herself a swim in the Southern Sea. The thought made her equally angry and sad—angry that there was such a rule, and sad that she felt shame. And, too, there was sadness that her people had been exiled to the islands, in the first place.

She swished her arms, focusing on the feeling of the wide sea moving freely around her body. Then she held her breath and flipped backward, flicking her tail above the surf. The movement felt good. It released some of her tension and brought her back to the moment.

She allowed herself to float, again, grinning down at her shimmering tail. She ran her hands along the smooth, silver-y flesh that trailed up her thighs and followed it with her fingers as it wound up to meet her midsection. There, it melded with the flesh of her abdomen, then it crossed over her chest and wove down her upper arms before fading into fair skin above her elbows. She fanned her long, reddish-brown hair above her head, gazing up at the wispy clouds. It was freeing for her to oscillate between two forms, to imagine living in two worlds, so different from one another.

She often wondered about that, living in two worlds. Elysia had never seen more of the Southern Sea than what she could view from the shoreline of the islands. She closed her eyes and allowed herself to dream of the beautiful and enchanting secrets of the sea below. Although she had never known them, her ancestors had, many cycles ago. But those days were long past, and the secrets they had known lay hidden from her view. She wondered what it must have been like before the exile. What had they felt like when her people were truly free?

Long ago, the selkies and merrows had lived in harmony, enjoying the abundance of the sea as one court. They had been united under one banner—the Court of the Sea. Their rulers had shared the throne, and one council had governed the courts' members in peace and prosperity. The clans had worked together in all things and had shared the abundance of the sea with one another without fear or quarrel, and without the hateful Treaty of Hiraeth.

But since her father's death, things had changed. The Selkie Court now lived in exile. They didn't know abundance, at least, not like their clan used to.

Most Quarters, they did just fine, but sometimes, goods stretched thin, and her mother's face was pinched with worry, as were those of the council. Her grandmother had said that life had once been easy, but they'd had to work to survive since the exile, and the Selkie people were too proud to ask their Merrow neighbors for assistance.

Many cycles ago, Lord Dolion, the Court of Merrows' former ruler, had sold her father, Lord Ríonan, to the Court of Orm. In those days, Orm had been searching for Amloga to feed the Rotha-Am, or Wheel of Time, in his bitter quest to stop Time and assume control of all creation.

All created beings possessed some measure of Amloga—their Flame of Time, given to them by the Source. But in Timekeepers, like her father, the measure of Amloga was quite large. So, naturally, her father was seen as an essential piece in Orm's plan of destruction. His foul court had paid Lord Dolion a hefty price for the Selkie ruler before sacrificing him to the Rotha-Am at its fallen place.

After he led Lord Ríonan to his death at Orm's hands, Lord Dolion's heart had turned black. He had become blind with greed. He wanted the Selkie lands for his own, and so, he struck down the Selkie Court in their weakened state. While their people still grieved, Lord Dolion seized control of both courts. He exiled the Selkie clan from their home in the sea and sent them south, to two tiny islands. Then he drafted the Treaty of Hiraeth, forcing the clans to live under his harsh rules.

Her grandmother often recounted those horrid days in the Histories, but they had happened so long ago. Elysia had been so young when her father was captured by Merrow Forces. She could barely remember what her father looked like, let alone how things used to be. Like most of the clan, she had spent her life on the Selkie Isles. Their little islands were home.

Even in its harshness, the Treaty of Hiraeth was a way of life, and the days of peace between the courts were long past. After Lord Dolion seized control, he forced Lady Malca and the councils to sign the foul document, which he had drafted with his own hand. Among other things, it was forbidden for a Merrow man to even look upon a selkie woman. The measure was not only a matter of pride, it was also a matter of hate.

As a result of the treaty, the clans clung to rumors and superstition. Ill feelings and false stories about the other abounded. In fact, the relationship between their clans was so strained that Elysia believed the clans would still follow the treaty to the letter, even if it weren't enforced on pain of death.

Despite her father's foul legacy, Lord Dolion's daughter did not agree with his plans. Lady Sirena was sorry for the harm done by her father to the Selkie Court, and she'd been trying for many cycles to make amends for it. Despite general ill-will between the people, and the harsh measures outlined in the Treaty of Hiraeth, she was friendly to the Selkie people. It was clear that Lady Sirena wanted things to change. Elysia didn't think there was anything she could do about it, but that hadn't stopped the ruler from trying.

After she assumed the throne, Lady Sirena had been instrumental in her own father's judgement. In fact, it was she who had sent her father to his death. Lord Dolion had been bound in shackles and plunged into the deepest canyon of the sea. There, he'd been forced to die a coward's death. According to her grandmother, the councils had watched as his body was crushed in the sea serpent's coils and dragged through the sea floor into the creature's lair, never to be seen again. Nathair had eaten him alive—a fitting death for such a black-hearted creature, or so her grandmother had said.

Since, Lady Sirena had often proposed other remedies to ease the tension between their courts. She had even gone so far as to invite Elysia to fight beside the Court of Merrows in the battle against the Court of Orm. Despite her mother's intense worry, Elysia had gone, with the unanimous blessing of both councils. Though the Court of Orm had been defeated, it had not done much to repair the relations between the clans.

Prior to the battle, Elysia had spent a brief stay in the Court of Merrows with her mother on court business. She still burned when she thought about it. She had been dying to explore, but unfortunately, she hadn't gotten to see much of the court past her own rooms. She'd tried to sneak out several times, but her mother had ensured she was under heavy guard, high in the fortress. Two Guards had even flanked her while she sat in the throne room, making it impossible for her to escape.

Usually, court business was a bore, but surprisingly, Elysia had enjoyed hearing the councils' debates. At first, she had chafed under her Guards, itching to be free, but eventually she had relaxed. Soon, she had found herself listening with interest. At one point, she had even thought the Treaty of Hiraeth would be amended, but the animosity between the clans was too great, even among the councils, and the debates had gone nowhere.

Despite Lady Sirena's openness to the Selkie people and the many cycles that had passed since Lord Dolion's evil acts, the Selkie people, and in Elysia's opinion, her mother, still did not trust Lady Sirena. They didn't trust *any* merrow, for that matter. Rumors and tales flew on both sides, unchecked, and, if anything, the relationship between the clans worsened with each cycle.

Even still, Lady Sirena persisted. Since Elysia's visit to the Court of Merrows and the battle with the king's army, the ruler had taken a special interest in Elysia. Last winter, she had even invited her to come to court alone for a visit. Elysia had been dying to go. Winter was notoriously bleak on the islands, and she had begged her mother endlessly. But, of course, she'd been refused.

Her mother had become furious when the letter arrived. Elysia had pleaded, but her mother had forbidden her to go. The council had agreed. According to them, the tensions between the clans were just too great, and it would simply be too dangerous for their future ruler to travel to the Court of Merrows alone.

Elysia had considered sneaking away or drafting her own letter in her mothers' hand and sending it to Lady Sirena, feigning her consent to the visit. But the treaty forbade a selkie from entering the Court of Merrows without expressed permission, and Elysia knew she'd be risking her own skin if she defied it. So, she had been forced to stay.

Lady Sirena had sent an escort with her letter. Of course, the young merrow was not allowed to set his foot on the Selkie Isles. The Guard had flanked the shoreline, and he had waited for her in the water, armed with a spear. Elysia had only been able to see the Guards' backs and the tip of his fierce spear from her window, but she had longed to climb down the lattice and follow him beneath the sea.

Unfortunately, that was impossible. The space below her window was under guard, and when she had tried her door, it was locked. She had only been set free to hand him a letter. Tears had pricked her eyes as she had placed it in his palm, declining Lady Sirena's invitation.

The merrow had stared just left of her feet. His face had been a hard line, and he'd given her a tight nod before his silver hair had flashed in the sun as he dove beneath the waves. His shimmering blue tail had flicked once, and then he was gone.

Elysia had stared after him in despair. Her heart had been as heavy as a stone. She had needed an escape, and she'd needed it right then. She had spun, headed for the woods, and she hadn't looked back as she thrashed through the forest to the river. Then she'd laid flat on her belly, burying her face in her arms as she allowed the churning waters of the Brook to carry her through to the cavern's other side.

When she had docked her small raft, she had run as fast as she could to the top of the highest hill. She had glared at the open water as she screamed with all her might. When her voice was gone, a silent landscape had answered her, and she had fallen to her knees, staining thick, hot tears onto the dirt. She cried until she was spent, and soon, she fell asleep.

Sometime later, Elysia had awoken to a faint tinkling sound by her ear. She opened her eyes to slits, listening. The quiet sound swirled inside her head, weaving softly in thin tendrils. They moved in and out of one another until, all at once, they met, coalescing into an ethereal sound. It was a gentle voice—soft, yet persistent.

Elysia had sat up on her palms, looking for the source of the voice. A breeze swirled her hair, and then, all at once, a sudden Wind whipped over the hillside. The soft voice swirled within it, curling around her like a large cocoon. Then the Wind stilled, and the voice collected itself onto the ground where her tears had stained the dirt. As she stared, a young tree pushed itself up though the damp patch of earth.

The young tree grew, higher and higher, before her eyes, until it was fully grown. Shaded by its branches, she had sat up on her knees, staring at the new tree in awe. It had been strange and unsettling, but a keen awareness of something larger than herself had stirred in her belly, and she had broken a sprig of pink flowers from the closest frond and carried them back to her grandmother, certain she would know what to make of it.

Ríona had touched the branch lovingly, and tears had pricked her crinkled brown eyes.

"It's a Tamarisk tree, young 'Lysia," she had said. "Whoever finds a Tamarisk tree, finds a good thing. The Histories tell us that the good fae, Ita, grew Tamarisk in her West Mountains gardens. She was the former healer of the realm, and it appears that the Source has seen fit to grant this sacred task to you. Ita has passed into the Hereafter, and there is no one to wield the healing power of the Tamarisk for the sick in body, heart, and mind.

Be ready, dear child, for this task may lead you to places and people you have never known. It will open doors for you that have long been shut, and lay secrets plain that have long been hidden. One day, the Histories may read that the healing powers you have been granted are greater than you or I now know."

Elysia could see her grandmother's raised finger in her mind's eye, crooked with age. Her dark brown eyes had peered solemnly at her from her wrinkled face.

"Always remember, Elysia, your gift comes with a promise, even though that promise has an enemy. If you access the gift, the promise will follow. Your enemy may be as wide as the Southern Sea, and the task before you may loom larger than the known worlds, but the promise will prevail. There is no stopping it. The promise is wider than the sea, and larger than the known worlds, by far. There is *no* thing, in all of creation, that can exceed it, for it comes down to you from the Source.

When you do not know the way, your gift will see you through. You may struggle in deep waters, but you will not drown. You need only access your gift. Hold to the promise, Elysia, and listen to the Voice."

Elysia had sat on the threadbare rug before her grandmother's armchair in the little sandstone house she called home. She had wrinkled her nose at her grandmother's words, not at all sure what she meant. So, she had decided to sit the branch aside for later. If she were being honest, she had all but forgotten the Tamarisk tree and her grandmother's discussion last winter.

Presently, she lifted her face to peer up the hillside. Since the winter, the hill had become a grove of Tamarisk trees. She watched the pink boughs waving in the breeze. The trees circled the top of the hill like a crown. Each time she visited, there were more and more.

A niggling feeling nipped in her chest at the sight, and she frowned up at them. She wasn't sure what to do with the information her grandmother had given her. She could barely handle the idea of her Presentation tonight, let alone taking on the task of healer for the realm. Besides, she didn't think her mother or the council would allow their future ruler to be the realm's new healer. Sooner or later, someone would fall sick in the Court of Merrows, and that wouldn't do for anyone.

She flicked her eyes to the sun. It was well past mid-morning. She sighed, flicking her fingers through the water in irritation. She had to go. If she waited any longer, Ena would alert the Guard. Regretfully, Elysia swam towards the shore. As she stood, her silver skin slaked off to dissolve in the shallow water behind her.

She turned back as she stepped barefoot onto the rocky beach, shielding her eyes to take one last look at the shimmering water. Some nameless, deep feeling pulled her towards it, and if she had followed it, she would have dived back in and let the Midsummer Ball, and *Connor,* be cursed. She would have loved nothing more, but she knew she couldn't do that. Not today, not ever.

Elysia felt trapped, and she made a promise to herself, then and there. Someday very soon, she would leave the Selkie Isles and search out the sea's hidden secrets. She didn't care about the treaty, or the fact that she would soon be betrothed. She didn't care about her mother's opinions or the council or what anyone on the Selkie Isles thought about it. Once she lived below the water, none of it would matter. She would escape it all—the land, the treaty, Connor, the court, and all the rest. She would be free from all of it.

Chapter 2

Kai flicked his eyes flatly around the throne room from his perch behind Lady Sirena's right shoulder. He sighed heavily, long-since passed being bored. The merrow man kneeling before the throne was droning on and on about some injustice or the other, but Kai wasn't sure what he was saying. He had tuned him out several sentences ago. Kai wished he would hurry, but unfortunately, Lady Sirena still sat at attention, nodding her head towards the merrow man with interest.

He tapped his foot impatiently. It was well past due for the court hearing to be over. He gazed pointedly at the side of Lady Sirena's head, urging her to stand. She didn't move, and Kai blew out a restless breath, causing her to flick her eyes to his side in warning.

Kai pressed his lips together in irritation. He couldn't help it. The man had been talking forever.

Court hearings were always the most boring days of the Quarter, and today was no different. Kai scanned the room, clenching his hands behind his back. They had been at this for an *eternity*. Surely, it was almost over. He had more important things to do, like fishing with Seamus.

Just then, he spied a mass of orange hair peeking from behind a glass pillar. Seamus poked his head out and furtively scanned the hall, then sidestepped behind a row of sentries. True to fashion, his quick motion bumped into the last sentry in the row, pitching the man forward. He caught himself just in time and glared backward at Seamus, who pretended not to notice. Kai grinned. Seamus had never been the stealthiest spy.

He and Seamus had been friends since they had passed eleven cycles. They had met at the Aptitudes Test, where Kai had shown considerable abilities as a warrior, guard, and spy. This was not surprising, given his heritage.

Kai's uncle was the leader of the merrow Forces and his father had provided service to the court as a guard and spy before his death. Kai bore his father's same long, silver hair and his uncle's piercing blue eyes, which hinted he might excel in the same abilities. And, to no one's surprise, he did. He'd flown through his testing, and he'd been thrust upward in the Forces ranks, almost immediately.

After Kai's parents had perished from exposure to a poisonous algae bloom, Lady Sirena had taken him in. She had known his family for many cycles, as his father and uncle had formerly served under her father's court. Since Lady Sirena had never born offspring, she had raised Kai as her own and guided him into the path he had chosen.

Kai could still remember those early days after his parent's death. Lady Sirena had been a constant to him, then, when he'd needed it most. If he was being honest, she had helped him survive it.

When he had passed his eighteenth cycle, Kai was due to select his station within the Forces. Lady Sirena had directed him to honor his heritage and choose a position worthy of his skills and abilities. So, he had chosen to serve the Court of Merrows as a guard and spy. Seamus had signed for the same station, but even *he* would have agreed his skills were probably better served somewhere else. Stealth was not Seamus' strong suit.

In addition to Merrow Forces training, Kai had begun privately training to inherit the merrow throne. Lady Sirena had been so kind to him. Kai loved her like his own mother, and he wanted to please her, but he just wasn't sure he wanted to the job. Not since last winter, anyway.

Despite his feelings of disinterest, he had reluctantly agreed to her plan. He had passed his days in a haze, numbly going about his training and escaping from the throne room for release, whenever possible.

The majority of his lessons were quite boring, like these blasted court hearings, but Lady Sirena insisted they were an essential element to learning the ins and outs of ruling the Court of Merrows. So, Kai was made to endure it.

Most in his position would have jumped at the chance to inherit the throne, but Kai didn't care about his status or a position of leadership, especially not since the accident. Silently, he squeezed his eyes shut, blocking out the memory. None of it mattered—not since he had lost her.

Just then, Seamus squeezed in between two sentries on the front line. He stuck his orange head out, motioning to Kai with his hand. *Come on,* he mouthed. Kai didn't acknowledge him, and Seamus sank to his knees in a mock plea for Kai's attention. His friend was causing quite the commotion, and an irritated sentry beside him gave his shoulder a hard nudge. Seamus grunted before he fell flat, crashing into two others as he fell face-first onto the glass throne room floor.

A hush fell over the throne room as he caught himself with his hands in a loud squeak against the glass. Lady Sirena lifted her face in irritation towards the sound. She narrowed her eyes at Seamus' orange head, and Kai watched a sheepish grin creep over his friend's face. The droning merrow man before her finally silenced at her expression. He spun, and then all eyes were on Seamus, lying on the floor.

Seamus scrambled to his feet. He flung out a palm, bowing in an exaggerated fashion as he backed slowly down the aisle.

"Apologies, My Lady. Please, continue," he said, dipping his head. His words echoed loudly in the silent hall, bouncing back from the glass walls and ceiling. Kai cringed at the sound, watching as Seamus bowed, once more.

Seamus flicked his eyes to Kai, just before he slipped out front door. *Hurry up!* He mouthed. Kai grinned, and Lady Sirena turned to stare pointedly in his direction. Quickly, Kai pulled a straight face.

"Sorry," he whispered.

He straightened his shoulders, and Lady Sirena sighed heavily, then she turned back to the droning merrow man. She smiled. "Please, continue," she said sweetly.

The merrow man droned on a while longer, until finally, he stood. He bowed to Lady Sirena and moved to the left of the throne room. Kai blew out a breath. *Finally.* The droning man had been the last one in today's group.

Kai jiggled his foot and tapped his fingers against his thigh. Technically, he wasn't allowed to leave until Lady Sirena dismissed the council. He flicked his eyes in their direction. The panel of merrows sat to his left at the council's bench, placidly chatting amongst themselves. He flicked his eyes to the ceiling in annoyance. They were in no hurry.

Finally, Lady Sirena stood. She tapped her scepter once on the glass floor, the glass orb gleaming beneath her palm.

"Court hearings are concluded. Council is dismissed."

Kai didn't wait to hear more. He hopped to the throne room floor, skidding across the glass as he hurried towards the doors. The taste of freedom was sweet on his tongue.

"One moment, Kai Bennet," Lady Sirena called sharply.

Kai sagged against the door handle. So much for sweet freedom.

He spun slowly, lifting his eyes to the throne. Lady Sirena smirked. Kai gave her a shallow bow, and she motioned him forward. His feet were heavy as stone as he trudged back up the aisle.

Lady Sirena stepped gingerly on her bare feet to meet him on the floor. She gazed up at him pointedly.

"Don't forget you have Night Watch this evening," she said softly. "Alistair tells me you've missed the last two." She studied his face, a hint of anxiety in her tone. "Tell me, where do you disappear at night?"

Kai folded his hands behind his back. He tapped his thumb rapidly against his palm.

"Nowhere," he mumbled.

Lady Sirena sighed. "Well, you're overdue to get serious about your lessons. Your training cycle is almost up. One day, it will be up to you to take your uncle Alistair's place and lead the Forces. And, when the day comes, the entire court, too." Kai dropped his eyes.

Her face softened, and she touched his arm gently with her palm. "I know you miss her, Kai, but this reckless behavior has got to stop." She lifted his chin with her hand. "The people don't trust me, as it is. They question my every choice. They won't accept you as my heir, if you keep this up."

Kai sighed, flexing his jaw. "I know," he said quietly. And he did know. What she was saying was true.

Lady Sirena nodded once and dropped her hand. "Good. I'll let Alastair know he should expect you."

Kai dropped his eyes. He gave her a nearly imperceptible nod.

"Off, then," she said, patting his arm. "Your friend is waiting."

Kai turned in time to see Seamus's red head popping in the door. "Let's go, Kai!" he shouted. His voice reverberated off the glass, bouncing harshly against Kai's ears. Kai winced, grinning sheepishly at Lady Sirena. She smirked, raising one eyebrow, then jerked her chin towards the doors.

Kai forced himself to walk calmly to the doors, but he couldn't wait to get outside of them. At last, the sentries shut them behind him, and he blew out a breath. Finally free.

Seamus grinned, punching him lightly on the shoulder.

"Took you long enough!" he shouted. The shorter Merrow bounded down the castle steps, pausing at the bottom. He turned back to Kai, raising his arms.

"Kai! Let's *go!* We don't have much time until the Night Watch. Alistair will be furious if I'm late again."

Kai chuckled. "Okay, I'm coming," he said. He jogged down the steps and stopped by Seamus near the street. Seamus folded his arms, peering up at Kai with serious eyes.

"You're coming, right? To the Night Watch, I mean? There's only so many excuses I can give Alistair." Seamus grimaced and flicked his eyes furtively down the street. "That guy scares me."

Kai sniffed. "We'll see," he said quietly.

Seamus rolled his eyes. "*Great.*" He flicked his eyes back to Kai curiously. "Where do you go every night, anyway? Maybe you're off on some *heir business?*" He chortled at his own joke, and Kai snuck a punch on his upper arm.

"Very funny," Kai said.

Seamus rubbed the spot Kai had punched, chuckling, then he dropped his hand.

"Come on Kai, seriously. Out with it. We've been mates long enough for you to tell me the truth. I mean, I thought I already knew all your secrets, but apparently there's still some you've yet to tell me." Seamus peered up at him expectantly.

Kai wet lips. He shook his head, dropping his eyes. "It's nothing. Seriously. I just," He sighed heavily, running a hand through his hair. "I need a break from it all is all. So, I go…out."

He put a hand on his hip, feigning interest in a vendor's cart across the street.

He moved towards it, exchanging a copper for a cluster of fat grapes. He popped one into his mouth as Seamus shrugged.

"Whatever you say. Just try to show up tonight, okay? Now, let's get a move on." He squinted his eyes and licked his finger, holding it up in the air. "Ah, yes, the river is ripe for fishing, tonight! Race you!" He punched Kai's arm before he took off like an orange flash.

Kai grinned after him, ignoring the sting of his punch. Then he jogged down the street, weaving left and right until he met Seamus in a small lane hidden behind a cluster of towering river birches. He followed Seamus' orange head to an opening in the rock wall at the back of the lane that had been tunneled into the stone of the fortress surrounding the court.

Long ago, the hidden tunnel had been a flourishing part of the court, but this section had long since fallen out of use. No one ever passed by this way anymore. No one except the Forces and a few stray fishermen ever dared enter it. Some even said it was cursed.

After the death of Lord Ríonan, the tunnel had been the path of the Selkie clan's exile. Lord Dolion had ordered it flooded after their passage. It was his final seal, a signal to the Selkie clan that their people would never return. Since, the rock ruins had lain partially submerged, and the section of the city that had once thrived there had all but been forgotten.

He and Seamus had found the secret tunnel several cycles ago, after Seamus had overheard some of the merrow Forces talking about it in hushed tones. They had mentioned an old section of the city that lay partially submerged in an abandoned tunnel behind a grove of river birch trees, where the fishing was prime.

Apparently, the tunnel was part of a series of undersea passages, and since it had been flooded, it was now connected to the undersea river system. Kai had been fascinated. The rivers connected all of Caelium through the underground caverns laced throughout the realm.

He had been amazed when he and Seamus had first visited. But now, the flooded tunnel and the other passages that zigzagged below the realm seemed perfectly ordinary. Deep, dark holes were good hiding places for evil to lurk after the fall of the Court of Orm, and the Forces traveled the passages almost every night, keeping watch on the river system, ensuring any creatures were kept at bay.

He and Seamus had searched for the secret tunnel for weeks, until Kai stumbled upon its shrouded door late one afternoon. After that, he and Seamus visited the tunnel as often as they could. Sometimes, they even made extra coppers selling their catch in Meallta's street market.

Of course, Lady Sirena didn't know anything about their fishing. No doubt she would have forbidden it. Just one more thing to keep his focus off his training and his future. A distraction, she would call it.

As *distracted* as he was, at least he was present during the day. Well, mostly present. And that was something, right? He never missed lessons on the Histories, court hearings, his defensive training, or skills in espionage. It was only the Night Watches he had trouble attending.

Kai hadn't mentioned the fishing, and she hadn't questioned him about it. *Yet.* Still, he knew he had better quit skipping the

Night Watch, or she would have him trailed. Then his and Seamus's fishing adventures would be over for good.

Kai carefully scanned the lane, then he ducked his head into the tunnel behind Seamus. The two descended in darkness for several steps, climbing down through the walls of the fortress until they emerged beneath the sea floor. There, the passage widened into a large, expansive cavern.

In the front of the cavern, a waterfall dropped down from over their heads, spilling into the undersea river below. Winding green vines crept over the rocks, and a variety of wildflowers and squat water thistles grew near the cave door, while moss and lichen made a patchy coat over the cavern walls. No ruins extended to the first cavern, but beyond it, the remnants of hollow stone buildings and abandoned Forces training grounds extended to the tunnel's far end.

Kai brushed his fingertips across a nearby fern, causing bluish, hazy light to illuminate from its fronds. The light traveled from the ends of it, scattering across the petals of wildflowers, the twists of green vines, patches of thick moss, and the crusts of lichen that clung to the cavern walls and ceiling. Kai grinned as he flicked the tip of a larkspur to his right, causing the petals to glow. In moments, he was surrounded by a kind of secret blue sun.

Tiny insects skated silently on the river's surface. They were barely perceptible, even for sharp merrow eyes. Seamus moved to the edge of the river and struck the surface with his spear, causing a rippling golden glow to bounce from beneath his blade. The water striders glowed when disturbed, causing a shimmering light to scatter across the water.

He turned to Kai and grinned. "Ready?" he asked, unbuttoning his shirt. Kai tossed his clothing onto the nearest rock and stretched his neck left and right. Then he blew out a breath, shaking out his arms. "Ready." he said evenly.

Kai dove as Seamus plunged in after him. He shivered as the tingle started in his toes, and then he was slicing through the water; his blue tail sending sprays of golden light skittering behind him.

He and Seamus raced through the river, winding left and right until they came to a high, domed cavern in the middle of the tunnel. The water there was still, but the river flowed beyond the pool, past a series of whitewater turns until it twisted out of sight.

They surfaced, and Seamus turned to him, the pale green scales on his temple flashing with his movement.

"This is where I found them, last time," he said. "The eels." He held up his thin, freckled arm, flexing. "Big around as my arm."

Kai chuckled.

"If you say, so," he said, smirking.

Kai held up a muscular arm, flexing his bicep. "Your arm or mine," he teased. Seamus scoffed and flicked his fingers, spraying golden water onto Kai's face.

"Ach, that's nothing! A tiny worm compared to these things." He held up his own thin arm again, flexing.

Kai laughed out loud, the sound echoing against the high rock dome. He flexed his other arm, wiggled his eyebrows in Seamus' direction.

"Yea, yea, keep it up, then," said Seamus. "We'll see who catches the biggest eel, giant's arms or no."

With that he dove, his pale green tale flashing as he disappeared under the water. Kai grinned and dove after him. The chase was on.

He sliced through the water, cutting through the tunnel as fast as he could swim. For a moment, he didn't see anything. Then all at once, just ahead, a bright-yellow ribbon of fin flashed before it ducked out of sight into a dark window in the rock.

Kai tucked his arms and pushed hard towards the place where the tail had disappeared. When he reached it, he stowed his spear over his back, then he settled back against the rock near the window where the eel had disappeared to wait.

Soon, the eel poked its yellow head through the hole. Kai lunged and grasped it around the neck with both arms. The eel thrashed, writhing left and right in his arms. It turned its large head, attempting to nip Kai's hand with its long yellow teeth.

Just when Kai thought he had him, a static hum tinged under his fingers as the animal built up a charge along his spine. Then the tip of the eel's tail began to glow brightly. The static humming intensified. Kai knew he had only moments before the creature gave him the shock of his life.

He twisted his legs around the eel's body, managing to grasp its head in his large hands. Just as the eel snapped its tail, shooting the charge through his yellow skin, Kai twisted its neck once, and the creature went limp in his arms. Then he stuck it through with his spear. Dark, mirky blood inked out from the wound into the water before Kai's face. He blew out a breath, relief soaking through him as he sank against the side of the tunnel.

He rested his head against the dark rock, letting his heart rate slow. A moment more, and he would've been floating lifeless in the tunnel, a prime target from someone, or *something's,* next meal. He sucked in a deep breath, then furrowed his brow.

It had been a while since he had heard Seamus. Normally, his friend was thrashing through the water loudly, but Kai couldn't hear him, now. He lifted his head to listen. The only sound he could hear was his own breathing. The water around him was quiet.

Silently, he carried his kill to the surface and laid it gently on the slick rock at the water's edge. He scanned the moss-covered shells of the hollow buildings formed out of the wall, but there was no sign of Seamus. Kai frowned. Something wasn't right.

Kai gripped his spear and ducked his head back beneath the water. Seamus had a favorite fishing spot, just ahead of where he had caught the yellow eel moments ago. He would check there, first.

Quietly, he crept along the passage, searching for signs of his friend. He passed Seamus' favorite fishing spot, frowning. There was no sign of him.

Just then, the glint of a silver blade hinted from the bottom of the river. Kai swam towards it and pulled Seamus' spear from the silt.

Not good.

Seamus would've never left his weapon behind, unless there was trouble. Kai flicked his eyes around him, scanning for movement. The water was still, so he clutched both spears and swam silently on.

Ahead, the tunnel widened into another large cavern. Kai swam through and peeked his eye above the water. Silently, he scanned the room, then he lifted his nose and sniffed at the air. A gag formed in his throat as the smell of rotten flesh hit him square in his face. He swallowed against it, grimacing. That smell could only mean one thing; he had found the sea trow, Grym. Ben breathed a curse. He could only hope Grym had not found Seamus, but he probably had, because Seamus was prone to neglecting his own safety—especially when fishing.

If he had, it would be almost impossible for him to get Seamus free. Grym lived a mostly solitary existence in the undersea caves, but when he had the chance, he loved to capture an unsuspecting passerby. Grym was a great fisherman, and his favorite catch were merrows.

Kai flipped through his memory, struggling to recall Alistair's lessons on sea trows. From what he could remember, trows were blind and mute, having lived so long alone in the deep, dark holes of the earth. They survived on their sense of smell, and of course, on sound. Hence, their love of music.

Grym had a habit of preventing his victim's escape by tying them to a stone and forcing them to sing while he played his lyre. Whether or not he liked the song determined how long the poor being might live. Seamus had a *terrible* voice, and Kai worried that he was in real danger of becoming Grym's next meal, or worse, the next skin in the cave trow's collection. Kai shivered. The only thing Grym liked better than music was collecting the skin of sea folk, which he displayed in a collected heap around his current dwelling place. Hence, the smell.

The Histories designated trows as base beings, concentrating on their own desires and ignorant of the harm they caused to others. Alistair had also mentioned that trows were particularly favorable to making an exchange. If his uncle was right, and Kai could offer Grym something worth more to him than Seamus's skin, he might let his friend go.

Might.

Quietly, Kai crept to the water's edge. Trows were fantastic at disguises, and more than once he'd heard of a merrow being trapped after mistaking Grym for a stone. He scanned the cavern, searching the rocks for any signs of movement.

There, in the back corner, Seamus' orange head bobbed behind a large circle of boulders. The huge rock in front of him moved slightly to the left as Seamus cleared his throat and began to sing.

His voice faltered and cracked as Grym began to play his crude instrument, echoing harshly off the cavern walls. Kai ground his teeth and squinted against the sharp notes. Seamus sounded like a scalded sea cow.

Silently, Kai lifted himself out of the water. Seamus caught sight of him, and he stopped singing for a moment, his eyes rounded like saucers. *Grym*, he mouthed. Kai huffed and nodded, bringing a finger to his lips. *I know*, Kai mouthed pointedly. Seamus nodded. He swallowed convulsively, his throat bobbing, then he resumed his song.

When Kai was close to the trow, he cleared his throat and tapped him on the shoulder. Grym started and dropped his lyre, causing a twang of sharp notes to emanate from the instrument. Then, he turned his head to the side. Two large holes gaped in his eye-less face where his nose should be. Kai grimaced at the sight, wishing he could close his ears to the clicking sound emerging from Grym's throat. The creature lifted his head as he sniffed at the air, forgetting Seamus tied to the stone behind of him.

Kai froze as Grym stood, shaking of his stony disguise and unfolding his segmented body to its full height. He lifted two of his six legs, pawing at Kai's face and head with their sticky, pointed tips. Kai didn't move as Grym bent low. He chuffed a breath, ruffling Kai's hair with his fanged jaws. The creature flapped its papery wings in delight, and Kai held his breath. Grym stank like the rotted skins he so favored collecting.

Kai reached behind him with one hand and lifted the enormous eel towards Grym's face. "I've brought a gift for you, Grym. Freshly caught, dead only moments ago." Grym sniffed the air and bent his front arms, grasping at the eel with his pinchers, but Kai held the eel back just slightly, tsking through his teeth.

"Not too fast." Grym's clicking intensified. "I-I mean, it's a gift, of course." Kai chuckled, feigning nonchalance. His heart was thumping against his throat. "You can have it. Only, let's make an exchange."

Grym turned his head to the side, clicking slowly through his fanged jaws. Kai continued.

"Uh, as you can see, erm, I mean *feel*, young Seamus there is a poor contest to this feast I've laid before you. Wouldn't want you to waste your appetite on such a *paltry* Merrow when you can have this." He plopped the eel onto the stone before Grym, who picked it up in his arms, rolling the slick eel over and through his pinchers.

Kai crossed his arms. "I'll even throw in a song." Grym lifted his head, clicking in Kai's direction.

"So, do we have a deal?"

Grym clicked excitedly before he turned and snipped Seamus' bonds, freeing him from the stone.

Seamus ducked against the wall, backing around the cavern until he stood just behind Kai's shoulder. Kai handed Seamus his spear, and the two slowly backed away from the trow.

Suddenly remembering the terms of his exchange, Kai fumbled for words. He was supposed to sing. *Sing something.*

He hummed for a moment, wincing. His voice wasn't much better than Seamus's. Grym clicked, turning his eye-less face in Kai's direction. Kai fumbled for another melody. Loudly, he restarted, humming a tuneless song that bounced flatly against the walls of the cavern. He grimaced as his own voice echoed back to his ears.

Surprisingly, Grym clicked with pleasure at the sound. Then he took his right pincher and disemboweled the eel with one slice. Seamus winced behind Kai's shoulder as the eels' guts spilled out over the stone. Grym fluttered his wings with delight and bent his jaws to the eels' tail. Slowly, he lifted its body in his claws and slid the entire eel down his throat, stripping its skin as he went with his grotesque teeth. Kai grimaced, swallowing bile, as Grym laid the eel's skin to dry on a nearby boulder. A few more moments and that could have easily been Seamus.

As quickly as they could, they cut through the water, fleeing towards the first cavern. Seamus turned to Kai when they surfaced there. His green eyes were round and full of dread. The look on his face was so serious that it struck Kai as hilarious, despite their narrow escape. An odd bubble of mirth formed deep in his throat, and he pulled himself onto the side of the pool, holding his middle as deep peals of his laughter echoed off the cavern walls.

Seamus buttoned his pants and stuffed his arms into his shirt. He pulled his head through the neck and stared down at Kai, who was doubled over.

"Oh, yes, it's *so* funny. Seamus almost gets skinned alive by the giant sea trow·and what do you do? *Laugh*." He buttoned his vest, rolling his eyes.

Kai tried to hold it in, but Seamus' round eyes and horrid singing voice popped into his mind, and he started laughing again. Seamus hissed.

"Yes, keep it up. I know, I'm an *endless* well of fun and enjoyment for you."

Tears rolled down Kai's face, and he swiped at his cheeks.

"I'm sorry, but you should have seen your face. You should have *heard* yourself!"

Seamus raised his hand, halting Kai's explanation.

"No need for apologies. Thanks for saving me. *No thanks* for laughing about it." His face turned serious. "And we'd better get going, or we'll to be late for the Watch. Alistair will have our tails."

Kai's laughter died in his throat, and he dropped his eyes. He sniffed. He could feel Seamus studying his profile, but he didn't look at him. Seamus dropped his hand and crossed his arms over his chest. "Don't tell me. You're not coming."

The muscle in Kai's jaw feathered. "Not tonight," he said quietly.

Seamus threw up his arms.

"Well that's just *grand*. Good luck to me, then, and nice knowing you."

Kai chuckled. "I'll see you tomorrow at training," he said. Seamus mock-bowed, fluttering his arm.

"I'll be there, Lord Kai," he said. Kai grinned.

"See you later," he said.

After Seamus had gone, Kai remained on the edge of the pool, thinking. He flicked his tail and watched the bright blue shade shimmer in the water's golden light. The splash mirrored the shine of the golden ring he kept tied around his neck. Absently, he touched it.

Maura had always liked his tail's color. *It matches your eyes*, she had said. Kai grinned. She had joked that his only true skill as a spy was due to his tail. She had said it blended him with the sea, making him look like a blue wave gliding through the water. His smile faded as he remembered her tinkling laugh. He thought of her reddish-brown hair floating behind her in the surf, and his heart squeezed. He missed her more than he could explain.

He and Maura had been inseparable. Their parents had died around the same time, after an algae bloom had poisoned the waters surrounding the Court of Merrows. Lady Sirena had called the healer, Ita, but with the continuous exposure to the poison, her Tamarisk Cakes had been unsuccessful. It had been a full cycle until the waters had cleared. Most of the court had fallen sick, and many had died. Maura's parents and his own had been among them.

After their death, Lady Sirena had taken Maura in. Kai had bonded instantly with her over their parents' deaths, and soon, they had become the best of friends.

Maura had known him like no one else. She had been the holder of all his secrets, the absolute love of his life. It didn't seem real that he had lost her last winter. One moment, they had been racing over a Sea Lily grove, and the next, she had been gone.

The giant Sea Lilies were beautiful. Kai couldn't blame her for getting so close. They carpeted the valley beyond the canyon and reached their colorful arms out towards the surface. Their feathery crowns were covered with a slick, sticky substance, made for catching prey. It was toxic, especially to sea folk.

"Watch this!" Maura shouted. She was only playing, but she dove too low, and her arms had caught in the fronds. They wrapped her in their deadly embrace, and instantly, she fell to the sea floor, choking and writhing in pain. Kai was frantic. "Maura!" he screamed, but there was nothing he could do. There was nothing anyone could have done to save her.

He carried her back to court in his arms. Tears streaked his face, and he begged for someone to help her. Ita came. She tried, but she was just too late. The skin around Maura's lips had already turned dark blue, and the scales on her temple had already begun to flake off. She coughed once, spurting dark blood, and her slender hand slipped off the bed, dropping the golden ring Kai had given her into his palm.

Kai had gotten very sick, after that—too much contact with the poison. Seamus had never left his side, and soon, he had taken to his own sick bed. Ita had patiently tended them both, feeding them small bites of Tamarisk cakes and whispering prayers to the Source.

Seamus had recovered quickly, but Kai had barely made it. After, his body was so weak, and his grief was so fierce, that he wished he hadn't. If he were being honest, there were some days when he still felt the same.

Since Maura had gone, nothing seemed to matter. His life was out of focus. Its edges were blurred. All the plans he had made, the dreams he had dreamed, they had all died with her.

Kai lifted the ring from his neck, holding it lovingly in his palm. Tears pricked his eyes as he closed his fist around the small golden circle. Tonight was Midsummer, he and Maura's would-be wedding night. He could still see the look in her golden eyes when she had said, *Let's do it on Midsummer. It's so beautiful, then, Kai. You can sneak to our island and get some blooms for my bouquet.* She had loved the feathery, pink blossoms from the Tamarisk trees that had sprouted suddenly on their secret island before her death last winter.

Kai tightened his jaw against a wave of pain as he tucked the ring back around his neck. He knew what he needed to do. He needed to feel close to her, especially tonight, and there was only one way he knew how. The Night Watch would just have to wait.

Chapter 3

The Midsummer Ball was the event of the season, and everyone who was anyone in the Selkie Court would be in attendance. Preparations had been underway for weeks, and with the day of the ball finally upon them, the palace grounds were buzzing with activity.

Among other things, the ball highlighted the first blooms of the island's famed Evening Star flowers. The Evening Stars' incandescent blooms always opened on Midsummer, just after nightfall. They were Elysia's favorite, the one thing she was looking forward to, tonight.

She tucked her raft back into its hiding place in the reeds, scanning the forest for guards. One crossed the path in front of her, and she swung herself behind a tree, holding her breath. It was late, later than she'd realized. Guards were everywhere. The tall guard passed, and she blew out her breath, then peered out from behind the tree into the palace courtyard, cursing herself for staying out so long. The grounds were crawling. She would have a hard time getting to her rooms without being seen. And if she was seen, endless questions would be asked.

At the moment, no one was looking towards the forest. There was not a moment to waste. Silently, Elysia slipped from her hiding place and jogged towards the clearing. If she didn't hurry up, Ena would have her tail—and so would her mother.

She tucked herself inside the garden gate and ducked behind a vine-covered stone column. She waited for a moment, then peeked out from behind it, grimacing. The garden was full of gardeners pruning and plucking and servants laying down the square dance floor in the garden's center.

A giant white tent had been erected to the right of the gardens, and countless servants were carrying large platters of food from the kitchens to place underneath it. Beneath the tent, people moved about in droves. Some carried table settings, candelabras, and lanterns, while others adjusted centerpieces or helped installed a giant floral arrangement decorating the tent's ceiling. In the back corner, a group of musicians stood, tuning their instruments.

A gardener knelt just beside her hiding place, clipping large, white roses for a table setting. Elysia waited until he stood and gathered his collection of blooms. He folded them under his arm, then turned and carried them towards the tent.

When he walked away, Elysia raced from behind the column and flattened herself against the side of the palace nearest her bedroom. The trellis of climbing rose vines beneath it pressed against her stomach, a sharp thorn digging into her hip.

She grimaced, ignoring the shooting pain from her side as she gripped her fingers to its bars and glanced furtively over her shoulder. The gardens were empty, for the moment, but they wouldn't be for long. It was now or never. She turned to the trellis and lifted her foot to the first rung.

Just then, her mother's voice hissed behind her. "Elysia Bryn, get down from there *this instant*, before someone sees!" Elysia dropped her forehead onto the trellis and sighed through her teeth. She was caught.

She dropped her foot to the ground and turned slowly, plastering a sweet smile onto her face. "Good afternoon, Mother," she said cheerfully. Lady Malca raised her eyebrow. She scanned Elysia's dirt-stained clothing and reached to touch her damp hair, smirking.

"Might I ask *why* you are climbing up the trellis into your rooms?" She paused, and Elysia didn't answer. "And *why* your hair and clothes are in such a state?"

Elysia opened her mouth to explain. "Well, I…" But Lady Malca held up her hand.

"No, please, *spare* me the details. I'm certain I do not wish to know." She flicked her fingers towards the back doors. "Just, please, enter the house like a proper lady. And hurry. Ena is in a state. She's been looking for you all day."

Elysia nodded. She smiled sweetly, earning a smirk from her mother before she dipped into a shallow curtsy. Then she hurried through the back doors.

Ena met her at the bottom of the steps. Her navy-blue eyes were frantic, and her fiery red hair hadn't been brushed. It stood out around her head like a halo of fluffy clouds.

"Finally! *There* you are. I've been searching all over. I nearly sent the Guard!" She scanned the hall, leaning into Elysia's ear. "*Where* have you been, all day!" She gripped Elysia's arm firmly with her small hand and hustled her up the polished stairs.

"We've got to hurry. We're already late, and Lady Malca is going to have my tail if you aren't ready by this afternoon." She frowned back at Elysia. "This is only my first cycle on this job, you know. Technically, I'm still on a trial basis. I'm doing my best, but you're really making it harder than it has to be, what with stealing off to the Source knows where all day."

Elysia sat heavily onto the bed as Ena moved to the vanity and grabbed a brush. She turned to Elysia, throwing up her hands. "I mean, I know the council has no female children to choose from, so obviously, there's not a lot of competition, but what's the point in convincing the council and your mother to let me be your lady-in-waiting if you make it impossible for me to keep the job more than one cycle?!"

She tugged Elysia to the vanity and sat her down, pulling the brush through her tangles as she peered seriously at her through the glass. "You *know* your mother expects a certain level of…" she looked up to the ceiling, rolling her hand in the air, "…perfection."

Elysia flopped back onto the bed and sighed. "Oh, believe me, I know," she grumbled. Ena sighed and moved to the bed. She tapped Elysia's leg with the brush. "You know I love you, 'Lys. I mean, you're my best friend. But tonight is really important, to your mother and to the court."

She grinned. "In other important news, I heard you're choosing Connor as your mate!" Elysia rolled her eyes, then tucked her arms over her face. "MMhmm," she mumbled.

Ena stood and moved to the bathing room. She frowned at Elysia as she sprinkled bathing salts into the large tub. "What, you're not excited? Connor's the catch of the Isles. He's anyone's dream." She held up a hand, ticking off items with her small fingers. "Rich, intelligent, gorgeous. What's not to like?" Elysia peeked at her from under her arm, pulling a face. Ena shrugged. "Well, I'm just saying, you could do worse."

Elysia dropped her arms, pushing herself off the bed. "I guess," she said glumly. She dropped her damp clothes to the plush carpet and stepped into the bath.

Ena folded her arms. "I'm just saying…" Elysia didn't wait

for her to finish. She plunged her head and flicked her silver tail, imagining she was floating in the sea. She stayed below, listening to Ena's muffled voice continuing its chatter until her red head backed away from the side of the tub. When she was gone, Elysia resurfaced and laid her head back against the tub's edge.

She knew Ena meant well, but her friend didn't understand. No one did. No one, not even Ena, could understand the pressure of being the heir to the selkie throne. Her friend would never understand what it was like to have her every move watched like she was a creature on display or to be forced into a marriage with a man she didn't love.

She flattened her lips into a thin line as she soaped her hair, thinking of the ever-expanding Tamarisk grove on her secret island. As if her other duties weren't enough, she was also supposed to be the healer for the entire realm? She frowned, dunking her head.

Tonight was worry enough. She couldn't think about the healer situation or her grandmother's odd words, right now.

She lifted out of the tub and wrapped herself in a towel, then moved to the bed. Ena had laid two gowns across the mattress, and mercifully, her friend had stepped out of the room, allowing her some much-needed peace.

Elysia ran her hand over the soft fabric of the closest one. Both gowns were stunning, but this one was her favorite. Ena had commissioned the dress designs to play on the botanical theme of the evening.

One dress was warm brown silk, with a shimmering gossamer overlay. Tiny flower buds were sewn into the neck and bodice, swirling down to colorful, open flowers on the full skirt.

The other, her favorite, was deep green silk, with delicate golden leaves and wispy vines woven throughout its slender column. A tiny Evening Star bloom had been woven into the top of each slender shoulder strap. Elysia grinned down at it. It was just her style, and it matched the green of her eyes perfectly. The golden threads would bring out the tiny flecks of gold in them. Carefully, she stepped into it.

She had just tucked the straps over her shoulders and moved before the mirror when Ena re-entered the room. Her friend grinned at her reflection.

"Ah, yes. I knew you would like that one."

Elysia spun, smiling at her friend's appearance. Ena had slicked her unruly, red hair into a tight bun at the nape of her neck. Her slim body was clad in a pale blue gown that shimmered softly in the light.

"Ena, you look lovely!" Elysia exclaimed. Ena blushed and smoothed the already perfect hair over her ear. "You think?" she asked sheepishly.

A deep blush colored her friend's cheeks, and Elysia narrowed her eyes. "What is it?" she asked. Ena bit her lip. "I just want to be ready. In case anyone, you know, *interesting* might be there." Elysia grinned, arching one brow. "You mean like Tyse?" she teased. Ena grinned. She grabbed Elysia's stays, biting the inside of her lip. "Maybe," she said, giggling.

Ena giggled as she tied the ends of them, ending in a loud snort. She covered her mouth, widening her eyes at Elysia's reflection. Then both ladies broke out in peals of laughter. "What?" Ena asked between laughs. "I can't let you be the only one to have any fun!" Elysia chuckled and rolled her eyes. Then she grabbed the brush and pulled it through her hair. Her grin faded as she studied her reflection. The events of tonight were starting to become real. At sunset, she would be forced to choose Connor, and then, her life would be over forever.

Elysia barely registered Ena's hands as she braided the top half of her long, red-brown locks into an intricate twist. She was too absorbed with thoughts of her bleak future. Emotions swirled rapidly inside her chest, beating against her ribs like a bird in a cage. Ena didn't comment as she ran the brush through the loose curls trailing down Elysia's back, but, more than once, she shot a worried glance at her friend's reflection.

Elysia slid her feet into strappy heels and fit her favorite golden hoops in her ears as Ena tucked an heirloom jewel around her throat. It was a gift, from her mother; the same stone she had worn when she had chosen Lord Ríonan for her mate. Elysia put a hand to her neck, fingering the pretty emerald stone. It lay at her midchest, but it felt too tight, choking. She swallowed against the feeling, lifting her chin to suck in a breath. Still, she felt closed in.

"I need some air," she whispered.

A cold sweat broke out on her back as she moved swiftly to the window and swung it out on its hinges. She braced her hands on the frame and closed her eyes, letting the evening air breeze past her face. It was twilight, almost time for the ball to begin. The band was beginning to play beneath the large tent, and gentle music wafted in on the warm breeze. Below her, a gardener lit the circular lanterns that had been strung above the gardens with a long torch. They illuminated the garden's blooms in a golden glow, and Elysia inhaled deeply, savoring the sweetness of the air.

The wooden dance floor lay in the middle of the gardens, just beyond the fountain. Already, people were milling around it, sipping punch and speaking in low tones. Sighing, Elysia stared at the splendor. She wished she could enjoy it without the cloud of *Connor* hanging over her head.

Ena cleared her throat. "Time to go, 'Lys," she said quietly. She placed a hand on her shoulder, and Elysia sighed, slowly pulling the window closed. She turned to Ena, her shoulders slumped. She sighed again, and Ena raised a finger.

"Ah, perhaps a *bit* less sighing, a little more smiling?" Elysia nodded. She lifted her shoulders, working to plaster a smile on her face. She could tell it was flat, and she raised the corners of her mouth even further.

Ena arched one brow and put a hand on her small hip. "Hmm, I'm not very convinced," she said teasingly. She grabbed

Elysia's hand, which was hanging limply at her side, giving it a squeeze. "You've got to do better than that. Okay? Everyone will be watching. You're their next ruler. Their futures depend on you, and they need to trust you, to have confidence in your decisions. Besides, Connor's not so bad." She tucked her arms around Elysia's back. "You'll see. Everything will turn out alright."

Elysia wrapped her arms around Ena, resting her chin on her small shoulder. She wished Ena's words were true, but she just didn't see how they could be. Nothing was alright, not one single thing.

She trailed Ena glumly down the stairs and followed her out the back doors and into the gardens. Tyse met them just outside the doors. It was obvious he had been waiting for Ena. He tugged nervously at his collar and raised his hand to her in a small wave. Ena waved back to him, then she spun to Elysia, grinning. Her cheeks were flushed, and Elysia smiled at the way her eyes sparkled. "See you later. At dinner, okay?" Elysia nodded, and Ena squeezed her hand, then moved down the steps on Tyse's arm.

Elysia cocked her head, watching them as they disappeared into the garden through a tunnel of flowering vines. She giggled, thinking about the two of them together. They were definitely a mismatch. Tyse had always been shy and quiet, and Ena had not been shy or quiet one day in her life. Elysia couldn't imagine them having a conversation. Tyse wouldn't be able to get a word in edgewise.

She moved down the steps where Tyse and Ena had gone, weaving through the tangled garden passageways in hopes of finding some quiet corner to hide out in until the dinner. She wasn't really expected until then, anyway, so no one would come looking for her. She hugged the high garden wall, avoiding the central fountain and dance floor. At the end of the wall, there was another, hidden fountain. It was smaller than the other and tucked into an alcove behind some high shrubs. No one was likely to pass that way. It would be the perfect place to hide for a while in quiet solitude. She moved silently in the hidden fountain's direction.

In a moment, she heard Ena to her left. Her friend giggled softly, then spoke in a low tone. She peeked through a hole in a lattice of vines, watching as Ena batted her lashes at the seat next to her. Tyse was sitting in it, ramrod straight on the wrought iron chair. He looked scared to death. Ena didn't seem to notice, and she placed her small hand on his knee, causing him to jump.

Elysia clamped her hand over her mouth, stifling a laugh. A mismatch made for the Histories. She backed away, hurrying along the wall before ducking behind row of rosebushes. She folded herself around the next corner, and then she was there, at the hidden fountain.

Thankfully, she had managed to sneak to her hideaway without being seen. She released a breath, pressing her back against the cool stone wall. A low bench had been built into it, and she sank onto the seat, settling in to her solitude.

Just then, she heard a soft rustling in the rose bushes to her right. She froze. The sound was followed by silence, then the crunch of footsteps on the gravel path. Silently, Elysia lifted off the seat. Someone was moving beyond the high bushes. She could see their vague outline, slipping towards her. She moved into a crouch, ready to steal away in the opposite direction.

Just as she leapt for the corner, her head bumped into something hard. Then two large hands grasped her upper arms and thrust her backward, pushing her back flat against the wall. She opened her mouth to shriek, but a large palm clamped over her lips, stifling the sound.

Connor's dark eyes gleamed over his hand, and he chuckled low through his teeth.

"Hi there," he growled, pressing his body against her. He pinned her thigh with his knee, and Elysia whimpered, pressing her body as flat as possible against the wall behind her. Connor grinned, pressing his knee harder. "Here we are, alone, at last," he purred.

Elysia glared at him over his hand. Her stomach twisted, and she was certain she was about to vomit. She hoped she did. She hoped it splattered all over him and his perfectly crisp dinner jacket.

He dropped his knee and tucked his free arm around her back, pulling her towards him. "Pretty soon, we'll be alone every day. What do you say…a wedding before the end of the Quarter?" Elysia's eyes flamed, and he chuckled low, running his fingers along her spine. "I don't want to wait too long, you see." She cringed against his fingers. Yep, she was absolutely going to vomit. Connor grinned. "Anyway, the people will be expecting a short engagement. We don't want to make them wait."

He tucked his face towards her neck and ran his nose along her jaw. "Mmm, you smell so good." Elysia squirmed, and he pulled back, roving his eyes over her dress. "And you look even better. I bet you're absolutely stunning in your sea form."

She glared as he lifted his hand off her mouth, whispering against her cheek. "Come on, Elysia, just a little taste. We'll be married soon, anyway." He moved his lips towards her mouth, and Elysia fisted her hands against the stone. She strained her face away and pressed her mouth into a hard line, swallowing bile. Connor's chuckle was low in his throat. "Playing hard to get?" he teased. "That's alright. I like the hunt."

Abruptly, he dropped his arms and stepped away from her. His eyes gleamed, and he stuffed his hands into his pockets. "I'll see you at dinner," he said, winking. Elysia jerked a nod, earning another chuckle from Connor. He held her gaze as he backed slowly away, reminding Elysia of the way a predator stalks its prey. Then he turned, walking back the way he'd come.

When she was sure he was gone, Elysia collapsed in a heap on the stone bench, holding her head in her hands. She was shaking. Her head was spinning, and her heart thrummed in her ears. Her stomach swirled as beads of sweat broke out on her forehead, and she leaned back against the stone wall, sucking down deep breaths of the cool evening air. Vomiting was the least of her concerns. If she wasn't careful, she was going to faint.

How was she supposed to survive this? Connor's very presence made her sick, and she was expected to *wed* him? The thought made the dizziness worse. Her vision tunneled, and she pushed the thought away, focusing on bringing air slowly in and out of her chest.

It didn't matter how she felt. Her mother and the council had made that very clear. They'd said so at the last council meeting. Connor was her choice. It was what was best for the court.

Despite Lady Sirena's insistence that things should change, that the Selkie Court might rely on the Court of Merrows, the council was adamant that they maintain strict separation. According to them, any close contact with the Merrow court could spell disaster for the Selkies.

What about Lord Ríonan? one had said. *Do we not remember what happened to him? What if Lady Sirena chooses to turn on us like her father did?* Another, a fat, squatty woman that Elysia had never liked had said, *We must not bend. Elysia must wed Ciar's boy. It is the only way to maintain our safety and our self-reliance.*

It was clear. It was up to her. Above all, their clan must do what it took to remain separate of the Court of Merrows, and, unfortunately for her, what it took was up to Elysia. No matter what, Connor was to be her choice. It was the only way for the clan to remain self-sufficient. At least, that's what Lord Ciar had said when he convinced them.

Lord Ciar owned several mines on the Selkie Isles, where precious jewels and rare sea glass were uncovered from the tunnels and underground river beds and shipped throughout Caelium at high price. In exchange for his son's seat at Elysia's side, Ciar promised to support the court with his lucrative trade. Because of this, her mother and the council were certain Elysia's union would add a necessary layer of protection for the court. It would help them uphold the treaty, prevent them from having to have additional contact with the merrows.

Elysia had always found Ciar rather slippery. He was too keen to grasp at power when it was presented, and she was sure he was only offering up his son for his own interests. She had never liked the way he looked at her. There was something sinister in his eyes. She shuddered. They reminded her of Connor's.

Even with Elysia's reservations, her mother saw no issues with Ciar *or* his son, and neither did the council. Classically, Connor was every Selkie woman's dream. He was tall, dark, rich, and handsome. Elysia guessed she could see it, but there was also an edge to him that she couldn't quite explain. More than once, she'd caught him ogling her at court with his beady black eyes, and just last Quarter, she'd seen him steal away with some young woman in the dark palace library, long after the court meeting was adjourned. She could still see the young woman's face, a mixture of fear and uncertainty, as Connor had pushed her back through the library doors.

She thought of their encounter in the garden moments ago and shivered. It sufficiently illustrated her meaning. Even the memory of Connor's body pressed against her made a sour taste come into her mouth and fear swirl in her belly. She was sure her face had looked just like the woman from the library.

She blew out a breath and stared up at the sky. It was getting late, and the moons were already visible in the pinkish-purple twilight. Dinner was scheduled for sunset. After, they would gather in the gardens to watch the Evening Stars open. That's when it would happen.

Her Presentation to the Selkie Court would occur, and every eligible suitor in court would line up on the dance floor. She would select one to join her in the first dance of the evening, and at the end of it, her suitor would be declared her mate. Soon, preparations for her wedding would begin. The thought made her heart flatten, and she gripped the edge of her stone bench, whitening her knuckles.

Elysia sighed. There was no point in hiding here any longer. She might as well get on with it. At last, she stood, smoothing the front of her dress. She forced herself down the garden path, then exited through an arched doorway in the stone wall towards the covered pavilion.

Despite her dark feelings, her breath caught in her throat at the beauty of the scene. The Midsummer Ball was the one event on the islands where no expense was spared, where nothing was left wanting. Summer harvests were always bountiful.

The large white tent billowed in the breeze, stretching wide over long banquet tables heaped with all kinds of food. Circular tables covered with crisp white cloths sat inside the tent and on the lawn, while decadent floral designs cascaded in the tables' center. Hanging floral vines twisted from the poles of the tent up to the roof, covering the inside of the ceiling with a mass of fragrant and colorful blooms, while the musicians sat on a platform in the far-left corner, filling the courtyard with the sound of soft strings.

At once, Ena appeared at her elbow. She tucked her small hand around Elysia's forearm, grinning. Tyse followed her closely, still stiff and silent. He pulled at the neck of his shirt, swallowing convulsively and causing his throat to bob.

Elysia stifled a giggle, then turned to her friend. Ena grinned up at her.

"Ready for the night that will change your life forever?!" Ena said excitedly. Elysia twirled her finger in the air, unenthusiastic. "Hurrah," she said sarcastically. Ena ignored her, tugging at her elbow. "Come on, then. Time to get this party started! Besides," she sniffed, "Everyone knows it's not a party 'til I show up."

Behind them, Tyse made a gurgling sound in his throat. Elysia cut her eyes to him. He looked like he might faint.

Ena pulled her through the yard until they were just outside the tent. Suddenly, she spun and peered seriously into Elysia's eyes. She took a deep breath and grasped Elysia's hands.

"Right. Now, you look lovely, this night is lovely, and everything is going to be *fine*. Remember to smile, look pleased, and *try* to enjoy yourself, okay?"

She studied Elysia's face closely. Elysia sucked in a nervous breath, then smoothed her dress and scanned the interior of the tent. "Yes?" Ena pressed, raising her brows. Elysia nodded once. "Yes," she muttered. Ena nodded. "Good. Now, I see your mother at the head of the room. There are two seats for us."

She started to walk away, then remembered Tyse was standing silently behind her. She stopped short and grinned at him over her shoulder. "I'll talk to you later, okay?" she said sweetly. Tyse grunted and gave an imperceptible nod. Then he turned and walked stiffly across the lawn.

Ena waited until he was out of earshot, then lifted her face towards Elysia's ear. "I'll be talking to myself, more like," she whispered. She puffed out a breath and shook her head. Elysia chuckled. "Not going well?"

Ena threw up her hands. "The man never speaks! How can he have absolutely *nothing* to say?"

Elysia bit the inside of her cheek, trying to stifle a laugh.

"I believe you have enough to say for the both of you," she teased. Ena shrugged. "Someone's gotta keep the conversation going."

Lady Malca was waiting for her at the table, along with most of the council. She gestured to the seat nearest her, scanning Elysia from head to foot. "Darling, you look lovely. Come, have a seat. Ena, dear, sit next to her."

Elysia smiled softly at her mother and sat in the open chair. "Hello, Mother. Everything looks lovely, as usual." Lady Malca smiled, turning her head to admire the splendor. "Yes, we've rather outdone ourselves this cycle," she said proudly.

She cut her eyes to Elysia, smiling conspiratorially. "But, this is no ordinary Midsummer Ball, right, my darling?" Elysia lifted her chin, smiling a flat smile. "No, Mother, it isn't." She lifted her napkin from her plate, focusing on arranging it neatly on her lap.

Lady Malca studied her for a moment, then leaned towards her, speaking low. "And we are agreed? Your choice will be Connor?" Elysia sniffed. She fisted her hands in her napkin beneath the table. "Yes," she said flatly. "We're agreed." Lady Malca nodded approvingly and patted Elysia's arm. "He's an excellent choice. Powerful, handsome. He will be an asset to you and to the court."

Elysia's heart burned, and she tapped her foot restlessly beneath the table. When she could bear it no longer, she turned to her mother, peering pleadingly into her face. "Mother, are you *certain* it must be this cycle? Can't we wait just one more before I have to make my choice?"

Lady Malca sighed as she lifted her hand to tuck a lock of stray hair behind Elysia's ear. "My dear, we have discussed this. You've already passed your eighteenth cycle. You're well over one cycle older than tradition dictates." She grasped Elysia's hand and squeezed.

"Tonight, you will officially become a Lady of this court. It is your duty as the future ruler to protect the clan, and that means you must do what it takes to preserve our way of life.

Ciar is wealthy and powerful, and so is his son, by association. You must choose him, and it must be tonight. Choosing Connor as your mate will strengthen the clan's confidence in your position and provide security for us. With Connor by your side, we can continue to live in safety. We won't need to rely on the Court of Merrows for anything."

Elysia nodded. She bit the inside of her cheek, holding back tears. Across the table, the fat council woman that Elysia detested whispered something to the thin woman on her right. Lady Malca lifted her glass, furtively scanning the table. "Chin up, darling," she whispered. "The people are watching."

Elysia turned her head from the council's prying eyes and dabbed at her damp cheeks with the back of her hand. She knew her mother was right. Connor was the obvious choice for the security of their people, the protection of the clan, but was he the obvious choice for her? She knew that certain expectations came with her position, but did her needs or wishes matter not at all?

She sighed as she lifted her glass to swallow through the lump in her throat. She wasn't certain what her wishes even *were*, but she knew for certain what they weren't. In no way, shape, or form would they *ever* include a land-locked life on the Selkie Isles with Connor as her mate.

Chapter 4

Elysia pushed her fork slowly around her plate, creating small piles of food near its edges. Usually, she enjoyed the delicious meal at the Midsummer Ball, but tonight, she had no appetite. All she could think about was what was required of her after.

Finally, she gave up and put down her fork. She took a sip of her tea and fought the urge to squirm in her chair. The dinner was dragging on forever. She would have given anything to escape. She sighed and crossed her arms, tapping her fingers restlessly on her elbows.

At last, it was over, and Elysia sprang out of her chair. She curtsied lightly to her mother, then turned and strode out towards the gardens. She wanted to get a good view of the first Evening Star blooms. It was likely to be her only joy of the night, maybe even the last joy she'd ever experience.

Evening Stars were never planted in the gardens. The strange flowers simply appeared there every spring. In fact, the whole island would soon be dotted with their bright blooms, which opened at nightfall to illuminate the countryside in a bluish glow.

Elysia posted herself to the left of the fountain, where a cluster of Evening Stars had sprouted next to the path. Their bright blue buds grew on long, curved stalks and hung like bells above her head, swaying gently in the evening breeze.

Soon, the garden was full of partygoers. They lumped themselves into small groups and sipped from their glass stemware, chatting quietly amongst themselves. A hush fell over the crowd as, at last, the sun dipped below the horizon and the first bloom burst open right above Elysia's head.

She watched in awe as the blue flower unfurled its long petals. In moments, they had curled back on themselves to form the shape of a five-pointed star. At once, a tremor began in the base of the stem, and a soft tinkling sound began as an iridescent light sparkled gently from the center of the bloom. The light spread outward in a soft blue glow, forming weaving lines along the petals, until the entire bloom bathed her face in its gentle light.

One after another, more flowers burst open, until the entire garden glowed with a faint bluish hue. Ena appeared at Elysia's side and tucked her small hand around the crook of her elbow. She smiled up at the closest bloom, then turned to face Elysia. "I'll be by your side, you know," she murmured. "No matter what." She gave Elysia's arm a squeeze, and Elysia covered her hand with her own, smiling down at her friend. "I know," she murmured. "And thank you." Ena smiled. Then she moved to take her place with the others who had begun to gather at the far end of the dance floor.

Lady Malca stood waiting in the center of the floor, facing the crowd. Already, the eligible suitors had begun to line up in front of her. Elysia sighed. It was the moment of she had dreaded. She squared her shoulders and smoothed the front of her dress, then moved to stand by her mother.

Quietly, she scanned her eyes down the long row of suitors. The young men smoothed their hair and adjusted their jackets under her gaze, and more than one of them winked. Her stomach turned at their actions, and she had to work to keep from rolling her eyes.

They didn't know they were wasting their charms. They couldn't have known that this wasn't really Elysia's choice. Her choice had been made for her.

She furrowed her brow and scanned the long row, once more. Connor was suspiciously absent. Lady Malca narrowed her eyes, searching the crowd behind the row. "Where is he?" she hissed. Elysia shrugged a shoulder. "Probably off somewhere with…"

Connor's appearance cut her off. He strode lazily into the garden, taking his place at the end of the line. His usually coifed hair was out of place, and he smoothed it with his palm before rebuttoning his jacket. The young suitor beside him gave him a nudge, pointing to the corner of his mouth. He flicked his eyes to Elysia before dropping his gaze and swiping at the lip stain with his thumb.

In a moment, a lovely woman with long blonde hair appeared from where Connor had entered. She slipped into the crowd, standing closely behind him. Elysia vaguely recognized her. Maybe her name was Delia? She tucked a lock of silky hair behind her ear and kept her eyes on the dance floor as the crowd around her whispered softly. Some of the suitors even chuckled, jabbing each other in the sides at the obvious situation.

Lady Malca stared at Connor in horror, and Elysia's face and chest burned. She was mortified. She tried to ignore the whispers and stares, but a large lump formed in her throat, and she was dangerously close to crying. She hoped the bluish light of the Evening Stars was enough to mask her expression, and she bit the inside of her lip and stared hard at the floor, willing her brimming tears not to fall. She had never been so humiliated.

Connor didn't seem to care. Actually, he appeared rather pleased with himself. Elysia watched as he laughed jovially with the young man to his left. Her anger flared, and she swallowed her tears, staring daggers at them.

Connor didn't look at her, but Delia did. For a moment, she pretended not to mind Elysia's stare. But then her face flushed, and she turned away, disappearing into the crowd.

Lady Malca clapped twice and cleared her throat. "Good evening to all, and welcome to the Midsummer Ball. We are delighted to have you all join us tonight to celebrate the beauty of the Selkie Isles and the first blooms of our famed Evening Stars." She gestured to the nearest bloom and clapped softly with the crowd.

"As you know, the Evening Star is a symbol to us from the Source of true love and great beauty. And what could be more beautiful than to celebrate true love tonight?" The crowd clapped softly, again, and Lady Malca paused, waiting for them to quiet.

"In a moment, under the symbolic Evening Stars, the future ruler of the Selkie Court will choose her mate." She gestured to Elysia, who nodded politely, wearing a flat smile. Her stomach was twisted in a hard knot.

"So now, without further delay, I present my daughter, Lady Elysia Bryn of the Selkie Isles." Elysia curtsied to her mother, as gentle claps resumed, and soft string music wafted through the garden. She stayed in her curtsy longer than was necessary, delaying the inevitable, and she could feel her mother staring pointedly at the top of her head.

At last, she stood. Without meeting Connor's gaze, she strode purposely to the edge of the dance floor and extended her hand. Connor grinned down at her lazily. Then he took her palm with a flourish and kissed the back of it.

Elysia stared at him with cold eyes as he lifted his gaze, grinning smugly. The familiar burn of bile returned in her throat, and she fought to keep down her vomit as Connor gripped her waist and twirled her across the dance floor. The crowd clapped with delight, but Elysia's heart was a silent stone.

Other couples soon joined them, until finally, the whole floor was full of whirling skirts and sharp suit jackets. Connor pulled her tighter, whispering hot breath into her ear. "So, is this how it's going to be?" he growled. "People are *watching*, Elysia. The least you could do is smile." She glared at him and flattened her mouth into a grimace. "Does that suit?" she said sharply.

Connor snatched at her waist, hurling her against his jacket. The breath pressed from her throat, and she wheezed, clamping onto his collar with both hands. At once, his expression changed. Elysia's mind rang warning bells, as he studied her face hungrily, lifting her chin with his rough hand. "It'll do. For now," he said hotly. He twirled her again and she clamped her eyes shut, sucking down deep chest-fulls of the cool night air. All the whirling was making her sick feeling worse.

Abruptly, and for no apparent reason, the band stopped playing. Connor stopped spinning, and Elysia immediately stepped back from his arms. She brought her hands to her stomach, trying to still the tea swirling inside of it as sharp voices erupted on the other side of the fountain. The people around them began to murmur and step back from the dance floor. Connor's eyes were focused at the shouts. His face was a mask of disbelief, and Elysia spun towards the fountain to see what the matter was. Her eyes widened at the scene. She was nearly as shocked as he.

Two merrow men with long spears stood stoically by the fountain. It was obvious by their weapons and dress that they were members of the merrow Forces. The one on the left was older, muscular and broad, with a crop of short silver hair and piercing, glittering blue eyes. The merrow on the right was younger, thinner, albeit still muscular, with fiery, red hair that was almost as bright as Ena's. Trails of translucent scales trailed up the men's temples, and they bore three inconspicuous slits in the skin just below their ears.

At once, the selkie Guard surrounded them both, aiming their spears at the merrows' throats. The taller one lifted his chin, studying the Guard with narrowed eyes. "Lady Malca, if you would be so kind. I am aware we are in breach of the treaty, however, we come at the request of Lady Sirena. We're here to deliver an invitation."

Lady Malca studied the tall Merrows in silence, then she lifted her arms and clapped twice. Immediately, the Guard dispersed, reforming in a neat row behind the selkie ruler.

Ena had moved to Elysia's side, during the commotion. She gripped the back of Elysia's elbow nervously. "What do they want?" she whispered. Elysia shook her head. "I have no idea."

The older merrow adjusted his posture as he pulled a rolled parchment from his vest. Then he held it in front of him and began to read. "The Lady Sirena, on behalf of the Court of Merrows, apologizes for this sudden intrusion. She requests that the honorable Lady Malca overlook this minor breach of the Treaty of Hiraeth, as she wishes to extend an invitation to her daughter, Elysia Bryn, the future ruler of the Selkie Court. It is the solemn wish of Lady Sirena that the Lady Elysia would come to stay at the Court of Merrows, alone, as her guest and ambassador of the Selkie Court."

A hush fell over the crowd, then all eyes turned towards Elysia. Elysia blinked at the taller Merrow in shock. Why was Lady Sirena so insistent that she come to court? She had already been forced to decline her invitation last winter. What could she possibly mean?

Lady Malca clasped her hands at her waist and addressed the older Merrow, who gazed respectfully down at the dance floor. "Alistair, thank you for your kind visit," she said proudly. "I regret to inform you that I must decline Lady Sirena's invitation, on behalf of my daughter. As you can see, this is a party, and your intrusion is in poor taste, not to mention a violation of the treaty. Please, return to your own court. And please ask that the Lady Sirena leaves us alone, in peace."

The tall merrow inclined his head politely to Lady Malca, keeping his eyes trained on the ends of her shoes. "Respectfully, Lady Sirena is under the impression that the Midsummer Ball marks the Lady Elysia's coming-of-age. She is now considered a Lady of the court. Is this not so?"

Lady Malca flicked her eyes to Elysia.

"It's true," she said flatly. Alistair nodded once.

"As the Lady Elysia is now of age, is it not the tradition of the Selkie Court that she be allowed to make her own choice regarding an ambassador's visit?" Lady Malca's shoulders slumped slightly. "Yes," she breathed.

Elysia's heart gave a little thrill. She hadn't known that. She had certainly never been taught that fact. She frowned, thinking. Perhaps she had. Maybe she had simply forgotten.

Alistair nodded. "As it is your tradition, Lady Sirena respectfully requests that the young Lady be allowed to make her own decision about whether she wishes to visit the Court of Merrows and that you consent to her coming as outlined by the treaty, if she accepts the invitation." He lifted his hand. "Of course, Lady Sirena will provide Lady Elysia with an escort, as she has attempted to do in the past," he added.

Her mother didn't answer. She stared hard at the dance floor as Elysia's mind reeled with possibilities. Ena eyed her warily, and she squeezed her friend's hand. "Lys, no," she whispered. Mixed emotions fluttered in Elysia's chest as her mother turned to face her. Her eyes were tinged with fear, and Elysia smiled quietly as she curtsied to her. Lady Malca dropped her eyes, worry lining her expression as Elysia moved to stand before the Merrow men.

A thrill of excitement tinged with fear swirled in her belly as she considered her next words. The possibility of adventure in the sea was thrilling, but she was still quite unsure of what she was about to do. After all, the Merrows hated the Selkies, and she couldn't forget their murderous behavior towards her father. Lord Dolion hadn't been the only one to despise her people, and she knew some if not most in the Court of Merrows still held the same view.

She frowned, working through her complicated thoughts. Despite the danger, she really wanted to go. She knew Lady Sirena, or at least, she thought she did. From what Elysia could tell, she was nothing like her father. It was clear the ruler wished to repair the relationship between the courts. Elysia was almost sure that she wouldn't personally inflict harm to her or the Selkie Court. Besides, she was sending an escort. Surely that was further evidence she meant to keep Elysia safe.

She studied the two visitors. They were tall and imposing, especially Alistair, and it was hard for Elysia not to shrink back from their large frames. Merrow men were known to be large and threatening, especially those in the Forces. If her escort looked anything like them, he could surely keep her safe.

She turned her head slightly, taking one last sidelong glance at her mother. The leader's face was ashen. It was as if she could read Elysia's mind, as if she already knew her next words. She peered quietly at Elysia's face, eyes brimming, before giving her a quick nod.

Elysia grinned. She turned back to the Merrows, straightening her shoulders and lifting her chin. She was going to take that small nod as consent.

"Thank you for your visit. Please relay to Lady Sirena that I appreciate the kindness of her invitation." She paused, glancing again at her mother. Lady Malca swiped a tear and

Elysia hesitated, wetting her lips. She knew the dangers the council had discussed this past winter, the ones about her visiting the Court of Merrows alone. The tensions between the courts were so high, that a visit to the Court of Merrows, especially as the future selkie ruler, meant she was risking her life.

Her heart thrummed in her ears, and before she could allow herself to think any further, she blurted out,

"I would be delighted to accept."

A hush fell over the crowd as someone grabbed her by her upper arm. Conner twisted it roughly, thrusting her behind him, his dagger drawn. "I can't allow that," he bellowed. "No Lady of mine will *dare* visit the Court of Merrows." He lunged towards the visitors as Alistair and the red-haired Merrow lifted their spears, crouching in defense.

Metal clanged against metal, and before Elysia knew what was happening, the red-haired Merrow had spun Connor into a headlock. He placed the blade of his spear against Connor's throat, drawing a thin line of blood, and Connor raised his hands, dropping his dagger onto the dance floor.

Elysia stepped towards him, but Ena blocked her path. The top of her red hair glowed in the blue Evening Star light, and she placed a hand to her hip, casually sticking out her small foot. "Now, now, boys," she said lightly. "There's no need for violence.

After all, this is a party."

She smiled sweetly at the red-haired Merrow, gesturing to him with her hand. "Sir…er, I mean Lord…" The red-haired merrow cut her off. "Just Seamus," he replied. Ena studied him thoughtfully. "Thank you, *Just* Seamus," she teased. Seamus widened his shoulders, the muscle by his mouth giving a little twitch. His bright green eyes were fixed carefully on the blade of his spear, which he still tightly against Connor's throat.

Ena grinned, then quickly stuffed it down. She clasped her hands at her waist, maintaining an air of seriousness.

"You'll have to excuse poor Connor, here. You see, he and Lady Elysia were betrothed this evening, and he was understandably feeling quite defensive about her being taken from him on such short notice. I'm sure he will behave himself, if you just let him free. Right, Connor?" She raised her chin at Connor expectantly.

The muscle in Connor's jaw feathered, and he swallowed against Seamus' blade. He flicked his eyes to Ena and gave a slight nod.

Ena smiled sweetly. "There, see? Nothing to worry about."

Seamus released his grip, sending Connor toppling to the floor.

Connor landed on his side with a grunt. He ground his teeth, then stood swiftly, dusting his suit jacket. He flicked his eyes to Alistair and Seamus, giving them a warning stare. The two glared back at him, their steely, glittering eyes sending shivers down Elysia's spine. Then he stalked off the dance floor, moving to stand by Delia at the edge of the crowd.

Elysia followed him with her eyes, watching as Delia swiped at an imaginary smudge on his collar. Connor found her gaze above Delia's shoulder, and a flush bloomed on Elysia's chest as a smug, lazy grin spread over his features. Swiftly, she lifted her chin, flicking her eyes back to their merrow visitors. She schooled her face into one of nonchalance, angry at herself that he'd caught her looking at him.

Seamus and Alistair were still at their posts. The two had an odd look on their faces. They were staring straight ahead, stiff and uncomfortable. Elysia moved her eyes to the ground in front of them. Ena had lowered herself into a deep bow, right in front of Seamus. Elysia blinked at her friend's back in shock. She had never seen a Selkie woman bow to a merrow man. Technically, she wasn't breaking any rules, but it just wasn't done. She flicked her gaze to her mother, who was staring at Ena with bulging eyes, and she covered her mouth, stifling a grin.

Ena stood, then, smiling coyly up at Seamus. The merrow grinned at the tips of her shoes in fascination. "Thank you, *Just* Seamus," she said sweetly. "Your kindness to Connor and the Selkie Court will not be forgotten.". With that, she spun and came to stand just behind Elysia's left shoulder.

Elysia inclined her head to Ena's ear, "Quite the performance," she teased. "A bit shocking, perhaps, but at least you saved Connor's skin. Seamus looked like he was about to slit his throat."

Ena sniffed, crossing her arms. "All in a days' work," she whispered smugly, eyeing Seamus.

"By the way, are you *sure* about this, Elysia? Visiting the Court of Merrows, *alone*?" Elysia grinned down at her friend. "Who says I'm going alone?"

For once, Ena was stunned and speechless. She put a hand to her chest.

"*Me*?" she wheezed. "You want *me* to accompany you to the Court of Merrows?"

Elysia shrugged. "Why not?" she asked. "You *are* my lady in waiting. It's perfectly reasonable that you would accompany me on my visit."

Ena stared hard at the two Merrows in front of them. Her eyes rested on Seamus, and she bit the inside of her lip. Elysia followed her gaze and grinned, whispering, "I'm sure Seamus will be there," she teased.

Ena's ears tipped pink, and she tucked in her lips, stifling a giggle.

"Leave it to you to make a joke at a serious time like this," she whispered, holding back a grin.

"Is that a yes, then?" Elysia prodded.

Ena flicked her eyes to Seamus and smiled a small smile. "Okay, I'll go," she said.

"I mean…Yes."

Elysia grinned. "Perfect."

The merrow men had moved to stand in a small circle with

Lady Malca. Alistair was speaking in a low tone, and Lady Malca's face looked pained. Elysia frowned and moved beside her, placing a hand on her shoulder. She squeezed, and her mother turned, putting her warm palm to Elysia's face.

"At least take Ena with you, my darling," she said. "You'll need a friendly face amongst the Merrows."

Elysia grinned. "My thoughts exactly," she replied. Lady Malca smiled weakly. She pulled Elysia into a squeezing hug. "Be careful," she whispered. "Promise me."

Elysia nodded against her shoulder. "I promise," she whispered. Her mother nodded.

Then she stepped away, swiping at her eyes as she moved to discuss the matter with her council near the garden wall.

By then, most of the crowd had begun to disperse. Elysia turned back to the Merrow men. "I have one more request, if you would kindly relay it to Lady Sirena?"

Alistair nodded, staring hard at the floor. "Of course, My Lady," he replied.

Elysia gestured behind her, where Ena stood demurely in the middle of the dance floor.

"You've already met my lady in waiting, Ena."

Ena lifted her hand, giving small wave.

"I would like her to accompany me, during my visit. That is, only if Lady Sirena doesn't mind."

Alistair shifted slightly. He studied the ends of Ena's shoes with his flinty eyes. Seamus did the same, but his lips twitched, and he lifted his gaze briefly to Ena's face.

Elysia stiffened. Seamus had looked directly at Ena. It was a clear treaty violation. merrow men's tails had been flailed for less.

She flicked her eyes quickly to the Guard. Thankfully, they hadn't noticed. They were still in position, standing behind her mother near the edge of the dance floor. She blew out a breath, moving her eyes back to Seamus. His face was fixed in a hard, sharp line, and he was back to staring pointedly at the floor near Ena's feet.

Suddenly, Seamus cleared his throat. "Sir, I would be willing to volunteer as her escort, if there is no other task you have for me tomorrow," he said rapidly.

Alistair peered sideways at him, raising one brow. The muscle in Seamus' jaw ticked, but otherwise, his expression was still a hard, sharp mask. Alistair narrowed his eyes, studying Seamus' expression.

"So be it," he said abruptly.

He flicked his eyes away, and a broad grin escaped Seamus' lips, before he pushed them back into a flat line. Alistair gestured to Elysia, keeping his eyes at her feet.

"Be at the shoreline at midday. Your escorts will be waiting," he instructed. Elysia nodded once. "We'll be ready," she replied. With that, the two Merrows disappeared out of the garden and into the night.

Elysia let out her breath and sat heavily on the edge of the fountain. She was shaking, and she braced her arms on the stone, as Ena plopped down next to her. "This is not at *all* how I expected this night to turn out," said Ena. Elysia crossed her feet, letting her head hang back as she peered up at the sky. Caelium's double moons were bright and full, and tiny stars dotted the darkness, twinkling down at her like miniature, glittering lanterns. She sucked in a calming breath. "Me either," she murmured softly.

Inside, her mind raced with the events of the evening, and she twisted her lips, working to straighten her jumbled thoughts. Should she have refused Lady Sirena's invitation? She still wasn't sure.

She still wasn't sure why she'd even been invited. What did Lady Sirena mean by it? Tensions were so high between their courts. She wondered if her visit would make it worse. She wondered if she would be safe.

Then, there was Connor. He was more than furious. She was sure she would pay for his public humiliation later. She bit her lip. Or maybe he wouldn't even care. He was probably off with Delia somewhere, again. She imagined them kissing against the garden wall, and her stomach burned. *Sickening.*

Suddenly, she couldn't stand the dry land for one more moment. She felt caged, and she ached to get out of her body, out of her feelings, and into some new ones. A swim was what she needed. Maybe then, she would feel better, and her mind would be clear enough to sort through her mass of tangled emotions.

Chapter 5

Kai lifted his eyes above the water, scanning the shoreline. Evening Stars dotted the hillside above him. Their first blooms had just burst open, and the bluish light of the bell-shaped flowers mixed with that of the full moons to illuminate the secret island in a soft glow. As usual, the coast was clear, and he lifted himself out of the water.

He stood in the shallow waves and cupped his palms, drawing tiny water droplets into them from the surrounding sea air. They hovered above his skin in two small orbs before he moved them into a long, thin line. Then he flattened his palms, waving them lightly over his frame. The fine droplets collected themselves, weaving into a dry, light fabric that covered his torso and legs. He stared down at the blue of the sleeveless shirt and long pants, clicking his tongue. He preferred his usual attire over the ones he made by water weaving, but it would have to do.

Alistair had taught Kai to water weave just before his twelfth cycle. It had been just after his parents' deaths, and he had just started training with the Forces. His uncle had brought him everywhere, that first cycle. He'd gone with him across the realm, patrolling the undersea rivers. It had been a welcome distraction from his grief, and Kai was thankful he'd been given the experience. On patrol, access to clothing wasn't always guaranteed, so Alistair had shown Kai how to water weave, and it had taken Kai several Quarters to perfect the skill.

He chuckled as he hiked up the hillside, remembering Maura's face the first time they had come to their secret island. At that time, Kai hadn't quite perfected water weaving. He'd been so nervous when he had come up out of the water that he'd fumbled the water droplets. They'd fallen from his palms into the sea, and Maura had turned red as an algae bloom. She'd spun away, covering her eyes, while Kai had hurried to hide behind an oak tree on the shore, beyond embarrassment.

When the initial shock had worn off, she had fallen over on the rocks, holding her stomach as peals of laughter shook her frame. Finally, she had stopped laughing. Then she had sat with her back to the oak tree, chatting with him and patiently waiting while he struggled to weave the tiny droplets over his skin.

After a few tries, he had gotten it right, and the skill had never left him. Later, long after she knew he had perfected it, Maura had insisted he still needed practice. They had used the excuse to come back to the island, and soon, they were escaping from court to visit there as often as possible.

After Maura's death, Kai had avoided the island. It was just too painful to visit. There were too many memories, too much sorrow. Instead, at night, he wandered the open sea, avoiding his Night Watch duties and the dreams of Maura that he so wanted to be his reality.

Being at court without her was bad enough, but the island? The island was so much worse. Kai's heart squeezed with memories. It was where they had told each other their secrets, where they had first held hands, where they had shared their first kiss, and where they had fallen in love. The secret island *was* Maura. It was everything.

One day, they had found a hidden grove of Cypress trees, nestled between two hills at the island's southernmost tip. A waterfall flowed down the rocky hillside from the stream above it, filling a small, clear pool at the base of the trees. *Paradise*, Maura had called it. And it had been, once.

On their fourteenth cycle, Kai had built Maura a treehouse there. He had used the logs of the grove, stripping the wood and sanding it until it was smooth. That cycle, she had been fascinated with the idea that one day they would grow up and live on the island together.

Just like the selkies.

Kai stopped at the edge of the grove, peering up at the treehouse. Now that Maura was gone, their secret place had lost its charm. The branches of the trees hung low, dejected, and even the window frames of the treehouse looked sad and vacant. They peered out at him with hollow, empty eyes.

Absently, he touched the golden ring that hung around his neck. He had given it to Maura when he had asked her to marry him, right there on the treehouse steps. He smiled softly at the memory. Their secret grove had felt so beautiful that night, so full of joy, so full of life.

Tears pricked his eyes, and he touched the wooden stair with a shaky hand.

He remembered Maura's *Yes*. She had flung herself into his arms, and he had pulled her against him, kissing her soundly. His joy had been untethered, and if he'd wished, he believed he could have sprouted wings. He could have flown, high above them, carried on happiness and dreams.

Kai's jaw flexed, and he stared dejectedly at the tiny pink blooms in his palm. On his way to the treehouse, he had stopped in the Tamarisk grove to collect some fronds. They were Maura's favorite. She had been so excited when the trees had sprouted on the island.

Look, Kai, it's a Tamarisk grove! It's a sign from the Source of good things to come.

Each time they had visited after that, she had stopped in the grove to collect a bouquet.

Lately, Kai had started visiting the grove, too. He would gather a handful of fronds and sit on the treehouse steps, thinking. Sometimes, he even talked to Maura about his life, or his dreams, or their memories.

At first, the practice had made him feel worse, and he had spent an entire Quarter in a deep gloom, lashing out at anyone within speaking distance. Unfortunately, Lady Sirena and Seamus had been on the receiving end of his abuse, more times than he cared to admit. But later, his visits had begun to hurt a bit less, and now he found himself looking forward to sitting on the treehouse steps and talking into the quiet darkness.

Kai leaned against the steps, chuckling to himself. He must really be losing it, if he thought that talking to himself in the darkness was an enjoyable practice. He shook his head and sat heavily onto the second step, laying the bouquet of Tamarisk fronds on the ground.

For a while, he was still, listening to the flow of the waterfall and the sounds of small animals scampering through the wood. The dual moons glowed softly through the branches above him, shining a lattice of light on the forest floor, and a strange sense of peace enveloped his mind and his body. He allowed himself to sink into it, closing his eyes.

Something occurred to him as he sat still, in the quiet. He hadn't been inside the treehouse since…before. At first, even the *idea* of going inside it had been more than he could bear. He had avoided the thought completely. But now? Now, he felt more comfortable with the idea.

He stood, turning to peer up at the silent doorframe. He wondered how it would feel to go inside. The more he stared, the more curious he became, until finally, he picked up the Tamarisk fronds and climbed the creaking wooden steps.

At the top, he paused. He closed his eyes, steeling himself for the onslaught of painful memories he was sure he would find inside. He inhaled, as an echo of Maura's laughter bounced from the doorway and into his head. His eyes popped open at the sound, and he scanned the treehouse's dark interior. Her laugh had sounded so real, so close. But the treehouse was empty, and the small, wooden room remained silent.

Kai blew out a shaky breath. He rested his forehead against the rough door frame, shaking his head. "I really *am* losing it," he whispered. He tossed the Tamarisk bouquet on the floor inside, then he braced himself on the door frame and pulled himself through.

Immediately, the scent of Tamarisk fronds mixed with cypress logs tinged his nose, and an onslaught of memories flooded his head. His eyes pricked, and his throat tightened, and he leaned heavily against the far wall. The weight of the memories was crushing. Pain sliced his chest, and he gripped it, sliding down the wall until he landed hard on the wooden floor. He was right back there…right back to last winter.

Maura sat with her back against the wall, just to the left of the door. Her hand was outstretched, examining the ring he had given her moments before. Her long reddish-brown hair glimmered in the moonlight, and she flicked her golden eyes to him, grinning. She giggled, then, and moved to all fours, crawling towards him on her knees.

She stopped just before him, hovering her lips over his face. Then she moved towards his ear. "I love you, Kai Bennett, and I always will," she whispered.

Kai smiled up at her grin. Her hair hung around his face like a long curtain, encasing him in its salty, floral scent. He reached to wrap his fingers in it…

Kai blinked as the memory dissolved before his gaze, and the space in front of him was, once more, empty and silent. He drew back his hand. Maura was gone. The memory had vanished, and he sat alone, again, in the darkness. Her floral scent still hung in the air just above him, and he brought his hands to his head, swallowing convulsively.

It had been so real. He had seen her, heard her voice. He had almost touched her.

Almost.

Kai felt his chest crack, and he brought his arms across it, bracing against the pain. Seeing Maura like that, feeling her, nearly touching her, had pulled open a deep wound inside of him that he had thought was nearly healed. The spot to the left of his chest, the place of his Amloga, his Flame of Time, ached and burned, and he grimaced, massaging his fingers over the spot.

After Maura's death, his suffering had been so deep, he had thought he would surely drown. The only way he'd survived was to push down his feelings, and with it, everything else. He had passed forward a spectre of his former self, a shadow—a shadow full of grief.

He locked himself away, not allowing anyone or anything to touch him. Because of it, he had managed to go whole days or full weeks without feeling anything at all. It was just easier that way, just a way for him to survive. He knew he couldn't live that way forever, but at least he could function in his day-to-day without his chest cracking open and its contents spilling out on the glass floor of the throne room for all to see. He didn't think he could take that. Better that he be this shadow of himself, a partial Kai Bennett, than to feel his grief fully and fall apart.

He inhaled deeply, struggling to stop what he knew was coming. Now that he had opened himself, now that he'd allowed in the towering waves of grief, he didn't know how to stop them. They rolled over him, pressing him flat against the floor.

Maura's memory had been *too* real, and his emotions were *too* raw. It was as if no days had passed, as if he was right back to the day of her death, lying on the bed beside her as she slipped away from him.

He tucked in his knees, folding into himself as great sobs wracked his frame. It was as if he was losing her, all over again. His insides were turning outside, and there was nothing he could do about it. They spilled out onto the cypress from the gaping hole in his chest, and he was drowning inside of it, being sucking down inside himself with her memory. He screamed as his tears flowed, pounding his fist against the floor.

Sometime later, exhausted, he fell asleep. He didn't know how long he had lain on the floor, but when he opened his eyes, silver streams of moonlight still glowed through the windows of the treehouse. He turned to his back, stretching his arms. His left leg still prickled with sleep, and he sat up, scooting against the wall and massaging his calf as tingles of feeling returned to it.

The Tamarisk fronds still lay to the left of the door, and he stared at them dejectedly, running his fingers through his hair.

A symbol of good things to come. Right.

Nothing good had come from the Tamarisk trees or his trip up the treehouse steps. Kai vowed, right then and there, never to climb up them again. He lifted onto his knees, moving towards the treehouse door. If this is what it brought for him, this onslaught of pain and suffering, then it was best he didn't come anymore.

He reached to grab the bouquet, just as a silver stream of the moons' light shone on the Tamarisk fronds. The flowers sparkled in the light from the window, and Kai blinked, pulling back his hand. He was certain his eyes were playing tricks on him again. He rubbed at them hard, trying to clear his vision.

The flowers still sparkled as the air inside the treehouse suddenly became charged. It prickled across Kai's arms, and he froze as the hair on the back of his neck stood on end. He frowned at the moonbeams, tracing their path to the fronds. Something was happening, something strange.

Suddenly, a funnel of Wind *whooshed* inside the treehouse door. Kai ducked as the Wind whipped around and around the small room, shielding his head from the gale. The Wind whirled, tugging at the hem of his water weaving and threatening to unravel it. Then it swirled to the left of the doorframe, settling above the Tamarisk fronds.

A buzzing sound pricked at his ears as the fronds rose from the floor. They whirled around with the Wind as the silver beams of the moons intensified. Kai shielded his eyes from the bright white light, as the Wind whipped the flowers into a funnel, faster and faster until they were nothing but a bright, sparkling blur.

All at once, the Wind made an exit. It zipped past the doorframe as the fronds floated to the floor. Kai froze. Silence blanketed the forest outside in the Wind's wake, and the air inside the treehouse was heavy with a mysterious weight.

Kai blinked, staring at the sparkling moonlight where the Wind had been. There, by the door, a transparent figure remained.

He watched as the sparkling light solidified, and then she was there, in the flesh, solid and whole. It was Maura.

His eyes bulged and he pushed backward on his palms, scooting rapidly towards the far wall. His heart hammered in his ears, and he fought against shock, staring blankly in Maura's direction. *Just my eyes playing tricks on me*, he thought. *Or maybe I'm still asleep.* He slapped at his cheeks, trying to wake himself.

Maura's figure sat staring at him as he squeezed his eyes shut. He held his breath, pinching his arm, then he opened one eye to a slit. Maura still sat by the door, grinning at him with her eyebrows raised. He blew out his breath and stared at her openmouthed, shaking his head. He was losing it, alright. He slapped himself. Hard.

Snap out of it, Kai. She's gone. Maura is gone.

Just then, a tinkling laugh escaped Maura's lips, and she covered it with her palm. Kai sat up straighter, staring at her in wonder. His cheek still stung from his slap, and he rubbed it lightly with his fingers. He was sure he would have a red spot there in the shape of his hand.

"Maura?" he croaked. Maura grinned at him through the moonlight and giggled again. "Yes, Kai?" she said brightly. His heart dropped to his knees, and he squinted, staring at her incredulously. He gestured to her figure. "How?" He swiped at his hair. "I—I mean, how are you…"

"How am I here?" she answered, grinning.

Kai nodded. He didn't speak, didn't want to. Maura's voice was so lovely that he didn't want to pollute it with his own. He waited, watching her. He hoped she would say something else. He wanted to hear her voice again.

She picked up the Tamarisk fronds, gently touching the pink blooms.

"Did you pick these for me?" she asked. She moved a lock of hair behind her ear, lifting the flowers to her nose.

Kai tucked his knees to his chest, nodding. He stared at her in amazement. He didn't know how, but she was here. She was really Maura, and she was really talking to him.

In the back of his head, it occurred to Kai that he might be dying. Or, at least, close to death. How else could he be seeing her and talking to her, if he wasn't? He couldn't make sense of it.

Maura grinned.

"They're lovely. My favorite, you know," she said.

She crossed her legs and laid the flowers back on the floor at her feet.

"It's the Tamarisk," she said, peering across the treehouse at him. He gaped at her silently, and she sighed, gesturing at the moonlight. "It's the Tamarisk and the moonlight, mixed with several other factors that are kind of hard to explain."

Kai rested his chin on his knees, smiling softly at her. He was trying to listen, truly, he was, but he kept getting distracted by the sound of her voice. He kind of hoped he *was* dying, so he could stay with her. That way, she'd never have to leave.

Absently, she twirled a piece of her hair in her fingers.

"Try," he said. She furrowed her brow. "Hmm?"

"Try to explain. Try to explain how I'm seeing you and hearing you, right now."

Maura sighed and sat back against the wall, crossing her arms. She wrinkled her small nose and squinted, like she used to in deep concentration. Kai grinned. He had always loved when she had done that, and he'd more than once grabbed her face, kissing her nose until she pushed him off her, laughing hysterically.

"Okay, I'll try," she said, pursing her lips. "It's like this: As you know, Tamarisk trees have certain…*unique* qualities. They have healing powers, yes, but it's more than that. When Tamarisk is mixed with moonlight, and a being is present with a deep desire, there is a chance, albeit a slim one, that the Source will honor that being's request."

Kai shook his head, leaning back against the wall.

"I don't understand," he said. Maura shrugged lightly.

"Like I said, it's difficult to explain."

She wrinkled her brow, staring up into the moonlight. Suddenly, she said up straighter, holding out her arms.

"Okay, okay, let me explain it like this. Death, here in Caelium, well, *everywhere* really, but especially here, is not what you think."

Kai swallowed, nodding. "Go on," he said quietly.

She grinned. "So, you remember when I died that day, after the Sea Lilies?"

Kai nodded. Of course, he remembered.

"Well, I was never really *gone.* I just sort of…moved from one place to another. Kind of like, swimming through a dark cave and emerging some place new on the other side." Kai stared at her blankly and she frowned, searching for more words.

"It's like passing through a door into another room. You can't see me from your side, but you know I'm over there. But now you *can* see me, because I've moved back through the door to your side. Does that make sense?" She raised her brows, and Kai nodded. He gestured for her to go on.

"Okay, so, you have an Amloga, or Flame of Time, in your chest, placed there by the Source. You remember, we studied it in the Histories." Kai nodded. He did remember that. Maura continued.

"Right, so, this Amloga, it's pretty powerful. So powerful, in fact, that under the right conditions, it can move the Rotha-Am or Wheel of Time. In our case, your desire was reflected in your Amloga, and that desire, mixed with the Tamarisk and the moonlight, moved the will of the Source. Time paused, for just a tiny moment, and I was able to move from the room I was in with the Source, to *this* room, with you." She tapped the wood of the treehouse. "See? This treehouse is like my other room. Because it meant so much to me in this life, and so many great things happened between us here, it's the room where I appeared."

Kai straightened his legs. He studied Maura intently, and she grinned at him, settling back against the wall.

"How long do we have?" he asked quietly.

Maura peered up at the moonlight for a moment, then flicked her golden eyes back to him.

"As long as the moonbeams shine on the Tamarisk fronds, I'll be here. But when the light turns, I have to go."

Kai swallowed convulsively, picking at an imaginary spot on his pants. Maura giggled softly, and he lifted his eyes, grinning.

"What's so funny?" he asked.

"Nice pants," she said, teasing. "Have you been practicing your water weaving skills, again?" Her giggle grew into a laugh, and she held her middle as the sound reverberated off the wood.

Kai ran a hand through his silver hair, reddening. He grinned broadly at the memory of their first island visit.

"Very funny," he replied.

A bubble of laughter was forming in his own throat, but he swallowed it. He didn't want to interrupt her own laugh's beautiful sound. Tears were squeezing from the corners of her eyes, and the sight of it caused the bubble to form again. Maura's laugh had always been contagious, and a chuckle rumbled in his throat, building until he was laughing loudly, right along with her.

At last, he sat back against the wood, sighing as he stared at her glowing frame. She looked at him the way she had always done, like he was everything she had ever wanted, and he crossed his arms, swallowing through his constricted throat.

"I…I don't want you to go," he whispered.

Maura dropped her eyes, picking a bud off a Tamarisk frond.

"I know," she murmured. He watched her quietly as she blew the petals gently off her hand.

"Maybe I can come again, to meet you here?" he asked.

She shrugged. "Maybe," she answered, staring down at the floor. She flicked her eyes up to him. "That's up to you and to the Source."

Already, the moonlight had begun sliding past the window frame.

Maura laid her head back against the wall. She gave him a sad smile.

Kai frowned.

"Maura, I…" His throat tightened around his words, and he paused. "I miss you so much," he whispered, his voice breaking.

She nodded, searching his face. "I miss you too," she breathed.

He shot her a quick grin before he sucked in a shaky breath.

"Just tell me, before you go…" His voice cracked, again, and she folded her hands, waiting patiently. Kai swallowed, struggling to tame the emotion in his words.

"Are you okay? I mean, are you okay where you are?"

She grinned across the room at him and hugged her chest, inhaling deeply.

"Oh, I'm more than okay," she replied. "I'm wonderful. Things are perfect in the Hereafter."

The silver streams of moonlight dimmed as they passed away from the window, and the wound in Kai's chest pulled as he watched Maura's sparkling body fade from view. Just as the last of her was vanishing from sight, she whispered, "I'll see you soon."

Kai smiled to himself in the dark silence. Despite the faint ache in his chest, he felt better than he had in a long while. Now that he'd seen her again, now that he'd heard her voice, he couldn't wait to do it again. It was all that mattered. It was all he wanted.

He moved to pick up the Tamarisk fronds, then scaled down the treehouse steps. He would come again to the cypress trees. He would come to be with Maura again, as soon as possible.

CHAPTER 6

Kai swung his arms, letting the tips of the tall grasses tickle his fingers. After his encounter with Maura, he felt airy, light. He wanted to prolong the feeling.

Right now, he was floating inside a bubble containing only himself and Maura. It would burst if he was forced to encounter anyone else. Solitude was key.

The sea breeze blew softly over the hillside, wafting the sweet scent of Tamarisk to his nose. He grinned. He would stop by the grove, again, enjoy his bubble for a little longer before returning home.

He hummed quietly to himself as he hiked, swinging Maura's bouquet in his hand.

But just outside the grove, he paused. A glint of movement

caught his eye, and he blinked, surprised. Something had moved inside the grove.

He pulled the nearest branch away and froze as the bouquet slipped from his fingers. His heart leaped into his throat, and he dropped the branch, silently ducking behind a tree. There was someone else in the grove.

Kai peeked past the tree trunk in disbelief. To his knowledge, only himself and Maura had ever come here. But apparently, he had been wrong.

In the grove's center, a woman with long, reddish-brown hair stood with her back to him. She held a Tamarisk frond in each palm as she stared silently out at the water.

Maura. His heart leaped as her name built in his throat, but he stopped himself from calling out to her at the last moment. The woman swayed her hips, and Kai narrowed his eyes, studying her frame. His heart sank. The movement wasn't right. The woman wasn't Maura. It was someone else.

She wasn't Maura, but the two of them could have been sisters. She had the same height, the same build, and the same hair, but there was something different about her motion. She turned her head slightly, and he ducked from her view. *Definitely not Maura.*

All at once, she dropped her fronds, and moved down the hill, headed towards the surf. Kai crept to the middle of the grove and sunk down on his knees beneath the low hanging limbs, watching her climb. She swung her hips lightly, letting her fingers graze the tall grasses as she went. Kai crept closer, peering down the hillside. The woman was singing, and it was a beautiful sound.

He watched her toss her long hair, then bend to pick up a small stone, skipping it into the surf. She had to be selkie. He was so close to the Selkie Isles, and she was so beautiful, she almost had to be.

Kai knew he was breaking the treaty by watching her, but he couldn't move now, could he? She would catch him for sure, if he did. Then she'd report him to the Guard. They would probably kill him on sight for this sort of infraction. They'd kill the Merrow heir, and then there would be a war between the clans. He was sure of it. Better to stay put, unmoving, out of sight.

He gripped the tree trunk hard, warring with himself. What he was doing wasn't right. He knew that. Still, he kept watching her, fascinated. She was lovely. He couldn't help it.

There were rumors that a selkie woman could lure a Merrow man to his death, and Kai was starting to believe it. Once you looked at one, you couldn't look away, or at least that's what Seamus said. Her beauty and voice would draw you in. Then you were caught, like a fish in a net, and you didn't care what happened to you after.

Kai raised his brows. Maybe Seamus was right. It was what he was doing, right now, wasn't it? Letting a selkie woman draw him in, not caring if the Guard took him out?

He watched her skip another stone, chiding himself. He didn't *really* believe the rumors, did he? Of course not.

He told himself he could stop watching her at any moment. And he could have, couldn't he? *Yes.* Of course, he could.

He could have, but he didn't.

He told himself he was only fascinated with her because she looked so much like Maura, and that was probably true. He studied the familiar line of her back, thinking. It was true, but maybe there was more to it. He wasn't sure.

Whatever the reason, he couldn't seem to help himself. He couldn't break his gaze. She tossed another stone and another, and Kai sat in silence, watching her.

She swayed slightly, as she sang, and Kai strained his ear to make out the words to her song. Its mournful melody stirred him, and he moved closer, to the very edge of the grove. Strangely, his Amloga began to burn in his chest with her words. He pressed his hand over it, grimacing.

The woman bent to the beach, picking up a handful of smooth stones. She tossed one as she sang:

> *Oh where, my love,*
> *Oh where, have you gone?*
> *Oh where, and why*
> *Did you leave?*
> *With hand upon heart,*
> *I'll ne'er again know,*
> *A love such as that one with thee.*

Kai's Amloga flamed with her words, and he gripped his hand over his left chest, grinding his teeth. The pain of his Flame was enormous, and he groaned softly.

The woman turned at the sound, and Kai clamped a hand over his mouth. He flattened himself to the ground, watching her eyes warily through the low branches as she scanned the grove behind her.

He didn't even want to *think* about what would happen to him if the Guard were to catch him, now. He held his breath as her eyes passed over his hiding place. She stopped, focusing on the air above him, where a branch swayed gently on the night breeze. Kai whispered a prayer, willing the branch to stop. They'd flay him alive if she were to catch him.

At last, she turned back towards the water. Kai let out his breath, relaxing slightly as she resumed her hum. Before he knew it, she was unfastening the stays at the back of her dress. *Blast it all.* She was going to *undress*, right here in front of him. He ducked his head, cursing himself for visiting the grove. He was certain, now, he'd be flayed alive.

He grunted quietly, massaging the spot over his Amloga Flame. Since the woman had stopped singing, the burn had cooled to a dull ache. He peered down at it. The left of his chest glowed dimly through the fabric of his shirt, like a dull ember in a pile of ashes. He frowned, wondering what had caused it to flare.

The woman untucked a shoulder from her dress, and he snapped his eyes away, turning his face towards the ground. He rested his head on his forearm, thinking. If he moved now, she would hear him, and he was certain she would alert the Guard. He wasn't sure who the woman was or how close the Guard might be, so he figured it was safer to stay put. He waited, staring hard at the dirt.

In a moment, he heard a gentle splash, and he lifted his eyes, resting his chin on his hand. He watched in silence, as the woman dove under the waves. Her silvery tail flashed as she flicked it gently, and she fanned her dark hair above her head as she laid herself flat on top of the water. Kai grinned. *Definitely selkie.* She was magnificent.

He had never seen a Selkie in her sea form before. She was fascinating. Her silvery tail didn't have scales, like his own tail did. Instead, slick, silver skin trailed up her lower frame. It wove up, crossing over her chest before it melded into the pale flesh of her neck and upper arms. He held his breath, watching her flip backward in a perfect arc. *Beautiful.*

After a while, she started back towards the shore. Kai tucked his head, allowing her some privacy as she lifted herself out of the water. He wondered what happened to her silver skin when she stood. Did it vanish, when she left the water, like his own did? Or did selkie women return to their land forms by some other method?

He was too absorbed in his thoughts. He almost didn't hear her moving up the hillside. She was closing in on him before he knew it. Silently, Kai moved to his feet and backed into the center of the grove. When he was sure she wasn't looking, he spun, then he dashed out the other side.

Just as he was passing the last tree, his foot hung on a twisted root, and he tumbled headlong down the other side of the hill. He grunted as he toppled end over end, landing with a thud at its base near the rocky shore. He heard the woman rustling through the tree limbs above him, and he hurried to stand, stumbling over loose stones as he splashed into the water.

"Hey!" she called loudly. But Kai pretended not to hear her. He dove silently into the waves, not turning to acknowledge her.

Chapter 7

Elysia stared down from the grove in horror as the silver-haired merrow dove beneath the waves.

"Hey!" she shouted. He didn't pause, and she fumed as his shimmering blue tail flicked once above the water. Then he was gone.

She narrowed her eyes at the spot, thinking of his silver hair and blue tail. He was vaguely familiar. She was almost certain she had seen him somewhere before.

She searched her mind, flipping backward through her memories. Maybe she had seen him at the Court of Merrows last winter? But certainly, she would have remembered him. He had too distinct an appearance for her to forget.

She shook her head, frustrated. Her thoughts were jumbled, at the moment, and she was having a hard time remembering. She bit her lip, flushing. Whoever he was, he'd been watching her swim from his hiding place in the Tamarisk grove. Her chest flamed at the thought of it, and she huffed, angry and embarrassed. Only Ena and her mother had ever seen her tail. Now, he, this *merrow* man, of all people, had seen it, too. Not to mention, he had seen her in her land form before she dove. The thought burned her, and she stomped her foot, yelling into the darkness.

She hadn't even known anyone else *knew* about her secret island, let alone visited it. She certainly wouldn't have expected the visitor to be a merrow man. She kicked at a stone, ticking off the list of rules the Merrow man had broken. Her chest blazed. She was so angry. She'd see to it that he was punished if it was the last thing she did.

She paced the hillside, seething. Certainly, he had broken the treaty, just by trespassing. Stepping onto Selkie lands without permission was enough for his punishment, without even mentioning the *other* law he'd broken. She frowned. She would tell her mother immediately and have him charged. They'd probably execute him before a crowd. He'd be flayed alive in his sea form, a wretched coward's punishment, just like the coward he was.

Elysia fisted her palms. She hoped she'd be there to see it. She grinned maniacally, as she jogged back to her raft. *Flayed alive.* It was a gruesome sentence, but it was no less than he deserved.

Suddenly, she stopped short, grunting in frustration. There were holes in her plan to have the merrow man flayed. Great, *gaping* holes.

To start, no one knew about her secret island, at least, no one but her grandmother, herself, and the merrow man. Telling her mother about his infractions would reveal her sacred hideaway. It would reveal her own visits to the island. Her visits *and* what she'd been doing there.

That was the other problem. It was forbidden for a Selkie woman to show her sea form in public. Well, not technically *forbidden*, but it was certainly frowned upon. Her secret island wasn't exactly public, but she was certain her mother and the council would argue it was. She was sure they would forbid her from returning.

No. She couldn't risk it. She couldn't risk her mother or the council finding out about her little oasis, or the fact that she had gone swimming there. There was simply no way to explain where the merrow man had been or what he'd been watching her do, without incriminating herself in the process.

Sighing, she pushed her raft from the shore. There was another hole, and it was a big one. She flipped through a map of the Selkie Isles in her mind. There, the two tiny Selkie Isles perched in a curling crescent shape over her corner of the Southern Sea. Unfortunately, her secret island wasn't part of them. And if it wasn't part of the selkie lands, then he hadn't even been trespassing.

She furrowed her brow, working through her jumbled thoughts. The Treaty of Hiraeth specifically stated:

Merrows are prohibited from trespassing on selkie lands without expressed permission from the councils and court rulers

If her secret island wasn't part of selkie lands, then he didn't need permission to come there. The island was a veritable free space, unencumbered by treaty law. He was free to visit there anytime he wanted.

Elysia huffed. It appeared he hadn't broken the treaty on that count—just on the one where he had watched her. But, clearly, she couldn't tell anyone about that.

Her plan to have him flayed wasn't going to work. She would have to scrap it and come up with another. She worked to craft one, as she pulled her oar hard through the water. By the time stowed her raft in the reeds, there was no new plan to be had. Unfortunately, it appeared she was going to have to keep their little encounter a secret.

The thought burned in her belly. It made her furious. She was furious that he had gotten away with it. It wasn't fair.

She crept slowly through the trees, moving as silently as possible. The edges of the sky were beginning to lighten past the branches, and soon, it would be daybreak. She broke free of the wood, casting worried glances at the sky as she hurried through the garden towards the lattice of climbing vines.

She hadn't meant to stay out so late, but after the ball, she had really needed a moment to herself. And she had gotten it, before she'd been so rudely interrupted.

She put her foot to the first rung, blushing as she thought about the merrow man. How had he known that she was coming there to swim? Had he been there before? Had he followed her there?

She thought not. Surely, she would have caught him before tonight. But Merrows were excellent spies, so maybe she wouldn't have. She pulled herself upward, thinking. Maybe he had come with the dispatch along with Alistair and Seamus. Perhaps he had stayed long after the other merrows had gone. Maybe he had trailed her through the Brook. She bit the inside of her lip, reddening at the thought of him seeing her without her dress. And then, even *worse*, he'd seen her tail. The thought made her sick.

She lifted herself through the window, closing the frame tightly behind her. Then she moved to the armoire and pulled out a nightgown. As she peeled off her dress, she thought about the song she had sung on the beach. She wondered where its words had come from. Something about the loss of great love, how there would never be another like it.

She pulled blue satin over her head and stuffed her feet into slippers then moved to the bathing room, brushing through her tangled hair. Her grandmother, Ríona, had told her a great many things the day Elysia had brought her the first Tamarisk frond. Most of it, she had tucked away, stuffing it down for another dawn. But one thing Ríona had said stuck out to her, now.

Being a healer is bigger and grander than you think, 'Lysia. It is a great gift, with great responsibilities. It requires ALL of ones' self to be used by the Source, else, the healing properties of the Tamarisk may not be complete. It has been this way from the very beginning, from the dawn of the gifts of the Source.

Being a healer looks different for every being to whom the charge is entrusted. It is based on that being's specific skills. Think of yourself, Elysia. What abilities do you possess, that might be of use? Mayhap these abilities will be of greater importance than you think, for special gifts do not often seem special to those whom the gifts have been given.

Elysia had nodded gravely, that day, but, to be honest, she hadn't really understood her grandmother's words. Now, as she climbed into bed, she considered them. She tucked her thick coverlet beneath her chin and frowned hard at the ceiling, thinking. What gifts *did* she possess?

Immediately, her mind drifted to the song she had sung tonight on the island. She had always loved to sing, but something about tonight had been different. She thought about the song's strange, mournful words, how they had floated inside of her head. Some outside force had driven them. She was sure of it. Too, her Amloga Flame had burned as she had sung, tossing stone after stone from the shore. She narrowed her eyes. She had sung often at the secret island, but that had never happened before. At least, not until tonight. She folded her arms, confused. What was different about tonight, then?

Realization dawned on her, and she snuffed out a breath. There was only one thing, only one thing had been different about the island this evening—the Merrow man. He had hidden behind her in the Tamarisk grove. That's when the words had come.

She pushed away her embarrassment at his presence, focusing on the issue at hand. Could it be that the merrow was the outside force? Could *he* have driven the words to her song?

She bit her lip, and stared hard at the ceiling, trying to fit the pieces of the puzzle together in her mind. Try as she might, she just couldn't make them snap into place. It was all still a mystery.

She sighed, frustrated. Suddenly, she felt very tired. Her head ached, and she flipped onto her side closing her eyes. The sun was coming up, and she had precious little time to sleep. Soon, her escort would meet her on the shoreline. Then he and Seamus would take her and Ena away from the islands.

Elysia smiled as she drifted away, carried on the wings of a dream. Tomorrow, she was going to the Court of Merrows. She would get her adventure beneath the sea. A real adventure, away from the islands. It was the adventure she had longed for.

Chapter 8

Kai pushed himself hard through the open water. If the Selkie woman had alerted the Guard, they would be on his tail, any moment. He peered ahead, where the partially collapsed entrance to the tunnel was hidden behind a tangled forest of giant kelp. He pushed through the towering, twisted plants, whose slick leaves wrapped his face and arms in their long tentacles. Then he tucked his head, spearing through the narrow opening beyond.

He shot through the rock in total darkness, pushing hard for speed. Just a few more moments, and he would emerge in the tunnel. Once he broke the river's surface, he would be safe on Merrow lands. No selkie would dare follow him there, Guard or otherwise.

At last, he surfaced in the tunnel, and he moved to the bank, bracing his arms on the rocky ledge. He rested his forehead against it, panting. He was out of shape. Skipping the Night Watch was starting to catch up with him.

Usually, it was nothing for him to swim the length of Caelium's deep river system in one night. In fact, he did it often when he was on patrol. It was no small feat. The subsea river beneath his Southern Sea home flowed to meet the waters below the land. It crisscrossed throughout Caelium, reaching the entire realm. But Kai had missed the last five Night Watches on his schedule. He hadn't swum as much lately. He was going to have to stop doing that.

He allowed himself to catch his breath as his mind wandered to his encounters on the secret island. At first, he had thought Maura was imagined, a creation of his own desperate mind. But she hadn't been. She'd really been there.

The way she had explained her appearance to him, like moving from one room to another, made sense. Somehow, she had moved from her side of the door, and she had ended up back in the treehouse with him. He still couldn't quite believe it.

Maybe it was because he wanted it so badly, or maybe it was because the elements—the Tamarisk, the moonbeams, his desire, had all been just right. Whatever the reason, she had been there, really *been* there. Kai was still in awe of that fact.

He rested his chin on his arms and grinned. *Maura*. He thought about the way she'd looked at him. It was like she always had, like he was the only one for her.

He couldn't wait to get back to her again.

There was only one problem with that—the selkie woman. On first glance, she had looked exactly like Maura. He had almost called out to her, and he would have, if he hadn't stopped himself. That would've been a disaster. He would have been flayed alive. Or worse. Images of Nathair's deep sea lair flashed in his mind, and he shivered. He certainly didn't want to meet with the giant sea serpent anytime soon.

Unbidden, another kind of image floated into his head. He thought of the woman's bare shoulder, how her silver tail had flicked above the water, and he shut his eyes, pushing the images down. He shook his head. He couldn't believe he'd been so stupid. Watching a selkie woman? What had he been thinking? He should have turned around when he saw her in the grove, dove beneath the waves and not looked back again.

The muscle in his jaw flexed as the sound of her voice drifted inside his head. He thought of the way she'd flipped backward, her tail forming a perfect arc. He wondered who she was. She was obviously selkie, but who?

Besides visiting the secret island, he'd only visited the Selkie Isles once before, and that time, he hadn't even touched land. He'd waited in the water, on some request of Lady Sirena to escort the heir to the selkie throne. He had kept his eyes carefully averted as the woman handed him a letter of refusal, and he had left just as fast as he'd come. He chided himself, wishing he had done the same on this visit.

It might not matter, though, that he'd touched land uninvited on this visit. He flipped through his memory, recalling a map of the Selkie Isles he'd been forced to study. He didn't think he had seen the secret island on it. In fact, he was sure he hadn't seen it. There were only two curved islands in the selkie lands. They looked like a sliver of a silver moon. So that was one less treaty law broken. He'd bring up that fact, if he was tried before the councils. Maybe then he could wriggle out of one charge.

As for wriggling out of his *other* infraction, it was her word against his own. His silver hair and iridescent blue tail made him easy enough to identify, since he and his uncle Alistair were the only merrows with such coloring. He could only hope that the selkie woman wanted to keep their encounter a secret, just as much as he did.

Kai thought about that, then he raised his brows, as something occurred to him. Lady Sirena had told him that selkie women were forbidden from showing their sea forms in public.

Well, she hadn't exactly called it *forbidden*, but she had insinuated that it was frowned upon. Apparently, it was considered too intimate. She had told him so when she had sent him to escort the heir.

He grinned as he dove into the water. The selkie woman wouldn't want to tell their secret, not unless she wanted everyone to know she had been swimming where someone might see. Surely that alone would be enough to keep her quiet.

Satisfied with this, he cleared his mind and cut through the river at maximum speed. It would be daylight soon, and Lady Sirena would be expecting him in the throne room at mid-morning. He groaned, thinking of his lack of rest. His Night Watch shift had been over since midnight, and he should have long since been asleep.

At last, he reached the final cavern. He pulled himself out of the water and pulled on his waiting pants, then stuffed his arms through his shirt and vest. Outside the tunnel, he scanned the sleeping court. No one stirred, and the lane was silent. Quietly, he wound his way up the lane towards the palace steps. There, he turned right, slinking into a narrow passage beneath a tangle of green vines and climbing his way high into the walls of the fortress, where his rooms awaited him.

Kai had always preferred simple furnishings, and his rooms reflected his taste. A large four post bed stood against the back wall, along with two small night tables. In front of it, an oval writing desk and a small chair sat in front of a large window, overlooking the open sea beyond the dome. A seagrass rug lay beneath them, and a stone fireplace roared from the hewn-out rock of the far wall.

Most of Kai's furniture had been crafted in the West Mountains, where the carpenter, Benjamin, made his home. Kai had met Benjamin two cycles ago, at a ball held in the Timekeeper's Court after the defeat of the Court of Orm. Kai had patrolled the river system during the battle, so he had not fought alongside the army in the plain beneath Leyth Castle that day.

At first, he'd been hesitant to attend the party. He hadn't known anyone that would be there. But Lady Sirena had insisted that he come, and he was glad. If he hadn't gone, he would have never met Ben.

Benjamin was a mountain fairy, and he had taken up carpentry after Orm's defeat. Though the Court of Mountain Fairies had long been destroyed by the giants and the fires of the drake, Benjamin still called the West Mountains home. Arturo, now Master Timekeeper to the king, had welcomed Benjamin and the few other survivors into the Timekeeper's Court, where they lived to this day.

It was there that Ben had honed his craft. Now, his carpentry skills were unmatched. Kai had instantly loved his creations, and later, Lady Sirena had commissioned his rooms' furniture, as a surprise.

Kai flopped sideways across the bed, closing his eyes. The night had taken its toll, and he was exhausted. He had barely shut his eyes before his breathing became even, and he was carried away to the secret island's shores.

It was day. He was hiding in the Tamarisk grove, watching the selkie woman. Her long, reddish-brown hair shimmered in the sunlight, and

she held the Tamarisk frond in each hand. She hummed as she moved her bare feet in a dance, swishing the fronds along the tops of the tall grasses. Kai was fascinated, and he crouched still and silent under the tree limbs, gazing out at her in the middle of the grove.

All at once, his left chest began to ache. He grimaced, shifting as he reached for it and causing his foot to slip on an exposed root. Kai stumbled, and the woman turned at the sound, only it was Maura standing amid the trees. He wanted to call out, wanted to move towards her, but his voice made no sound and his feet had somehow become wrapped in the tree roots. They curled around his ankles, gluing him to his spot.

Maura studied the trees silently, scanning for movement. The tree roots were climbing up his arms, now, and he struggled silently against his bonds. The more he struggled, the tighter they became, until he was forced to be still, still as a stone.

He watched helplessly as Maura turned away. She dropped the fronds as she moved down the hillside, and he tried to scream her name, but his voice came out in a whisper. "Maura," he breathed, but she couldn't hear him. He started to panic. He was losing her all over again.

As she moved into the waves, the transformation began, and she dove under the water, her tail flashing in the sun. When the last of her was gone, the roots released him. They slipped from his limbs, and he fell heavily to the earth, his eyes shimmering with unshed tears as the words to the Selkie woman's song floated dreamily through his mind.

Oh, where, my love,
Oh, where have you gone?
Oh, where, and why
Did you leave?
With hand upon heart,
I'll ne'er again know,
A love such as that one with thee.

CHAPTER 9

Kai sat up, rubbing his eyes. Sleep had evaded him for most of the short night, and what little sleep he had gotten had been fitful. Groggily, he pulled himself to the end of the mattress and swung his feet to the floor.

Sunlight was already streaming through the sea outside his window, casting golden rays to the floor through the glass. Kai hitched on his pants from last night as he shuffled towards the basin. He frowned at his tired reflection as he splashed cool water on his face, then raked the excess through his hair. He looked exhausted, but he would have to do. Lady Sirena was expecting him in the throne room, any moment.

He pulled a clean shirt over his head before he fastened his vest and hurried down the hall, then he slipped silently through a side door near the end of it. Hidden passages were crisscrossed all over the fortress, and Kai often used them when he was in a hurry or didn't want to be seen. This one led to the waterfall behind the palace gardens.

In a moment, he emerged there. He swiped a couple of blooms from a nearby rosebush as he jogged towards the back palace steps. He was already late. If anybody asked, he would say he had lingered in the gardens too long. Besides, if Alistair had alerted Lady Sirena of his, now sixth, absence from the Night Watch, maybe the flowers would put her off her guard and lessen his punishment.

He straightened his shirt as he jogged up the steps, nodding once as the sentry pulled the right door wide. Then he paused, wincing, as Lady Sirena's voice echoed down the long glass hall in front of him. She was already holding court.

Kai blew out a breath. She was going to be furious. He had already been late to too many court meetings this Quarter to count.

Quietly, he crept down the corridor, then he edged silently past the towering glass of the throne room doors. He snuck in behind the back row of sentries, laying himself flat against the wall. Then he flicked his eyes to the throne. Lady Sirena was continuing her speech. So far, she hadn't seen him. He slid further left, towards the throne. If he could just slip behind the dais, he might appear at her shoulder undetected.

Just then, she caught him with her sharp green eyes. *Too late.*

"Ah, *there* you are Kai Bennet," she announced loudly. "What *perfect* timing." She gestured to Alistair, who stood in front of her on the floor. "We were just discussing your next mission."

Kai slumped against the wall. He was caught. Sheepishly, he slipped between the sentries, then sank wordlessly to the floor before the dais on one knee.

Lady Sirena glared down at him.

"It has come to my attention that you have, *once again*, failed to participate in your duties to the Forces on the Night Watch," she said sharply.

Kai flicked his eyes to Alistair, who now stood to Lady Sirena's left. His uncle stared hard at him with his flinty blue eyes, and Kai dropped his gaze, embarrassed at his uncle's disappointment.

Seamus stood to Alistair's left, squirming. Kai flicked his eyes to him. Obviously, Seamus had squeaked about his Night Watch absence.

Seamus met his gaze. He shrugged. *Sorry* he mouthed silently. Kai nodded once in his direction. He didn't blame him for squeaking. His uncle Alistair could be very…convincing. Kai had been on the receiving end of his steely stare, more than once. It was terrifying. So, he knew it wasn't Seamus' fault.

Lady Sirena cleared her throat in irritation, and Kai quickly moved his attention back to her. She raised an eyebrow.

"As this is a repeat offense, I am sure you are aware that there must be a consequence?" she asked sharply.

Kai shifted uncomfortably. He was aware, alright. He

swallowed, then nodded.

"Yes, my Lady," he murmured quietly.

"Good," she said, nodding.

"To that end, for your next mission, the council and I require that you serve as escort and guard to the heir of the selkie throne, Lady Elysia Bryn of the Selkie Isles."

Kai's heart fell to his feet. She expected him to go *back?*

"This post will extend indefinitely, until such a time as I see your mission is complete. This means that you will forfeit *all* free time you might've otherwise had with your regular duties, in service to this court."

Kai bowed his head. On the outside, he appeared calm, every bit the willing and collected Selkie escort. But inside, his mind was racing. What if the selkie woman saw him when he returned to the islands? What if she reported him to the Guard?

A flash of the selkie woman's silver hip flickered in his mind, and he flexed his jaw, staring hard at the floor. He had thought of another problem, and his face paled at the idea of it.

Maybe Lady Sirena already knew about the selkie woman. Maybe this was only the start of his punishment. Maybe she was forcing him to go back so that the Guard could apprehend him.

Images of a long spear slicing his tail in two played behind his eyes, and he winced. He hoped he was wrong. He hoped she didn't know. It would mean his death, if she did, even if he was the heir to the merrow throne.

The thought chilled him, but he straightened his shoulders, staring up at her silently.

Surely, she wouldn't allow that. It seemed a little harsh, even for such a blatant infraction as Kai's had been. Her green gaze chilled him to his bone. It was harsh, but he'd seen her do worse.

She pursed her lips and rested her hand against the bluish orb of her scepter, gazing down at him from her nose. A hint of a smile flicked over her lips, but she quickly masked it, settling her face into studied seriousness. Kai narrowed his eyes. Was she actually *enjoying* this? He might be sentenced to death, and she was fighting a grin?

She lifted her chin, addressing the throne room.

"As you may or may not already know, I have invited the Lady Elysia Bryn, heir to the selkie throne, here, to the Court of Merrows, for an extended stay. She will serve as an ambassador and our honored guest. I am sending Kai Bennet as her escort, as it is likely that she will be in danger, a target of court tensions."

Astonished whispers wove through the throne room, and Kai turned, trying to catch the words. "A mistake"… "What is she thinking?" "It's too dangerous"… "Breaks the treaty"… "A selkie in the Court of Merrows? It will never work."

Lady Sirena tapped her scepter hard on the floor. "Silence!" she shouted.

Instantly, the chatter ceased, and the room fell quiet. Kai lifted his head, looking up at her expectantly.

She waited in silence, flicking her sharp eyes about the room in warning.

"I am aware that this invitation could be perceived as a breach of the Treaty of Hiraeth. However, the visit comes at the agreement of myself, the councils, and Lady Elysia. As heir to the Selkie throne, Elysia has come of age to make her own decisions, and she has accepted my invitation with the blessing of her mother, Lady Malca and the selkie council. Therefore, no treaty laws have been broken."

She waited, pursing her lips, daring anyone to speak.

"It is no secret that it is my desire to heavily amend the treaty, or even throw it out entirely. And it is true that I harbor sorrow that our courts have not agreed on such amendments at this stage. There is too much hard history between us, and I fear if we allow things to continue as they are, our courts will come to blows, or, at the very least, we will be doomed to live in separation, forever at odds with our neighbors.

Therefore, it is my sincere wish that this court welcomes the future Selkie ruler with open arms. I trust I can rely on you all to uphold this wish, and for that, you have my thanks." She smiled kindly, a sharp contrast to her hard features moments ago. "I am hopeful that her visit will be the first step towards the restoration of our two great clans. So, now, I will release you to prepare for our honored guest. Please, begin your work. This court is now dismissed."

She tapped her scepter twice, and the throne room buzzed once more with chatter about the forthcoming Selkie heir's visit. Lady Sirena sat, and Kai watched her warily as she motioned for him to approach. He grinned up at her, and his heart sank at the serious look on her face. She knew. It was obvious by her face that she knew what he had done. He trudged up the dais, then stopped before her, folding his hands at his waist as he stared hard at the floor.

She studied his features with a worried crease of her brow.

"You look tired, Kai," she whispered. "Please tell me, where are you going during the Night Watch? Is there something I should know?"

A muscle feathered in Kai's jaw. Maybe she didn't know what he'd done, after all. He shrugged.

"It's nothing. I promise. I'm just…working through some things," he murmured.

She peered up at him anxiously, grasping his palm.

"I'm worried about you," she said quietly. "Alistair is, too. Lately, you're gone every night. You've missed your last six Watches. It's just not like you."

Kai nodded wordlessly, looking anywhere but her eyes while she studied his face.

"I know you miss her, Kai. It's understandable." She squeezed his hand. "But Maura is gone. Skipping your duties and refusing to participate in the very things which will prepare you for your future life on the merrow throne isn't going to bring her back."

Kai's eyes brimmed, and she touched his cheek gently with her hand.

"I know you loved her. We all did. I miss her, too. But you *must* move forward. You can't stay in the past with her forever. She wouldn't want it. She would want you to move on with your life, to be the leader she knew you could be. Do you understand what I am saying?" Kai's throat tightened, and he clenched his teeth, fighting back tears. She was right. She just didn't know how right she was. He had been living in the past since last winter, and, last night, he had *literally* opened a door through Time to be with Maura, again.

Lady Sirena was worried, and she had every right to be. Even *he* knew his behavior wasn't healthy. He knew he shouldn't visit the treehouse again, but after last night, after he had seen Maura, had talked with her, he didn't know how he would stop.

He sniffed, then looked up to Lady Sirena's face. Her glittering eyes were full of fondness, and she smiled softly, chucking him gently under his chin. He smiled weakly, nodding.

"Good," she said.

Satisfied, she straightened. "Now, you and Seamus are expected in the Selkie Court at midday."

Kai cast his eyes to Seamus, who was absently thrumming his fingers against his spear blade. Seamus was coming? *Why would she ask Seamus?*

She held up a finger to Kai in warning. "*Don't* be late. Lady Malca is probably at her wits end, as it is. This will be Lady Elysia's first visit to our court alone, and her mother is likely very nervous. Do your best to be respectful *and* punctual."

She flicked her eyes to Seamus, who was slumping lazily against his spear. "You too, Seamus," she said sharply. Seamus jumped at his name, scrambling to attention. He bowed deeply from his waist, nodding furiously.

Kai chuckled at Seamus under his breath. He didn't understand why Lady Sirena would ask his hapless friend to come along. Did the *illustrious* selkie heir require two escorts? If so, surely, Alistair would've been the better choice.

Lady Sirena answered his thoughts before he could consider them further.

"Seamus has volunteered to escort Lady Elysia's attendant, Ena. I agreed to this plan, as I understand Lady Elysia is very close to her. This is Elysia's first time traveling alone, and having Ena close by during her stay will likely make her much more comfortable during her visit."

Kai smirked. Seamus had *volunteered?* This was news. Seamus never volunteered for anything. The question was, why had he now? He folded his arms, searching Seamus' face. Seamus' kept his eyes carefully turned away, but his neck splotched red and he cleared his throat uncomfortably, picking an imaginary piece of lint from his vest.

Kai narrowed his eyes. There was something Seamus wasn't telling him. He knew it, but instead of pressing, he let the matter drop, certain he would find out what had caused this sudden onset of *courtly generosity*, later.

Kai's thoughts whirled as he and Seamus dove into the river of the abandoned tunnel. Seamus hadn't spoken a word to him since they had left the throne room. Still, Kai didn't push. Wordlessly, he followed Seamus' glittering green tail through the tunnel, weaving in and out of the turns until they emerged in the giant kelp grove on the other side.

Kai followed Seamus to the surface, where his friend studiously scanned the shoreline, humming a flat tune absently to himself. At last, Kai couldn't take it anymore. He narrowed his eyes at Seamus' profile and flicked his fingers through the water, splashing the side of Seamus' orange head. Seamus recoiled, then frowned, splashing him back.

"What was that for?" he asked.

"You tell me," Kai said, challenging.

"Tell you what?"

"*Tell me* what made you volunteer to be a Selkie escort for an unknown duration, thereby forfeiting any breaks you may have had in your regular duties to the Forces." He raised his brows as Seamus stared at him blankly. "As in…no fishing?"

Seamus' shoulders sank, and he stared disappointedly into the distance.

"Hadn't thought that one through," he said forlornly. He cut his eyes to Kai and gave him a mischievous grin. "But no matter about the fishing," he said excitedly. "It's the lady in waiting. Ena? She's gorgeous, mate. I mean *truly* gorgeous. I saw her the night of the Midsummer Ball. Alistair and I came to deliver the invitation to Lady Elysia. And, well..." He shook his head.

Anyway, I tried not to look at her, you know, because of the treaty, and all, but..." He grinned. "When Lady Elysia suggested that Ena should come, I couldn't help myself. I volunteered, on the spot."

Kai chuckled. *Of course.* It was a woman. It was always a woman with Seamus. Once, he'd given up six nights of fishing to attend dancing lessons with Lord Charlie's daughter. As if Seamus would ever need to know how to dance. Kai grinned at the thought. Seamus dancing. Now, *that* he would've paid a net full of coppers to see.

"Alright, then, we'd better go," said Kai. "Don't want to keep this...*Ena* waiting." He flicked water at Seamus' nose and dove under, laughing at the surprised look on his friend's face.

"Ha, yes, *so* funny. You're hilarious, Kai," Seamus called. "You won't be laughing when you see her!" Kai never turned, but his hearty laugh floated backward through the waves, trailing in his wake.

In a moment, they neared the shore. They waited in the shallow water as the ladies descended the hillside towards the beach. Seamus and Kai kept their eyes politely averted, respecting the outlines of the treaty. Surprisingly, no one was with the women, and the two waited awkwardly on the shore as he and Seamus stared into the distance.

From the corner of his eye, Kai could see that one was petite, with fiery red hair. He grinned. That had to be Ena. She cleared her throat.

"Good morning, boys. I presume you are our escorts?" she said pertly.

Seamus could barely contain himself. He grinned broadly at the sound of Ena's voice, and Kai could tell he was dying to look. Lady Sirena had requested they be respectful, so before Seamus could turn his head, Kai interjected.

"Yes. You must be Ena?"

"Yes. That's me." She gestured to the taller woman at her side. "And this is Lady Elysia."

Kai inclined his head. "Pleasure to meet you, Ena, Lady Elysia."

"A pleasure," said Ena kindly.

Lady Elysia said nothing, despite Ena gesturing for her to speak. For a moment, they argued under their breath. There was hissing whispers, and then Lady Elysia spoke, apparently against her will.

"The pleasure is all mine," she said flatly.

Kai hesitated, frowning at her tone. She sounded angry. In his periphery, he could see Ena turn her orange head, whispering quietly. Lady Elysia hissed a response and folded her arms, looking away.

Ena cleared her throat. "Okay. We're ready," she said cheerily.

"What about your bags?" Kai asked. Ena raised a small bag from her shoulder, dangling it so Kai could see. "This is enough for overnight. Lady Sirena has already sent for the rest in her glass-covered carriage. It's the same one Lady Elysia and Lady Malca rode in on Elysia's, er, I mean, *Lady* Elysia's first visit. Our bags should be waiting for us in our rooms when we arrive."

Kai nodded, then he turned to Seamus, giving him a hard stare. His friend was cutting his eyes at Ena. He was trying his best to get her attention. Kai hissed, and Seamus flicked his eyes away, raising his arms.

Kai blew out a breath as he moved his gaze across the shoreline. If he didn't stop, Seamus was going to get them killed. He was certain the Guard was hiding just over the hillside, waiting for one of them to break the treaty laws. They would like nothing better than to punish a couple of Merrows. He was sure of it.

He was scanning for the Guard, of course, but he was also scanning for the Selkie woman. Luckily for Seamus, the Guard was nowhere to be seen, and lucky for him, neither was she.

"Very good. Let's be on our way, then." Kai said quickly. He gestured to Seamus, who reluctantly joined him in turning his back as their escorts readied themselves in the water.

There was shuffling behind him, and a quiet splash as Elysia's voice hissed a whisper.

"Ready?" Kai called. "Almost," Ena answered sweetly. Their

shuffling resumed, and he frowned. Was Lady Elysia coming to court against her will?

"Everything okay?" he asked.

"Okay, okay, we're ready now," Ena chirped. Kai nodded. "Follow me."

Slowly, he retraced the familiar path back to the giant kelp forest, then he wove in and out of the towering plants, searching for the tunnel entrance. Kelp forests were disorienting, and he took several wrong turns before he located the small opening. He wiggled his way through, then pushed down through the darkness.

Soon, he was trailing upward, and finally he surfaced inside the last cavern. He waited by the riverbank for Seamus, Ena, and Lady Elysia, keeping his eyes turned to the closest wall. After much longer than he had anticipated, the three surfaced behind him.

Ena and Elysia gasped as they broke the surface, collapsing onto folded arms against the riverbank and sucking down deep gulps of dry air. Kai waited patiently, allowing them to catch their breath. Selkies' sea lungs were notoriously weak from disuse, or so he had heard. By the sounds of the women's gasps, that rumor must have been true.

He knew the feeling from experience. Sea lungs had to be exercised, or they would become shriveled and weak. Land lungs could be used instead, but they required breaks. You were forced to continuously surface if you used them over long distances.

He scanned the tunnel ahead of them. Usually, he tried to hurry through this route, to avoid Grym and the other creatures that favored his and Seamus' fishing spot. Today, he would have to take it slow. Otherwise, the women couldn't make it.

He waited a few more moments for their breathing to slow, then, he dove, following slowly along the winding river's path. He was being careful to keep his speed in check, and Seamus matched his rhythm, but his friend stared sidelong at him with a puzzled expression. Seamus gestured for them to increase their speed and swam slightly ahead of him, but Kai shook his head.

Kai knew he was making Seamus nervous, and he knew why. He felt the same. There were things worse than Grym lurking below them in the darkness that he'd rather not have to meet.

The once dry passage, previously used by the Court of Merrows as an extension of the city, had long since been flooded by the river system. As such, the underwater terrain was mostly a maze of towers and buildings, long out of use. After Lord Dolion had ordered the water table raised, the merrows had abandoned this section, leaving the labyrinth of buildings as the perfect hiding places for foul creatures he'd rather not think about.

He'd no sooner pushed the thought from his mind, than one such *thing* made its appearance. Ena and Elysia had trailed behind, even struggling to keep up with his slower pace. All at once, Kai heard a small screech, and when he looked behind him, the women were gone. He exchanged a look with Seamus, and they readied their spears, backtracking through the tunnel towards the sound.

Mostly, the creatures left the merrows alone. There was plenty to eat at the bottom of the river, and merrows were often more of a threat than they were worth. But two slow, weak selkie women? Kai could think of several creatures that would find them to be just the right treat. He grimaced at the thought and clutched hard to his spear, pushing for speed.

Ahead was a domed coliseum, hewn directly from the cavern walls. Many cycles ago, it had been used as a training ground for merrow Forces. Now flooded, it had fallen out of use, and a new, larger arena had been built within the Court of Merrows' dome.

Half of the abandoned ring's stone seats and shallow rooms lay beneath the water and half were exposed to air, higher up in the rock. They were partially crumbled and overgrown with sea grass, moss, and lichen. Kai and Seamus crept to the edge of them, peering around a cracked column connected to a stone arch marking the domed entrance.

Seamus muttered an oath, and he exchanged a foul look with Kai, blinking rapidly with his glittering green eyes.

"*Why*, in the name of the Source, were you going so slow, Kai?" he hissed. "If we'd just moved a little faster, we wouldn't be in this mess right now."

Kai frowned, his anger flaring. "You really think I *wanted* to go slow?" he whispered. "When's the last time you saw me go slow, Seamus?" He gestured towards the middle of the coliseum.

"I was doing it for the ladies. They've been land-locked for so long that their sea lungs are weak. They aren't used to using their tails. We would've lost them, for sure, if we'd kept up our usual pace."

Seamus rolled his eyes. "So you say," he muttered. "But I'm not so sure."

"Oh, you're not sure?" Kai raised his hand in a mock salute. "So sorry, I didn't know I was in the presence of an *expert*." Seamus frowned and brought his nose close to Kai's face, hissing his words. "Me? The expert? Maybe if you'd kept *your* expert ideas off the selkie ladies and on swimming a little *faster*, we wouldn't have to fish them away from whatever foul thing has them hidden in this arena," he spat.

Kai brought his nose close to Seamus' face. He raised his voice. "Who *me!? I* need to keep *my* attention off the selkie ladies? Oh ho, you're one to talk!" He ground his teeth. "At least I'm not drooling all over one of them. As if Ena would ever have anything to do with you!"

He pushed Seamus hard in the chest, knocking him backward against the rock wall of the tunnel. Seamus' green eyes blazed, and he slashed at Kai with his spear. Kai blocked him, and then metal clanged against metal as they wrestled out of the tunnel and into the center of the arena.

Kai grunted as the tip of Seamus' spear swiped his upper arm. A thin line of blood seeped from the spot as he swiped the butt of his spear against Seamus' thigh. His friend shouted in pain, then he ground his teeth, driving the heel of his hand straight up into Kai's jaw. Kai's head bounced back against his shoulders, and he tasted iron. He swung his head straight, his jaw throbbing as blood pooled on his tongue. *That's it.* He fisted is hand, ready to swing at Seamus' ear…

A small whimper escaped from their right as he brought his arm around. Kai froze. He spat blood as Seamus held up his hands in surrender. "Did you hear that?" Seamus whispered. Kai nodded. He put a finger to his lips and the two of them hovered in the water, breathing hard. They strained for another sound, and when they heard a second whimper, they exchanged a glance, nodding gravely in an agreement to forgo their argument. Silently, they pushed through the water towards the sound.

As they moved closer to the terraced walls of the coliseum, a gruesome sight came into view. Kai flexed his jaw. If this was what he thought it was, then they were in trouble. Thick, sticky webbing laced along the stone seats and across sections of the shallow rooms. Inside the white cocoons, a variety of lifeless creatures were held frozen, their eyes open in vacant stares.

Lovely. It was as he had feared. The women had been captured by a diving spider, a particularly nasty creature, capable of paralyzing a Merrow with a single bite. Afterward, the spider would bundle its prey in a silk cocoon, preserving it until the lucky victim was selected for their captor's next meal.

Diving spiders were known to be very greedy, often preserving more meals than they could devour. The extra prey would usually waste away in their cocoons, dying of starvation or lack of air, whichever came first. Mostly the latter, if they didn't call the sea their home.

Kai scanned the silent faces, a host of haunting stares. One of the cocoons wriggled to his right, and he locked eyes with the cocoon's emaciated occupant. He couldn't tell who or what was inside, as sticky webbing covered all but one eye. But he could see they had been there for a long while.

He shuddered, looking away. There was nothing he could do for them, now. They had been there so long that their body had already melded with their wrappings. In fact, the only thing holding them together was the webbing of the cocoon itself. If he stripped it, it would be like stripping a second skin. Their insides would slip outside, and they would die instantly.

For a moment, he hesitated, warring with himself. Was it better to send the poor victim to an early death, to put them out of their misery? Or let nature take its course?

He didn't have to war long. As he watched, the single, visible eye grew glassy. Then the cocoon went still, its occupant passed on.

Kai turned away. He studied the path ahead, trying and failing to keep his mind off the unfortunate, still cocoon. He didn't know which was worse, dying a slow, trapped death like the one he had just witnessed, or being eaten alive by the diving spider.

He stopped when he reached the stone seats at the far edge of the ring. Seamus appeared silently beside him. Above them, a small room was partially obscured by strands of web. Kai jerked his head towards the opening, holding a finger to his lips.

Inside the room, a faint purplish light glowed, a sure sign that a diving spider was inside. Kai and Seamus crept silently to the edge of the opening. Then they brought their eyes just above the frame. The diving spider was there, alright, and so were Ena and Elysia.

Ena caught sight of them from her spot on the far wall, where she was pinned flat in a mass of tangled web. She let out a little squeak, but Kai put his finger to his lips. Tears sprang into her eyes, and, she slid them to the diving spider in terror. The monstrous beast was facing away from the door frame, spinning a paralyzed Elysia into a cocoon.

The diving spider was a massive, horrifying creature, the stuff of Kai's nightmares. Her eight spindly legs ended in long, sharp spikes, and her velvety bottom was equipped with a skirt of delicate fins that flittered in the purplish light her glowing lantern. The light dangled from the front of her head, hovering above eight beady, black eyes, and a mass of inner and outer black fangs covered her lower face. They chomped at extra bits of webbing, as she spun Elysia tighter into her sticky wrapping.

A large, silk bubble clung to underside of the spider's abdomen. The air inside it wobbled, shimmering in the purplish light as the spider worked. Kai eyed the bubble as he climbed over the window sill. If he was going to save them, he would have to be fast. When the diving spider detected his presence, she would work rapidly to puncture him with her fangs. One bite, and he would be helpless. Then, he and the others would never escape.

Kai readied his spear as he stalked behind the spider. He could feel Seamus on his tail, and for the first time during this mission, he was glad his friend was here. He could use all the help he could get, and two spears were certainly better than one against a diving spider.

He lifted his spear, ready to slice into the spider's back leg, when the foul creature spun towards him. She roared a rasping screech. Then she lunged, spearing the edge of his tail with her front spike. Kai yelped. Her spikes burned like a flame. Quickly, he swung hard with his blade, slicing off the offending leg.

The spider roared as she recoiled, holding up the severed stump. Purplish blood streamed from her wound's jagged edge. It muddied the water in front of Kai's face. Kai couldn't see through all the blood.

Now, it was Seamus' turn. Through the murky water, Kai could see him baring his teeth. Seamus bellowed as he swung his spear, slicing a wide gash in the spider's velvety back. More blood poured as the spider screeched. She turned to Seamus, spearing at him her remaining front spike. Seamus ducked at the last moment, narrowly missing her spear. Then he thrust his own spear upward, driving it squarely in the spider's side, where it stuck deep in her flesh. Purplish blood was nearly filling the room now, but she barely slowed. The giant spider fluttered her fin, raising herself up onto her back legs.

Then she opened her hideous jaws as wide as possible and lunged at Seamus, sinking her teeth into his right shoulder.

Kai watched in horror as Seamus fell limply to the floor. The silk bubble of air was still clinging to the spider's underside. If Kai could open it, she wouldn't last long. He blinked through the haze of blood as he swung his spear, slashing it open on the spider's belly. The sack ripped, and he watched as the bubble glided out the door, lifting towards the surface above.

When she realized her air was gone, the spider panicked. She spun in a circle, searching for her lost lifeline. Purple blood leaked from her wounds with her motion. It made the already murky water thick, and Kai coughed against the haze of bitter, metallic water.

In a moment, the spider paused. She wobbled, the loss of her blood and air too much. Then she fell, toppling towards Ena on her one front leg. Ena screamed as the spider tumbled towards her place on the wall. The creature was going to crush her against it. She squeezed her eyes shut as the spider slid forward, her giant back pushing up against her chin. Then, the diving spider was still, and Ena was silent.

Kai blinked through the murky water, hurrying towards her. He raised his spear and slashed the spider's abdomen from its body, then rolled it away from Ena's trap on the wall. Finally free, Ena wheezed as her head sagged in relief. She sucked in a long breath, as Kai cut her sticky wrappings away.

In a moment, the bloody water began to clear, and Kai surveyed the room. Elysia was still inside in her cocoon in the far corner. Ena rushed to her side as Kai stepped over the diving spider's severed body, moving to cut her down from the wall. He stared at her closed eyelids as he stripped the sticky bands covering her face and body, then he turned his back to search for Seamus while Ena peeled the silk away.

His friend lay in the opposite corner with his face to the wall. Kai moved to him, rolling Seamus onto his back. Seamus' eyes were vacant, and his lips had a purplish hue. Kai moved him gently, examining his shoulder. Luckily, it was a shallow bite. The diving spider's fangs had barely broken the surface of his skin. He patted Seamus' arm. He would be alright. The venom would wear off before nightfall. Elysia, on the other hand, would have bigger problems.

He slung Seamus over his shoulder, then he carried his limp body to the surface. A small shell of a former dwelling sat just outside the arena. Carefully, Kai hauled Seamus to the bank. He moved past the door of the small house and deposited Seamus on the floor of the front room. Then he returned to the diving spider's lair, ready to collect Lady Elysia.

Elysia's silver body lay in a limp heap near the back wall. Ena sat behind her. She murmured quietly in her friend's ear, softly stroking her dark auburn curls. They draped across Elysia's face like a curtain. Kai appeared in the doorway, just as Ena pushed the curtain of hair away.

For a moment, he stared blankly at the scene. Then his eyes centered on Elysia's profile. His vision tunneled as he examined her face, and his heart skipped a beat. He had seen her before; he had watched her from the cover of the Tamarisk grove. It was her. It was the selkie woman from the secret island.

CHAPTER 10

All at once, Kai realized he had been staring at her. Quickly, he looked away, focusing pointedly on the stone floor in front of him. Ena rolled her eyes. Gently, she moved from her spot with Elysia. She swam to the doorway, peering up at him.

"I think we're well past the formalities of the Treaty of Hiraeth, don't you, Kai?" she asked. "You just saved our lives, after all." She folded her arms, arching one brow.

"Besides, we won't tell."

Kai wet his lips. Ena was right. They were well past the treaty laws, now.

Slowly, he lifted his gaze. Ena's blue eyes sparkled mischievously. He smiled at her, and she grinned back at him.

"That's more like it," she said.

He watched her long hair billow above her head as she turned to look at Elysia. Seamus was right. Ena was rather beautiful. But then, so were all Selkie women. It was how he had gotten into trouble with one in the first place.

He turned his gaze to Elysia, who still lay unmoving on the stone floor. It felt odd to him to study her so openly, but, like before, he couldn't look away. Soft, silver skin wound up from her tail, crisscrossing her chest and melding into the porcelain skin of her neck and upper arms. Her abdomen was bare, and he watched her stomach rise and fall with her breathing. Then he trailed his eyes to her face.

Winged, dark auburn brows lived over her eyelids, a perfect match to her reddish-brown hair. She had quite large eyes for such a delicate face. Their color was a mystery. He hadn't been able to see them that night on the island, and, for a moment, he lingered, wishing she would open them. She didn't, and he continued his examination, following the line of her nose. It was sloping and narrow, at odds with her full lips, which parted slightly above her small chin.

Suddenly, he realized Ena was watching him. She was grinning at him with her eyebrows raised. Quickly, he looked away, pretending to be fascinated with the wall of the small room.

Little did Ena know; this wasn't the first time he had been caught staring at her friend. Ena turned, and he dared another glance at Elysia. He wondered what she would think of him staring at her now. Would she be angry, like before? He imagined her features pulled into a furious face, and he dropped his eyes. It was safe to say she would be just as angry as she had been that night.

An image of her ball gown laying in a heap on the shore flashed in his mind, and he grimaced. If she remembered him, he was doomed. He would meet with Nathair or be flayed alive. Maybe both. He could only hope that she didn't.

He was ticking through the list of possible tortures he would have to endure when he realized Ena was asking him a question. She was waving her hand at his face.

"Kai? Kai, are you listening to me?"

Kai started. "Um, yes, I'm listening." He shook his head. "I mean, uh, what did you say?"

Ena sighed, rolling her eyes. "What are we going to do about Elysia? Is she going to be alright? Will Seamus?" Kai nodded, "She'll be fine, and so will Seamus. I'll carry her to the surface, let her sleep it off. The venom from her bite won't be gone until tomorrow morning, so we'll have to spend the night in the tunnel. After that, I'll carry her the rest of the way. Diving spider venom is vicious, and its effects are long-lasting. Even after it wears off, she'll be too weak to make the swim without my help."

He moved inside, then lifted Elysia off the floor. To be so tall, she was surprisingly light. She turned her head to his chest and moaned slightly as he cradled her close. A good sign. She wasn't completely paralyzed. He expected her to be conscious before morning.

He stared down at her profile. Her eyelids fluttered, then closed again. She would be awake soon—too soon. Kai wasn't sure if he was ready for that. If she was awake, then she might recognize him. He frowned. Or maybe soon was a good thing. That way, he would be able to assess whether she remembered him before they reached court. The last thing he needed was a public display. That would seal his fate for sure. No, he needed to be able to talk her down before they arrived.

He lifted Elysia easily from the water, tucking her to his chest as he gathered water weaving for them both. Then he moved towards the abandoned house. Her body chilled rapidly in the dry air, and her lips were deep purple by the time he reached the door. Kai tucked her closer as she began to shiver. The colder she got, the worse she would be and the longer it would take for her body to fight the venom.

As he moved into the front room, the effects of the venom intensified. Elysia was becoming delirious. A cold sweat dampened her skin, and she fought against his grip. He tried to calm her by loosening his arms, but her muscles contracted in a spasm, and she groaned, tucking her face into the crook of his arm.

He wrapped her to him as he knelt to the floor, rocking her slowly back and forth. Elysia moaned, and he flicked his eyes down to her, shushing her softly. Dark strands of auburn hair clung to the pale skin of her forehead, which gleamed softly with a sheen of sweat in the dim light. He brushed the strands away, and despite their perilous situation, he couldn't stop himself from studying her face.

She was beautiful, too beautiful. She looked even more like Maura than he had first realized. It made his stomach burn, and as quickly as he could, he laid her on the stone floor near Seamus. He turned for the door, but Elysia moaned behind him, and he paused. He was worried she could feel the sting of the venom surging beneath her cold skin.

Kai tapped the side of his leg, thinking. What she needed was warmth. The warmer she was, the better she would feel. Too, some extra warmth would burn the venom faster, and she would be quicker to recover.

Quickly, he moved towards the back of the house, searching for a coverlet. He passed through a series of hallways and empty rooms, until finally, he came to the kitchens. An abandoned cupboard perched against the far corner. Its door was half-off the hinge. He pulled it free and tossed it aside, rummaging through the cupboard's contents. He tossed out empty baskets and bottles, until, at last, he emerged with two ragged blankets from back of the shelf.

Ena was sitting in the front room with Seamus and Elysia when he returned. She had already unpacked her small bag and was now wearing a silk dress in deep blue. She sat by Elysia's side, her thumbs rubbing worried circles over her friend's cold fingers.

Quickly, Kai flung the blankets across Elysia and Seamus. Then, he set about building a fire. Crusts of lichen coated the surface of the room's walls, and Kai scraped some of glowing crusts free, mixing them with several dried fern fronds to create a small mound of kindling on the front room floor. These he lit by dragging a piece of flint across the stone beneath them, creating a spray of bright sparks. Soon enough, he had a small blaze.

He stoked the fire to a quiet roar, and within moments, Elysia stilled, her breathing even. Kai stared down at her sleeping frame. He was thankful she was comfortable. Now, all he could do was wait.

Kai settled against the wall by the door and braced his spear across his chest, just in case any other foul, cave-dwelling visitors decided to pass their way. The warmth of the fire felt good, and he let his head rest on the wall as he gazed across the room. Ena lay on the floor beside Elysia, her arm slung protectively across her coverlet. The room was quite warm, now, and large beads of sweat shimmered on Elysia's forehead. Good. She would sweat out the venom, soon.

Seamus stirred for a moment, then he lay still again, his breathing slow and even. Kai grinned. Pretty soon, his friend would be up and ready for fishing. Kai's stomach grumbled. He was starving. Hopefully, Seamus would catch a giant eel for breakfast.

Kai closed his eyes, trying to relax. Fatigue from the day and his recent string of nights with little sleep had left him exhausted. He drifted, but within moments, Seamus was shaking him awake.

"Kai, wake up. I'm better, now. I'm gonna go fishing. Want to come?"

Kai opened one eye. He peered up at Seamus groggily, then closed it again.

"No, Seamus. You go ahead. I'll stay right here." He jerked his head at Elysia's sleeping frame. "I need to stay with her, anyway."

Seamus nodded, then he turned his gaze towards Ena.

Ena sat up, stretching. She rubbed her eyes, staring across the fire at him. She grinned, and Seamus stared back at her open-mouthed. She raised one eyebrow.

"What is it, Seamus?" she asked sleepily.

Seamus scratched the back of his head. "Well, I, er, I'm going fishing. Just wondered if maybe you'd like to come? Kai's going to stay here with Elysia, so she'll be safe." He waited as Ena watched him, shifting uncomfortably. "So…do you want to?"

Ena glanced down at Elysia uncertainly. She bit her lip.

"I don't know, Seamus. I mean, she looks better, but still."

"She'll be fine," Kai said. "I'll make sure of it. Plus, Seamus is a great fisherman. You won't be gone for long."

Seamus tucked a hand over his heart, speaking with mock feeling. "Why, Kai Bennet, that's the kindest thing you've ever said to me. I think I'll die right here of pure joy."

He collapsed against the wall, fake choking as he slid to his seat. Ena giggled softly, and Kai punched Seamus in the arm, rolling his eyes.

"Get going, oh, *Great Fisherman*," he teased. He nodded towards Ena. "You too, Ena. I promise, Lady Elysia will be fine."

Ena tucked the blanket tighter under Elysia's chin. Then she flicked her eyes to Seamus, grinning. "Alright, let's go."

Seamus beamed as she moved towards him. He was clearly delighted. When she was right in front of him, she pointed her small finger at his chin, narrowing her eyes.

"And let's make it fast."

Seamus grinned as he hopped to his feet.

"Certainly, my Lady," he teased. He bowed low from his waist, and Ena rolled her eyes. She brushed past him, trying and failing to hide her grin.

She straightened her lips as she paused in the door, gesturing for Seamus to follow. Seamus waited until she had turned away, then he wiggled his eyebrows at Kai, happily trailing after her.

Kai chuckled as he watched him leave. He shook his head. It was always a woman for Seamus.

He stood, stretching, then he collected some more lichen for the fire. He sprinkled the dried crusts over the embers, coaxing the burn to a small blaze. Beyond the flames, he could see Elysia stir. Kai froze as she fluttered her eyes. Then, she opened them.

She rubbed her lids, sighing a yawn as she stretched her arms up over her head. Kai didn't move. He waited, watching as she tucked the coverlet tightly around her.

Slowly, she sat upright, and for a moment, she appeared disoriented. She blinked rapidly at the abandoned stone walls of the dimly lit house and scratched her mussed hair, clearly confused at her whereabouts. Then she pulled the cover over her shoulders and stood, moving away from Kai to gaze out the front window.

Kai wasn't sure what to do. She hadn't noticed him yet, and he didn't want to startle her. Quietly, he adjusted his position.

"Hi," he said in a low voice.

But it didn't work. He scared her anyway.

She spun at the sound and brought a shaky hand to her chest, stumbling backward against the wall. He smiled softly as he held out his hands. "Sorry, I didn't mean to scare you."

Elysia was still weak from the venom. At least, that's what he told himself. She went pale as she lost her strength, sliding down the wall onto her knees.

She started to fall forward, and her eyes rolled back as Kai hurried to catch her. He was afraid she was going to hit her head, and she would have, but he caught her just before her cheek smacked the floor. He turned her gently onto her back, holding her head in his lap as her eyes fluttered open. They found his face, and she stared up at him in shock. Then her eyes drifted closed, and she lost consciousness.

Kai peered down at her porcelain face, bracing one hand behind her head and the other around her shoulders. For a moment, she laid completely still, limp in his arms. Her hair still clung to her forehead, and Kai brushed a long curl from her eyes. Elysia sighed softly, opening them.

She stared at him blankly, for a moment, studying his features with her greenish-gold gaze. Then, all at once, realization registered on her face. Kai opened his mouth, but before he could speak, she shot out of his lap, pushing his arms away. She hugged the coverlet tightly around her as she shuffled towards the far wall. Then she turned, glaring.

She was moving too quickly. The diving spider venom wasn't completely out of her system yet. Kai held out his hands.

"Take it easy," he said, cautioning.

She blinked at him incredulously, then narrowed her eyes.

"Are you seriously trying to tell *me* what to do?" she spat. Her body wobbled, and she stuck out a hand, bracing herself against the wall. Kai reached for her reflexively, even though he wasn't close.

"Careful," he warned softly.

She rolled her eyes, and Kai dropped his arms.

"Listen, I'm just trying to help you, okay?" She flicked her eyes to him, still seething, and Kai nodded encouragingly. He pressed on.

"You were bitten by a diving spider, so you're not at your strongest, right now. Her venom was intense, and your body's still weak."

Elysia was ignoring him. She had moved from the wall and was searching around the room. "What are you…"

"Where are my clothes?" she barked.

She gave him a withering look, tucking the blanket up to her chin.

"Or did you dispose of them while I lay helpless on the floor?" Her eyes blazed, and Kai stared blankly. "I didn't…"

"I guess you *enjoyed* looking at me without my knowledge, again?" She glared at him in disgust, folding her arms.

Kai opened his mouth, then closed it again. *So, she does remember.* He shook his head.

"I didn't throw out your clothes. I wouldn't do that. They're…" He started to point to the back corner where Ena had left the small bag, but Elysia interrupted him.

"Okay, *sure*. And I'm supposed to believe you? After you watched me on the island the other night? After *that*, you expect me to trust *you?*" She chuckled mirthlessly, shaking her head.

"Yeah, I remember you. You're pretty easy to spot, Kai. First of all, you're huge." Elysia flicked her eyes over his large frame. She faltered slightly, flicking her eyes to his muscled arm before fluttering her hand at his head.

"And—and with the silver hair." She looked away, shaking her head.

She tapped her foot for a moment, then spun back to him, pointing her finger at his face.

"You know what? I could have you flayed alive for what you're doing right now. You're looking straight at me, and that's a *clear* treaty violation."

Kai's anger flared. Who did she think she was? He had just risked his life to save her from the diving spider, and she wanted to talk about having him flayed? A muscle feathered in his jaw, and he fisted his hands at his sides. *Ridiculous.*

He took a step towards her, and she stepped back, flattening herself against the wall.

"Do you *really* want to go there, Elysia?" he growled. He glared down at her, not breaking his gaze as he pointed back over his shoulder. "I just risked my *life* back there to save you from the diving spider, and all you can say is you'll have me *flayed?*"

He stepped closer, nearly bumping her chest. His eyes flashed as he parroted Ena's words.

"I think we're well past the treaty's rules now, don't you?"

Elysia swallowed. She set her jaw, but flicked her eyes away, biting the inside of her lip.

"And, by the way," he added, lowering his voice to a whisper. "What were you doing swimming in the sea that night?" He put his lips to her ear. "Isn't showing your sea form…*frowned upon*, in the Selkie Court?"

He pulled away slightly, watching the emotions play across her face. She flushed deep crimson before her face went pale, and she gripped the cover tightly, turning her knuckles white. He grinned. Now, he was getting somewhere. He pushed on.

"I bet they don't even know you visit that island, am I right?" She squirmed, and he grinned. "And they certainly don't know you go swimming there." He brought his lips towards her ear again. "So, if you tell, Elysia," he growled, "You'll have to tell it *all*, and that wouldn't be good for you, now, would it?"

He stood straight, watching as she swallowed convulsively. *Good.*

Elysia glared up at him, her eyes a stormy green sea. "It's *Lady* Elysia," she ground out. She brushed past him as she pushed away from the wall, searching the floor.

"And, *where* are my CLOTHES?!"

Suddenly, she went pale. She wobbled as she gripped her forehead, then she stumbled backward, tripping over her coverlet and nearly falling into the fire. Kai lunged onto his knees, catching the edge of the coverlet in his palm. He pulled it to him, flinging her backward into his arms.

Elysia blinked up at him, panting hard. Her forehead gleamed with a sheen of sweat, and her lips were pale. She frowned, then pushed his arms away as she scrambled to scoot towards the far wall. She wrapped the blanket tighter.

"I *don't* want your help," she spat. "Nor do I need it." She sniffed, lifting her chin as she stared into the fire.

Kai flexed his jaw. She was seriously unbelievable. He raised his hands in surrender.

"Fine by me," he hissed. "Not like I really wanted to help you, anyway."

He started towards the door, jerking his thumb over his shoulder.

"Clothes are in the bag in the corner."

CHAPTER 11

Elysia shuffled to the bag of clothes in the corner. While she changed, she watched Kai's back from the window. As she pulled on the soft dress, she chided herself. She didn't know why she was bothering to make sure he wasn't looking. He obviously did whatever he wanted.

She narrowed her eyes as he picked up a stone and tossed it into the river, sending a perfect arc of golden water splashing downstream. The muscles of his back rippled under the thin blue fabric of his shirt, and she frowned. He was so infuriating.

He turned his head to the side, and she moved cautiously to the window, examining his profile in the dim light. His jaw was thoroughly square, and his nose was straight and tall, like it had been perfectly carved from hard stone. Just then, he flicked his iridescent blue eyes towards the window, and she shrunk behind it, her heart leaping into her throat.

At last, he turned away, and Elysia blew out a small breath. He picked up another stone, and cautiously, she peered out at him again. She watched as he sailed the stone into the current, then sat down on the riverbank. He rested on his palms and let his head fall back against his shoulders as he stared up at the high ceiling, blowing out a long breath.

Elysia scrunched her nose. It was just that he was a bit *too* perfect. His features were put together in exactly the sort of way that made her chest flutter. Presently, it did, and she frowned, crossing her arms over it. She had met his type before. He was just like Connor. Or maybe he was even worse.

Men like Kai were used to being adored. Their good looks seemed to make them think they could do whatever they wanted—just like Connor had in the garden. Her face burned as she thought of him pushing her against the high wall, and she turned away, seething.

She remained in the house, ignoring the temptation to glance out the window, until Ena and Seamus returned. Elysia could hear Ena's high voice from where she leaned against the wall. She was chattering on, like she normally did.

"You should have seen him, Kai, he was amazing!" she said, gushing.

"Hear that, Kai? I'm *amazing*," said Seamus. "Well, you were!"

said Ena. "Tell him, Kai, he's a great fisherman." "Yea, *tell me*, Kai," Seamus teased.

Kai's deep laugh drifted past the doorway, and Elysia huffed, rolling her eyes. "I'm sure you were perfectly…adequate, Seamus," Kai said.

Elysia heard the faint *thunk* of fist on flesh. Kai grunted, and she stood, peeking out the window. He was rubbing his arm, chuckling at the side of Seamus's orange head.

"Breakfast!" Seamus called.

Elysia's stomach grumbled, and she glared at Kai's back from her window. As much as she didn't want to be near him, she was famished. She'd have to go out.

Just then, Ena appeared in the door. She was breathless, grinning from ear to ear. Elysia stared at her flatly, and Ena's grin fell.

"What's wrong?" she whispered. She stuck a hand to Elysia's forehead, worriedly studying her features. "Kai said you were much better, but you look upset. What's the matter?" Why are you waiting all alone in here and not sitting outside with Kai?"

Elysia peered out the window. Kai and Seamus were joking loudly, exchanging more punches to each other's arms. She hesitated, then flicked her eyes back to her friend. Ena's blue eyes were searching her features for answers. Elysia opened her mouth, then closed it again.

She couldn't tell her.

Elysia shrugged, shooting Ena a grin. "It's nothing Ena. Truly. I'm just exhausted from the swim and the diving spider." She brushed past her, moving towards the door.

"Come on, let's eat. I'm absolutely starved."

Ena narrowed her eyes. "Okay…if you're sure?" Elysia nodded, faking a larger grin. "I'm sure." Ena smiled, sweeping her into a tight hug.

Blessed Ena. She really hadn't wanted to tell her about the ordeal with Kai and the secret island. She trusted Ena, but still, she wasn't sure her friend would understand. She didn't want to share her secret island with anyone else…even Ena. She already had to share it with Kai, and that was bad enough. Anyway, the whole situation was embarrassing.

Ena moved through the door, resuming her familiar chatter.

"'Lys, I'm *so* glad you're okay. You had me worried back there. Listen, you wouldn't have *believed* it. Seamus is an *amazing* fisherman. He caught two eels without even trying." She giggled. "He even let me spear the last one. I've never gotten to spear an eel before, you know? I am *so* glad you asked me to come with you! I mean, what an amazing adventure, right?"

Elysia chuckled. She wrapped an arm over Ena's shoulder. "Right," she said, smiling. "An amazing adventure."

They approached the edge of the river, and Kai turned to look at her. She glared.

"Just amazing," she said flatly. Kai pressed his perfect lips together, then he turned to resume chopping up the eel. Elysia watched as his sharp spear cut the flesh into neat squares. Already, a fresh pile of meat was assembled at his right.

Seamus lifted a square, balancing it on the end of his spear as he held it out to Ena. She grinned at him, then gingerly lifted the piece, dropping it into her mouth. Seamus gaped at her as she chewed, fascinated, then he quickly reloaded the spear with another bite.

Elysia grinned at their coy exchange, until the blade of Kai's spear appeared in the edge of her gaze. She stared pointedly at the piece of meat balanced on its tip, then turned away, crossing her arms.

Ena frowned, flicking her eyes back and forth between Kai and Elysia.

"'Lys, don't you want a bite?" she asked. "It's delicious." Elysia raised her chin.

"No thank you. I'm not hungry."

Ena frowned, flicking her eyes from Kai to Elysia. "But you just said…"

"I *said* I'm not hungry, Ena!"

Elysia's voice echoed off the cavern walls, and for a moment, everyone fell silent. Elysia bit her lip, then dropped her arms. "Ena, I'm sorry. I didn't mean it." She turned to face her, grinning apologetically. "It's just the exhaustion talking. And I probably still have some spider venom coursing through my veins. It's poisoned my tongue." Ena nodded.

"It's okay," she said, smiling softly.

Kai cleared his throat. "Spider venom can be pesky like that," he said quietly.

Elysia turned to glare at him. He had to be the most infuriating man she had ever met.

He stared at her flatly, shrugging. "Just saying." He held a square of meat out to her again. "Your poisoned tongue may say otherwise, but you need to eat. We've got a long swim ahead, and you're very weak. I plan to carry you most of the way, but still. You need your strength."

Elysia's eyes bulged. She raised her voice. "What do you mean, carry me?!" Her voice bounced against the cavern wall again, and she winced. She was talking louder than she intended, but she couldn't help herself. He made her so angry. She crossed her arms, narrowing her eyes.

"I certainly don't need you to carry me," she spat. "I'm perfectly capable of swimming on my own."

Kai sighed. He flicked his eyes over the river, then returned her gaze.

"I mean just what I said," he said calmly. "I'm going to carry you the rest of the way. There's no way you'll be able to make it, in your state. Anyway, we can move faster if I do. There are other creatures in this tunnel that would like to eat you, and I'd rather not meet with another one, if you don't mind."

Elysia's green eyes flashed with rage, and she fisted her palms at her sides.

"I'll not be needing your help, thank you very much." She bent to the pile of meat and lifted two bites, stuffing them into her mouth. "See?" she said in a muffled voice. "Already getting my strength back." She chewed quickly and swallowed. "Satisfied?"

Kai watched her flatly, then shook his head. "No.". Elysia raised her brows. "No?!" she screeched. "What do you mean, *No!*?"

Kai stood slowly. He crossed his arms, staring down at her from his straight nose.

"I *mean*, it doesn't matter how much eel you eat, you won't be strong enough to make it through the tunnel."

"Seamus, let's go," he said evenly.

Seamus frowned. He had several bites of meat balanced on his spear. Two were already in his mouth. He chewed them quickly and swallowed. "But, Kai, what about the eel?" Kai shot him a warning look.

"Leave it, Seamus," he said flatly.

Seamus stared at the meat longingly, then scooped up a palmful and stuffed it in his mouth. "Very well," he said, muttering through his full bite. "Seems like a waste, though."

Kai didn't give Elysia time to argue before he had scooped her off her feet and turned towards the river. "Hey! Put me down!" she screeched. She kicked hard with her legs, but he held the backs of her knees firmly against his chest and dove headlong into the water.

Elysia was furious. She lay rigidly in Kai's arms, holding her body as stiff as a spiny coral. Kai lowered his lips to the side of her head as he swam. "Relax, Elysia," he said gruffly. She frowned, glaring up at his square chin. There was a small cleft in it she hadn't noticed before. It was rather distracting. She ground her teeth, looking away.

"It's *Lady* Elysia," she snapped.

Kai didn't answer, and she pushed a little further.

"At least in the Selkie Court, our Guard knows their station," she said, sniffing. "Anyone in the Merrow Forces should know the same. *Lady* is a term of respect, and I *will* be respected, especially by someone like you."

Kai scoffed. The tiny muscle in his jaw flexed, and he stared down at her incredulously. "Someone like me, huh."

Elysia pursed her lips. She turned her gaze, sulking down at her wet clothing. He could've at least allowed her to pack it away. Hopefully, she would be able to change before meeting Lady Sirena. She hated the thought of meeting her host in wet clothes, especially on her first solo visit. It would be embarrassing to drip water all over the glass throne room floor. She opened her mouth to ask Kai if she could visit her rooms when they arrived, but he glared down at her so severely that she closed it again.

Elysia frowned. *Fine. That's just fine. I didn't want to ask for your help, in the first place.* She huffed, squirming in his arms. His body was hard as stone, and her side was beginning to ache from being held so long against it in a curved position. If she could just move her hip a bit. She shifted. *There, that's better.*

The edge of her hip grazed against Kai's ribs, and he grunted softly. "Sorry," she muttered, flushing. He didn't answer and moved her hip roughly away with his palm. Elysia frowned. *Typical.*

She focused on the tunnel ahead, working to keep her mind off her aching side. She hoped they were almost to the Court of Merrows. Then, she would be rid of him.

Once they arrived, Kai would resume his normal duties with the Forces, so she wouldn't have to see him very often. She would see him at court, of course, but that was to be expected. Most of the Guard were present for their court meetings on the Selkie Isles, and she was sure the Forces did the same. She flicked her eyes to his jaw, thinking. Maybe she would see him even less.

She couldn't recall Kai's presence with the Merrow Forces on the ground in the battle with the court of Orm, which meant he had either been guarding the court or patrolling the underground rivers. If it was the latter, that meant he was a spy. Spies were often gone from court, weren't they? She smiled a small smile, imagining Kai on patrol. Maybe she would barely have to see him at all.

She shifted slightly, and Kai gave her a warning stare. She glared up at him, then turned her focus to the tunnel ahead, cursing the diving spider. If it weren't for that foul creature, she wouldn't even be in this situation. Their journey couldn't end fast enough. Only a few more lengths of this blasted tunnel, and then she would be free. Free of Kai and his too-perfect face and his annoying blue eyes. Free of his smug looks and unwanted help. She narrowed her eyes. Once they made it to court, she would never have to deal with him, ever again.

Chapter 12

No signs of the abandoned ruins extended to the last cavern, save the symbol of the Court of Merrows, a swirling, silver water thistle, which was carved into the rock face above the door. A high waterfall emerged from the rock to the right of it, spilling into the pool below, and fresh, dry sea air blew through the doorway, moving easily through the section of shimmering dome that wavered across the it.

Tall shield ferns, clusters of larkspurs, and squat water thistles grew heavily near the exit, while soft, glowing moss lay in a thick carpet around the rocky riverbank. Kai lifted Elysia from the water and plopped her onto it. She landed on her back with a thunk, causing a *whoosh* of air to push from her chest.

She blinked up at the cavern ceiling, openmouthed. Her throat was fixed, and her chest wouldn't move. She grasped at her neck, panicking. She couldn't breathe.

All at once, the spasm ended, and she sucked in a breath. She sputtered and coughed, glaring up at Kai's back as he brushed past her. He didn't need to be so rough.

He was wearing the gauzy blue clothing he had worn this morning. She watched as he swiped his clothes from a waiting rock and moved silently behind a large boulder. Seamus did the same, and the two men returned moments later, clothed in the leather vests and slim, dark pants that marked them as merrow Forces.

Elysia held out the front of her dress. It was rumpled, and strips of green algae clung to her hem, but, thankfully, it wasn't damp. She frowned, brushing her hand against the fabric. In fact, it was completely dry. She raised her brow. She still needed to change, but at least she wouldn't be dripping water on the floor of Lady Sirena's glass throne room.

Dark boots appeared beside her, and she lifted her face to their owner. Seamus stared down at her with a wide grin. He pointed at her skirt.

"Neat trick, eh?" Elysia looked to her skirt and back to him. "What is?"

"The dry clothes! Once you get out of the water, they dry on the spot."

She stared blankly, and he chuckled, pointing above his head. "It's the dome that does the drying. Special combination of keeping the sea water out and letting the dry air in. Sucks the damp right out of the fabric."

Elysia nodded. She remembered the large, shimmering dome. It encircled the Court of Merrows like a giant upturned bowl. The wide court sat on the sea floor beneath it, as dry as the land above the surface.

Seamus tapped the side of his orange head. "And you thought there was nothing to me but my good looks," he said, winking. Elysia chuckled. He extended his hand, and she took it, standing as she dusted the dried algae crusts from her skirt.

Seamus moved to Ena and bent his head, whispering something in her ear. She giggled, and Elysia smiled. She already liked Seamus immensely. It was hard not to. Everything about him made her laugh, from his wild orange hair to his lopsided grin. And she suspected that he was right. There was more to him than met the eye. She wondered why he would be friends with someone as awful as Kai.

Just then, Kai cleared his throat from behind her left ear. Elysia startled and spun to face him, nearly bumping his broad chest with her nose. She frowned up at him, and he stared down at her flatly. He wove his eyes slowly from the hem of her skirt to her neck. Then he cocked his head, frowning. Elysia's throat blotched crimson, and she folded her arms over her chest, glaring.

He sucked in a breath before flicking his eyes to her face.

"I'd suggest a change of clothes before we meet in the throne room. Just, something less…mussed, would be good."

Elysia's cheeks blazed. She jutted out her chin.

"I wouldn't *need* to change, if you hadn't dragged me through the tunnel fully dressed," she hissed. Kai flexed his jaw. He stared down at her with his steely eyes.

"I'm only trying to help you," he said evenly. "But if you don't want my help, then that's just fine. You can figure it out yourself."

He flicked his eyes to Seamus and Ena.

"Let's go," he commanded. "We're already late for morning court, and Lady Sirena doesn't like to wait."

With that, he disappeared through the stone doorway.

Elysia stared after him in disgust. She ground her teeth. He was unbelievable.

Ena appeared at her side, staring up at her with wide eyes.

"Will you *please* tell me what is going on with you two?! You're at each other's throats!"

Elysia sighed. "It's nothing, Ena," she said tiredly. "Just drop it, okay?"

Ena eyed Elysia dubiously before turning to peer at the doorway where Kai had disappeared. She shrugged. "If you say so," she muttered. She turned back to Elysia.

"But you need to calm down before morning court, okay? The last thing we need on this visit is more hostility. We have enough of that between our people, as it is."

Elysia glared at the doorway, folding her arms. She knew Ena was right. Their people didn't need another excuse to fight.

She sighed, nodding.

"I'll try," she said softly.

The words nearly choked her, but she knew she would have to do just that. Kai would likely be out on patrol anyway, so he shouldn't cause her many more problems. At least, she hoped he would be. The less he was in her presence, the better. It would be much easier to ignore him and keep her anger in check if he was out of her line of sight. For now, she would just do her best.

Kai was waiting for them just outside the door. His shoulder was propped against a river birch, and he looked past her when she emerged, training his eyes carefully on the shallow stream that wound beneath the cobblestone street.

Good. She lifted her chin as she brushed past him, moving out of the thick cover of river birches and into the lane. Now that they were back in public, the treaty guidelines had reappeared. It would be easier for her to control herself, if he wasn't staring at her with his irritating blue eyes.

She paused as she stepped from beneath the branches, her breath catching in her throat. Even though she had been to the Court of Merrows once before, the beauty of it all was still mesmerizing. The shimmering dome soared over her head, a glittering, bowl-shaped barrier to the wide sea beyond. Streams of sunlight shone down through its surface, extending their warm rays like golden fingers from the surface of the Southern Sea to the ground.

A towering wall of ancient rock extended inside the dome's edge. It encircled the massive court like a fortress, and the top of it was overhung with trails of dark green moss. Inside the walls, glittering glass houses and towering stone structures dotted the lush landscape, which boasted trees and flowers of all sorts. Cypress clustered around clear blue pools, while willows wove their branches low over winding streams. Patches of large ferns and wildflowers grew from every available patch of ground, and climbing vines covered the stone houses that were hewn directly from the round fortress wall. Elysia smiled as she counted twinflower, sea pinks, lady's mane, and several orchids, which also grew in the palace gardens at home.

In the distance, the glittering glass palace perched on a high slab of rock before a towering waterfall, whose wide stream flowed from high on the fortress wall. It cascaded over the sheer face before disappearing behind the shining palace. Elysia gazed up at it, admiring the beauty and harmony of nature mixed with Merrow design.

Ena appeared beside her, and Seamus trailed close behind. Her friend gaped openmouthed at the scene. She spun in a circle on the cobblestone path, and Seamus watched, grinning widely at the air to her left. "It's fantastic!" Ena gushed. "So lovely, I couldn't have imagined it, if I had tried!" She smiled at Seamus, and he chuckled, leaning on his spear.

"I'm glad you like it," he replied.

Suddenly, Kai brushed past Elysia. He bumped her shoulder in the process, and she pitched forward, narrowly missing scraping her palms on the path before Seamus caught her by the arm. She frowned up at Kai, who stared just slightly to her right. "Watch where you're going!" she spat. For a moment, he looked as if he might apologize, but then he squared his shoulders. The muscle in his jaw flexed, and he didn't say anything.

Seamus cleared his throat uncertainly. "Well, ladies, Kai and I will show you to your rooms, now." He moved to Kai, nudging his arm. "Right, Kai?" Kai twisted his mouth. "Sure," Kai muttered.

Without saying more, he marched towards Elysia. He grasped her firmly by the arm, then began dragging her down the lane at break neck speed.

"Hey, let go of me!" she shouted. But Kai ignored her.

Curious merrow women peered out at them from the windows of stone houses and stopped in the lane to stare as they passed. Elysia could feel their glittering eyes on her, but when she returned their gaze, they looked away. She frowned at the lane ahead, stumbling behind as Kai pulled her on. It was obvious he was taking the long way around. She grunted, straining against his grip.

"What do you think you're *doing*?" she said through gritted teeth. "Let go!"

She twisted out of his grasp, just as a merrow man with an armful of packages stopped on their left. He was staring at her openly. Kai grasped her arm, pushing past him and dragging her along behind. "I'm *trying* to get you safely to the palace, *Lady* Elysia," he said under his breath.

Elysia dug in her heels, pulling against his hand. He tugged her arm, flicking his eyes nervously to the staring man. "Come on," he muttered.

Elysia stiffened. "I don't need your help," she hissed. "I thought we had established that fact."

Kai gripped his spear with white knuckles. He glared at the air to her right and brought his face close, his nose almost grazing her cheek.

"If you want to walk in the streets alone, fine," he said gruffly. "But be warned, the people here don't take kindly to a Selkie in the Court of Merrows. Especially if she's the heir to the Selkie throne."

Elysia flicked her eyes to the sides of the lane. Angry merrow men glared just shy of her actual frame, while the women gaped, whispered to one another in a winding hiss. She swallowed, relaxing her pull against his hand. "Fine," she muttered.

Wordlessly, Kai turned, continuing his path with Elysia trotting behind. Just then, she heard Seamus shout. "Kai, behind you!"

Kai stiffened, and before she knew what was happening, the merrow man who had stared was at her back. She froze as he wrapped a large arm tightly around her throat and placed a crude dagger to the edge of her chin. "Kai?" she squeaked. The man pressed down hard with the blade, and she lifted onto her toes, terror coloring her expression.

Kai had already spun into a defensive position. His spear was lifted just to her left, aimed at the merrow man's jaw. He bared his teeth, and his blue eyes flashed with rage.

"It would be in your best interest to let the Lady go," he said evenly. He jerked his chin, and Seamus rounded the man's side, pointing his spear against the side of the man's neck.

The man flicked his eyes to Seamus "Or what?" he spat. "What will you do to me, if I don't?"

A growl grumbled from deep in Kai's throat. He lowered his spear to the man's chest.

"Let her go, or you'll be flayed alive, right here in the street."

The man laughed mirthlessly. "I couldn't care less if you flay me alive. I only care about protecting the purity of the Court of Merrows. Any *selkie* who enters here pollutes these waters." He gestured to Elysia. "She is here, thus our waters are polluted. And she has broken the Treaty of Hiraeth. She is subject to be punished." He shrugged flatly. "I'm only doing my part to uphold the law."

Kai punctured the tip of his spear through the man's shirt, and the man groaned as a dark spatter of blood landed on Elysia's shoulder. She whimpered quietly, and the man tucked the blade tighter against her throat, just nicking the surface.

Elysia sucked in a breath as pain seared her throat, and Kai flicked his eyes to her neck as a thin line of blood trailed down it. He ground his teeth. "She's broken no law, as she is here with expressed permission of the councils and court rulers." He smiled grimly. "But you, my friend, *you* have broken the treaty today. I watched you stare at her from where you stood." He jerked his chin to Seamus. "My friend Seamus, there, will corroborate my story, won't you Seamus?"

Seamus nodded. "Aye, I will. Saw it with my own two eyes."

Kai grinned darkly at the large man, just as several other members of the Forces arrived. On Kai's command, they circled the man, aiming at Elysia's captor with the tips of their spears. Kai gave a signal, and one of them hit the man hard in the back of the legs with the flat of his blade.

The man howled as he dropped to his knees, breaking his grip on Elysia's neck.

She pitched forward, but Kai lifted her easily with one arm before she could drop to the cobblestones. He turned, breaking into a run, and Elysia didn't protest. She bounced limply against his back until they reached the end of the lane. There, Kai turned into an opening in the fortress wall, hidden under a cluster of hanging green vines.

Inside, he sat her down gently. Then he braced his arm on the opposite wall and stared sidelong at her, sucking in deep breaths of air. Elysia tucked her hand to her neck. She pulled it away, examining the dark blood on her fingers. Silently, she wiped them on her dress and craned her neck around the opening, trying to see back the way they had come. She bit her lip. "What about Ena?" she asked. "And Seamus?"

She turned to look at Kai on the opposite wall, but she nearly bumped her nose on his chest in the process. He had moved close behind her. Elysia tucked herself back against the wall as he braced one arm on the rock above her, peering out in the same direction. The air inside their hiding place was close, and the scent of river water mixed with tangy sweat lifted from his skin. Furtively, she studied his face, waiting for him to answer.

He was close enough that she could see the tiny scales trailing up his temple, and she focused on them, following their path as they wound up above his ear into his hair. He flicked his eyes down to her, and she looked away, attempting to focus on the world outside their hiding place.

For a moment, he just stared at her with his cold blue gaze. At last, she turned to him, watching as a series of emotions played across his face. Then his eyes softened. Something about his look sent off warning bells, but Elysia couldn't move. She was frozen, and she blinked up at him, watching the fiery blue of his eyes glittering in the dim light as he moved to balance his spear against the far the wall. He flexed his free hand, never breaking her gaze, then, he took a step towards her.

A flush rose on her chest as put his fingers to her chin. He lifted it softly, turning it left and right as he examined the shallow slice from the man's blade in the dim light. A tiny muscle in the corner of his jaw flexed, then he met her eyes.

"Is it hurting?" he asked quietly.

Her heart throbbed in her ears, and she swallowed, grasping for a coherent thought.

What was he doing? And why was she allowing it? She felt light-headed. The world was slightly off-balance, and she couldn't think. She nodded. "Yes," she whispered, then shook her head. "I mean, no, it's not hurting."

Kai nodded slowly. "Good."

Silently, he dropped his palm, trailing his fingers lightly along her bare forearm. He paused near her wrist, pressing lightly, and Elysia sucked in a breath. There was a faint bruise there where he had gripped her moments ago. His fingers hesitated over it, brushing lightly, and Elysia's heart thrummed.

"What are you doing?" she whispered.

He flicked his eyes to her face. "What about here?" he asked. He pressed lightly over her bruise, again. "Does it hurt?"

Elysia felt as if she were falling backward, tumbling headlong into a great expanse from which she might never escape. He studied her face for a reaction, and Elysia dropped her eyes, watching his fingers trail lightly over her bruised skin. His touch was like fire, and she flicked her eyes back to his, flustered. "It's fine," she squeaked.

Slowly, he raised his palm to her shoulder. He pressed it gently, rolling her back against the wall. Elysia laid her hands flat against the damp stone. She didn't speak as his eyes moved slowly over her limbs, face, and hair. She didn't know why he was studying her, why she was allowing it.

At last, he rested on her eyes. "You don't seem to be damaged anywhere else," he said gruffly. "Sirena would be furious if you were. She would have my tail, so I had to make sure you were alright before we reached the throne room."

She nodded mutely, and Kai grinned. He dropped his lips to the side of her head, grazing her cheek with his own. His breath tickled the shell of her ear, and she gripped tightly to the stone wall, unable to move. "Ena will be fine," he murmured. "Seamus will see to it."

Elysia didn't answer. She couldn't if she had wanted to. She couldn't believe what had just happened. She didn't quite understand it, but she got the feeling that something had just passed between them that couldn't be undone. Why in the known worlds hadn't she stopped him? What was wrong with her?

Suddenly, Kai pulled away. He frowned as he leaned past her, peering out into the streets. Elysia blinked rapidly, then furrowed her brow. She lifted herself from the wall. "What is it? What's the…"

Before she could finish, Kai gripped her roughly around the waist. He flung her back against the wall, trapping her body under his. He was heavy, and she strained and squirmed under his weight. "Kai?! Wha…"

He clamped his large hand hard over her mouth. "Quiet," he hissed. Elysia glared at him over his palm, but he didn't acknowledge her. Instead, he peered silently through the hanging vines into the street.

Outside, two Merrow men moved past their hiding place. They scanned the wall with their sharp eyes, holding roughhewn spears. One of them paused, examining the hanging vines over their hideout's opening. His glittering grey eyes narrowed, and Elysia gripped her hands against the damp stone as he gestured to his friend.

Kai watched him warily, then he flicked his eyes to Elysia. He held a finger to his lips, then removed his hand from her mouth. She nodded mutely as he reached for his spear.

The men moved silently around the door as Kai crouched into a defensive position. He aimed at them with his spear, his muscles taught, like a wound spring. One of the men started towards the door, and Elysia braced herself, ready to run. Kai bared his teeth, but at the last moment, someone called to the men from down the lane, and the two backed away from the opening.

Elysia sagged against the stone as Kai stood upright. He sighed heavily, leaning on his spear.

"Who were they?" she whispered.

Kai grimaced.

"Friends of your attacker. They're radicals—merrow men that cling to Lord Dolion's foul wishes. They would like nothing better than to see the heir to the selkie throne lying dead in our streets."

Elysia curled herself tighter against the stone wall. She frowned. Maybe she had underestimated the danger in coming to the Court of Merrows. The diving spider had been bad enough.

Now, she had been attacked almost as soon as she had come into court. She chewed her lip. So much for an adventure beneath the sea. It was more like a nightmare. And at this rate, she wasn't sure she would make it back to the islands from her adventure in one piece.

She flicked her eyes to Kai, who was peering through the hanging vines. He looked back to her over his shoulder. "It's clear, for the moment. And after your attack, the Forces will be out in droves. We should be safe to make it into the palace."

He scanned her clothing.

"You won't be able to visit your rooms until after morning court. News of the attack will have already reached Sirena's ears, and she'll be near panic. She'll want to see you first."

Elysia nodded, and he looked away. She shifted uncertainly. "Thank you," she said softly. Kai raised his eyes. "For what?"

Elysia twisted her mouth. "For saving me. Both times."

Kai shrugged. He dropped his eyes, folding his arms across his chest.

"It was nothing. Just doing my job."

Elysia gave him a small smile, and he straightened, clearing his throat. "Come on, let's go. We'll take the fortress passages and come in the palace the back way."

Elysia followed as Kai slipped beneath the hanging vines. He scanned the streets, keeping a firm hand braced against Elysia's back as they slipped away from their hiding place. Behind them at a distance, deep shouts mixed with the clash of metal blades. Elysia's heart leaped at the sound, and she hurried along as Kai pressed her forward, trying to keep her mind from inventing another attacker around the next corner.

Just before they reached the castle steps, the shouting intensified, and suddenly, a sharp, shrill scream cut through the fray. Elysia's steps faltered.

"Ena," she whispered.

She turned to search towards the sound, her eyes landing on a throng in the center of the court. There, merrow Forces jostled for position against the angry mob. Elysia searched the sea of faces, just glimpsing the tips of Ena's flaming hair in their midst. Her heart lurched, a scream mounting in her throat. Ena was being held between the two men who had almost discovered her and Kai moments ago.

Elysia moved to run towards them, but Kai caught her hard by the upper arm. She ground her teeth, struggling against his grip as he propelled her forward. "Let go!" she shouted, but he ignored her. He pulled her on, turning right into a wide tunnel hewn out of the stone fortress wall. Two tall sentries were posted at its opening, and Elysia flicked her eyes helplessly to the men as she passed. They never moved and peered straight ahead, holding a tight grip on their long spears.

Once inside, Kai spun her hard to face him. He gripped tightly to her upper arms, and she yelped. She was sure she would have two more bruises to further decorate her limbs. Kai clamped a hand tightly over her mouth.

"Quiet," he hissed, glaring. "The last thing we need is an angry mob of merrows on our tails."

Above their heads, a row of iron lanterns hung from hooks at intervals, casting a yellowish-gold glow along the narrow corridor. Elysia blinked through their dim light, frowning at him over his hand. He dropped it, then turned to lift a lantern from the wall.

"But Ena," Elysia hissed at his back. "I saw her. She was being held by those men."

Kai spun. He held the lantern up to her face, narrowing his blue eyes as Elysia recoiled.

"Ena is the least of my concerns, right now. My only job is to protect you, and even *that* is proving to be more than I can handle." He took another step towards her, backing her against the wall. "If you weren't so *stubborn* and would *listen* to me, Ena might not be in this situation." Elysia blinked at him in shock, and he brought his face closer, growling.

"One selkie in the Court of Merrows is enough to cause chaos. Especially the heir. It would've been best if you'd left the other one at home."

Elysia stared at him openmouthed, and he stood straight, glaring down his nose.

Elysia's anger flared, and she fisted her hands at her sides. Who did he think he was?

She stepped towards him, lifting her chin as she nearly bumped his chest.

"Ena is my best friend and my lady in waiting," she hissed. "It's expected she would come with me on my visit. You would know that if you knew anything at all." She pointed her finger at his chest.

"And as for the angry mob? If that's anyone's fault, it's yours."

Kai raised his brows as she dropped her hand. He scoffed.

"Seriously? How is this *my* fault?" He pointed his own finger at her chin.

"*I'm* not the one that threw a *tantrum* in the middle of the street. If *you* would have just followed me obediently, you wouldn't have been attacked in the first place!" He shook his head, laughing mirthlessly.

"No, Elysia, it's not my fault. But it's absolutely yours."

Elysia was fuming. She glared, raising her voice. "*Excuse me*, but I've studied the Histories, just as I would *assume* a member of the Forces, like yourself, would have done. And it was *your* Forces that captured *my* father when he was killed by *your court*. That's the whole reason we have the Treaty of Hiraeth and the animosity between our people, in the first place!" She narrowed her eyes. "And aren't those in the Forces usually from the same families? So that would mean, it was, who, *your* father who led mine to his death?" She paused, raising her brows. "Or am I wrong?"

Kai stared down at her in shock. He opened his mouth, then

closed it again, shaking his head. Elysia continued before he could gather his words.

"I thought so," she said flatly. "Seeing as you hail from such a family, it's not like you care, either way, what happens to me." She glared, grinning as she watched the emotions skitter across his face. She pressed on.

"You're probably just protecting me for your own benefit. Either you want to get your foot in with Lady Sirena and gain a higher position in the Forces, *or*, and I'm almost *sure* it's this one, you're doing it to get yourself out of some trouble."

He glared at her in disbelief, and she smiled a flat smile. She'd hit a nerve. Time to press it a little further. "All you care about is yourself," she spat. "I knew that from the first moment I saw you on my secret island!" She narrowed her eyes. "What were you doing there, anyway?" His eyes were round *O's* as Elysia chuckled mirthlessly. She shook her head. "I can tell you exactly what. You were following me." She folded her arms. "You trailed me so you could watch me swim!"

The thought of it pushed her over the edge, and she stomped her foot hard against the stone. "You're just like all the rest!" she shouted. "You do *exactly* as you please, no matter who it hurts! Your choices are based on your own whims, and you give no thought to the consequences. So, tell me, Kai, who are *you* to tell *me* what to do?!"

Kai's hand was gripping his spear so tightly that his knuckles had gone white. His cheeks were flushed, and he glared down at her furiously through the lantern light. His look was so menacing that Elysia shrank slightly under his stare.

"You don't know *anything* about me," he said evenly. "I have no need of increasing my regard from Lady Sirena, and I certainly don't care what someone like *you* thinks of me," he growled. He brought his nose close to her face. "You may think what you like," he breathed, "But your opinion is of no difference to me. I have a job to do, and I will complete it. After that, you won't have to worry. I won't have anything more to do with you."

With that, he turned away, moving swiftly down the long corridor. Elysia glared after him. "Good!" she called to his back. "When this is over, I hope I never see you again as long as I live!"

Kai didn't acknowledge her, and it made her anger surge. She ground her teeth, fighting the urge to punch the stone wall.

She glared at Kai's back as he turned to the left. He was moving rapidly out of sight. She had no idea where she was going, so she had no choice but to follow him. She muttered angrily, starting after him.

Never in her life had she met a man more frustrating than Kai. She half-hoped he'd fail in his mission to protect her. Sure, she'd be maimed, or worse, but at least he'd be punished. Surely, if he failed, he would lose his rank, or maybe he would even banned from the Forces, depending on what kind of trouble he was in.

Whatever the case, she imagined he would be punished severely. She grinned. That would teach him. And at least she would have to deal with him anymore. After an epic failure to protect the heir to the Selkie throne, he certainly wouldn't be her escort on her next visit. That is…if she survived for a next visit.

Her mind drifted to the angry mob. Things were much worse between their clans than she had realized. The last time she had come to the Court of Merrows, she had mostly stayed in the palace or her rooms. She hadn't been allowed to explore or interact with the people at all.

She had thought it was simply her overprotective mother that had demanded they ride in a covered carriage to and from court and be housed in private rooms, away from the court's eye. But now, she saw that Lady Sirena had been shielding her and the other Selkie visitors from the peoples' hostility.

What Elysia had said to Kai was true. Animosity between their clans had been increasing since her father's death, and things had only worsened since Lord Dolion had drafted the Treaty of Hiraeth. After he exiled her people, he had forced Lady Malca and her council to sign it, on pains of death, and the hatred between the clans had only spiraled since then.

Elysia had never experienced such hatred directly. Sure, she had heard tales of deadly encounters with their Merrow neighbors, rumors of hate-brewing factions, but until today, she had never truly believed them. Now that she had seen such a faction up close, had felt the crude blade of hate pressed against her throat, she wondered, what could Lady Sirena possibly expect to gain from inviting her here?

If the merrow ruler was expecting Elysia to improve relations between their clans, she was going to be sorely mistaken. It was obvious her presence was only causing more problems. Certainly, this disaster of a visit had already illustrated that fact famously.

She flattened her mouth into a grim line. She hoped Lady Sirena knew what she was doing. Otherwise, her first visit would prove to be an epic failure. In many ways, it already was. Besides inciting an angry mob and possibly injuring her best friend in the process, Elysia had made a mortal enemy of her escort.

She frowned. That couldn't be helped. Everything about him made her furious, from his eyes, to his face, to his stupid silver hair. Besides the few moments in their hiding spot, Ena was right, they were constantly at each other's throats.

Kai hooked a right up ahead, and she ground her teeth, speeding her steps. It was simple. She and Kai were a disaster together, and there was only one answer for that: avoid him, as much as possible. Elysia grinned. Morning court couldn't come fast enough. When it was over, she would do just that.

CHAPTER 13

The passage emerged from beneath the waterfall, where a smooth, winding path led through the palace gardens. Two large oak trees grew at its rear entrance, which was marked by a high stone arch. Their roots cascaded over the path, while a circular stone wall lined the garden's outer edge. It was shadowed by a green hedge on the interior, and dark green moss clung to the stones, while winding honeysuckle vines trailed over its edges. Buttercups, bluebells, foxglove, primroses, twinflowers, and water thistles grew in clusters around the path, and a large, white rosebush clung to a long trellis on each side. Heavy blooms dotted its greenery, filling the garden with a sweet, heady scent.

Elysia smiled, letting her fingers brush a large, white bloom. She wished she had more time to linger. The large white rose bushes were very similar to the ones at home, and their beauty made her strangely homesick for the Selkie Isles garden below her window's trellis. But there wasn't a moment to spare, and regrettably, she moved on.

Throughout the garden, hidden alcoves had been secreted between the hedge and the wall. Elysia passed a low stone bench tucked inside of one. It created the perfect hideaway for those who'd rather not be seen.

She flicked her eyes over the bench, bristling as her encounter with Connor at the Midsummer Ball flashed in her mind. She could still feel the press of his heavy body against her, pushing her against the high wall. Her stomach turned, and she swallowed against the sick feeling. She wondered how many times Kai had used the hideouts for something similar.

A winding stream flowed from the base of the waterfall, twisting through the menagerie of plants until it ended in a glassy blue pool at the garden's center. A circle of purple iris lined the water's edge, and large green lily pads were spaced across it at intervals. Kai stepped to the first one, then skipped ahead, moving nimbly from one pad to the other in a single stride.

Elysia put her toe gingerly to the first lily pad and pressed, testing her weight, then she held the closest orchid stem, moving her back foot to join it. She waited as the pad wobbled slightly, then carefully, she let go of her orchid. Softly, she lifted her other foot, taking another step, then another as she worked to balance with her arms. She grinned. *Easy.*

She flicked her eyes across the pool, then frowned. Kai was already waiting on the other side. He leaned boredly against the trellis, facing away from her. She glared at his back, then bit her lip, measuring the distance to the next pad with her eyes. Then she stepped one foot across.

She moved to lift her back foot, but the surface of the second floating plant was slippery, and her front shoe slid sideways as she lost her balance. She flailed her arms, grasping at the air, but there was nothing to hold. Then she pitched sideways, her whole body splashing under in the shallow pool.

Kai spun at the sound, instinctively drawing his spear. Then moved towards her swiftly, scanning for danger with his sharp eyes. Quickly, Elysia tucked her silver tail beneath her soaked skirt. She scrambled for the edge of the pool, her chest flaring under his sharp, blue gaze.

She pulled herself to sit on the bank as she flashed him a threatening frown. "Enjoying the view again, Kai?" she snapped. Her wet dress clung tightly to her slim frame, and, for a moment, Kai stood dumbfounded. He gaped down at her blankly, then moved as if to lift her, but she flicked her fingers, brushing him off.

"Look *away*, please!" she growled.

Kai blinked as realization dawned, then he turned slightly to the side, relieving her of his stare.

"Sorry," he muttered.

Elysia flicked her eyes over the palace courtyard as her chest splotched crimson. Thankfully, she and Kai were alone, so no one else was witness. Still, it was embarrassing, even if only in front of him. Quietly, she lifted herself from the edge of the pool and emerged at his side.

He cleared his throat as she held out her skirt, which was quickly drying under the air of the dome.

"I didn't see anything. I swear," he said to the air to her left. Elysia rolled her eyes. *Sure.*

She didn't answer as she brushed past him, headed for the palace doors. Kai frowned after her.

"*Again*, I'm only trying to do my job," he called. "Which is to keep you safe."

She shook her head. Behind her, Kai was muttering angrily to himself.

"Of course, *you're* the one who's angry. It's all about you, isn't it Kai," she grumbled quietly.

Kai barked a huff as his anger surged, and he marched after her, clenching his jaw. "But, *of course*, you think I was trying to get a look at you," he muttered. "*Yeah*, Elysia, I just can't control myself. Because you're *exactly* the kind of woman I like." He held up his hand, marking his words with his fingers. "You know: selfish, unfeeling, rude, self-centered, causing a problem wherever she goes…"

Elysia rolled her eyes. He had just named all his own illustrious qualities. She reached for the door handle, then paused uncertainly.

She had never come in the palace back way, and she suddenly realized she had no idea where to go. Still fuming, she pulled her hand back in a huff, facing the glittering glass with crossed arms.

In a moment, Kai appeared silently at her side. He glared at the glass doors, then spun towards her, opening his mouth. "I…"

Elysia cut him off. She held her palm towards his nose, and he blinked down at it, gripping white knuckles on his spear. She didn't look at him, and Kai scoffed, shaking his head.

"Forget it," he growled. Then he brushed past her, pulling the heavy glass doors open.

Elysia sniffed, lifting her chin. She wouldn't let him agitate her. He wasn't worth it. Kai was no one. He was only a member of the Merrow Forces—an extremely annoying member, but still.

Silently, she stepped through the doorframe, watching Kai's retreating back with narrowed eyes. As usual, he was moving ahead of her at a breakneck pace, and Elysia trotted after him, cursing his long stride. It made her mind wander to Ena, whose petite legs always hurried to match her own quick steps.

Ena's scream from inside the angry mob echoed in Elysia's mind, and her pace increased. She hurried down the corridor to meet Kai at the throne room doors. Hopefully, Lady Sirena would know something about what had happened to her friend. Two tall sentries pulled the high doors outward, and Elysia followed Kai closely as he stepped through. She would ask her about it immediately.

She couldn't stop herself from craning her neck to admire the towering hall. Glittering panes of green and blue glass spanned high above to the vaulted ceiling, where wide strips of sunlight streamed down past the dome from the sea's surface. They refracted through the glass, landing in dancing prisms of color on the glimmering, columned walls before reaching the throne room floor.

The morning court was full of waiting spectators. Rows upon rows of sentries stood guard against the walls, while noblemen and noblewomen were seated to the left and right of a long aisle. Near the front, the Merrow council was positioned in a curved row of seats to the left of Lady Sirena's throne. Elysia recognized some of their faces from previous meetings.

Every eye turned towards them as she followed Kai into the aisle. Elysia wanted to shrink under the Merrows' sharp gazes, but Kai walked confidently to the base of the dais. He bowed softly from his waist, and when he stood, Lady Sirena nodded, smiling.

To Elysia's surprise, she beckoned him forward, and he took the steps two at a time before he bent to kiss her cheek. Then, he took the post directly to her right, standing with one hand on his spear and the other folded behind his tall back.

Elysia flicked her eyes from Kai to Lady Sirena. She was confused. He had kissed her cheek, and now he was standing beside her, much like the place she took at their own court meetings at home. She frowned up at him, wondering if he had already received his promotion for delivering her safely. Maybe

Lady Sirena had made Kai her personal guard as a reward. But that still didn't explain the kiss.

She studied Kai's proud frame, thinking. Maybe the kiss was a merrow custom. But if it was, she had never heard about it, and she had never seen it in practice. Not until today.

Lady Sirena broke her thoughts.

"Lady Elysia, how lovely to see you again," she said warmly. "It has been too long. I am so glad you agreed to come for a visit. Please, come closer, so that I may have a look at you."

Elysia kept her eyes carefully away from Kai as she stepped up the dais. She could feel his presence radiating from the side of the throne. Lady Sirena stood, embracing her softly as she kissed her on the cheek. Elysia smiled at the gesture. Perhaps it was a merrow custom, after all.

Lady Sirena grasped her hands, peering at her with a concern.

"I apologize for so poor a welcome into our court. I understand that your lady in waiting, Ena, has been injured in the attacks this morning," she said softly. Elysia paled. "Yes, my Lady," she whispered. Lady Sirena dipped her chin, her green eyes glittering as her dark hair swished near her waist. "Rest assured; we are doing all we can for her. She is resting, now, in her rooms, and is receiving the best care. My sources tell me she is doing well, but she will likely be bedfast for several days."

Elysia swallowed convulsively, and Lady Sirena squeezed her palms.

"Seamus has been charged with guarding her doors, along with several others. You may go to her as soon as our court is adjourned."

Elysia nodded. Her throat was tightening. She was afraid she might cry.

"Thank you, for all of it," she murmured, her voice wavering.

Lady Sirena smiled softly, then pulled her in for another embrace. "She will be alright," she said quietly. Elysia nodded against her curtain of dark hair. She hoped she was right.

She moved back to the floor as Lady Sirena tapped her scepter once on the dais.

"Morning court will now come to order," she said in a strong voice. She flicked her sharp eyes around the room as the already quiet hall fell into silence.

"The first order of business is the heightening animosity between our two great people: Selkie and Merrow. As many of you know, we in the Court of Merrow have welcomed the future Selkie ruler, Elysia Bryn, to our court as an ambassador. As Elysia is now of age, her mother and the Selkie council graciously agreed that she be allowed to make her own decision regarding this visit, and we are thankful that she has bravely accepted our invitation." She dipped her chin to Elysia before she continued.

"As you know, many cycles ago, my father, Lord Dolion, betrayed our great Selkie neighbors. He murdered their leader, Lord Ríonan, and took their lands, exiling them to the Selkie Isles, from which they could never return. Shortly after, he drafted the Treaty of Hiraeth and forced the councils and the newly installed Selkie leader, Lady Malca, to sign it, on pain of death.

The results have been disastrous. We who were once two clans living in harmony have now become so at odds that an ambassador from one court may not visit the other, without fearing for her life." She flicked her eyes solemnly to Elysia, then returned them to the hall.

"I have never been a proponent of the treaty, and I had hoped that the passage of Time would prove to heal wounds so long ago formed. But it seems our two courts are trapped in the past, doomed to relive the treachery of my father, cycle after cycle. For if we forbid a merrow man to even look at a selkie woman, what hope for restoration can there be?"

She studied the court room with her sharp green eyes. "I have tried, many times, to amend the Treat of Hiraeth and its harsh conditions, but so far, I have not been successful. Too much has happened, and it seems there are too many harsh feelings between our people to make things right.

If we hope for change, we must shorten the gap between what has been and what we hope will be. Change may come slowly, but come, it must. For we can no longer afford to live in the past, nursing old wounds." She paused, gathering words. "A new day dawns on the Southern Sea's horizon, and with it, a new path will be forged. Though dark days may come, we will walk this path with confidence, for our only way out of the grip of darkness is to proudly march through.

It is to this aim that I have called on Lady Elysia. Even now, she walks this new path as ambassador of her people, here in the Court of Merrows. I am hopeful that her presence will open the hearts of the clans and show them a way forward."

She smiled down at Elysia.

"Elysia is a bright ray of light in a very dark place, and I hope that, with her presence, the unification of the selkie and the merrow will begin. In fact, I am hopeful that this future of unity has already begun. That is why I have placed her under the care of my ward, the heir to the merrow throne, Kai Bennet."

Elysia's face paled and her heart dropped to her feet. She flicked her eyes to Kai, blinking. *The heir?!* Kai was the heir to the Court of Merrows throne? Why had he not told her?

She moved her gaze over him, seeing him with new eyes. He looked strong, powerful…regal, even. Elysia didn't know how she hadn't seen it before.

Her chest flared with a mix of embarrassment and anger as she flipped back through their interactions. She had said some things that she might not have, had she known who he was. But how could she have known?

She narrowed her eyes, hoping he could feel their burn. He should have told her. There had been plenty of opportunities. Kai remained still and silent, but the muscle in his jaw flexed slightly under her stare.

Lady Sirena continued. "I chose Kai for several purposes. First, I have installed him as Lady Elysia's keeper and guard, and he will remain by her side for the duration of her visit. He has already proven to be very capable of her protection, as he demonstrated in the attacks this morning.

Second, I hope that their close contact proves to form a relationship that is intimate and long-lasting. With their equal positions of leadership, my wish is that they would be able to find a way forward, where I and others have so long failed."

Elysia fought the urge to scoff. Lady Sirena was going to be sorely disappointed if she thought she and Kai were the key to mending relations between the courts. *Intimate? Long-lasting?* There was absolutely no chance of that. How could there be, when they could barely say two words to each other before they were at each other's throats?

"And third," Lady Sirena added, "I am hopeful that this mission will be beneficial for Kai on a personal level." She turned her head to smile briefly at his profile. "There comes a day in every young merrow's life when the future comes calling, and that day for Kai Bennet is now. One, day, it will be his responsibility, along with Lady Elysia's, to lead our great people into a new era—one that I hope will mark the Histories with peace and harmony."

With that, she tapped her scepter once on the glass floor.

"If Elysia's visit proves ineffective, I will be forced to take more drastic measures. In the meantime, we will ask the Source to bless her coming. Morning court is now dismissed. Thank you all for your attention to these desperate matters. We will reconvene at our next scheduled meeting to discuss our future plans."

At once, the hall began a quiet chatter. Harsh words snaked past Elysia's ears, and she tried to tune them out. To her right, several noblewomen studied her curiously with their iridescent eyes. Elysia shifted uncertainly, hugging her arms against her chest.

"There's just no sense in it," one whispered. "If Lady Sirena thinks a visit from a *Selkie* woman is going to overturn cycles upon cycles of foul feelings, she's quite mistaken."

"Right," replied another. She flicked her eyes over Elysia in distaste. "And she's so…*young*.

If the others have been unsuccessful, what can *she* do to amend the Treaty of Hiraeth?"

Lady Sirena's strong voice cut through their sharp words. "Elysia," she called, beckoning her forward. Elysia's face burned with embarrassment as she passed the noblewomen. She bit the inside of her cheek, staring hard at the glass floor to avoid their harsh stares. Secretly, she felt the women might be right. After all, she had only just passed her eighteenth cycle, and her presence had caused an uprising almost as soon as she had stepped her foot past the dome.

Lady Sirena grasped her hands, dipping her face to Elysia's eyes.

"Pay them no mind, Elysia," she said softly. She flicked her eyes to the cluster of women, who made a studied attempt to look casually in another direction. "They are steeped in the past, trapped in a cage of their own making, and they cannot see their way out."

She lifted Elysia's chin, peering deeply into her eyes.

"Hold your head high, my dear. You are the daughter of Lord Ríonan and the heir to the selkie throne." She smiled. "I knew your father, all those cycles ago. He was a great leader: proud, strong, and brave." She paused. "I see much of him in you."

Elysia flicked her eyes to Lady Sirena's face, and the ruler smiled warmly.

"And much of your mother. She has held her own on the selkie throne, since your father's death. Though we have not always seen eye to eye, she has done what she thought was best for her people. That is the mark of a great leader.

You, Elysia, are the best of both of them. There is no limit to what you can do. Do not allow the attack, the prejudices of some nasty noblewomen, or your own fear to hold you back from becoming who you are supposed to be. Stand tall. Assert yourself. Show them your strength, even if you must fake it." She chuckled lightly. "I speak from experience, as you might have guessed."

Elysia grinned, and Lady Sirena nodded. She gave her hands a squeeze. "I was once a new leader, too.

"Now, Kai will show you to your rooms. If you should need anything, he will be close by. I have had you installed in the rooms adjoining his own, and he has been instructed to remain by your side for the duration of your stay, however long that may be. We will determine that in the coming days."

She folded her hands at her waist. "I expect you are tired from your journey. I won't hold you any longer." She smiled softly. "You need to rest before your welcome dinner."

Elysia did her best to smile back at her before she gave a small bow. Kai was supposed to stay beside her for her *entire* stay? She flicked her eyes to him. He seemed unphased by this news, which meant that he had known it beforehand.

Calmly, he left his post and moved to stand beside her. He bowed to Lady Sirena, then held out his arm, ready to escort her down the glass steps. Elysia took it stiffly, narrowing her eyes at his profile as they slowly descended. Outside, she was the picture of calm, but inside, she was raging. Not only had he kept his identity as heir a secret, which explained the kiss and his position by the throne, he had also neglected to tell her that he would be with her for her *entire stay* as her personal guard.

He dropped her arm as they stepped to the floor, moving swiftly ahead to the doors. Elysia followed dutifully behind him, glaring daggers at his back. As soon as they were out of earshot, she was going to flay him alive. She grinned at the thought. She would enjoy every moment.

Lady Sirena might trust him, but there was no way she was going to. He was clever, she would give him that, but he was also sneaking and secretive. He had proven that fact twice, now, both by hiding his identity and skulking around her secret island.

She didn't care if he *was* the heir to the throne. Rulers couldn't always be trusted. After all, Lord Dolion had murdered her own father, and he had been a merrow ruler.

What really mattered were his actions, and Kai's actions had shown her his true identity, no matter what image he tried to portray. He might act like he was the obedient heir to the Merrow throne and the picture of a trustworthy member of the merrow Forces, but she knew better. It was very simple. If hiding the truth was as good as a lie, then Kai Bennet was a liar.

And liars couldn't be trusted.

CHAPTER 14

Elysia kept silent until they stepped beneath the waterfall. Then, she sped ahead of Kai and spun back to face him. She glared at him furiously. "Why didn't you tell me?" she demanded. Kai kept his face a flat mask. He stared blankly back at her. "Tell you what?" he asked innocently.

Elysia fumed. *So typical. Feign innocence, and you might get away with it, right, Kai?* She fisted her palms. Not this time. "*Why* didn't you tell me about your position at court," she pressed. "Or the fact that I'd be stuck with you for the entirety of my visit?"

Kai didn't answer. He simply stared, then he brushed past her, moving further along the corridor. Elysia blinked at his back. Then she marched ahead again and spun to face him, holding a hand to the center of his chest. She lifted her chin, accusing.

"You let me think you were just a Merrow Forces escort, paying your punishment for some infraction or trying to win a higher position."

Kai chuckled mirthlessly. "No, Elysia, that's what *you* thought. *I* never told you that." He stepped back, folding his arms. "And I didn't think it necessary to lay out every detail of your visit. I figured Lady Sirena would've already done that. It seems obvious that you would need a guard for the duration of your stay. Especially if you're going to be inciting a riot every chance you get."

Elysia blinked at him in shock, and he shook his head, grinning flatly. "You should be *glad* that you're under my guard. If you hadn't been, you'd probably be dead right now and our two courts would be at war."

Elysia narrowed her eyes. What he said made sense. She was embarrassed she hadn't thought of it herself.

"Never mind that," she snapped. Kai moved to step ahead, but she blocked his path.

"If you're the heir, then why didn't I see you, when I was last at court?"

Kai stared at her evenly, then he flicked his eyes to the ceiling, twisting his mouth.

"I wasn't…well then," he said quietly. He paused for a moment, opening and closing his mouth, then shook his head. "It doesn't matter. I just…I wasn't often at court meetings, okay? I took a…I took a break. But now I'm back." He shuffled his weight, staring at the ground.

Elysia studied his expression. He was frustrated with her, for sure, but there was a glint of sadness at his edges. She bit the inside of her cheek. Her anger died a bit, and she lowered her voice. "Where were you, then?"

The tiny muscle in his jaw flexed, and he stared at the floor before he met her gaze. "It doesn't matter, now. I'm here, I'm the heir, and we're stuck together for the Source only knows how long. We might as well get used to it, however much we may hate it." He wet his lips, waving uncertainly with one arm. "Apparently, Sirena thinks we can do some good for our people. Although, I have no idea how we might do that."

He dropped his arm, and Elysia thought of the riot in the street. She sighed. He was right. They at least needed to try. If nothing else, for Lady Sirena. She bit her cheek.

"Fine. I'm willing to try if you are."

Kai nodded. "We're agreed, then. Let's go. Our rooms are just above us. After you've changed, I'll take you to Ena."

Elysia followed him until they were high in the stone wall of the fortress. There, he stopped at a curved end in the rock. Before him were two large, polished wooden doors with an ornate iron lantern hanging between them. Kai moved towards the first door and pulled it open wide.

He flicked his eyes to Elysia. "This is your room." He gestured towards the other wooden door. "The other is mine. They join in the middle by way of a two-sided door, though, you don't ever have to open it."

They moved inside, and he pointed to the adjoining door. "There's locks on both sides," he explained quietly. He flicked his eyes to her. "I would ask that you keep your side unlocked, in case I need to come in quickly." He shifted uncomfortably. "You know, if," He waved his hand. "If there's an intruder," he mumbled, dropping his palm. He cleared his throat. "It's highly unlikely, since we're so high in the fortress. Most people don't even know these rooms exist. But, just in case."

Elysia stared uncertainly at her side of the unlocked door, then flicked her eyes to Kai, raising her brows. He stared at her blankly. "What?" he asked. She grinned. "So, let me get this straight. You want me to keep *my* side of the door unlocked, so *you*, the one who has a history of watching unsuspecting Selkie women swim, can come into my room, anytime you like?"

Kai stared at her in disbelief, then rolled his eyes. "Good grief, Elysia, I didn't actually *see* anything, okay? I didn't even know you were there, in the first place."

Elysia narrowed her eyes. "The real question is: Kai, what were *you* doing there, in the first place?"

Strangely, Kai's face blanched at the question, and Elysia watched as a myriad of emotions passed over his features. The tips of his ears flushed, then he looked away, frowning as he swallowed convulsively. He took a moment to gather himself, and when he looked back to her, he wore his familiar hard expression.

"I'll leave you to get changed," he said flatly. "You'll want to see Ena, before dinner."

With that, he strode quickly from the room and shut the door to the hall tightly behind him.

Elysia stared after him in confusion. He was obviously upset, but she had no idea why.

She crossed her arms, thinking. Something about her question had bothered him.

Maybe it was the fact that he had broken the treaty. Was he worried she would tell someone about it? She bit her cheek. Surely, he knew she wouldn't do that.

Of course, she had only just decided that she wouldn't do that, moments ago, while in the throne room. Discovering that Kai was the heir to the Merrow throne had somewhat complicated her plans to have him flayed. She twisted her mouth. Before, she had taken comfort in continually plotting his demise.

But Kai didn't have to know that.

The wood of their connecting door was thin, and she could hear him moving on the other side of it. He was muttering softly to himself. Elysia pressed her ear against her side of it, but he had already stopped muttering, and she couldn't hear anything. She pulled away, frowning. There was something else Kai wasn't telling her. She was certain of it.

For the moment, she let it drop, and turned back into her

rooms. Her stomach grumbled, and she pressed it with her palm. She needed to get ready for her welcome dinner. She was starving, and Kai was right. She *did* want to see Ena, beforehand.

She moved to the large, gilded mirror by the adjoining door and studied herself. Silently, she touched her tangled mass of hair, clicking her tongue. It had dried in a twisted mound from her fall in the garden pool, and her clothes were rumpled and dirt stained. She looked a mess. No wonder the noblewomen from morning court had talked badly about her.

She moved to the polished wooden armoire in the corner, pulling it open with its swirled seashell handles. Several pieces of her clothing hung neatly inside, and she rummaged through them, searching for something to wear.

Her eyes landed on a pale blue gown with silver beading, and she grinned, pulling it from the chest. It would be perfect for dinner, and she knew just the shoes to match it: strappy, flat sandals woven with silver thread. She snagged them from the neat row beneath her dresses padded over the plush cream rug to lay her selections across the bed.

The bedframe was large and circular, and the high mattress was topped with fluffy pillows in various shades of blue and cream. She gazed at them longingly, brushing her hand along the soft fabric of the coverlet. Her body was exhausted, and she longed to pull it under her chin, but she knew the moment that she did, she would fall asleep, not waking until morning.

She sighed as she moved to the bathing room and turned on the tap. While the water ran, she moved in front of the large picture window in her bedroom. The high window faced outward, and she had a private view of the open sea past the glittering dome. Coral backed chairs and a small table sat before it, and Elysia lowered into one, admiring the beauty of the undersea landscape.

She smiled as a school of fish swirled past in the deep water. Together, their bodies made a large, moving, oblong shape that glistened and glimmered in the sunlight. A silver dolphin twisted in and out of them, cutting rapidly through the small school. His presence through the group into chaos, and Elysia giggled as the fish darted back and forth, avoiding his path.

Suddenly, she remembered her bath, and she raced to the bathing room just in time to cut off the water before it sloshed over the side. She rolled her eyes at herself and drained some of the water before stripping off her stiff clothing and stepping into it.

After she felt clean, she hurried to dress, then sat at the vanity to weave her hair into a thick braid. She curved the long plait around her head and secured it with pins, leaving little slips of dark curls to frame her face. When she'd finished, she moved to the large wall mirror, and turned left and right.

As usual, Ena's dress selections were excellent. Elysia especially loved this one. The pale blue satin column clung lightly to her delicate curves before dropping to her ankles in a cascade of small, gauzy ruffles. Tiny, silver beads lined a trio of delicate straps which fell lightly off her shoulders, while silver beading swirled over the bodice and trailed down the front and back of the gown in the pattern of a silver tail, a nod to her Selkie heritage.

Elysia smiled at her reflection, smoothing a wayward lock of hair. Ena was the true master of hair design, but Elysia felt good about her efforts. She had chosen well to arrange it high and off her face. The updo complemented the off-shoulder style of her dress perfectly.

Just then, Kai gave a rapid tap on their adjoining door, and before Elysia could respond, he stepped through. She raised her brows, then frowned at him.

"Kai! You can't just burst through the door before I've said, 'Come in'! You could've caught me undressed!" She crossed her arms, huffing as she rolled her eyes.

"I guess it wouldn't be the first time, right?" she muttered flatly.

Kai didn't say anything, and she flicked her eyes back to him. He was standing completely still. And he was staring. Elysia blinked up at him, shifting slightly under his gaze. Her chest burned, as silently, he wove his eyes from her feet to her bare shoulder. For a moment, he lingered there. Then he moved his eyes to meet her gaze. He opened his mouth, then closed it again, swallowing.

"You look, ah…you look lovely, Lady Elysia," he said quietly.

Elysia stood frozen. His evaluation had unnerved her, and, for a moment, she wordlessly held his gaze. His long, silver hair was smoothed behind his shoulders, and the shade of stubble on his square jaw had been closely shaven. She dropped her eyes, flicking them rapidly over his dark suit. A wide, silver sash crossed over his shoulder, a nod to his position as heir to the merrow throne. She returned to his face, smiling softly. "You look well, yourself, *Lord Kai*," she said teasingly.

Kai rolled his eyes. He held up his palm. "Please. Just Kai, okay?" Elysia giggled.

"Okay," she agreed. "Then, just Elysia, too."

He flicked his eyes to her shoulder, again, then returned them to her face. "Okay," he said quietly. He smiled a small smile, extending his arm. "Are you ready?" Elysia nodded. Then she took his arm, and they moved together into the corridor.

In a few moments, they scaled past the waterfall and arrived at Ena's rooms. Several sentries were posted outside her door, just as Lady Sirena had said, but there was no sign of Seamus. Kai nodded once to the sentry on the right, and the tall merrow pulled the door open.

Elysia's eyes landed on the large bed as she rounded the room's corner. Ena small body sat propped with pillows in the middle of it. Seamus sat just to her left on a low stool. He was gesturing animatedly, and Ena was giggling weakly at his antics.

Elysia cleared her throat, and Seamus dropped his arms as Ena turned towards her, eyes sparkling "Hi," Ena said, grinning. Her face was wan, and Elysia smiled softly as she moved to climb up onto the mattress. She snuggled against Ena's right side and took her hand. Her skin was damp and cool, and Elysia hugged her small fingers tightly inside her own. "Hi," she whispered.

For a moment, Elysia said no more. She stared hard at Ena's lavender coverlet, and tears sprang into her eyes as the events of the day played again in her mind. Her throat tightened, and she swallowed against it, gripping tighter to Ena's hand. "I'm so sorry, Ena," she whispered. "I..." She took a breath. "It was my fault, what happened." Ena studied Elysia's profile with her large blue eyes. Then she turned her small body towards her, wincing. She unwound her hand and tipped Elysia's chin towards her face, smiling softly as Elysia blinked through her tears. Ena's skin was tinged pale yellow, and greyish shadows hung low beneath her eyes. "It's not your fault, Elysia," she said hoarsely. She furrowed her delicate brow. "How could you even think that? You can't control what other people do."

Elysia nodded mutely. She was on the verge of sobbing. "I'm just... I'm just so sorry you're hurt," she choked, her voice breaking. She swallowed, swiping a tear as it trickled down her cheek. "I heard you scream. I wanted to come to you, but Kai said it was too dangerous. He said Seamus would protect you, so I..." The tears started again, and she pressed her lips together, sniffing.

Ena nodded. She grinned at Seamus. "He did," she said, holding his eyes. She turned back to Elysia, her blue eyes wide *o's*. "One of the rioters stabbed me with his blade."

She pulled down the coverlet, showing large strips of bandage wrapped tightly around her middle. A dark patch of blood stained a thick swath of the material on the right.

Elysia pursed her lips. "Do you mind if I see?"

Ena blinked in surprise, then shrugged. "Sure." She reached a hand to Seamus, grimacing as he helped her sit upright. Then, carefully, Elysia unwound the tight strips of linen. When she was done, Seamus eased Ena to her back, a little groan escaping her lips as she settled onto the soft bed. She was paler than she had been a moment ago, and a sheen of sweat had broken out on her forehead with the effort. Seamus dabbed it with a clean cloth, as Elysia peeled the last bandage away.

Elysia stared hard at the open wound, fighting the urge to gasp. Dark blood oozed from the corner. It trickled down Ena's side, and Elysia pressed the bandage to the spot, causing Ena to groan.

The wound was deep and jagged, and a harsh, acrid scent wafted from the opening. An edge of dark, ominous, purple tissue crept out from the center, trailing up towards Ena's chest.

Elysia flicked her eyes to Seamus. His orange brow was furrowed, and he dabbed Ena's brow with a cool, damp cloth. "Is it poison?" Elysia asked him. He nodded. "Yes. The attacker used a ray's barb. The stab is very painful, in any case, but it can be quite toxic. Especially to land dwellers."

Elysia peered worriedly into Ena's pained face. "What else is being done for her?"

Seamus pointed to the small night table. Various tinctures, teas, and bandages were clustered on top of it. "We're doing all we can," he said quietly.

"And it needs to stay open?" Elysia asked him. Seamus nodded. "It's best to keep the wound open, for an injury like this one," he said. "Otherwise, the poison spreads faster. The hope is that the fresh air exchange from the dome will cleanse the wound and dissipate the offending toxin. Later, it can be sutured shut."

Ena gazed at him sidelong and Elysia raised her eyebrows, grinning. Seamus stared at them blankly, moving his eyes rapidly back and forth from one to the other. "What? Impressed?" he asked, grinning. He flicked his eyes to Kai. "I paid attention in my training, unlike *some* people we know." Kai rolled his eyes and Seamus sniffed, crossing his arms. "Told you there was more to me than my good looks."

Elysia giggled and Ena laughed outright, causing a trickle of blood to flow from the wound's edge. Elysia pressed it, and Ena inhaled sharply. "Ouch," she hissed.

Seamus lifted Ena's back gently from the bed as Elysia quickly rebound her bandages, then he settled her carefully back onto her pillows. Elysia tucked the coverlet under her chin and gave Ena a spoonful of tea from the mug Seamus handed to her. Ena sipped a small drink, then she closed her eyes, exhausted by her efforts.

Elysia brushed a damp lock of hair from Ena's forehead. "I'll be back to check on you, soon," she whispered. Then she moved towards the door. She paused in the doorway to call over her shoulder. "Seamus, why don't you come with us to dinner?" she asked. Seamus was busy dabbing Ena's forehead. He glanced quickly up at her, then returned his gaze. "I think I'll stay right here," he said quietly. "I'm not hungry, anyway."

Elysia nodded. She understood his feelings. After seeing Ena in such an awful state, she had somewhat lost her appetite, too.

Her mind raced as she and Kai moved through the corridor. Her friend was in terrible shape. Hopefully, the tinctures and teas on the night table and the fresh air from the dome would prove effective, and Ena would soon be right again.

But what if she wasn't? Elysia frowned as the niggle of doubt forced its way into her mind. What if Ena grew worse, or, the Source forbid, what if she died? Elysia shuddered, stuffing her fears down. Ena would be alright. She *had* to be. And if she wasn't, well, Elysia wasn't sure she could bear it.

CHAPTER 15

The circular dining hall was nestled past the throne room, at the end of a long, curving corridor. Its walls were opaque blue, and its glittering domed ceiling was made of a single piece of clear glass. Thick, green vines climbed over it, hanging heavy with trumpet-shaped moonflowers. Their sparkling white blooms were open wide, draping the dining hall in a fresh, floral scent.

Countless Evening Stars lined the rooms edge, their bell-shaped blooms intensifying the bluish hue of the walls. Elysia smiled as she touched the high stalk of the nearest one. She was sure Lady Sirena had had them imported from the Selkie Isles to make her feel more at home.

A long table with a thick, white cloth sat in the room's center, surrounded by upholstered silver chairs. White roses and silver water thistles floated in a large crystal bowl at its center.

It was an intimate gathering. Only Lady Sirena, Kai, Elysia, and the members of the council were in attendance. Elysia sat to Lady Sirena's right, while Kai sat in the seat next to her. She sighed as she sipped from her glass stemware, staring forlornly across the table at Seamus' and Ena's empty seats.

Lady Sirena placed a hand over her arm. "How is she?" she asked. "She's not well," Elysia answered softly. She sat her glass back onto the table, biting the inside of her cheek. "I'm really worried about her."

Lady Sirena and squeezed her arm. "Ena will be alright." She eyed Elysia's thin arm. "Now, you must eat. We can't allow you to become drawn during your visit. Lady Malca would have my tail." She lowered her voice. "Then we will never get the treaty amended."

She chuckled lightly and Elysia grinned.

Large silver platters heaped with warm bread, colorful fruit, fresh fish, and creamed greens sat before them on the table. Elysia eyed them greedily, then she reached for a piece of bread. Despite her earlier lack of appetite, she felt hungry, and it occurred to her that she hadn't had a proper meal since before the Midsummer Ball.

Kai's plate was already heaping. He needed no instructions, and by the time Elysia had taken her first bite, he had nearly cleaned his plate. She chewed her mouthful of bread and grinned sidelong at his profile, raising her brows.

He scooped the last of his greens onto his fork, then paused with the bite in midair, staring at the air in front of her. "What?" he said around a mouth full.

Elysia giggled. There was greenery stuck between his front teeth. "Nothing," she teased.

She lifted her fork, savoring the flavors that exploded on her tongue, and before she knew it, she had cleaned her plate, too. She could feel Kai's eyes on her plate, and she stopped mid-chew to stare at him. Her voice was muffled as she covered her full mouth. "What?"

Kai shook his head, grinning. He shrugged. "Nothing," he teased. Elysia rolled her eyes as he grabbed another roll and stuffed half of it into his mouth. She giggled, watching as he gave an exaggerated sigh of contentment around the full bite.

Lady Sirena flicked her eyes from one to the other and folded her hands beneath her chin, smiling.

"I'm glad to see you two are getting on so well together," she said happily.

Elysia gave a knowing glance to the side of Kai's head, and he stiffened. Lady Sirena continued. "I confess I was somewhat worried, on the beginning."

Elysia stared at her mutely, and Kai stuffed the rest of his bread into his mouth. He barely chewed it before he swallowed.

"Worried?" he asked innocently. Lady Sirena nodded. "Yes. You two are so similar. It seemed a recipe for either extreme compatibility or extreme distaste. I'm glad to see it's the former."

Elysia nearly choked on her last bite of fish. Lady Sirena thought them compatible? *Surely not.* She felt Kai shift in his seat. He cleared his throat. "Erm, ah, yes, we are getting along just fine," he stuttered. "No issues." He picked up his glass, gulping a drink as Lady Sirena nodded. "That's wonderful, because I confess I…"

Just then, Seamus burst through the dining hall doors. His fiery hair was sticking up in all directions, and his face was a mask of pale panic. He searched the room frantically, before his eyes landed on the air to Elysia's left. "It's Ena," he said rapidly. "She won't wake."

Elysia's fork tumbled from her hand as she scrambled from her seat. Her worst fear was coming true. Her best friend, her sweet Ena…She rushed out of the dining hall with Kai close on her heels.

Seamus threw the door to Ena's rooms wide and stood aside as Elysia ran towards the bed. Ena's red hair clung to the pillow in limp strands, and her small body was as still as a stone. Elysia put a hand to her pale cheek. It was damp and sickly hot. Elysia brushed a strand of hair from Ena's eyes.

"Ena?" she said softly. "Ena, it's me, Elysia. Wake up." Ena didn't move, and Elysia turned back to Seamus. "She's burning," she said worriedly.

Seamus sank to his knees on the other side of the bed and placed a hand on Ena's forehead. All the color drained from his face, and he flattened his mouth into a grim line. "How long does she have?" Elysia asked him.

Seamus shook his head. "I can't be sure," he said quietly.

"Usually, around two days, once the fever sets in. I've seen someone make it three, but that was a strong Merrow man. He did just fine, after the healer came with the Tamarisk Cakes."

Seamus stared forlornly at Ena's small frame. He brushed a wet lock of hair from her forehead. "Too bad Ita died," he said quietly. "I don't think she has a replacement." He shrugged. "Anyway, if there is a new healer, we couldn't find them on such short notice. Ena needs the healer now, if she has any chance."

Elysia blinked rapidly. She flicked her eyes to Kai, who stood at the end of the bed. He raised his brows in question.

Elysia swallowed, then opened her mouth. The words wouldn't come, and she closed it again. She pressed her lips into a thin line, then took a deep breath, trying again. "I know," she said quietly. Seamus flicked his eyes to her, and Elysia bit her lip. She looked from Kai to Seamus. "I know who Ita's replacement is. It's me. I'm the new healer."

Kai stared hard at the side of Elysia's head. He remembered the first night he had seen her, dancing in the Tamarisk grove. Pink blossoms had hung heavily from the low tree limbs, and he had watched her from the shadows as she swirled. She had held a blossoming Tamarisk frond in each hand.

He thought about how the trees had multiplied across the hillside of the secret island, after they had begun sprouting two cycles ago. He had never considered it before, because he had been so engrossed in spending time with Maura. But now that he thought about it, their growth on the island coincided with the death of the realm's former healer, Ita, who had died in an attack by the Court of Orm in the stables of the Timekeeper's Court.

According to the Histories, the new healer would be known by the growth of a new Tamarisk grove. Once the Source had chosen a healer's replacement, new trees would blossom in the place the new healer held most dear. It made sense to Kai that the Source had placed the trees on the secret island. Obviously, it was a special place for Elysia. After watching her that night, he could see that. Much like himself and Maura, the island was Elysia's hideaway and refuge. It was clear to him, now, as clear as the calm evening sea. Elysia was the new healer, and the secret island's Tamarisk grove proved it.

Elysia bent to kiss Ena's damp forehead, then stood and faced Kai. "We have to leave for the island," she said evenly. "Tonight." She turned back to Seamus, speaking to him over Ena's still frame.

"Take care of her," she whispered.

Seamus nodded then bent back to Ena. He dabbed her forehead with a cool cloth. "I won't leave her side," he said solemnly.

Kai had moved outside the door and was speaking to a sentry in low tones. The tall Merrow nodded once, then he moved swiftly down the corridor. Elysia met Kai at the door, and together, they ran, emerging moments later from beneath the waterfall.

"I've told the Forces that we're making an emergency trip back to the Selkie Court," he said quietly. "They'll send word to

Lady Sirena." Elysia nodded. They moved into the garden, and Kai turned to face her. He inhaled expectantly.

"I know I've not given you much reason to trust me, so far," he said slowly. "But I need you to trust me, now. Things are dangerous for you here. There are radicals hiding on every corner. They want nothing more than to see you dead." He gripped her palm. "Please, Elysia, for your own safety and for the sake of the courts, stay with me and do just as I say. Alright?"

Elysia nodded. The memory of her attacker's crude blade against her throat was still fresh in her mind. She didn't want to repeat it. "I understand," she said quietly.

Kai squeezed her palm, then let his hand drop. "Good," he whispered. "Let's go. Stay to my left at all times."

Elysia hugged Kai's side like a shadow as he moved silently past the garden wall. He slipped beneath an arched breezeway at the left side of the palace, laying himself flat against the stone as he moved inside. Elysia trailed him closely, her shoulder brushing his upper arm as he paused at its end to peer into the streets. They were empty, and he slipped his arm around Elysia's back before they scaled down the palace steps in the waning light.

Kai kept to the side lanes, his sharp eyes on high alert. Up ahead, the merry lights of a small tavern spilled into the street. Jaunty music wafted from the doorframe, and a cluster of broad Merrow men stood just outside the door, laughing loudly. Kai brought his lips close to her ear.

"Do just as I say," he murmured.

The men fell silent as Kai and Elysia approached, and Elysia's heart skipped as the men turned. Four pairs of glimmering merrow eyes were suddenly fixed on her. The man closest to her grinned, and Kai tucked her slightly behind him as the man reached into his vest, producing a jagged blade.

Kai snarled as the man lunged, baring his teeth. He met the man's blade with his spear as the three others circled, blocking their path. Kai slammed the man's back with the flat of his blade, then he made a broad sweep with his spear, clearing the center of the lane. He thrust Elysia forward as he spun back to face the men, flaunting his spear. "Make for the tunnel!" he shouted. "Run!"

Elysia fled as fast as her feet would carry her. Behind, she could hear Kai's shouts and his spear clanking against crude metal. The grove of river birch was just ahead. The trees were thick, and if she could just make it past the edge, she would be hidden from sight. Her heart thumped in her ears as she pumped her legs towards it, not slowing to see if anyone had followed.

She was going too fast. All at once, her feet tangled beneath her. The left one caught on the edge of a cobblestone, and suddenly, she pitched forward. She shrieked as her feet flew up behind her, and she tumbled headlong onto the cobblestone path, her shoulder smacking hard against the stones. It throbbed as she rolled onto her back, and she squeezed her eyes closed, shutting out the pain. Then, suddenly, she froze.

Something cold was pressed against the center of her throat. Elysia blinked up in the dim evening light. One of the tavern men grinned above her, holding her to the ground with the tip of his jagged blade. She grimaced against the cold metal, and the merrow chuckled mirthlessly, pressing his blade tighter against her skin.

She whimpered as the crude tip bit into her skin, and a thin line of warm blood trickled from beneath it. The merrow grinned down at the blood, then fixed her with his glittering green eyes.

"What's a *selkie* like you doing on merrow lands?" he hissed. Elysia squirmed, and he pressed his boot hard into the front of her thigh, causing tears to spring into her eyes.

"It's a violation of the treaty, 'init? On pain of death, don't it say?" He flicked the end of the blade, making the shallow cut slightly wider. Elysia winced and he grinned. "Might just take it upon myself to uphold the law." He twisted his boot against her thigh, and she howled.

"And when you're dead, I'll send your rotten flesh to pollute the sea *outside* my dome."

Elysia squeezed her eyes shut. There was nothing she could do. He was going to kill her. She braced herself, ready to die.

"You'll pollute it yourself, if you don't let the Lady go."

Elysia's eyes popped open. *Kai.* Kai stood close behind the merrow's right shoulder. His blue eyes were as cold as Elysia had ever seen them, and his spear was against the man's throat.

The man flicked his eyes to him. "Or what," he spat. He

looked to Elysia with disgust. "She's naught but a *selkie*. So, what do you care?"

Kai gripped the man's hair, pulling it back as he further exposed his neck to his blade. The man yelped as a trickle of blood ran down from beneath it. "I *said*, LET the Lady go!" he shouted thunderously.

Elysia's heart leapt into her throat. She had never seen Kai so angry. He was every bit the fearful member of the Merrow Forces. It was terrifying.

The man swallowed gingerly against the blade's grip. "Never," he spat. He glared down at Elysia with contempt. "She pollutes this court with her very presence."

Elysia's eyes widened as he lunged towards her. She screamed, bracing for impact, but Kai held him fast. She heard a gurgling sound and then the *shing* of the spear as Kai's blade slit his throat.

Immediately, the man's eyes went flat. His own blade dropped. It clanged against the stone as he fell to the street.

Elysia scrambled backwards, scooting away until her back hit the trunk of a river birch. She pressed at the shallow wound on her neck, watching as Kai stared down at her lifeless attacker. Behind him, the Forces were binding the arms of the remaining three men in front of the tavern.

Curious members of the merrows' court had come into the streets to watch the exchange, and Elysia scanned their faces with wary eyes. Most of them glared at her in disgust. They gestured to Kai in confusion, and more than a few shouted obscenities in their direction.

Kai ignored them. He dipped his blade into the stream, rinsing the blood, then, he moved towards her. He dropped onto his knee, staring into her eyes. Wordlessly, his rough hand lifted to her chin, turning it gently left and right. She winced, her eyes filling with tears as he flicked his eyes to her face. His blue eyes flashed intensely as he studied her expression.

"Are you alright?" he asked gruffly. Elysia pinked under his stare. She moved her eyes past him to the people in the street. "Kai, people are watching," she whispered. "You're looking directly at me."

He never moved his eyes.

"Sink the blasted treaty to the depths," he said evenly. "It's an evil that need be long past us."

Elysia flicked her eyes nervously behind him as Kai stood. He reached out his hand, and she took it as he pulled her to her feet. He turned briefly to the lane, where people still huddled in groups, whispering, then he turned back to her.

"Let's wait deeper in the grove, until everyone clears. Then, we'll head for the tunnel," he said quietly. Elysia nodded, and he put a guiding hand to the small of her back as he ushered her into the cover of the thick grove.

Kai crouched behind a tree, and Elysia sank down beside him. Wordlessly, he reached inside his shirt pocket and pulled out a cream-filled pastry she had been eyeing at the dinner table. Then he tore it in two, giving her a half. She flicked her eyes to him in surprise, then grinned as she took the sweet.

Elysia watched as Kai took a huge bite. He bit his half pastry in two, chewing loudly as he peered into the lane from behind the tree. A bit of cream stained the corner of his mouth.

It could've been her near brush with death, but suddenly, he struck her as hilarious. A giggle formed in her throat, and Elysia clamped a hand over her mouth.

Kai frowned over at her. "What's so funny?" he whispered.

She turned the pastry half over in her hands. "It's just…" She grinned, pointing to the corner of his mouth. Kai swiped the cream, and she giggled. "Very funny," he whispered.

Elysia continued to watch him as he eyed the lane. She smiled.

"You're a pretty good spy, you know," she said quietly. Kai looked at her blankly, and she giggled again. "I mean, watching people from the cover of trees is one of your specialties, right?"

Kai rolled his eyes. "Full of jokes tonight, aren't we?" he whispered. Elysia giggled again before she took a bite of her pastry. Its sweetness practically melted on her tongue, and she sighed, laying her head back against the tree trunk. She swallowed, then shrugged, grinning to herself. "Just lightening the mood," she said lightly.

They sat eating their pastry halves in silence for a few more moments, while Kai continued to peer through the branches. Finally, the lane was still and silent, and he stood quietly, dusting his hands.

He held one down, and Elysia took it wordlessly, but this time, he didn't let go. He gripped tightly to her palm as he wove through the trees, guiding her through the dark grove towards the hidden tunnel.

Elysia pursed her lips as she stared down at their joined hands. No one had ever held her hand before. At least, not off the dance floor. And, certainly, no one had ever held her hand while they were alone.

Kai's palm was large and rough, and it dwarfed her slender one in size. For a moment, she felt somewhat like a small child being pulled along, and she considered pulling her hand away. But the close trees were disorienting, and she was afraid she would lose Kai's path and end up back in the lane by accident. Besides, his hand felt sort of nice. She relaxed a little, allowing herself to enjoy it.

Kai glanced back at her, and she bit the inside of her lip. He smiled, and she flushed, flashing him a tight grin. She hoped he couldn't read what she had been thinking.

Soon, they slipped into the hidden tunnel, and Kai dropped her hand. Elysia felt somewhat bereft as he moved to sit on a large, flat rock near the waterfall. He pulled off his dark boots before tossing his jacket, then he stood and began unbuttoning his shirt.

Elysia tucked her arms over her chest, reddening. Was Kai expecting her to change, right out in the open? She flicked her eyes to him as he peeled off his shirt, then he stood facing her with his hands on his hips.

His mouth twitched as she blinked at his chest, then his lips slowly broke into a grin. Elysia's face burned, and quickly, she dropped her eyes as she crouched to untie her sandal strap. Her hands shook, and she fumbled with the ties, but she refused to look up again.

Kai chuckled under his breath, further increasing her blush. But she ignored him, and at last, she heard him splash into the river. She let out her breath, then stood, kicking off her sandals. From the corner of her gaze, she could see Kai's flashing blue tail, and she watched as his head broke the surface near her side of the riverbank.

She hugged her arms across her chest, and when he didn't break his gaze, she huffed, frowning at him as she stuck out her foot. "Really, Kai?" she grumbled. "Could I ask for a moment of privacy, please?" She glared hard at his stare, then spun away from him, fuming.

Kai chuckled. "Alright, alright."

Elysia heard him turn, but she peeked over her shoulder, just to check. He had turned away and was bracing his arms on the opposite riverbank.

Quietly, she lowered her gown's straps from her upper arms, then flicking her eyes to the back of Kai's head before stepping out of the dress. She laid it neatly on a nearby stone, peeking back at him. He hadn't moved, and she shimmied out of her underthings, then hid them beneath her dress on the rock.

Covering herself with her arms, she tiptoed to the riverbank, then slipped over the side. She splashed into the water, then she counted to three, allowing the silver flesh to form up her frame, before she broke the surface.

Golden sprays of light broke the river as Elysia flicked her tail, and Kai half turned as she stared at him across the water. He held her gaze, the glow bouncing off his silver hair before he sank beneath the water.

He emerged right in front of her. The end of his tail grazed her own, and she stiffened, watching nervously as he braced his arm on the riverbank. Her heart hammered in her ears at his nearness, and the air was heavy with some deep connection Elysia couldn't name. He studied her expression, and the muscle in his jaw feathered as he glanced down at her tail. She flushed as he watched it swish softly in the water. Then he wove his eyes slowly up to her face.

"I wanted to tell you…I, ah…" He cleared his throat, then shook his head, starting again. "I wanted to tell you that I didn't see anything that night." He slicked his hair and wet his lips. "I mean, I *did* see you swim…" He gestured to her tail. "In your sea form. But I, ah…" He stuttered. "I, I didn't see anything else."

He met Elysia's gaze, and she grinned up at him, then moved her eyes away. She studied the surface of the water, gliding her fingers along its golden current. She could feel Kai's eyes moving over her again, and she didn't stop him. She smiled.

"You know, in the Selkie Isles, it's considered more…intimate to see a woman in her sea form than it is to see her…the other way. That's one of the reasons we don't swim." She submerged her lips, then resurfaced, watching quietly as the emotions played across his face. She smiled softly, shrugging. "It's my own fault, really, that you saw me. I mean, I didn't know anyone else was there, but still. I knew better than to swim. Anyway, we would both be in trouble if anyone knew." She widened her eyes. "Might even start a war."

She stared down silently, and Kai cleared his throat. He held out his hand.

"Agree to keep each other's secret? For our own good and the good of our courts?" He gazed down at her regally, and she laughed at his formal expression. "It's agreed," she said. She shook his hand, then held up one finger.

"On one condition."

Kai grinned. "What condition is that?"

"You tell me what you were doing on the secret island."

Kai's grin faded as he studied her face. He lowered his eyes. "I, uh…" He swallowed, shaking his head. "It's a long story, and anyway, it's probably best we get moving. Ena needs us to get to the island and back as quickly as possible." He flicked his eyes to her solemnly. "I promise I'll tell you. Just…let's get to the island, first, okay?" Elysia nodded. "Okay."

She studied his face. His expression was shrouded. She couldn't read it.

He twitched his lips. "One more thing, and you're not gonna like it." Elysia frowned up at him. "What?"

Kai stared at her flatly. "I'm going to carry you the whole way."

Elysia rolled her eyes. "Is that *really* necessary, Kai? I mean, I *can* swim." She smirked. "You've watched me, remember?"

Kai ignored her jab as he scooped her into his arms. She wriggled in his grip as he stared down at her decisively. "Yes, Elysia, it's really necessary. You've been land locked all your life, and your sea lungs are weak. We want to get through this tunnel and to the island as fast as possible, right?" She sighed, nodded mutely. He was holding her too tight, and she wiggled slightly, trying to find a comfortable position.

"Right," he said decisively. "I'm right, and I'm faster, so stop wriggling."

He grinned smugly as he dove under, while Elysia glared at his chin. He was so infuriating. If she hadn't been afraid of another diving spider experience, she would have shown him who was faster, weak sea lungs, or no.

She held herself stiffly away from him, fuming. But as he sped through tunnel, she soon relaxed in his arms. As much as she hated to admit it, he *was* faster. And besides, this was for Ena.

Her eyes drifted to his neck, where a thin chain floated in the current. It carried a thin golden ring. Elysia studied it quietly as it hovered against his chest. It was small, a woman's size. She moved her eyes to the square of his jaw, thinking. She wondered whose it was.

Elysia flicked her eyes back to the golden circle. Maybe Kai was seeing someone. Maybe the ring was hers. She wondered what the woman looked like. She wondered if Kai loved her.

Elysia tried to imagine his mate as she moved her eyes over his features. Kai's perfect, chiseled face stared straight ahead, and she smirked. With a face like his, she was probably quite lovely. Probably, she looked like Delia.

Images of Delia's quiet face and long, silky hair flashed in her mind, and she frowned.

She thought about how she had appeared in the garden behind Connor at the Midsummer ball, how he had straightened his jacket, how his hair had been mussed. Elysia sighed as embarrassment bubbled up in her throat at the memory. It didn't matter that the ball had been the night of her and Connor's betrothal. That hadn't stopped him from doing the Source knew what in some dark garden corner with Delia.

She pressed her lips together. Maybe Connor wore a ring around his neck, too. Maybe it was meant for Delia. Maybe he loved her. Her stomach churned, and she wrapped her arm across it, earning a quick glance from Kai.

She frowned as he looked away. And why should she care? It didn't matter if Connor loved Delia or not. She was his betrothed. She would marry him for the good of the Selkie Court, and his father would provide all the support the court needed by way of his mines. And Connor would…well, she didn't much care what

Connor would do. Anyway, it wasn't like she could stop him.

Elysia ground her teeth, focusing on the path ahead. She couldn't think about that right now. Ena needed her. Her friend would die, maybe in as soon as two days, if she didn't make it back with the Tamarisk.

She flicked her eyes to Kai's chin. He was already swimming through the tunnel at a breakneck speed, but a niggle in the back of Elysia's mind urged him to go faster. They had already been delayed by the Merrow men at the tavern. If anything else were to happen, they might get back too late. Elysia's stomach sank at the thought. If Ena died, she would never forgive herself.

Mentally, she urged Kai on, wishing she had done things differently. If she had only heeded her grandmother's words, if she had been quicker to embrace her role as the new healer, she might have had the Tamarisk on hand after Ena's attack. By now, her friend might have even been well. She closed her eyes, wishing she had done just that.

But she hadn't. And that couldn't be helped, now. She couldn't focus on what might have been. Silently, she breathed a prayer to the Source. She asked that Ena be spared. Then, she gave thanks for her gift. She only hoped she hadn't accepted it too late.

Chapter 16

Inside the kelp grove, Elysia peered up at the moons through the towering plants. Their light glittered softly between the slick fronds, streaming strips of silver ribbons onto her skin. It was just after midnight. Kai tucked her to his chest as he wove in and out of them. "Almost there," he murmured softly.

He sped on through the open water, and soon, he surfaced, releasing her in the shallows near the secret island. Elysia peered fondly at the familiar landscape, as Kai began lifting himself out of the water. The island was much the same as it has always been, but like all familiar things seem after a long journey, tonight it looked different.

Blue Evening Stars dotted the hillside under the moons' bright glow, and dusty pink Tamarisk blossoms waved from their circular perch on the hilltop like a sparkling crown. Elysia remembered sitting beneath their fronds. She had wistfully gazed out over the sea, wishing she could swim away for a distant adventure.

She lifted herself to stand, thinking over all that had occurred. She had nearly had enough adventure. Now that she had returned, she couldn't wait for her feet to touch the dry earth.

Suddenly, she had a horrifying thought. Her clothes. She had left them on the rock in the tunnel. Quickly, she splashed onto her belly, flicking her eyes to Kai nervously.

He was facing away from her, already on the shore. The gauzy blue fabric of his clothing shimmered slightly in the moons' silver light. Slowly, he turned, searched the shallow surf until he landed on her bobbing head. He put a hand on his hip and grinned.

"Something wrong?" he teased. Elysia burned under his gaze. She huffed. "Obviously." He chuckled low, and she rolled her eyes, turning to the side to relieve herself of his smug grin.

"Want me to show you a trick?" he asked lightly. She didn't answer, and he shrugged. "It's fine, if you don't. We all know you don't need my help." He leaned casually against a large rock, crossing one foot over his ankle. "If you change your mind, all you need to do is ask."

He stared off in the distance, humming softly to himself, and Elysia waited, grinding her teeth. She wet her lips, thinking. She really had no choice. If she wanted to get out of the water, she would have to let him help her.

"Alright," she said softly. Kai put his hand to his ear. "Ah, I couldn't hear you. Did you want to ask me something?" he asked, too cheerfully. Elysia huffed, pursing her lips. "I *said, alright.* I want your help," she ground out.

Kai grinned, holding up his arms in mock offense. "Okay, no need to get huffy. I'll help you." Elysia shook her head and rolled her eyes. He was impossible.

"Okay. Every young Merrow learns this skill, so it shouldn't be too tough. It's a simple maneuver we learn as a safety, for just this sort of scenario." He grinned broadly, settling back against the stone as he crossed his arms. "On second thought, maybe I shouldn't teach it to you," he said teasingly.

Elysia gaped at him in shock, and Kai laughed out loud. He stood straight.

"*Relax*, Elysia. I'm only joking." He turned away from her. "Okay, go ahead and stand up." Elysia frowned, watching his eyes warily as she stood slowly up out of the water. She covered herself as best she could, and she watched as his cheek lifted with his grin. She rolled her eyes. "Just, get on with it, Kai," she spat. He chuckled. "Alright, alright. Let me explain.

First, you hold out your hand, palm up, like this." He cupped his hand and held it out in front of his chest. Elysia mimicked him, holding out her own palm. "Okay, got it," she said flatly.

"Good," he said, nodding.

He closed his eyes and took a deep breath. "Now, the air holds water just like the sea does. I want you to envision all the water in the air around you gathering into your palm."

Elysia did, imagining tiny, invisible water droplets collecting into her hand. She opened her eyes and frowned. Her palm was empty.

"Don't be surprised if it takes a few tries," Kai called. Elysia sighed. She closed her eyes, concentrating.

In a moment, a tiny, almost imperceptible *woosh*, disturbed the air around her, and when she opened her eyes, a large bubble of water droplets hovered just above her cupped hand.

"I got it!" she called excitedly. "Good! Now, the next part is tricky. Take the water that you've gathered in your hand and line it into long strands. Once you've done that, weave the strands into a covering of your choice. Pass your hand in front of your body, and the water will collect itself into the pattern you envision."

Elysia frowned hard at her hand. She willed the water to move into a long strand, then she passed her palm over the front of her body. Instead of collecting itself, the strand fell flat, and the water droplets splashed back into the surf. She huffed. "Kai, this is taking too long," she complained. "Just try once more," he called over his shoulder.

Elysia straightened, holding out her palm. She closed her eyes. This time, the water gathered easily, and she wove it again into a long strand. Then, she imagined a gauzy top with thin straps and a pair of loose pants. She focused hard on her design as she passed her hand over the front of her body.

To her surprise, she felt the water collecting neatly against her frame. She opened her eyes, smiling down at her glimmering creation. The fabric was opaque blue and light as the air, and she tested its movement as she stepped out of the surf, spinning in a circle.

Kai heard her moving on the rocks, and he spun towards her, smiling broadly. He passed his eyes over the shimmering fabric, moving slowly from her feet to her face. Elysia struck a pose. "What do you think?" she asked him, grinning. He lifted his chin, gesturing lightly to her clothing. "Nice," he said gruffly.

Elysia pinked under his stare. She dropped her eyes. "Thanks," she murmured. She could feel his eyes studying her face, and she bit the inside of her lip. For some reason, Kai's stare made her stomach do funny flips. It was a different feeling than the one she got when Connor stared at her. She frowned, then bent to pick up a smooth stone. "So, you said you would tell me what you were doing here, that night," she said lightly, tossing the stone. It made a smooth silver line in the surf as it skipped across the water. Kai broke his stare as he gazed out after it. He nodded.

"I did," he said quietly. He paused for moment, studying the surf. "But it's probably easier if I just show you."

Wordlessly, he gestured for Elysia to follow. He turned, and she trailed him a far distance along the shoreline, before he turned into a narrow pass in the hills at the island's far end. The light from the moons and Evening Stars was muted inside of it, and Elysia held out her hands to steady herself on the uneven ground.

They climbed higher and higher inside the rocky pass, until a sheen of sweat dotted Elysia's forehead, and her breath came in short bursts. She peered up at Kai's back. She was certain he had forgotten the way and was leading her towards a dead end. But he moved ahead on sure feet, so she continued to follow him.

Soon, the pass opened onto the banks of a narrow stream. The stream grew into a rushing river, and Elysia followed Kai to its edge, where it spilled over a shallow fall into a still, quiet pool.

A set of natural, narrow stone steps led down to the pool's edge. Kai stepped to the first one. He extended his hand, and Elysia grasped his rough palm, turning her feet sideways to scale down after him. She stopped at the edge of the water, gazing in wonder. As long as she had come to the secret island, she had never known this place existed. It was an idyllic hideaway, to be sure, and she imagined Kai's little corner of the island was even lovelier, in the daylight.

The high hills circled the sparkling pool like a crescent moon, and a thick grove of Cypress trees shielded the ground beyond it. Kai moved silently towards them, while Elysia followed. She studied his back, wondering what he was thinking. He hadn't said a word, since they had left the shoreline.

He stopped at the edge of the grove, where a treehouse perched among the low branches. Its foundation rested on three large Cypress trunks, and a set of roughhewn wooden steps extended from the ground to the open doorframe. Elysia peered up at it.

Two silent windows flanked the opening. They stared back at her, like two hollow eyes peering out of the darkness.

Kai stood mutely at the base of the steps. He clenched his fist, staring up at the door. Elysia watched as a wash of emotion traveled rapidly across his exquisite face. She tried to read it, but the feelings passed too quickly, and then they were lost in the darkness.

Kai sighed as he dropped his eyes. He sat heavily on the second step.

"This was our place," he said quietly. "Mine and Maura's."

Elysia stared at him mutely, and he paused, brushing a hand through his damp hair.

"Maura was my…everything." He lifted his eyes to peer up at the low hanging branches.

"We found this place on one of our adventures." He half grinned, then his face dropped. "Maura loved adventures."

Elysia peered hard at his face. "What happened to her?" she asked softly. Kai's mouth twitched, then he set his jaw, flattening his lips into a thin line. He cleared his throat.

"She…" He inhaled, meeting Elysia's eyes. "She died." He swallowed convulsively.

"It was the Sea Lilies," he said gruffly. "She swam too low. Got caught in the fronds. She was gone in a matter of days."

Elysia sank to her knees as he hung his head. She reached a slim hand out to cover his forearm. "Kai, I'm so sorry," she breathed. "I didn't know." Kai smiled a flat smile. He moved a shaking hand to the stairs, picking at a narrow slat in the wood. "I built this treehouse for her, just before I asked her to marry me," he murmured. He gazed up at the open door.

"Now, I come here to…to be with her."

Elysia nodded. So, Kai had been seeing someone. Only, that someone was gone, now.

The ring had been Maura's, and now that she had died, he wanted to keep it close. That's the reason he kept it around his neck. "I see," she said softly.

Kai frowned. Elysia thought she understood, but she really didn't. She thought he had been coming here to visit Maura's memory. That had been true, before. But the last time he had come? The last time, he had visited her for real. She had been here, in the treehouse with him. The thought still amazed him, and he hoped he would be able to meet with her again, before he and Elysia went back home.

He opened his mouth to explain, then closed it again. Elysia wouldn't understand, and he wasn't quite ready to share that much of it, yet. Anyway, she would probably think he was crazy, if he told her the whole truth. He studied her hand on his forearm. Maybe when she went to collect the Tamarisk, he would collect some, too. Then he could come back and see Maura.

Elysia frowned. Kai's jaw was clenched, and he was staring hard at her hand on his arm. "Is there something else?" she asked him.

He flicked his eyes to her, then looked away, sliding his arm from beneath her grasp.

"It's nothing," he said quickly. He stood abruptly, half-turning from her view. "Ready to go get the Tamarisk?"

Elysia frowned up at his back. He had already started walking back the way they had come. She narrowed her eyes. It was obviously something. He just didn't want to tell her.

She stood, starting after him. "If you don't mind, I might come back here while you're collecting the Tamarisk," he called to the air in front of him. "I'll collect a bit myself and bring it back to lay on the steps. It was Maura's favorite."

Elysia moved behind him to climb the narrow stone steps. "Of course," she said to his back, watching him scale above her. "I'll cut it for you myself."

Kai rested his shoulder against a low tree trunk, as Elysia moved quietly through the Tamarisk grove. She lifted her fingers to the feathery fronds, running them gently over the tiny, pink blossoms. In the silence, a quiet melody stirred in her chest, and she hummed the tune absently as she moved through the low branches.

Softly, a sea breeze began to wind its way through the grove. Elysia paused, and Kai watched as the breeze swirled through her damp hair. The strands curled about her face, partially blocking it from his view. She closed her eyes and lifted her hands, and his heart squeezed at the sight.

For a moment, she was Maura, but then he blinked, and the breeze changed course. The hair blew from her face, and she was Elysia, once more. Softly, she hummed her gentle tune, weaving in and out of its quiet melody until words began to start.

The words stirred in Kai's chest, and just like before, a burn began to the left of his heart. He pressed his hand to the spot, expecting the pain to grow. But the burn was different from the first time. It was painful, yes, but it was a somewhat welcome feeling. The sorrow that had tinged Elysia's words at their first meeting was softer, this time, and strangely, as he listened, Kai found his own sorrow was easier to bear.

He watched her sway from beneath the low hanging limbs, and lifted his palm, allowing the gentle burn of his Amloga to spread outward.

My love, she comes,
To meet with me,
Beneath the quiet
Cypress trees.
Though long, she's gone,
She'll ever be,
Beneath the quiet
Cypress Trees.

The words faded out as Elysia resumed her gentle hum, and Kai moved out into silver streams of moonlight. He met her in the center of the grove, and she peered quietly up at his face. His voice caught in his throat, and he choked his question through its restriction. "The words, where did they come from?" he asked her gruffly.

Elysia furrowed her brow. She hadn't thought about it. The words had just formed on her tongue. It was as if they were always a part of her and had found the right moment to come out. She shrugged.

"They just…are," she said softly. He stared down at her blankly, and she bit her lip, thinking.

"It's like…the words were always a part of me." She placed a hand to his chest, just to the left of his heart, where the flame of his Amloga rested. "Here. It's as if the words live here, inside my chest. They're like little flames of silver fire. Those little fires have minds of their own. They burn inside of me, longing to escape, until finally, I can't contain them. You see?"

Kai frowned, and she dropped her palm, searching about her. She knew what she meant, but she didn't quite know how to explain.

At once, something her grandmother had told her sprang into her mind, and she smiled softly. "My grandmother calls it the Selkie's Song," she said quietly.

Kai narrowed his eyes. "The Selkie's Song?"

Elysia nodded. "It's like…a whisper, a stirring inside of you that you can't contain. Each word is a little flame that longs to be set free. My grandmother says it's a gift. Most Selkie women have it, though it's long fallen out of use. She says the little fires are the words of the Source. She calls the words the Voice. The words name things unknown—secrets, desires of those listening, desires of the Source."

Kai blinked hard, thinking. He had heard rumors of what Elysia called the Selkie's Song, but he had thought that they used it for a more sinister reason, like trapping a merrow man as Seamus had explained.

Elysia shook her head. "There are lots of myths about the Selkie Song, but most of them aren't true." She shrugged. "I don't really understand it all, but my grandmother is usually right about these things." She picked some pink petals from a Tamarisk frond and watched them blow away in the breeze.

Kai rubbed the spot to the left of his heart. The burning there had almost subsided. He thought about the words to Elysia's song, both moments ago and the first night he'd seen her. She was right about the Voice. It was as if it had known his pain. By some miracle, the words she had sung had both acknowledged his suffering and allowed it a release. He raised his brows. Seamus had been wrong about the Selkie's Song, but what Elysia's grandmother had said was the truth.

A sudden rustling to their left shocked Kai from his reverie, and, at once, three Selkie Guards burst into the Tamarisk grove. One pushed Elysia behind him, while the others fixed their spears on Kai's throat. He raised his arms in surrender as Elysia glared at up at them.

"What is the meaning of this?!" she bellowed. "I am the daughter of Lady Malca, and *this* is Kai Bennet, the heir to the merrow throne. Unhand him, at once!"

The Guard to Kai's right spoke. "I'm sorry, my Lady, but we have orders from your betrothed to kill trespassing Merrow men on sight. Your mother has received word of the attacks in the Court of Merrows, and she is concerned that the unrest there will soon reach our own shores. She's ordered additional patrols. Lord Connor placed himself in charge of them all."

Elysia rolled her eyes. Of course. *Connor*. "Take us to Lady Malca," she said flatly. No one moved, and Elysia glared at the Guards. "Unless you want to slit the merrow heir's throat? I'm certain that was not my mother's intention, as it would undoubtedly start a war." She glared at the Guards with their spears to Kai's throat as they waffled uncertainly. They exchanged a quick glance with one another, then lowered their spears.

Elysia followed as the Guards propelled Kai down the hillside, glaring daggers at their backs. A small boat waited for them there, rocking gently in the shallow waves. Kai stared down at it incredulously. He rolled his eyes, chuckling mirthlessly at the wooden vessel as the Guards pushed him on board.

Elysia pressed her mouth into a thin line and sat down primly beside him on the narrow seat. Kai scoffed, and she glanced sideways at him. "Even your *Guards* avoid getting in the water?" He shook his head as he eyed the stern-faced selkie in front of him. "Ridiculous," he said loudly. The Guard's jaw clenched, and Kai folded his arms. "Your sea lungs are probably weaker than Elysia's," he spat. At that, the Guard behind him jabbed him hard in the back with his knee. Kai winced.

"Hey!" Elysia shouted. She glared up at the Guard in warning, then flicked her eyes back to Kai's profile. She swatted his forearm. "My sea lungs are just fine," she said quietly. Kai scoffed. "Oh *yes*, I'm sure the diving spider would agree," he teased.

Elysia folded her arms. "Well, maybe I could use a few lessons, then, seeing that you're the *expert*, and all." She narrowed her eyes. "We'll see who's fastest, after a little practice."

Kai nodded, smirking at the open air. "I agree. You need lessons…*desperately*. We'll practice on our way back to the Court of Merrows." He glared up at the Guard facing him.

"We could be practicing now, if we hadn't been so rudely interrupted." He jerked his thumb at Elysia. "You do know she was trying to collect Tamarisk to save her *selkie* lady in waiting, right?" The Guard didn't answer, and Kai folded his arms. "I'm sure Lady Malca would *love* to hear how you three held up the new healer in her efforts to save one of your own." He grinned as the Guards flicked their eyes to each other, but they made no reply.

For a few moments, they floated along in silence, then Kai cleared his throat. "Your betrothed?" he asked gruffly.

Elysia bit the inside of her cheek. She dropped her eyes, picking at the wooden seat.

"Yes. His name is Connor."

Kai jerked his chin but didn't answer. For several moments, he stared ahead in silence. "And what's he like? This Connor?" he asked her. Elysia folded her arms across her chest. "He's…rich and handsome, by all accounts," she said flatly.

Kai nodded slowly. "And Lady Malca? What does she think of him?"

Elysia narrowed her eyes. "She…urged me in his direction."

Kai turned his head slightly. He stared at the air just in front of her. "Why?" he asked.

Elysia sighed. "Because, Kai's father Lord Ciar is very wealthy. He owns nearly all the islands' mines. Our court needs his support if we are to sustain ourselves without input from your own."

Kai looked ahead, considering her words.

"And you? What do you think of him?" he said quietly.

Elysia bit her cheek. "He's…fine," she said, shrugging. "My mother always says we do what we must for the good of the court. That's what I'm doing: what I must."

Kai nodded slowly. "And what about what you want?" he murmured.

Elysia turned to look at the side of his face. His square jaw was set in a hard line, and his silver hair glinted softly in the moons' light. She swallowed hard, facing forward. "What I want doesn't matter," she muttered. "I'm to marry Connor. It's been decided."

Her throat constricted as the garden behind her mother's sandstone palace came into view. Before the Summer's Eve ball, she had almost been resigned to her fate as Connor's wife. Now? Now, she knew she would never be able to accept it. After all that had happened, both with Connor and, if she were being honest, with Kai, it just wasn't possible. She swallowed against her aching throat as she studied Kai's profile, lowering her voice to a whisper.

"What I want isn't even possible."

CHAPTER 17

Kai struggled against the Guards' hands as they pushed him roughly through the throne room doors. Lady Malca was waiting for them at the room's end, standing quietly before her gilded throne. It was obvious she had been summoned from bed. Her eyes were puffy from little sleep, and her auburn, grey-streaked hair tumbled loose down the shoulders of her dark purple dressing gown.

The Guards thrust Kai to the foot of the dais, where he knelt to one knee. Lady Malca stared down at him with a flat expression, then she flicked her eyes to Elysia. Concern filled her gaze as she ran her eyes over Elysia's body.

"You're alright, my darling?" she asked. Elysia nodded, and Lady Malca smiled briefly, then turned back to Kai with a stony expression.

"You are Kai Bennet?" she asked sharply. Kai focused on the stair just below her slippered feet. He nodded. "Yes, my Lady."

Lady Malca sat. "And what, might I ask, are you doing on selkie lands?" She narrowed her eyes. "You *are* aware that your presence is in violation of the Treaty of Hiraeth, yes?"

The Guard to Kai's left placed the flat of his blade on top of Kai's shoulder, and Kai flicked his eyes towards it, swallowing convulsively. He turned back to the stair beneath Lady Malca.

"With all respect, my Lady, I wasn't aware that the island I visited was part of the Selkie lands."

Lady Malca flicked her eyes to the guard on his left. "James, where was this young merrow apprehended?" James shifted uncomfortably. He cleared his throat.

"We, ah, we found him as we patrolled the shallow waters, my Lady. On an unoccupied island just to our south."

Lady Malca narrowed her eyes. "What island was this? Was it part of our lands? If not, why were you patrolling in an such an area?"

James swallowed convulsively, and Lady Malca continued. "You were given specific instructions to patrol the *Selkie Isles.* Please tell me you were not doing otherwise." She glared down at the now squirming Guard, and he dropped his eyes.

"We found it by way of Lord Connor, my Lady. While it's not technically part of the Selkie Isles, Lord Connor felt it necessary to patrol the area, as it is a favorite of his betrothed." He flicked his eyes to Elysia sheepishly, then returned them to the floor. Elysia's eyes bulged. Connor *knew* about her secret island? James continued.

"He says the young Lady goes there often." He shuffled uncomfortably, flicking his eyes to Lady Malca and back to the floor. "To swim," he muttered.

Elysia wanted to crawl beneath the floor. She watched her mother's face pale, and she dropped her eyes to the Guard, who was frowning down at the side of Kai's silver head.

"Lord Connor said he'd seen this one there once before." *Oh no.*

Elysia flicked her eyes to Kai nervously, watching as the tiny muscle feathered in his jaw.

Charles continued. "He said this merrow was watching her swim."

Kai stiffened, and Elysia moved her eyes worriedly to her mother. Lady Malca flushed as she sank further her seat, obviously embarrassed.

James was still speaking, but Elysia's hearing had gone. Her ears were ringing, and her mind raged with *why's* and *what if's.* Her heart was thrumming out of her chest, and she fisted her hands, glaring at the side of the Guard's plump face. She wished he would be quiet. He had said enough already. But James had always been one to talk. He was too eager to rise in rank. It made him have a loose tongue.

Elysia wanted to scream for his silence, but still, he kept going.

"Connor saw the whole thing. He asked us to watch the island to the south for a silver-haired Merrow, because he's broken the treaty by watching the Lady, on selkie lands, or no."

Elysia's face burned, and she folded her arms against her chest, staring hard at the floor. So, Connor had been watching her, too. The thought made her stomach churn. *Disgusting.*

She lifted her eyes briefly to Kai. His jaw was set in a hard line, and all the color had fled his cheeks. He was holding himself so tight, he looked like a wound spring. Elysia understood the feeling. Nervous energy was coursing through her muscles. She was ready to jump on the Guards, should they make a false move. She was terrified for him. merrows who violated the treaty were shown no mercy on her the islands, and it hadn't been the first time a merrow heir was flayed by the Guard.

Once, she had heard an awful story. It had been shortly after Elysia's father was taken by the merrow Forces. After the exile, Lord Dolion's son had fallen in love with a Selkie woman. Despite the treaty, the two had a child. His mother hid him away on the Selkie Isles, and for a while, no one knew about him. But eventually the baby grew, and it was clear that he had merrow blood. His iridescent eyes shimmered in the sunlight, and he bore scales on his temples, three slits beneath his ears, and a fine, sheer blade along his spine that marked him as part merrow.

No one mentioned the child until the merrow heir came to

shore. He had only wanted to see his son, but he was captured by the Guard on the beach. They flayed him alive before the selkie woman's face, and then his shredded body was sunk to the depths.

The selkie woman had thought there was no end to her grief, but she had been wrong. Soon after, it was her son who was taken. Of course, it was only Lord Dolion's retaliation for the death of his own son. He was upholding the treaty, too, but, still, Elysia found it hard to imagine that he would kill his own, treaty or no. The baby was part merrow—Lord Dolion's own kin. Sadly, the boy was never seen or heard from again. It spoke volumes about the black depths of Lord Dolion's twisted heart.

Elysia shivered. Kai had broken the treaty, just like the merrow heir in the story. The Guard were well within their rights to flay him. And, just like horrid tale, it wouldn't matter if he was the heir to the Merrow throne, or not. One word from her mother, and he would be slashed in two, right before her eyes. Elysia searched her mind. She had to say something, do something, even if it meant she would flay her own tail, in the process.

Just then, she heard the creak of the heavy throne room doors. She lifted her eyes, her heart twisting as Connor thrust a hand in his pocket and strolled casually towards the dais. His smug face made her sick, and bile rose in her throat as he passed her, winking.

She glared at him in disgust. He had followed her, *watched* her on the secret island, and he had never said a word. Her face burned at the thought. Now, he was trying to kill Kai for the doing the same, just because he was merrow. Elysia narrowed her eyes at him. She thought not.

She moved towards the throne, stepping protectively in front of Kai's knees.

"Mother, you must know, it was a mistake. He didn't know anyone was there, and he didn't even see anything, right Kai?" She peered down at him over her shoulder, raising her brows. Kai wet his lips. He opened his mouth, then closed it, shaking his head slightly.

She turned back to her mother, who was staring down at her skeptically. "He saved me," Elysia said hurriedly. "More than once. First, it was a diving spider, then it was two merrow attackers. The men would've slit my throat if not for him. He even cut the last one down with his spear."

Lady Malca tapped her finger on the arm of her throne. She flicked her eyes to Kai, thinking as Connor moved beside Elysia. He ignored Kai's presence as he draped his arm lazily over Elysia's shoulder. Then he bent, kissing her cheek. "Hello, my love," he crooned. "It's good to see you again, so soon."

Elysia pushed him away. She stepped sideways, glaring as she swiped her cheek roughly with her hand. It left a splotched, red mark in the place where his lips had been.

Connor raised his brow, stuffing his hand lazily back into his pocket.

"Are you angry with me, my darling?" he asked innocently. He scoffed, pushing Kai's knee sideways with his boot. "Surely you're not upset over this merrow fellow."

Kai's knee bent at an odd angle, but he barely showed notice. He held himself fast to his position as Connor circled him. He jerked his chin to Kai. "I saw…this one…watching you that night." He shook his head, frowning. "A filthy, filthy thing to do. I knew he would show up again, sooner or later." He smirked down at Kai, then his grin spread wide, showing all his gleaming teeth. "Lady Malca, tell me, wasn't it a silver haired Merrow that led Lord Ríonan to his death?"

Kai glared daggers at Connor as Elysia flicked her eyes to her mother. Lady Malca's fingers were white on the arm of her throne, and she stared hard at the top of Kai's head. Her face was a mask of pain.

Elysia's heart sank. Her suspicions had been correct. Kai's father had served Lord Dolion. He had been there when they took her own father away. She turned her eyes to Kai. But that didn't matter now. Kai hadn't had anything to do with it.

Elysia dropped to her knees.

"Mother, please, this has nothing to do with that. Kai wasn't there all those cycles ago, and he had nothing to do with what his father did. He would never do something like that. I know he wouldn't. Especially not now." She peered at Kai over her shoulder, watching as he stared hard at the floor. She turned back to her mother. "He's done nothing but help me, and tonight was no different."

Her mother studied her silently, and Elysia continued. "We were only trying to collect the Tamarisk. It's Ena…she's sick. She might die, if we don't return with the Tamarisk, soon." She took a breath, peering into her mother's eyes. "I…I'm the new healer. The Tamarisk trees grew on my secret island. The Source has chosen me." She took a breath. "I came to collect it, so that I could save her, and Kai came with me. He's like my Guard. He's sworn to protect me. Lady Sirena bid him so, and he's quite loyal to her." She flicked her eyes to him. "And I know him to be incapable of willfully harming me. In fact, quite the opposite."

Lady Malca tapped her fingers, staring thoughtfully at Kai's bowed head. She didn't say anything, and, for a moment, her eyes were far away. Tears glistened at their edges as Elysia moved towards her. She kneeled at her mother's feet, then she took her hand, speaking in a low tone.

"He's not him, Mother," she whispered. "Kai wasn't there when they sent my father to his death. In truth, Kai has done the opposite. He has saved me from mine."

She gazed pleadingly as her mother dabbed her eyes. "Please. Grant him mercy."

Lady Malca sighed. She eyed Kai wearily, then ceased her tapping on the arm of her throne. Elysia gave her hand a squeeze. The end of her tapping meant her mother had made a decision, and hopefully, it was the one Elysia wanted.

Lady Malca studied Kai's solemn face for a long while. Then, at last, she spoke.

"It's our custom, in the Selkie Court, to repay a kindness with the like. If you have done as my daughter says, if you have saved her life, I will grant you mercy for the night," she said quietly. "In the morning, collect the Tamarisk and go. But be warned, my mercy will expire. If you remain, it will not last." Connor moved to protest, but Lady Malca held up her palm. "The decision is made," she said calmly.

Connor glared up at her, and Elysia flinched as he fisted his palms. He kicked the bottom step of the dais, then turned, eyeing Kai angrily as he passed. Lady Malca followed him with flat eyes. She watched as the throne room doors slammed shut behind him, then she stood, nodding to Kai and Elysia.

"You may go, but heed my warning." She stared sharply at Kai's face. "I will not extend such a kindness again."

Elysia leapt to her feet. She kissed her mother's cheek as Kai bowed low from his waist. "Thank you, my Lady," he said quietly. His Guards dispersed as Elysia jogged towards him. She grasped his arm, propelling him quickly through a side door behind the left of the throne.

Swiftly, Elysia pulled him up the staircase. She turned left, moving rapidly to the end of the hall before she paused at a set of wide wooden doors at the end. She pulled the right one wide.

"This is your room." She gestured to an identical set of doors across the hall.

"And that's mine." She peered gravely up at him. "Don't come out, until I come to get you in the morning. The selkies *detest* merrows. They will be furious that my mother has granted you mercy, especially James and the rest of the Guard. So the less you're seen, the better."

"By *they*, do you mean Connor?" he said, smirking. He folded his arms, leaning against the doorframe. "You shouldn't be worried about him. I could take him, James, and the rest with one arm tied behind my back."

Elysia rolled her eyes. "Of course, you could, Kai. Now, go to sleep. I'll see you in the morning."

With that, she moved across the hall. She stepped inside her door, shooting him a quick smile before she quietly closed it behind her.

Kai waited, staring hard at her doorframe, until she grew silent behind it. He tapped his fingers against his arm, thinking. Elysia was right. He knew he should take her advice. But Maura was so close. He had to go back and see her, while he had the chance. Quietly, he pushed his own door closed. Then he crept down the hallway. He paused at the top of the stairs, peering over them. The entry hall was empty, and he moved swiftly down the steps, before stealing out the back doors and into the garden.

He didn't make a sound as he followed the winding path past the fountain and moved towards a low arch in the garden's back wall. Kai paused beneath the arch, scanning the landscape, then he shot out of the garden, running full speed past the sleeping village towards the forest beyond.

Deep in the cover of trees, he met a wide stream. Kai slid his legs over the side, testing its depth. It was surprisingly deep. Quickly, he stripped his clothing, then he slid over the bank, dropping under.

Instantly, a hard current swept him forward, and he swirled end over end in the rapid water. He fought to pull himself upright, swishing his tail and curving his hands in a large arc, but nothing would right him. His head spun as he struggled to get his bearings. He was moving so fast that he couldn't tell which way was up or down.

There was nothing for it. He was helpless in the rapids. Closing his eyes, he allowed his body to relax. He hurdled along the water's path, focusing on sifting the swirling depths with his sea lungs.

He was certain he was bumping every rock and sharp corner along the way, until, at last, he reached the deceptive river's end. There, his bruised body flipped end over end as he was flung violently outward into the open sea. He breathed heavily, working to right his swirling head as he let himself sink down to the sea floor. Then he stretched himself flat, blinked up towards the surface.

His ears rang, and he laughed quietly to himself, as he shook the dizzy feeling from his head. The shock of his wild ride still burned in his aching limbs, and gingerly, he flicked his tail, pulling himself towards the surface.

He emerged near the beach of the secret island, scanning with his sharp eyes for movement along the shoreline. The landscape was still and silent. Cautiously, he stood, collecting his water weaving, then he climbed the hill to the Tamarisk grove. He cut an armful of the pink fronds, then he started the walk to the Cypress trees.

Excitement and apprehension filled his chest as he climbed the wooden treehouse steps. Quietly, he stepped through the opening, blinking in the dim light of the small room. Silver streams of the dual moons' light shone sideways through the window, and Kai propped the Tamarisk fronds against the wall in them. Then he settled against the far wall to wait.

It took longer than it had before, and Kai almost fell asleep before Maura appeared. He sagged against the wall, until at last, he glimpsed a thin outline of her delicate frame. She raised her wispy hand in a wave as he scrambled upright. "Hello, again," she said quietly.

She gave him a small smile as Kai flicked his eyes over her. Her outline was hazy, and her voice was thinner than he remembered. But it didn't matter. She was here. He grinned. "Hi," he replied. "I'm sorry it's taken me so long to get back to you."

Maura laid her head back against the wall. She was quite pale. "T'sokay," she said tiredly.

Kai frowned at her worriedly. She looked weak. "What's wrong, Maura?" he asked her. Maura sighed. Slowly, she turned her head to gaze out the window.

"It's kind of hard to explain," she murmured, shrugging. "I'm just not as strong, here, as I was before."

Kai frowned. "Why not?" he asked softly. "Did I do something wrong?"

She flicked her eyes to him weakly. "Course not, silly. It's just, I don't belong here, anymore."

Warning bells signaled in Kai's head at her words. His heart began to thrum in his ears, and panic threatened to grip his throat.

"Of course, you do, Maura," he said desperately. "You do. You belong here. With me." He pressed his hand to the left of his chest. "I called you here, remember? My Amloga called you."

Maura gazed at him weakly. Despite the moons' direct beam, her body was growing more transparent by the moment. "I know you did," she whispered. "But you didn't call as strongly, this time." Kai studied her quizzically, as she hugged her knees into her chest. "It's okay, Kai, really. It's normal, the natural way of things." She gave him a small smile. "There's someone else."

Kai froze. He was horrified at her words. His heart sank into his stomach, and he shook his head rapidly back and forth.

"No," he said quickly. "There's no one else. There's only you, Maura. Always, it's been you."

Maura gave him a patient grin. She shrugged one shoulder. "Of course, there is." Her smile brightened. "I heard her Selkie's Song."

Kai blinked at her in horror as realization came. "You don't mean *Elysia*?" He shook his head, scoffing. "Maura. Be serious. We can't go two sentences without fighting. We can't stand each other."

He threw up his hands. "I can't believe you would even say such a thing, after all that we've been through. You think I can move on, after us?" He put his tongue in his cheek, folding his arms. "Never."

Maura gazed at him patiently through the moonlight. Her voice was growing hollower with each word.

"There is a season to all created things, Kai Bennet," she whispered. "For the Source has made it so." She paused, studying his face.

"And we Merrow are no different. We are not exempt from the laws of the Source."

She tucked a hand to her chest. "My season with you has passed, and now, I belong with the Source. Where I live, in the Hereafter, my season is eternal." Kai's eyes filled and she smiled. "It feels to you like I am lost." She shook her head. "But I'm not. I've only just stepped through the open door. There, I am found in the other room, in the place with no sorrow, where my life has no end."

Kai swiped his eyes as she continued, her voice waning.

"Listen to the Selkie's Song, Kai. It reveals the desires of the Source. The Voice contains a knowing that cannot otherwise be known. It will lift you from sorrow and help you to see. Listen closely, and you will know. Allow the Voice to lead."

Kai lunged towards her desperately as she disappeared.

"Don't leave me," he cried. But Maura was already gone. The

silver moons' light shone brightly on the Tamarisk fronds, and he stared in anguish at the open space as tears sprang into his eyes, willing Maura to reappear. But the space remained empty, and his throat tightened around a lump as he laid his head flat against the floor, sobbing.

Kai cried until he had no tears left, long after the moons had faded, and a thin line of pinkish-orange light hovered over the horizon. He lifted his head, blinking dejectedly through the window at the morning sunrise. Sighing, he flicked his eyes to the Tamarisk fronds. The space around them looked bare, and he turned away bitterly, hauling his stiff body from the floor.

As he hiked back towards the beach, he considered Maura's words. He couldn't deny that she was right. Elysia's presence had been a distraction from Maura's memory. And the words to her Selkie Song had made his pain less acute.

He gripped his fists at his sides. Apparently, that was the problem. Elysia was to blame. And he knew exactly how to fix it.

If it was Elysia keeping Maura away, then he knew what to do. He would distance himself from her, as best he could. Even when they were alone, he would follow the treaty to the letter. He wouldn't look at her again, and he wouldn't speak to her, unless absolutely necessary. And he certainly wouldn't listen to her Selkie's Song.

After her visit to the Court of Merrows, he would never have another thing to do with her, ever again. When she was gone, maybe Maura would come back to him. He smiled, imagining Maura's appearance as bright and crisp, like she had been the first time he had seen her. Her voice would be strong, and her tinkling laugh would carry sweetly to his ears.

Kai frowned. There was nothing he wanted more than that. Nothing was more important than Maura. And he would do whatever he had to do to be with her like that again.

CHAPTER 18

The merrow held his blade tight against her throat. He grinned down at it, pressing, as a thin line of blood trickled from Elysia's neck. His mouth spread wide, a ferocious line of glinting, sharp-pointed teeth. Then he opened his jaws. They were too wide, unhinging to a dark abyss beyond. The darkness was swallowing her.

Elysia sprang up in bed, gasping. She searched the air in front of her, her heart thrumming in her ears, as she pressed at her neck, swallowing convulsively. But there was no Merrow man. There was no dark abyss, and on her throat, only a small, crusted scab remained where his blade had been.

She dropped her hand, blowing out a breath. It had only been a dream.

Beneath her window, a thin, whisper of light seeped past the frame. She lifted herself groggily from the mattress and pulled back the drapes. The sun was just coming up. She and Kai needed to leave.

She dressed quickly, then moved to the vanity and wound her hair into a long braid. If they hurried, they could be back in the Court of Merrows with the Tamarisk, by midday.

She raced across the hall and rapped lightly on Kai's door. He didn't answer right away, and she waited a moment longer, then tried again. She rapped harder this time, then pressed her ear to the door. "Kai? It's Elysia. We need to go."

He didn't answer, and Elysia frowned. Quietly, she turned the handle and peeked her head inside. His bed was still made, and she moved towards it, frowning. It didn't even look slept in. She huffed, tossing a pillow at the place where his body should have been.

"What were you thinking, Kai?!" she growled.

Fuming, she hurried down the steps and out the back doors. She knew exactly where Kai had gone. The question was, why had he gone in the middle of the night? She stepped into the garden, fuming. Connor's men would be out in droves. She was sure they were still patrolling the secret island. And they would be waiting for him.

She shook her head, muttering under her breath. Now, he had gone back to the scene of his crime. She only hoped he hadn't already been captured. James and the others wouldn't wait for her mother's mercy, this time. They would flay him on the spot. Or worse.

As she slipped past the garden fountain, something rustled to her left. Elysia froze at the sound, then she ducked behind a large rose bush. She peered out from between the thick leaves, her heart skipping in her ears. She could see movement from behind the high trellis. Someone was there, hiding beneath the pavilion.

A tumble of flowering vines had wound themselves across the pavilion's high columns. They created a thick canopy, which partially shielded its inside from view. There, the figure of a woman moved beneath them. She giggled, tossing her long blonde hair, then she threw her arms around another figure. Elysia squinted. It was a dark-haired man, standing beside her.

Just then, a breeze parted the vines, and Elysia watched as the woman's face turned towards her view. It was Delia, and the man beside her was Connor.

Elysia's stomach sank as Delia planted her lips directly on Connor's mouth. Connor wrapped his fingers into her long hair as he lifted her toes off the ground. He spun her in a circle, then he pressed her against a vine-covered column, kissing her fiercely.

Angry tears stung Elysia's eyes, and she swiped at them furiously. She didn't even know why she was crying. She hated Connor. She hated everything about him.

At last, Elysia could bear it no longer. She stepped from behind the trellis and cleared her throat, watching as their heads whipped in her direction. Connor stared at her flatly as Delia's face flushed crimson. She pushed Connor away, then she slipped from beneath the vines, fleeing the garden as fast as her legs would carry her.

Connor watched her leave, leaning casually on the nearest column. Then he crossed his arms, grinning smugly in Elysia's direction. "Enjoying the view?" he asked teasingly.

Elysia squared her shoulders.

"Much less than you enjoyed watching me swim, I'd wager," she snapped.

Connor examined a nail, then lifted his gaze. "I've seen better," he said flatly.

Elysia ground her teeth. Despite her best efforts, her throat tightened, and a hot tear slipped down her cheek. She swiped it, hoping he didn't notice. He was disgusting.

"Maybe you have," she ground out. "But you can be *sure* you won't be seeing me that way, *ever* again."

Connor lifted his chin. He stuffed his hands in his pockets as he stalked out of the pavilion. Then he stopped right in front of her, cocking his head to the side. Elysia's chest burned as he wove his gaze lazily up from her feet, and she crossed her arms, glaring.

Connor narrowed his eyes. He stalked her in a half-circle, causing a tingle of fear to bite at her neck. There was something predatory about Connor. He reminded her of a wild animal, and she was his prey. It made her knees rattle, but she refused to let him see her quake. He closed the distance as the fear moved down her spine.

It wrapped her chest in a vice grip, but she lifted her chin.

Connor stopped near her ear. He grabbed her roughly by the waist and pulled her against him, his hot breath spewing against her cheek. Then he gripped her upper arm with his free hand, squeezing mercilessly. Elysia whimpered, straining away. Tears sprang into her eyes, again, and she ground her teeth as a bruise blossomed beneath his fingers, willing them not to fall.

He brought his lips close. "I'll do *whatever* I wish, with *whomever* I please," he hissed. "That includes watching you, *whenever* I like. Once I'm your mate, there'll be nothing you can do to stop me. I'll be joint heir to the Selkie throne. I'll look at you in any way I please, and any others, including Delia, as often as I want. And you will allow it. Is that understood?" He tightened his grip on her waist, planting a sloppy kiss on her collarbone. Elysia winced, and he continued.

"If you don't, it won't go well for you. Because once we're married and we take the throne, all your power will revert to me, should you…" He pressed his face close, baring his teeth. "Meet an untimely *death*." He spat the word, squeezing her arm until Elysia's fingers tingled. He chuckled, shaking his head. "It wouldn't be the first time a selkie ruler has been deposed. And what will happen to your precious merrow then, do you think? When you're no longer here to defend him?"

Elysia wrestled against his grasp, and he twisted her arm behind her back, spinning her away from him. He held her fast against his chest, binding her arms to her sides.

"I'll get rid of every obstacle in my way, including your *mother*, to make *sure* he is reprimanded properly for his crimes." He chuckled mirthlessly. "I'll even take Lady Sirena down with him. As a matter of fact, I'll destroy any merrow that dares cross me!"

Elysia kicked at his shin, but he planted his knee hard in her thigh, making her leg go limp. She stumbled, but he held her upright. "In the end, it will be *me* that controls both courts. That's been my father's plan, all along. Once you and the others are gone, all of it will be mine!"

He growled a laugh as he tugged hard on Elysia's braid, glaring greedily as he exposed her neck.

"For now, I'll settle for taking *this* for my own." He bent his lips, and Elysia squirmed against his grasp. She ground her teeth as his mouth met her skin, and kicked her foot upward, landing a hard blow between his legs.

Connor groaned as her foot made contact, releasing her from his grasp. He stumbled backward, landing hard against the trellis, as Elysia pitched forward onto her hands, scraping them hard against the stone path.

"That is *quite* enough!" Lady Malca shouted.

Elysia flicked her eyes towards her mother. Her face was furious as she descended the steps and moved regally to Connor's side. She glared at him in disgust and pointed her finger in his face. "If you think you will *ever* have my throne, let alone my *daughter*, then you are sorely mistaken," she spat.

Members of the council had just arrived for morning court. Silently, they gathered at the top of the steps, witnessing the display in the garden below. Lady Malca continued.

"Lord Connor, you are released of your position in this court, forthwith. You are no longer betrothed to my daughter, and you are hereby stripped of your duties to the Selkie Guard."

Connor opened his mouth to protest, but Lady Malca held up her hand.

"Do. *Not*. Speak. Silence is your friend. You have threatened the heir to the Selkie throne, as well as my own person with your vile words, and I will hear no more of them! You, and your *despicable* father, are hereby banned from my court. He will no longer serve on my council, and you will no longer be welcome in my or my daughter's presence. I never want to see your face on these grounds, again. Do you understand? Be gone!"

Connor stared at her with an evil grin. "You'll regret this, *my Lady*. Mark my words." He stalked to her lazily, stopping a breath from her nose.

"You're just as weak as your husband was," he spat. "My father said he went to his death *willingly*, after Lord Dolion put a price on his head. Supposedly, he did it to protect his people, his life for our lives in trade. It was either him or us all, when Orm needed Amloga to control the Rotha-Am, and his life was worth more than ours put together because he was a Timekeeper." He frowned.

"Lord Dolion promised to protect us, after Lord Ríonan was gone, but we were all exiled, anyway. The treaty was crafted, and we were stripped of our lands, so what was it worth? Tell me, what does Lord Ríonan have to show for his sacrifice? *Nothing.* Nothing but his own foul death."

Lady Malca slapped his cheek hard with the back of her hand, but he glared down at her, still grinning. "You'll find the same fate for yourself, if you're not careful," he snarled.

"We shall see," Lady Malca said solemnly. "Now leave my gardens before I have you removed by force."

The Guard surrounded him, but Connor held up his hands. He backed away from them both, glaring a warning stare, as the council looked on from above. The Guard trailed him to the village gate, watching as he turned left onto a back lane, stalking out of sight.

Elysia stood, watching him disappear as she dusted her scraped palms. Her mother appeared at her side. She wrapped Elysia in a hug, then she pulled back, peering seriously into her eyes.

"I'm sorry, Elysia," she said quietly. "I thought we had him well in hand." She turned to look the way Connor had gone. "The council and I thought he was the best choice for our…situation, but apparently, we were wrong."

Elysia bit her lip. She squeezed her mother tightly again. "It's okay," she whispered.

Lady Malca pulled back, frowning. She scanned the garden. "Where is your merrow guard?"

Elysia smiled. "He's waiting for me on the island," she replied. "I must go. If we don't make it back with the Tamarisk soon, Ena won't make it."

Her mother nodded. She kissed Elysia's cheek. "Be safe, my daughter, and may the Source go with you."

Elysia's raft was waiting for her in the reeds. Quickly, she pulled it free and climbed aboard. In moments, she was navigating the familiar rapids with expertise. But as she moved into the cavern, her focus wandered from her task, and the interaction with Connor in the garden swelled in her mind.

The feeling of his hands on her lingered, and she shivered in disgust. His arm had bound her waist like an iron chain, and the sick feeling of his lips on her neck made her want to scrub the spot with soap until it went raw. Instead, she did the next best thing, moving one hand from her oar to wipe hard at her throat and leaving a smudging red mark.

She was nearing the end of the cavern when she saw Kai from the arched opening of rock. He was standing on the shore of the secret island. His arms were lifted above his head, like he was ready to dive into the water. She raised her hand to wave, and he looked directly at her, then dove under, ignoring her presence.

She frowned at the flick of his blue tail. He had seen her. Or, at least, she thought he had.

The water beneath her swirled in its familiar pattern, but she was so caught off guard by Kai's odd behavior that she let her oar slip. She lunged after it, narrowly missing as her raft spun sideways in the tumbling water. It careened wildly in the last rapid, and Elysia clenched her teeth, bracing for impact as the raft's front edge slammed into a large rock jutting out of the side of the cavernous opening.

Elysia yelped as she pitched forward into the surf. Immediately, the swirling waters of the Brook pulled her under. Her skirts billowed about her head, and she tumbled end over end in the dark water. She hadn't taken a good breath, and as she spun, her chest burned from lack of air. Vaguely, she remembered what Kai had said about her sea lungs being weak. She attempted to engage them, but she couldn't think clearly in the thrashing surf, and she took in sea water instead of filtering it out.

Helplessly, she fought for control, but it was no use. The Brook pulled her deeper and deeper, until, suddenly, she pitched violently sideways, hitting her head on a jagged rock on the riverbed. She winced at the contact, blinking as red blood pooled about her peripheral gaze. Then her vision went hazy, and darkness overtook her as her body went limp and lifeless.

Elysia didn't know how long she was out, but when she came to, Kai's face hovered hazily above her head. She blinked her eyes and coughed weakly, spewing out salty water, as Kai frowned down at her. He was speaking, but her hearing was muffled. Weakly, she clawed at her chest, ignoring his moving mouth. Her lungs were on fire. It was distracting, and she groaned as she was forced to take a sharp inhale of dry air. Kai spoke again, and she blinked up at him in confusion. She wanted to tell him that she couldn't hear him, but her throat burned, and she couldn't breathe well enough to force her voice out, anyway.

He slapped at her cheeks as her vision crossed. "Elysia?! Elysia! Can you hear me? Wake up! Open your eyes, blast it! If you ever listen to me once in your whole life, can it be now? Can it be this time?" He shook her shoulders gently. "I promise. Later, I'll let you do what you want, but now you have to listen to me. Can you do that?"

Elysia groaned. She could hear him, now. She tested her chest, taking in a deep breath and ignoring the burn she fluttered her eyes open. She grinned up at him.

"Whatever I want?" she said groggily.

Kai rolled his eyes. He sat back on his knees, blowing out a relieved breath.

"Within reason," he said, grinning.

Elysia coughed weakly. She sucked in another breath. "Well, I choose a swimming lesson, then," she croaked. "Looks like I need it."

Kai chuckled. He put his back to the wall of the cavern, and Elysia sat up on weakly onto her palms. She peered tiredly at the side of Kai's face. He wasn't looking at her, and she frowned at his profile.

"Swimming lesson, it is," he said quietly. He reached to grab her oar where it churned in the water against the cavern wall, then he stood and moved to retrieve her raft. "Just..not today." Elysia hauled herself to her feet, bracing against the damp rock wall. She frowned.

"Why not?" she asked him.

Kai shook his head. He moved the raft to rest in front of her as he hopped aboard and braced one foot on the bank, holding it steady. Then, he stared straight past her, extending his arm.

"Just, not today, okay?" he said. "You're too weak to swim, anyway."

Elysia narrowed her eyes. "Why aren't you looking at me, Kai?" she asked him.

The small muscle in his jaw flexed, and he opened his mouth to speak, then closed it again.

Elysia waited, staring pointedly.

Kai cleared his throat. "I just…I'm already in enough trouble, as it is." He dropped his head, blowing out a breath. "Connor is angry, and so is the Guard. I don't want to cause either of us any more problems. I think…I just think it would be best, if we keep our distance."

Elysia's blinked at the top of his silver head. She stuck out her foot, lifting her chin as she crossed her arms.

"If you think I care what that vile idiot thinks, then you're wrong. Besides, he's not my betrothed anymore."

She didn't wait for Kai to answer as she stepped quickly onto the raft. It shifted sideways with her movement, and Elysia's weak muscles failed to balance. She pitched backward towards the churning water, but Kai lunged, catching her around the waist at the last moment. He tugged her swiftly against him with one arm, balancing their weight as the water swirled beneath them.

Elysia's hands were braced against his chest. Her heart hammered in her ears, and she shivered, despite the warmth of Kai's body. He met her gaze, peering deeply with his too-blue eyes. Then all at once, he looked away.

Carefully, he lowered her to sit on the raft. Then he stepped away, never meeting her eyes.

"Are you alright?" he asked gruffly.

Elysia peered down at her trembling hands. To be honest, she wasn't. She was getting tired of her adventures. There were too many close brushes with death. She braced her hands on her arms, then returned her gaze to Kai. He was still refusing to look at her. His eyes flicked from one spot to another, focusing on the oar, the wooden raft, the cavern wall—anywhere but her face. It made her furious. She dropped her eyes.

"Yes, I'm fine," she snapped.

She swallowed, flicking her eyes to the side of Kai's head. "We still need the Tamarisk," she said quietly. Kai nodded, patting his shirt pocket. "I picked several blooms, when I went to the grove earlier," he said coolly.

Elysia studied his profile. His jaw was set in a hard line, and his eyes were hard as flint. She frowned. He was being so distant, like when they had first met. Something had changed, but she didn't know what. She watched as he avoided her gaze, pretending to be fascinated with the swirling water.

She watched as a muscle feathered in his perfect jaw. Maybe it was just like he had said. Maybe he really *was* worried that he had broken the treaty, and he didn't want to cause any more trouble. Even though her mother had granted him mercy, it was certainly possible that he was afraid for his life, especially with Connor and the Guard. She could understand that. Besides, she was sure that he didn't think she was worth the risk of any more infractions.

Whatever his reasons, it was obvious her presence made him uncomfortable. Her heart sank a bit, at the thought, but she stuffed the feeling down. She couldn't worry about whether Kai Bennet thought her worthy enough to risk his attentions, right now. Ena needed her.

She stared hard at his back as he pulled the oar, moving them slowly upstream. The muscles in his shoulder flexed with the effort, and she frowned, flicking her eyes away. If Kai wasn't interested in looking at her, then she certainly wasn't going to look at him. She sniffed, lifting her chin as she pretended to be interested in the dark brown rock of the cavern wall. She could ignore him, too. It was easy.

Anyway, she wouldn't have to worry about his opinion of her for much longer. Soon, her stay in the Court of Merrows would be over. Then, he would only have to ignore her once per cycle, at the meeting between their courts.

As they emerged from the cavern, she couldn't resist a glance at the sunlight glittering on his silver hair. Kai turned his head to the side, and she dropped her eyes. Though he wasn't looking, she could feel him assessing her from his peripheral gaze. She ignored him, picking at a chip in the raft's wood until he turned away.

He cleared his throat. "You need to learn to engage your sea lungs," he said quietly. Elysia lifted her face, frowning at the back of his head. "What?" she said flatly. Kai sighed.

"I said, you need to learn to engage your sea lungs. If you don't want to almost die like you did back there, you need a lesson." Elysia twisted her lips. "Fine," she muttered.

Kai continued to pull the oar, speaking over his shoulder. "It's easy. You already have everything you need. You just need to focus on filtering the air out of the water. Once you quiet your mind, it will seem simple. You're so focused on trying to hold your breath with your land lungs, that you're missing how easy it is. Try it, next time. You'll see."

Elysia didn't answer. She knew he was just trying to help, but he was really starting to annoy her.

Soon, they arrived at the reeds. Kai braced one foot on the bank. He kept his eyes fixed on the oar as he held out his hand.

Elysia sniffed. She looked away, ignoring his hand as she brushed past him, stepping easily from the raft to the ground. Kai huffed behind her, and she grinned to herself as she walked into the trees. Who needed him anyway?

She turned right at the tree line, moving swiftly towards the shore. She could ignore him for a few more days. Then, it would all be over. Kai would return to his life, and she would resume her own. Soon, she wouldn't have to deal with him anymore. And that was just fine with her.

Chapter 19

Elysia sat waiting on a large flat rock by the shore as Kai stowed her raft in the reeds. She grumbled in frustration, turned her head back towards the trees. He was taking forever.

"Hurry up, Kai! We need to go!" she called.

He didn't answer, and she stood, huffing. What was so hard about stowing a wooden raft?

Grumbling, she marched up the hillside, glaring angrily at the tree line. By now, they should have already been well into the tunnel. Ena was less than a day from imminent death, and if he didn't hurry, they weren't going to make it.

Elysia crossed her arms, tapping her foot anxiously. She wished she had the Tamarisk. Then she could have gone ahead, by herself.

Her side ached, and she stretched, wincing. Then again, it was probably best that she didn't go on alone. She was still weak from her ordeal with the Brook. Her limbs ached, and her already weak sea lungs still burned from taking on water. She knew she would move too slowly, and she certainly didn't want to get stuck in the tunnel, all alone, while some beast or another threatened to eat her alive. She would just have to wait.

Sighing, she trudged back to the forest path. She scanned the trees as she moved inside, but there was no sign of him. Elysia frowned. She should have met him by now. Warning bells triggered in her mind, and she increased her pace, winding back towards the stream.

She stood on the bank, searching the dark water. He wasn't there, either. The Brook's surface ran undisturbed, and her raft bobbed safely from its hiding place in the reeds. "Kai?" she called uncertainly. He didn't answer, and she peered worriedly through the still forest beyond as her heart hitched in speed. She was starting to get nervous.

She backtracked along the path. Maybe Kai had gone back to the palace. Why? She had no idea. He knew that they should have been gone, by now, and she had made it very clear that the less he was seen, the better.

Elysia ground her teeth as she stomped towards the tree line. He never listened. He just kept going his own way, putting himself in danger for no apparent reason. It was infuriating.

Just then, a large, dark figure emerged from behind the tree in

I control the Court of Merrows." He grinned down at her evilly, then flicked his glittering black eyes to the Brook. "Perhaps I'll get a head start," he said, hissing. "One less selkie for the merrows to flay." He reached for her, baring his teeth.

For a moment, Elysia was frozen to her spot. Her mind reeled. Kai was with Nathair, in his lair at the bottom of the sea. She had no idea how to find him, and if she died right here in the forest, no one would ever know who had actually sent him there. If Connor had his way, he would drown her in the Brook. She'd be sucked down in the dark water, nevermore to be seen.

She imagined her lifeless frame being tossed in the dark rapids as he swiped for her arm. He was right. There would be war if she didn't find Kai before he was eaten. Lady Sirena would have no way of knowing it was Connor who had sent him to his death. The merrow court would retaliate, and she had no doubt that Connor and Ciar would use the situation to fight their way to control of both courts.

She sprang to action as Connor lunged at her waist. She danced out of his grasp, and he narrowly missed her as she spun. But the maneuver threw her off balance, and he kicked her feet from under her. She landed hard on her stomach, knocking out her wind.

For a moment she lay flat, watching as Connor's feet circled her side. But then her breath returned, and a deep, guttural roar built in her throat. A small, jagged stone lay in front of her face, and she latched onto it, releasing her battle cry as Connor reached for her throat. Then she flipped herself hard, swinging her arm as she connected the stone with the side of his face.

It hit with a sickening crack, and for two breaths, Connor's expression registered shock. He swayed, moving his hand shakily to the spot. Dark, red blood flowed from beneath his palm, and she watched warily as his eyes rolled back. Then, he fell forward, landing on top of her.

Elysia wheezed as his weight pressed on her chest. She gripped his shoulder, and he groaned as she pushed hard, rolling him away. Then she scrambled to her feet, fleeing towards the shoreline.

She ran hard, not turning to see if he had followed. Most likely, he hadn't. She had hit Connor hard over the temple—hard enough that he might even be dead. She almost hoped he was.

She flung her clothes in a heap on the rocks, then dove headlong, swimming furiously. The sea about her was quiet, and she didn't slow, slicing through the water until the islands were two small dots behind her. When she was certain she hadn't been followed, she ducked into a large reef, slipping silently behind a wide orange coral.

Her breath came in short bursts through her burning sea lungs, and her heart thrummed in her ears as she peeked out from behind it. What if she *had* killed Connor? Ciar would surely retaliate, and maybe even some of the council. She was sure not everyone had supported her mother's decision to ban both Ciar and Connor from court, and if they hadn't, they would be angry—even angrier if Connor was dead.

She winced as she filtered another large breath, studying the reef about her. The landscape was foreign. She had no idea where she was, and no way of knowing where Kai might be. Even if she somehow managed to find the way to Nathair's lair, with her battered limbs and burning, weak sea lungs, she wasn't sure she could make it there. Of course, she had heard of prisoners being executed in the sea serpent's canyon, but she had never been there herself. She didn't know how she could find it.

She shivered as she imagined an enormous, slithering snake sliding out of a dark hole. His enormous frame circled Kai, wrapping him in thick coils. Nathair squeezed, and Kai's bones cracked. He screamed, and the snake opened his massive jaws, ready to devour him.

Elysia closed her eyes, swallowing convulsively. She tried to clear her head of the horrid images, but they wouldn't leave. She had to find him, before it was too late. But with no one to guide her, it didn't seem possible.

She opened her eyes, concentrating as she pulled in another breath. It was difficult, and she sat still, focusing like Kai had suggested. As she struggled to filter air bubbles from the water, she frowned. One thing was for sure. She needed to practice her breathing. If she couldn't properly filter a breath, there was no way she would ever find him.

She settled further into the rocky reef, trying to relax as she recalled Kai's advice after the Brook. Silently, she made herself still, focusing as she clamped her land lungs down tight. Immediately, her body panicked. Her air was already thin, and now, she had deprived herself of breath entirely. Her heart raced, and her mind screamed for relief, but Elysia ignored her body's response.

She grappled for her mind's attention, pretending she was part of the shimmering Merrow dome. It filtered the dry air with ease, keeping the sea water out and fresh air inside. Elysia was determined, she would do the same.

Slowly, she opened her sea lungs wide. She inhaled, filtering a large chest of water as she extracted the tiny air bubbles from within it. To her surprise, her body relaxed, and her heart rate slowed. She grinned. Kai was right. It was easier than she had thought. She opened her sea lungs again, trying another breath. It was even easier this time.

After several more breaths, she felt confident in her technique. Her body was calm, and her air supply had returned, so she focused on her other problem. How was she going to find Kai?

She considered going back to the palace. Surely, her mother knew where Nathair would be. But it was too risky. She couldn't go back. Not after what had happened with Connor.

She closed her eyes, thinking. All around her, the sound of the sea weaved to and fro. She leaned into its familiar rhythm, allowing her mind to drift with its tides. Soon, her head cleared of all distraction, and as they often did, words her grandmother, Ríona, had spoken echoed clearly in her memory.

"Your enemy may be as wide as the Southern Sea, and the task before you may loom larger than the known worlds, but the promise will prevail. There is no stopping it. The promise is wider than the sea, and larger than the known worlds, by far. There is no thing, in all of creation, that can exceed it, for it comes down to you from the Source.

When you do not know the way, your gift will see you through. You may struggle in deep waters, but you will not drown. You need only access your gift. Hold to the promise, Elysia, and listen to the Voice."

Elysia's eyes opened wide. She thought about what Kai had asked her, about the words to her songs. He had asked where they had come from, and she had explained that they were the Selkie's Song—words from the Source, a whisper, called the Voice.

Elysia frowned. There was something she was missing. Something…big, that she didn't quite grasp yet. She concentrated on the sea's tide, allowing its rhythm to lull her to a place of concentration as a question formed in her periphery.

What if the Voice was more than just words? Her grandmother had said the promise was wider than the sea, so surely, the Voice was even greater than she imagined. When Kai had asked, she had called the Voice a whisper, but when she thought about it, that wasn't exactly all that it was.

Before, with her songs in the Tamarisk grove, she had *felt* the Voice, rather than heard it. The words had come like tiny, silver fires burning in the left of her chest. She frowned. What if the Voice was more than that? What if the Voice was in all creation? What if it spoke through the sea, and rocks, and waves? What if the Voice had been speaking all around her, all along, and she just hadn't been listening.

She closed her eyes, focusing, as she silenced her mind into a smooth, clean slate. Outside, the sounds of the sea tides remained. But there were other sounds, too. To her left, a school of fish swished as the passed, and before her, the orange coral waved crisply in the reef. In the distance, the mournful call of a pod of whales sang out to her ears.

She allowed herself to absorb each one. Carefully, she pulled her mind across their edges, feeling for the sounds' sizes and shapes. Little silver flames flicked in her chest with each one. It was true, the Voice whispered in each of them, but none of the sounds were what she was looking for. Slowly, she tuned them out, one by one.

In her head, a white, silent slate remained. Its blank surface was vast, and it rippled and shimmered like a deep pool of water. Elysia pushed herself further into it, exploring its depth. She attached a light feeling to the blank space, and her awareness heightened as she smoothed the fingers of her mind across its surface.

All at once, a faint, whispering splash disturbed the pool in the left of her mind's periphery. A pinpoint of silvery-blue color formed there, and she focused on the spot, watching as it expanded. It rippled outward, as if she had thrown a stone into the sea. The ripples spread, and soon, they covered the surface of the blank pool. Then, the landscape of her mind took shape.

At first, the landscape was blurred. The sounds whispered, and the shapes were devoid of color. But as Elysia released her grip on herself, she toppled headlong into the scene, and the sights and sounds of the Voice became clear. She allowed them to overwhelm her, and she gasped as Kai's gruesome state played behind her eyes in sharp relief.

Deep within the bowels of the sea, Kai's hands were bound behind his back, and he stood on dry ground between two Selkie Guards. The canyon walls were steep and slick with thick, dark mud, and an oppressive darkness covered the entire scene. Corpses of creatures and sea folk, alike, littered the canyon floor, and before him, a yawning opening in the dark rock marked the abyss of Nathair's lair.

Kai's long, silver hair was flung over his face, and as she watched, a thin, winding strand of it fell to the ground. The strand stretched itself, expanding along the canyon floor, as it transformed into a long, silver ribbon. The silver strand wove through the mire, climbing up the canyon walls. There, it collected itself on the sea floor, waiting, searching.

Elysia focused on the glinting strand, and soon, it unwound itself, like a long piece of string. It whispered as it weaved to and fro in the sea's tides, marking a narrow path until it reached the tip of her ear.

Elysia's eyes snapped open. She knew exactly where Kai was. Carefully, she steadied her sea lungs and peeked from behind the coral, breathing a silent prayer to the Source that she would make it to him before it was too late. Then she swam hard in the direction the Voice had shown her.

Her muscles burned, and her chest ached, by the time she reached the edge of the canyon, and she hid herself in a bed of sea grass, catching her breath. In front of her, the mouth of the canyon was covered with a rippling surface of sea water. Below it, dry land lay in the canyon's deep. Silently, she crept towards the edge.

She pushed her face through the surface and peered down into the darkness, searching for Kai along the dry sea floor. It was stinking and dark, and she could barely see anything, as a stern voice lifted from the canyon depths. Elysia froze, listening. Kai's quiet response rose to hear ears, and she flicked her eyes towards it, straining to locate him with the sound.

"Just keep speaking," she whispered. She closed her eyes, creating the smooth, white landscape, in her mind, once more. Kai murmured again beneath his breath, and the sound disturbed the rippling pool of her mind. She focused on the spot, and the silver ribbon again stretched from his voice to her ears. She opened her eyes. He was just to the left on the canyon floor, and his arms were bound in chains.

Silently, Elysia tucked herself over the edge. Dry air pricked her tail, and her silver skin melted away as she stepped her feet onto a high rock ledge. She lowered her head beneath the surface, paused to collect her water weaving, then she continued her slow descent down the steep canyon wall.

She pressed herself as flat as possible, hoping to blend in with the shadowy darkness. Mud and mire clung to her bare skin, and another slick, sticky substance coated her palms. She pulled one free. "Ech," she whispered, shivering. Thin lines of pale, stringy filth trailed from her hands to the wall, and she wiped them on a towering, rough rock as she stepped onto the canyon floor.

Her hands came away from the rock with another slick coating, and she blinked down at them in the darkness, frowning. Then, as her eyes adjusted, she took in the gruesome scene. Ahead of her, a tall, towering pile of foul, smelling things rose from the ground. And beyond it was another, and another.

Countless bones and half-eaten corpses of fish, eels, and sea folk surrounded her in towering, jumbled heaps. She had wiped her hands on the nearest one, swiping across the body of a slick eel. Its sallow skin was in various stages of decay, and she gasped as she examined her palms. They were covered in stinking eel guts, and she sank to the canyon floor, scrubbing her hands hard on the slick dirt. The mud and mire didn't do much good, but it was better than the alternative, and she scraped her palms until they were red and sore, not realizing that her gasp had reverberated off the canyon walls.

Past the tumbling heaps, at the yawning canyon's other end, two Guards stood to Kai's right and left. One of them turned, and Elysia paused, flicking her eyes in the Guard's direction. It was James. His plump, ruddy face was peering past the gruesome towers, searching.

Silently, she sank further behind the nearest corpse heap, pressing her back against the canyon wall. She waited, listening for footfalls, as the clouded, glassy eye of a dead Merrow man stared vacantly out at her from the heap's middle. Elysia met his gaze, then squeezed her eyes shut, avoiding him.

No footfalls came, and in a moment, she crept from her hiding place. She sneaked further towards Kai as James turned away, ducking behind a closer heap and then, a closer one. There were two heaps in front of her now, and as she lunged behind the left one, her foot squished into a trail of the slimy filth from the wall. She winced, lifted her foot as the stringy, opaque trail strung towards the ground. Quickly, she swiped her foot along a patch of dark moss, then she followed the trail of slime with her eyes. It wound past Kai's feet, before disappearing into a dark, yawning cavern in front of him.

Elysia shrank from the wide opening, returning her eyes to Kai. She frowned. His Guards were arguing behind his head. Their whispers hissed, and she strained to hear, but she couldn't catch their words.

All at once, the two became quiet. James whistled low, then he dashed for the canyon wall, slipping and sliding as he went. The other Guard waited, poised to run as he stared hard at the yawning opening. Then he moved to follow him.

Halfway to the wall, he slipped in the slick mud. He landed hard on his side, but he quickly righted himself. He scrambled to his feet, following James as he climbed swiftly up a set of rough-hewn steps in the wall. Then the two breached the surface, disappearing out of sight.

Only Kai remained. He squared his shoulders, staring hard into the dark abyss in front of him. In moments, a low, rumbling growl echoed through the canyon, and Elysia watched in horror as the enormous sea snake, Nathair, appeared.

He slithered out of the opening on his slimy, slick belly, and his dark, iridescent scales glittered in the muted light. Nathair stopped at Kai's head, dipping his mouth as he ruffled his silver hair with a deep hiss. Then, slowly, he wound himself in a wide circle.

Nathair wrapped Kai's chained body with his long one, looping himself into three loose coils. Then he lifted his head above them, staring down at Kai with his dark, intelligent eyes. "MMMmmm, what have we here," Nathair hissed. His long, dark tongue darted in and out of his mouth with his breath. "It'ss a sssweet merrow, jussst for mee."

One by one, Nathair tightened his coils, and Elysia watched in horror as Kai was squeezed in the snake's tight grip. Kai squirmed, and Nathair grinned wide around his long, yellow fangs.

"There'ss no ussse trying to break free, little one. No one esscapesss me." He squeezed, and Kai groaned. "You've broken the treaty, and now, you mussst pay the priccce." He grinned, licking with his pointed tongue. "But today isss your lucky day. I'm ssstarved. SSo, I'll make it quick. I'll eat you in jussst one bite."

Nathair squeezed even tighter, and Elysia winced. Kai's face was growing purple from the pressure. His eyes rolled back as Nathair reared upward, opening his fangs wide.

Elysia was frozen. She had to do something, or Kai was going to die. At once, she snapped her eyes shut. She focused hard, closing out all sound.

In the white, shimmering landscape of her mind, she could see Nathair's jaws descending towards Kai's head. She breathed in and out, concentrating, and then a whispering melody snaked backward from Nathair's frame to her ears. Silently, she allowed it to coil inside of her chest. Then she pressed her lips together and began to hum.

At first, the melody was soft and slow, but, as she continued, the Voice in her mind grew, and soon, her own voice grew with it. She should have been afraid of the horrible sea snake, but as she stepped from her hiding place, she realized her fear was gone. She squared her shoulders as she moved into view, staring directly into the sea serpent's eyes.

Kai roused momentarily as she appeared. A look of shock passed his face before his eyes rolled back, and he fainted under the snake's squeezing pressure. Nathair ignored him. He was fixated on Elysia. His dark eyes glimmered, and she stared back at him as she continued to sing, her voice undulating in a series of *Oooos.*

All at once, the snake loosened his coils. He moved toward her as Kai fell to the canyon floor in a heavy heap. He began to circle her, and Elysia stared deeply into his eyes as the snake wound himself around her three times, just as he had done with Kai.

She held his gaze, unflinching, and as he watched her sing, Nathair's eyes began to soften. Elysia grinned. Slowly, she lifted her hands, swirling her fingers above her head to the melody. The snake followed their path, swaying his head lazily from side to side. Then, slowly, she lowered her hands towards the ground.

Nathair followed them. His eyes were growing heavy. They were almost slits as he relaxed himself against the canyon floor. Then they closed completely, and he grew still and quiet.

Elysia watched him warily as his mouth went slack. His breathing was even, and she continued to hum as she climbed up and out of his coils. Kai was waiting, just outside. He was sitting limply on the ground, and she took hold of his arm, pulling him upright. He started to speak, but she held a finger to her lips, continuing her hum as they backed away. Then, together, they climbed the rough steps up and out of the canyon, with the sleeping Nathair none the wiser.

Once they were safely out of sight, Kai held out his arms. He braced his chained wrists on a flat stone as Elysia lifted a large rock, smashing them in two. Then they swam furiously away from the horrifying snake's canyon.

Soon, they approached Elysia's reef. Kai's Guards were perched where she had hidden, behind the large orange coral. Kai frowned in their direction. He started to swim their way, but Elysia stayed his arm. "Let me handle them," she said quietly.

James had already spotted them. He moved quickly toward Kai with his spear raised, but Elysia blocked his path. She held up her palm, glowering.

"I wouldn't do that, if I were you," she said flatly. James flicked his eyes to the other Guard uncertainly, and Elysia folded her arms, glaring at them.

"When this ends…and it *will*, whose side would you rather be on? Two disgraced, Selkie nobleman, with enemies all around? Or the heirs to the selkie and merrow thrones?"

She jerked her chin at Kai. "Lord Kai and I have agreed to pardon you, but only if you let us go." She peered casually over her shoulder, where the surface of Nathair's canyon glittered ominously in the distance.

"If not…well, the sea snake won't sleep forever. And he'll be hungry when he wakes."

The Guards shifted nervously, and she raised her brow, watching as they lowered their spears. James bowed slightly. "As you command, my Lady," he said gruffly. Elysia nodded, and the two bowed low. Then they turned away, swimming far into the distance.

Kai stood stiffly beside her, staring after the Selkie Guards. Elysia turned to him, grinning. Relief washed over her in waves at his narrow escape, and she forgot that they weren't really on speaking terms. "I've saved you twice, now," she said, teasing. "We're even."

She waited for him to smile, studying the turn of his jaw. A muscle feathered there, under her gaze, but his lips didn't lift, and, *still,* he refused to look at her. She huffed, rolling her eyes.

"Actually, I've saved you four times," he muttered. "One diving spider, two attackers in the Court of Merrows, and the river."

Elysia ground her teeth. He had saved her so many times, she had forgotten a couple of them. "Fine," she said flatly. "Let's go."

She started to swim away, but Kai cleared his throat. "I lost the Tamarisk," he muttered.

"It fell from my pocket when we hit the water." She flicked her eyes to him, frowning, as he stared blankly past her tail. His refusal to look at her was *most* irritating. "By now, it will have washed to shore on the Selkie Isles. It's probably close to where I dropped my spear. We'll have to go there, first."

He brushed past her, swimming furiously, as Elysia glared daggers at his tail. Its glittering blue hue reminded her of his frigid, vacant eyes. "Fine," she whispered to his retreating frame. "If you want to ignore me, then I can ignore you, too." She ground her teeth, trailing after him.

They reached the shoreline quickly, mostly due to Kai's furious swimming. Elysia lifted her head tentatively from the water, scanning the shoreline. The coast was clear, and she stood, gathering her water weaving.

Kai was already on the shore. He swiped his spear, examining the blade as Elysia moved behind him. There, she combed the small rocks, searching for Tamarisk blooms. The tiny blossoms were scattered across the rocks like a miniature constellation of tiny, pink stars. She picked up one, and then another, and another, until her hand was full.

Behind her, the sun was beginning to lower on the horizon. She shielded her eyes, peering warily at its pink-tinged rays, which glittered sideways across the water. Their horrifying visit to Nathair's dark canyon had taken much longer than she anticipated. If Ena was still alive, she only had until the end of the day, and even still, Elysia wasn't sure they could make it.

Quickly, she searched the shoreline for something to hold the tiny blooms. They had to hurry, or it would be too late. She spied an abandoned gull's nest tucked beneath a large boulder, and she lifted it, examining its size and shape. The small nest had a cup-like design. It had been tightly woven with tough sea grasses, and Elysia decided it would do nicely to carry the Tamarisk. She began dropping the pink blossoms into it.

Kai noticed what she was doing. Silently, he unwound a thin, leather strap from the shaft of his spear. He moved towards her, holding out his hand. She glared at his palm, then looked away, holding out the small nest. Wordlessly, he took it, then he wove the thin strap through the top and sinched it like a purse string. Silently, he handed the purse back to her, and Elysia tied the strap snugly around her waist. Then he dove under as Elysia followed, headed for the tunnels.

Kai was waiting for her, when she surfaced inside the first cavern. He cleared his throat, staring flatly at the air to her left. "I'll carry you the rest of the way," he said coolly. "We need to hurry. Ena doesn't have much longer."

Elysia twisted her lips, but Kai didn't wait for an answer. He swept her swiftly into his arms, then dove headlong beneath the water. She glared at his jaw as he worked his powerful tail. He sped through the tunnel, holding her stiffly, being careful to keep his steely blue eyes trained on the path ahead of them.

Elysia held her body taught against Kai's forearms, avoiding contact. He couldn't bear to look at her, and she was sure, he would rather not be carrying her, now. Absently, she shifted her hands protectively over the small nest at her waist, causing her fingers to graze his chest. Her hand blazed, and she pulled it away, glancing to his chin. She watched as his jaw tightened, and she looked away, flushing. She was right. He couldn't bear her touch either.

Slowly, she lifted her eyes to the ring on his neck. The tiny circle glittered gold against his skin, and she imagined him sitting on the steps of the treehouse, thinking of Maura. She was sure that was what he had done when he had gone ahead to the island last night.

Elysia dropped her eyes, thinking. Since then, he would barely look at her, and he spoke to her even less. She frowned. She didn't know what she had done to make him so upset.

At last, they reached the final cavern. Their clothes from Elysia's welcome dinner still lay on the rocks. Kai discarded her absently, quickly lifting from the water as Elysia turned her back. He moved behind a rock, stuffing his arms and legs into his dinner clothing while Elysia did the same. She smoothed her gown against her abdomen, clutching the small nest tightly in her palm. She peeked inside. The tiny flowers were slightly damp, but otherwise unharmed.

She started for the door, but Kai stayed her with his palm. She turned to him, grimacing, as he stared blankly at the air to her left.

"I'll go first," he said gruffly. "And don't leave my side."

Without another word, he brushed past her, moving silently through the surface of the dome.

Elysia followed him, fuming, and moments later, they emerged quietly from the birch grove. Below her, a dark patch still stained the cobblestone street. Elysia stared down at it, remembering how thick blood had pooled beneath her attacker after Kai slit his throat. The bite of his cold blade against her neck still made her stomach lurch, and she swallowed convulsively, turning away.

Ahead, merrow Forces were stationed at intervals along the small lane. They stood at attention with their spears at their sides. Elysia furtively scanned their stoic faces from beside Kai's shoulder as they passed. They never looked at her, but the lane was full of those who did. Angry merrow faces glared at her from windows and doorways, their owners whispering amongst themselves.

Ahead, on her left, a cluster of Merrow women hissed in her direction. Elysia's eyes were fixed on them, watching as they glared in disdain. All at once, she felt something wet spatter the right side of her cheek, and she jumped, thinking she had been stabbed. She swiped hard at the spot, then pulled her hand away. There was no blood. Only a wet gob spat from another angry merrow woman's face.

Immediately, Kai pushed her behind him. He spun on the woman, just as her merrow mate materialized from the shadows of the alley behind her. The mate lunged at Elysia with a large blade, and Kai sliced the crude weapon in half with his spear. The woman screamed as the Forces descended, yelling obscenities as she and her mate were dragged away. More angry voices joined the shouts, and wordlessly, Kai lifted Elysia. He slung her over his shoulder as he broke into a run, leaving the angry mob of Merrows in the lane behind them.

He ran until he reached the vine-covered tunnel. A heavy iron grate had been placed across it, and two sentries stood near the opening. "Open the gate," Kai commanded, and the right sentry did so, moving it aside as Kai stepped through. The sentry shut the grate soundly behind them, and Kai placed Elysia gently onto her feet, just inside the opening.

He sucked down a breath as she smoothed her hair, staring hard at the wall beside her head. "Are you hurt?" he asked gruffly.

Elysia frowned at his worried expression, massaging a new bruise from his grip on her waist.

"I'm fine," she said flatly.

Kai nodded once, dropping his gaze. "Good," he muttered.

Elysia rolled her eyes. She brushed past him. "As if you even care," she whispered.

They didn't speak again as they climbed high into the fortress wall, and soon, they were back at Ena's rooms. Elysia dropped to her knees next to the bed. Ena's small frame was withered in its center. She was pale yellow and barely breathing.

Seamus was curled on the bed next to her. He had fallen asleep with his arm protectively across her coverlet. Elysia eyed it as she fumbled to open the small nest purse. Kai had pulled the leather so tight that she was having trouble. "Drat," she whispered.

Seamus lifted his head at her voice. He squinted at her groggily, scratching his hair as he sat upright.

"Did you get the Tamarisk?" he asked her. He gazed down at Ena worriedly, moving a damp lock of hair behind her ear.

Elysia nodded, lifting a small bloom. "I got it."

Seamus reached to hand her a small bowl from the night table, and she poured the pink blossoms into it. She glanced up at Ena's ragged breathing as she smashed them into a fine paste. Her chest was moving in shallow gasps, and each breath sounded full of water.

Elysia sat the small bowl on the bed with a sigh.

"I just hope I'm not too late."

Carefully, Seamus lifted Ena's shoulders, and Elysia unwound the stained bandage from her waist. Seamus lowered Ena to the pillow, and Elysia pulled the last piece of linen free, gasping.

The wound had festered. It was dark and streaking, and the putrid smell of death filled the air above it. Elysia held her breath as she swiped the length of it with Tamarisk paste. It was much worse than the last time she had seen it. She wasn't sure Ena would survive.

Seamus lifted Ena once more, and Elysia wound a clean bandage around her middle.

She fixed it in place, and Seamus laid her back. He tucked the coverlet under Ena's sallow chin, brushing her damp hair with his fingers. "What now?" he whispered.

Elysia settled down on the coverlet. She put her hand over Ena's cool fingers.

"Now, we wait," she murmured. "The rest is up to the Source."

Just then, a quick knock sounded at the door. Kai answered it, and a sentry handed him a small parchment. It was tied with a silver ribbon. Kai pulled it free, then he unfurled the small missive. He frowned as he read it silently, then lifted his eyes to Elysia.

Her face paled at his expression. "What is it?" she asked softly. Quickly, Kai flicked his eyes back to the parchment, frowning.

"The Selkie Court has been invited to a dinner, here, in the Court of Merrows. Lady Sirena is calling it…" He scanned the message. "*An urgent meeting.* She has invited your mother and grandmother, as well as the council. They are all coming here. Tonight."

Elysia frowned. There hadn't been an urgent meeting between their courts since the days of her father's death. She stared at Kai in confusion, and he shrugged at the air to her left.

She turned to Seamus. "Go," he said quietly. "There's nothing more you can do for Ena, now. I'll stay with her. I promise."

Elysia nodded. Ena's breathing was still labored and ragged, and tears filled Elysia's eyes as she bent to kiss her forehead. "Seamus will take care of you, while I'm gone," she whispered. "Just promise me you'll be awake when I come back."

Chapter 20

Elysia's hands shook as she pulled a dinner gown from her armoire. She stared down at the shimmering, emerald dress uncertainly, then put it back, frowning. What was she supposed to wear to an *urgent meeting* in the Court of Merrows?

She pulled and replaced several other dresses before she decided on a strappy, silver gown. It was formal enough to be appropriate, she hoped, and yet, it was still understated. The narrow column of silk danced lightly over her slim curves, and the skirt fell just above the floor, highlighting her silver heels. Tiny white roses swirled across the hem, and Elysia chose a simple pair of drop earrings to match them. The white rose was the crest of the Selkie Court, and her mother was very fond of the flower. Elysia had chosen her dress with her mother in mind, as a thanks for saving Kai's skin.

She selected a matching tiara, a thin circle of silver that dipped over her forehead, then moved to the full-length mirror.

Elysia smiled at her reflection. Despite a few rough days, and a few bumps and bruises, she was rather pleased with her appearance. As she had hoped, the color of her dress enhanced the creaminess of her skin, and the tiara drew attention to her wide eyes, which she had enhanced with a delicate shimmer of pearl powder. Her hair had been brushed until it shone, and it hung loose down her back in a dark mass of curls. She ran her fingers through it, then tucked a lock behind her ear. Despite herself, she wondered what Kai would think.

Just then, a soft knock sounded on the hall door, and a little thrill shot through Elysia's belly. That would be him. She took one last look at herself, straightening her already straight tiara. She had told herself that she was dressing for her own satisfaction, but she knew that wasn't entirely true. Despite her wish to make it otherwise, Kai's opinion of her mattered—more than she dared to admit. She knew he didn't think of her, in *that* way, but she couldn't help imagining the look on his face when he saw her, in a moment.

She took a deep breath as she stepped towards the hall, then she pulled the door wide. Kai stood waiting for her in the middle of the hall. He was facing slightly away from her, gripping tightly to his spear. Elysia flicked her eyes over him, smiling quietly at his appearance. He was dressed much the same as he had for her welcome dinner, but this time his suit was a deep blue. It made the blue of his sharp eyes seem even brighter.

"Hi," she said shyly.

Kai peeked at her from the corner of his gaze. Silently, he wound his eyes up her frame, gripping white knuckles on his spear. For a moment, he lingered on her hair. As he studied it, a look of despair, then disgust, crossed his features, and he flicked his eyes away. His jaw flexed and he cleared his throat. "Hello," he croaked.

His face was back to its hard mask as he held out his arm. Elysia took it reluctantly, falling in line as he marched stiffly beside her. She bit her lip, casting furtive glances in his direction as they moved down the hall.

Kai never acknowledged her. Instead, he stared straight ahead, the picture of a perfect Merrow Forces escort. Silently, Elysia moved a hand to her hair. Surely, she wasn't *that* unappealing.

By the time they reached the gardens, she had had enough. She pulled away, moving in front of him to block his path. She glared up at him, crossing her arms.

"What's wrong with you?" she hissed.

Kai frowned lightly at the air to her right. "What do you mean?" he said quietly. Elysia huffed, tucking a lock of hair behind her ear. He knew very well what she meant.

"You know *exactly* what I mean," she spat. "Ever since you left in the middle of the night to visit the secret island, you've been acting strange. You won't look at me, and you barely speak." She shook her head, flicking her eyes to the dome and back. "Even after I *saved* your *life* with Nathair, you *still* act the same!"

Her face was hot, and her throat was getting tight. She swallowed, then took a calming breath, steadying her voice.

"I understand that you might not find me…appealing, but you don't have to be so rude about it."

Kai scoffed. "Oh, *I'm sorry*, you saved me all of *one time*, and now I'm supposed to be indebted to you?!" He chuckled mirthlessly. "What a laugh! You can't go ten steps without me saving you from one calamity or another! If anything, *you* are the one who owes *me!*"

Elysia narrowed her eyes. "Twice. I saved you twice, Kai. And you *still* haven't answered my question."

Kai glared wordlessly at the air to her right. She stepped in front of his line of vision, and he dropped his eyes, staring at the ground. Elysia clenched her fists. She wanted to shout, but she pressed her lips together, struggling for control. "Why won't you look at me, Kai?" she said quietly.

Kai blew out a breath. Silently, he brushed past her to balance his spear against the trunk of the oak tree that flanked the entrance to the garden. Then he stood before her, clenching his fists. He started at the ground near her feet. Then, slowly, he wove his eyes upward.

Elysia watched, studying his expression. His face was a mix of anguish and longing. She could see he was fighting for control, but from what, she couldn't decide. Either he wanted to look at her, or he didn't. She wasn't sure.

His expression changed when he met her eyes, and he paused there, holding her in his grip. His blue eyes glittered in the evening light. They were deep pools, and as Elysia studied them, she was worried she might drown. Wordlessly, he stepped towards her.

The air became heavy as Elysia stepped backward, the only sound their breathing. She stumbled over a tree root, catching herself against the trunk as Kai reached to catch her.

Silently, he grasped her waist, tugging her close. Then, he brought one finger to the edge of her chin.

Slowly, he lowered his face to her ear. "I'm looking at you now, aren't I?" he said gruffly.

Elysia's chest flared as Kai pulled slowly away, brushing the stubble of his beard lightly against her cheek. She shivered. "Yes," she breathed.

He peered down at her heavily as he balanced his free hand on the tree above her, watching as she studied his face. Silver moonbeams streamed through the branches, illuminating the tiny, translucent scales trailing up the skin in front of his ear. She followed their path, as silently, he brought his fingers to her hair.

He studied a strand of it as he wound it into his palm, then he flicked his eyes to her lips. Elysia's heart leapt into her throat. She was sure he was going to kiss her.

He lowered his face, then all at once, his eyes went dark. The muscle in his jaw flexed, and he dropped his hand, stepping away.

Elysia collapsed weakly against the tree trunk. Her heart was thrumming against her ribs, and she swallowed hard, willing it to slow. She blinked in confusion, watching as Kai brought one hand to smooth his hair. His face was grim, and his eyes were back to the steely blue stare. He cleared his throat as he straightened the collar of his jacket.

"We're late," he said gruffly.

Elysia didn't answer. She wasn't sure she could have if she had wanted to. Wordlessly, Kai stepped beside her, swiping his spear. Then he turned away, striding purposefully through the garden.

The feeling of his beard on her cheek lingered, and Elysia put her hand to the spot, frowning after him. She was more confused than ever. A moment ago, she would have sworn that he was going to kiss her. He had studied her so deeply; she was almost sure of it. Then, for no apparent reason, at least none that she could fathom, his behavior changed. He had switched his act, returning to the stoic Merrow escort, again.

She glared at his retreating frame. Was that all that it had been? Just an act to make her stop questioning him? Her face burned, and she straightened, smoothing her dress. Well, he wouldn't find her asking anything of him, ever again. Not. Ever. She lifted her chin, skirting the lily pads as she followed him to the palace doors.

Kai was waiting for her, just inside. He was facing away from her, leaning casually against the glass wall. As she neared him, he extended his arm, but she ignored it, brushing past him as she moved briskly towards the dining hall.

Once there, Elysia folded her arms, glaring at the door. She would have just gone inside, but she couldn't very well enter without him. He was still her escort, after all. Everyone would expect him to be at her side, especially Lady Sirena.

In a moment, he appeared beside her. Elysia kept her eyes trained on the door as he cleared his throat. He faced her, then, and opened his mouth, "I…" but he didn't finish. He sighed as he studied the side of her head, closing it again. Still, she ignored him, and he growled under his breath as he spun to face the doors. Then, he pulled them open.

The dining hall was even more lavishly decorated than the last time Elysia had seen it. Moonflowers hung heavily from the domed ceiling, filling the room with a heady scent. They had doubled in size and number, and Evening Stars took up every available space along the wall.

Silver chairs lined the long table, while bone white plates, fluted glasses, and silver flatware rested on a thick white tablecloth, before each seat.

Elysia moved towards her chair. A single white rose, the crest of the Selkie Court, floated inside a votive before her plate. It was encircled by a single, flowering water thistle. She recognized the thorny, silver thistle as the crest of the Court of Merrows.

She flicked her eyes to the place next to her, frowning. An identical votive sat on the table in front of Kai's plate. She examined it as she took her seat and Kai pulled out his chair, watching as the floating thistle circled the rose. Something about the combination set off warning bells, but she couldn't place why.

Elysia's mother was seated at the opposite end of the long table, while Lady Sirena sat at the other. The selkie and merrow council members took the seats at the sides. They talked softly amongst themselves, while servants poured glittering, bubbly drinks into their fluted glasses.

To Elysia's surprise, Lord Ciar was among them. She froze as he pulled out his seat, watching him warily before she flicked her eyes to her mother. Lady Malca sat stiffly, staring daggers at him as he took his chair. He inclined his head to her before he grinned flatly at Elysia, then he flicked out his napkin, his dark eyes glittering angrily.

Elysia watched him, wondering how he had weaseled his way into this meeting. Her mother had made it clear that Ciar and his son were relieved of their duties to the Selkie Court. That included Lord Ciar's position on the council. Elysia was sure he would be hearing from her mother about his intrusion, later, but right now, Lady Malca wouldn't dare disrupt their gathering, and Ciar knew it.

Elysia's grandmother was seated just to her mother's right. She sipped from her glass, peering across the table at Kai, then she sat down her drink, smiling softly in his direction. Elysia raised her brows as she gave her grandmother a small wave. She flicked her eyes to Kai and back in confusion. Had her grandmother just *smiled* at Kai—the son of the silver-haired merrow who had taken her own son away? *Strange.*

A light *ting* drew her attention to the other end of the table. Lady Sirena stood there, tapping her glass softly. She smiled when she had the table's attention.

"Good evening, to all, and a special welcome to our friends from the Selkie Isles. Lady Malca, Mother Ríona, members of the council, we are most pleased by your presence here tonight.

As you well know, both of our courts have experienced much discord in recent days. In fact, it has come to my attention that there have been riots in the Selkie Court, much like we have experienced here, in the Court of Merrows. These uprisings are a signal to us of what has long festered beneath the surface of our tenuous relationship.

Since the murder of your blessed leader, Lord Ríonan, by my cursed father, Lord Dolion, we two courts have been at odds. Gone are the days when our clans lived in peace. Indeed, many of our people do not recall those days. Bitterness and hate are all they have ever known.

Much of this is due to the Treaty of Hiraeth, which was crafted by my own father and forced upon our two clans, on pain of death." She paused, scanning the table with her sharp green eyes. "However, a new day dawns."

Elysia flicked her eyes to her mother. She didn't understand where Lady Sirena was going with her speech, but something about it was making her nervous. Lady Malca gave her a small nod. She smiled encouragingly, and Elysia gave her a small grin.

Her mother looked away, and Elysia furrowed her brow. She scanned her mother's face, watching as she lifted her glass. She seemed completely at ease. It was strange, considering how unsettled her mother had been in past meetings.

Lady Sirena continued. "For several Quarters, the esteemed Lady Malca and I have been crafting a plan with the help of our councils. But for fear we would sow more discord; we have been forced to keep it a secret. We couldn't risk anyone knowing, until we were certain our plan would succeed." She flicked her eyes to Kai and Elysia, smiling. "Not even our own heirs knew anything about it. However, I am proud to say, our little trial has proven a success."

She raised her glass to Elysia's mother, smiling. "I must first thank Lady Malca and her council for so graciously allowing the beautiful Lady Elysia to visit our court." She nodded to Elysia. "Elysia, you believed you were simply here on an ambassador's visit. But we all had something more in mind."

Elysia flicked her eyes to her mother, then her grandmother. Both were beaming at her with pride. Elysia frowned. Something was happening, but she didn't know what.

Lady Sirena put a hand to Kai's shoulder, addressing the room. "We had planned to give these young ones a few more days together before we revealed our plan, but due to worsening tensions and the recent threats of harm to us all, we feel we should make our plans known." She paused, glaring at Lord Ciar's seat before turning her gaze.

"On this night, we have come together for a dual purpose. Our first aim is to amend the Treaty of Hiraeth. Long has this foul document kept our people in bondage, and long it has been my wish to see it destroyed. The day has now come for us to move beyond my father's treaty, and I hope its amendment will restore what he has broken."

She turned to Kai and Elysia, smiling brightly.

"The second purpose may be more important than the first. I…well, we *all* wish it to be a symbol of our restoration, a beacon of hope in a sea of darkness."

Elysia's heart was beginning a strange thrum. She watched as Lady Sirena's hand lightly squeezed Kai's shoulder. The ruler's face beamed down at her, and Elysia felt her insides turn out. She struggled to lift her face in a grin. What in the known worlds was happening?

Lady Sirena raised her glass. "I am pleased to announce that our heirs, Kai Bennet and Elysia Bryn, will join our courts in a bond of marriage. And let me be the first to say, congratulations."

Elysia felt her face fall flat. Panic rose in her chest, and her hearing turned to a buzz. Lady Sirena continued.

"This will be the first marriage between our courts in many cycles, and Lady Malca and I are hopeful that such a sacred bond will aid in the unification of our people. In efforts to expedite this process, the wedding will be held here, in the throne room, tomorrow evening."

Elysia sat stunned as the patter of light applause fanned around the table. Murmured congratulations pinged against her ears, and she pasted on a flat smile, struggling against the panic rising in her throat.

Suddenly, the hard scrape of a chair sounded against the floor. The room fell silent as Lord Ciar stood. He glared at Lady Sirena as he threw his napkin onto his plate, flicking his eyes over Kai and Elysia in disgust. Then turned to her mother, pointing his finger. "Like my son said, you'll regret this," he hissed.

Then he stormed out of the dining hall.

Elysia's ears still buzzed as she watched the door slam behind him. She had heard nothing after the *bond of marriage*. Her eyes pricked, and she swallowed around an enormous lump as she flicked her eyes to Kai. He appeared just as horrified as she. Stiffly, he reached for his fluted glass, then he swallowed the bubbly, golden liquid in one gulp.

Lady Sirena raised her own glass. "A toast, in celebration of the new couple. Kai, Elysia, may your marriage be the first step towards the healing and unification of our clans; the Selkie and the Merrow."

Every glass raised high, and Elysia lifted hers weakly to join them. Silently, she stole a glance at her grandmother beneath it. Ríona smiled encouragingly, and Elysia returned the gesture, although she struggled to lift the corners of her lips.

Things were starting to make sense. At first, she hadn't understood why Lady Sirena would ask her to visit the Court of Merrows, or why her mother and the councils would agree to it. At the ball, she had thought it odd that Alistair had mentioned a rule she had never heard, but she had just assumed it was true that Selkie rulers could make their own decisions when they came of age. Apparently, she had been wrong. There was no rule. The rulers and their councils had been planning her marriage to Kai, all along. She wondered if he had known.

She peered sideways, braving another glance at him. By the looks of it, he hadn't known anything about it. His arms rested weakly on the table, and his face was a strange shade of pale green. She was sure he looked like she had after the diving spider.

Elysia sank limply into her chair, as Lady Sirena led her mother and a line of council members to a small table in the far corner. On top of it, two large parchments lay side by side. Lady Sirena lifted one gingerly. She smiled broadly as she tore it in half, and the room erupted in applause. She let the pieces flutter to the floor, then she signed the new document with a flourish, as did her mother, and every single council member.

Elysia gripped her napkin beneath the table. She turned her eyes to Kai, watching as he unbuttoned the collar of his crisp dinner shirt. He didn't look happy. His face was flushed, and though she tried to ignore him, his presence in the chair beside her was amplified in light of their recent news.

Their wedding was *tomorrow*, and it was obvious he was disgusted with the idea. He blew out a breath, flicking his eyes briefly in her direction, but when she met his gaze, he looked away, flattening his mouth into a hard line.

He stood as Elysia folded her arms, sinking further into her seat. She wished she could disappear or flee the room. Anything would be better than sitting next to someone that wanted nothing to do with her. Of course, she wasn't exactly thrilled with the prospect of being with Kai, but at least she could look at him. How were they supposed to unify the courts, to be married, with all that entailed, if he couldn't even look at her?

Silently, she dragged herself from her seat. Her feet felt like stones as she followed Kai to the small table, where they would finalize their futures and those of their Selkie and Merrow homes. She watched as Kai took the quill steadily from Lady Sirena's hand. He didn't pause to look at its words. Instead, he scrawled his name quickly at the bottom.

His face was a stony mask as he spun. Wordlessly, he held out the quill, staring blankly at the air to Elysia's left. Elysia took it with a shaking hand. Before she signed, she flicked her eyes over the page.

THE TREATY OF HIRAETH
WITH HOPE FOR THE LOST LANDS OF PEACE
BY DECREE OF LADY SIRENA AND LADY MALCA

Henceforth,

❀ *Merrows and selkies shall pass freely between both courts, without necessity of permission.*

❀ *A merrow man may look upon a selkie woman, provided she is accepting of such advances.*

❀ *If such advances are accepted, courtship and intermarriage between selkie and merrow is permitted. Likewise, any children borne of such a relationship may stand.*

We hereby agree to the changes made in this document by the sign of our hand and seal its words with the forthcoming marriage of the respective heirs: Kai Bennet and Elysia Bryn.
Furthermore, we abolish the separation of our courts, and renew the harmonious relationship that we once knew. Let us no longer be called Selkie Court and Court of Merrows. Let us, once more, be joined

under a single name, the name of our forebearers.
Let our clans be known as
The Court of the Sea.
We recommend these changes,
as a right to life,
From this day,
Until the end.

With a shaking hand, Elysia signed her name beneath Kai's script. And with her signature, she bound herself to him for the remainder of her days.

Chapter 21

Kai climbed the treehouse steps with heavy feet. Wearily, he laid the Tamarisk fronds in a stream of moonlight by the door, then he sank down against the far wall to wait. He sighed, closing his eyes as he let his head rest against the wall. The events of the night weighed heavily on his heart and mind, and his emotions were raw and ragged.

A long while passed, and Kai almost gave up hope before Maura's tenuous frame appeared. Her colors were more muted than before, and her face was drawn and sallow. In fact, Kai could see straight through her to the wood wall behind.

He studied her worriedly as she lifted her lips in a wan smile. Their edges were tinged with a faint hint of blue. Weakly, she lifted her hand. "Hi," she whispered. The sound echoed, as if she spoke from a far distance.

Kai smiled back at her, waving. "Hi. It's good to see you."

Maura closed her eyes, and he studied her translucent frame, shifting uncomfortably. She didn't look good. He cleared his throat.

"I…I have some news," he said slowly.

Maura opened her eyes to slits. "You're to be wed," she said distantly.

"To that lovely selkie. Lady Elysia Bryn." She gave him a broad smile, but Kai could tell the expression exhausted her. She sighed heavily, shutting her eyes again. "Congratulations, Kai," she mumbled.

Just then, her frame flickered, moving briefly out of view. Kai scrambled to the middle of the treehouse floor. "Maura, please, don't leave me," he pleaded.

Maura's color had faded to sheer grey. She peered at him tiredly.

"My Time here with you was only ever limited, Kai," she said weakly. "And now, it has come to an end."

Tears filled his eyes as Kai shook his head violently back and forth. His throat was constricting, and he swallowed past the large lump. "But, I…I need you here with me. I can't live without you, Maura."

Maura eyed him patiently from her place on the wall. The color around her lips was darkening, and her breathing was labored. She gave a little cough, then slowly cleared her throat.

"Kai, I want you to listen closely to my words," she said gently.

"My days here have passed. Now, I belong with the Source. In gracious love and kindness, we have been allowed these few visits." She smiled lovingly as she shook her head slowly back and forth. "But it was never permanent. Nothing is, in this life. Only those things which are eternal can remain, in the end."

She pulled in a ragged breath. "You and I, our love, was a tiny, glorious piece of those eternal things. Its mark will never leave you. You are forever changed. But after I go, the days of former things will have long passed, and it will be time for you to experience something new. You must open your heart, Kai. Let go and allow yourself to be free."

A racking cough shook her frame, and her already grey color drained almost completely. Kai shook his head furiously as tears spilled over, staining his cheeks. "I could never be free," he choked. "Our love was too big. It was too deep, and my pain is too great."

She nodded. "A burden borne alone is often too heavy to bear. You were never meant to carry it alone. Give it to the Source and give Elysia a chance. Allow yourself to be open with her. You might be surprised what comes of it."

She paused as Kai wiped his tear-stained cheek with the back of his hand. "I don't know how to do that," he muttered. He blew out a breath, and Maura twisted her mouth to the side, stifling a grin. "You might start by allowing yourself to look at her."

Kai shot her a look as Maura's tinkling laughter echoed against the treehouse wall. She smiled through her fading lips. "She loves you, you know. She just doesn't know it yet."

Kai flicked his eyes up to her, frowning. She nodded encouragingly. "And you might love her, too, if you'd allow it."

Kai dropped his gaze. He picked absently at the floorboards, and she waited a moment, studying his face.

"I want you to make me a promise," she murmured. "A real one. And just because I'm a translucent patch of moonlight on this side, doesn't mean I am on the other." She lifted her finger accusingly, narrowing her eyes. "I'll know if you break it."

Kai grinned through his tears. He nodded slowly, still wishing she could stay, as Maura pulled in a ragged breath. "It's a dual promise, okay?"

"Okay," Kai choked.

She watched him closely. "I don't want you to try to bring me here, again," she said slowly. "I want you to let me go, once and for all." She paused, waiting.

Kai folded his arms across his middle. He had to, or he was going to fall to pieces. He bit the inside of his cheek, his voice wavering. "Okay," he whispered.

Maura visibly relaxed. Her frame flickered in and out again. "Good," she said, nodding. "Because I need to stop coming here. I have things to do, in the Hereafter."

Kai frowned. "What things?" Maura twisted her lips. She peered out the window, thinking. "I'm not really supposed to explain it to you, but...I have a job to do."

She turned her head weakly to face him, smiling. "You'll

understand. One day."

She sighed contentedly as she sank further into the wall, eyeing the golden ring around his neck. "And for the other part of the promise." She flicked her eyes to his face.

"I want you to let yourself love Elysia Bryn."

Kai sagged heavily against the other wall. He studied Maura's sheer face, his heart squeezing. "I'll try," he murmured. "I'm not sure I can do it, but I promise I'll try."

Maura smiled broadly. She was fading quickly, despite the strong stream of silver moonlight.

"Good. My work here is done." she said teasingly. Kai rolled his eyes. "Very funny."

Maura's limbs were rapidly disappearing. Her left leg and right arm were already half gone. Kai scrambled to his knees. He swallowed through another lump, hurrying to get out his words before Maura faded out of sight.

"I love you, Maura. I'll never not be able to love you. You can't ask that of me," he choked.

Maura peered at him distantly. Her voice was very thin, and he had to strain to hear her words. "I would never ask that, Kai. I know it's not possible. But your capacity for love is much bigger than you think.

Our hearts will always be connected through the door, from your room on this side to mine in the Hereafter, like we're tied with a long string. It's true of everyone who has loved and lost. But you can't let what we had make you close the doors of your heart to all others, or you may miss something great. You might even miss your destiny."

At last, Maura faded completely from view, her final words a distant echo in the bright moonbeams. "Open the doors of your heart, Kai. Form a new bond. Let yourself love again."

Kai peered, heartbroken, at the wall where Maura had been. The Tamarisk fronds sagged forlorn against it, and as he watched, the pink petals began to wither and fall. The string tied from his heart to Maura's tugged, and he hung his head, sobbing.

He cried for Maura's untimely death, and for the future they would never experience. He cried for the love he had lost, and for all his hopes that had been dashed to pieces on the rocks of Maura's absence. Then, finally, he cried from the deep aching place in his chest that burned with Elysia's songs—his Amloga, his Flame of Time, his connection to the Source. The ache flared to the left his heart, and Kai pressed it with his fingers, wincing.

Despite his best efforts to keep her, Maura was gone. He would never see her again. At least, not on this side. He sat up, wiping his cheeks. Tomorrow, he would marry Elysia and start a new life. The thought seemed unimaginable.

On his way out the door, he brushed the withered Tamarisk blooms lightly with his fingers. Then he pulled his hand away, leaving them lying in their place as he climbed down the wooden steps.

He paused at the bottom, leaning against the stairs as he pondered Maura's words.

Elysia Bryn was lovely, to be sure, and interesting, in an irritating sort of way. He couldn't deny that he had feelings for her. He might even love her if he allowed it. Maura was right about that.

He half smiled, thinking of her greenish-gold eyes glaring up at him. She certainly had a temper to match his own, and something about her angry expression made him want to wrap her in his arms. In fact, when she had glared up at him in the garden last night, he had almost kissed her. Almost.

Kai swallowed hard. It seemed Maura knew his own feelings better than he did himself. Absently, he threaded his finger through the small golden band at his neck. Maura had made him promise he would try with Elysia, and he had agreed that he would. Anyway, he might as well. She was going to be his wife, whether he liked it or not.

He peered up through the Cypress branches. The dual moons had faded from view, and a faint pinkish purple line fringed the horizon. As best he could, he would keep his promise to Maura. As hard as it was, he would try to open the doors of his heart to Elysia. But after how he had acted, he was almost sure she wouldn't do the same.

Chapter 22

Elysia stared uncertainly into the long mirror. It was late afternoon, and her mother was fluttering about her head, putting the finishing touches on her hair. Her grandmother sat behind her on the bed. She smiled at Elysia through the glass, then she turned to the window, sighing tiredly. Elysia frowned. She looked rather pale.

Her mother stepped away, and Elysia twisted her lips, studying her own reflection. Her hair was pulled back, and a slim, silver tiara with a pendant of glittering sea glass dipped over her forehead. Small, dark curls framed her face, and the rest of her hair cascaded down her back in a fishtailed design. She patted her head, then spun, holding out the skirt of her wedding gown. Her mother had brought it along for after their *urgent meeting*. Elysia still couldn't believe it.

The long gown was white satin, and delicate beading swirled in a pattern of tiny, silver scales from the strapless top to the trumpeted skirt. Its waist was sinched with a wide band of white roses, and behind, the hem trailed out in a wide train.

The train was Elysia's favorite part, by far. The pattern of tiny scales grew smaller and smaller, until finally, they melded into a smooth, silver tail. She twisted to examine it, then turned back to her mother and grandmother.

"What do you think?" she asked, grinning.

Lady Malca's eyes brimmed. She smiled broadly at Elysia.

"You're perfect, my darling," she said quietly. Elysia flicked her eyes to her grandmother, raising her brows. "Grandmother?"

Ríona brought a shaky hand to her chest. She sniffed, dabbing her damp eyes with a delicate lace handkerchief. "I've never seen a lovelier betrothed," she whispered.

Elysia moved towards her. She sank onto her knees, frowning up at her grandmother's features. They were drawn, and a fine sheen of sweat blanketed her brow. Worriedly, Elysia placed her hand to it. Her grandmother was too warm. Lady Malca sank down beside her, placing a cool palm to Ríona's cheek. She creased her brow, her voice full of concern.

"Grandmother, are you feeling alright?" she asked.

Ríona fluttered her hands, dismissing the two younger women.

"Yes, yes, I'm fine. I just need a lie down before the festivities begin." She dabbed at her forehead with her handkerchief, then met

Elysia's gaze. "But before I go, I have a little gift for you, Elysia."

A small, beaded clutch lay in her grandmother's lap. Quietly, Ríona reached a plump hand inside of it, producing a small velvet wrapper. She pressed the wrapper into Elysia's hand, closing her own palm on top of it.

Her soft brown eyes crinkled at the edges as she smiled down at Elysia.

"This is a wedding gift," she said quietly. "From your father."

Elysia peered down at the small gift in surprise. Reverently, she brushed her fingers over the soft blue velvet. It was rolled like a scroll and closed in the center by a thin, silver ribbon. Tears pricked her eyes, and she blinked past them. "What is it?" she murmured softly.

"It's a message," said her grandmother. "To be opened when the moment is right."

Elysia frowned at the silver ribbon. "But how will I know when the moment is right?"

Ríona tipped her chin, and Elysia blinked up at her soft brown eyes. "Only you may answer that question, 'Lysia. I don't know the answer, or even what your father's message contains. He left it with me, for safekeeping, just before he was taken away. He said I would know what to do with it, but for a long while, I had no idea. Now, I feel certain. This gift belongs to you."

Slowly, her grandmother brought a shaky hand to her chest. She pressed the spot to the left of her heart. "I feel it, here, that the Time is right. It's for you to keep safe, now, and for *only* you to open."

She closed her eyes, patting her gnarled fingers over her Amloga. "You ask how you will know when to open it." She opened her eyes, smiling.

"You will know, because the Voice will speak."

On her way to the door, Ríona held up a crooked finger. Slowly, she half-turned, holding tightly to Lady Malca's arm. "I inquired about your friend, Ena. It seems your healing gift has benefitted its first body."

Elysia broke into a smile. Ena was going to be alright. Her grandmother chuckled. "It's the first of many," she said happily. She tapped her left chest, winking. "I am sure of it."

All alone, Elysia studied her father's gift. She turned it over and over in her palms, then she moved to her jewelry box and lifted the lid. Carefully, she tucked the velvet wrapper inside of it. She would think about her father's mysterious gift later. Right now, she had more pressing matters on her mind. Matters like her wedding.

CHAPTER 23

Around midnight, Elysia had heard Kai slipping into the hallway from his rooms. He hadn't returned until the early morning sunlight streamed lightly through the water outside her window, his mattress squeaking as he collapsed on top of it. He had only recently begun to stir, and Elysia sat on the bed in her wedding dress, staring at the adjoining door and wondering where he had been. Just then, a soft knock came from his side of it. Elysia looked away.

"Come in," she said flatly.

The door swung open, and Kai stepped through. He stood in the doorway, shuffling his feet nervously as Elysia stared out the window, refusing to look at him. He sighed, then cleared his throat, stepping further inside. "I want to say something," he said gruffly.

Elysia frowned down at the silver beads on her skirt. A tiny one was loose near her knee, and she picked at it absently, twisting her lips.

"Well, that's quite a change," she spat. "Especially since you've barely spoken to me the past few days." She flicked her eyes to him angrily. "Tell me, Kai, what could you possibly wish to say to me, now?"

Kai peered at her silently with his steely blue gaze. She dropped her eyes, and he moved towards the mattress. He sat down beside her, and she crossed her arms, scooting slightly away from him as she glared out the window.

He studied the side of her head. "It's more than one thing actually," he said softly.

"First, I…I wanted to apologize."

Elysia bit her cheek. Tears were already welling up in her eyes, and she willed them not to fall.

"I want to say sorry for how I've treated you, over the past few days." He paused, running a hand through his hair. "Really, for how I've treated you since we met."

He waited, watching Elysia tap her fingers rapidly against her forearm. Then he continued.

"I…I owe you an explanation. I realize I've been…distant, the past few days. It's just…well, you remember, I told you about Maura, right?"

Elysia nodded, and Kai wet his lips. "Well, you know how I told you I visit the treehouse, sometimes…to be with her."

Elysia nodded, frowning slightly. She wasn't sure where he was headed with this. "Yes," she said uncertainly.

Kai nodded. "Well, there's something I left out of the story," he said quietly.

"Something you should know."

Elysia flicked her eyes to him. "What do you mean?"

Kai hesitated, then started again.

"Lately, when I visited the treehouse, Maura was really there. I mean," He scoffed, staring up at the ceiling. "I know it sounds crazy, but she *was*, Elysia. It wasn't just her memory. It was her."

He shook his head slowly from side to side. "I put the Tamarisk fronds in the moonlight, and I wished with everything I had that she was with me, and then she just…was." He rested his elbow on his knee, cradling his forehand in his palm. "I know I sound insane, but I'm telling you the truth."

Elysia half turned to him. She studied his expression, twisting her lips.

"I believe you," she said quietly. Kai sat upright. "You do?" Elysia shrugged. "Of course." He stared at her blankly, and she grinned. "I hear the Voice of the Source, remember? Strange is sort of my normal." She frowned. "What I don't understand is what this has to do with me, or rather, what it has to do with your behavior towards me."

Kai swallowed. He angled his body to face her, studying her face with a strange expression. Then, slowly, he brought his hand to her ear. He tucked a lock of hair behind it, causing Elysia to blush.

"I…" he paused, his eyes roaming her face as the muscle in his jaw flexed. "I've been cold to you because I thought it would help me keep Maura." He dropped his eyes. "She started to fade, after the night I saw you in the Tamarisk grove." He shook his head, meeting her eyes. "You have to understand, Elysia. I loved her. I *still* love her, and I would've done anything to keep her from leaving me."

Elysia nodded slowly. She understood where he was coming from, but the words stung, especially from the man she was about to marry. A thick lump formed in her throat, and she stood from the mattress, crossing her arms. "I understand," she choked.

Kai stood quickly behind her. "No, you don't," he said gruffly. "That's not the whole story. Not by far." He swallowed, running a hand through his hair. "I have…feelings for you, Elysia. I don't know what they mean, yet, but I know that they're there."

He took a step towards her, brushing her shoulder with his chest. "That's why I tried to avoid you. It's why I tried not to look at you or speak to you. It was because I knew there was something between us. I was afraid I would lose Maura, because of it. She even said as much. She could see that something was developing between us. But now, I see the loss of her was inevitable. She doesn't belong here, anymore." He swallowed, dropping his voice. "She doesn't belong with me, now. But you do."

He reached for her arm, but Elysia shied away. She spun,

backing up against the mirror.

Slowly, Kai moved closer. He never broke his gaze, and Elysia pressed her palms to the cool glass, frozen, as he braced one hand above her. She tried to maintain her composure, but he was too close. She could feel the heat from his chest, could smell the soap lingering on his skin.

Her heart began to thrum when his eyes rested on her lips. She let her own eyes drift to his mouth, and as much as she hated it, as much as she knew he was in love with someone else, she wanted him to kiss her.

Kai watched her closely as she sucked in a breath. His eyes moved to her shoulder, then he lifted a hand to her forearm. Lightly, he ran his fingertips over her skin, trailing them to her upper arm. He lingered there for a moment, rubbing lazy circles near her shoulder with his thumb.

Her heart was pounding, now. She was losing her grip, and if she allowed him to continue, she would be lost. Her thoughts were muddled, and she shook her head, forcing them to clear. Then, slowly, she pressed a shaky hand to his chest.

She ignored his racing heart as she pushed him gently away from her, slipping beneath his arm to move towards the window. As she stared out into the open sea, her words felt thick in her throat. They nearly choked her, but she said them anyway.

"I'll wed you, for the good of our clans, but it will be nothing more," she said softly.

Kai frowned at her profile. "What do you mean?" he said quietly.

Elysia gripped her fingers into her palms, her nails digging tiny half-moons into her skin.

"I won't be *wed* to you, in any real sense." She sniffed and crossed her arms tightly over her chest. "I can't…I won't."

Kai strode towards her. He crossed his arms, glared down at the side of her face as Elysia lifted her chin. "I just poured my heart out to you," he growled. "I told you everything, and *this* is how you respond?" He scoffed, shaking his head. "Unbelievable."

Elysia spun, frowning up at him. "It's obvious, to me, that you wish you'd never met me," she said evenly. "And I'm sorry that your feelings for me have taken the love of your life from you. Truly, I am."

She paused, fighting to control her rising voice. "But I can't… *pretend*, with you, Kai. You love Maura, not me." Kai dropped his eyes, and she continued.

"It isn't necessary for this to be a *real* marriage. All we need to do is perform the marriage ceremony and live as if it is one. We are only a symbol of unity for the clans, anyway. So as long as we play our part, the rest doesn't matter."

She waited, watching as Kai studied the floor. "Are we agreed?" she asked him.

Kai blew out a breath. He lifted his gaze to the window, then back to her, nodding slowly. "Good," she said quietly. "Then we'd better go. We don't want to be late for our own wedding ceremony.

That certainly wouldn't be the best start."

She brushed past him, then, moving briskly out into the hall. She waited, focusing on the halls end, until she heard Kai shut the door. He stepped beside her, wordlessly extending his arm, and she took it, walking stiffly beside him with her features arranged in a careful, placid mask.

Kai gazed at her sidelong. He waited, but she ignored him, and he drug his gaze forward, sighing. It was obvious she wasn't going to look at him unless she absolutely had to. He narrowed his eyes. But, after everything, there was no reason he couldn't look at her, was there?

He bit his cheek, casting his eyes in her direction. Despite her fake smile, she was lovely—as lovely as he had ever seen her. He ran his eyes over her features. Now that he was allowing himself to really examine her, he was having trouble keeping his eyes away.

He flicked his gaze to her hair. It was arranged in a style he had never seen. An intricate braid fell softly down her back, and some pieces were loose on her shoulder. She tossed them over it, and he ground his teeth. He wanted to wind the strands in his hand again, like he'd done in the garden. Silently, he eyed her face. She probably wouldn't like that, though.

In a few moments, they arrived at the palace's back doors. Wordlessly, Kai stepped ahead, opening one as Elysia brushed by. He watched her retreating frame as she moved down the hallway, thinking.

Things had changed for him, since he had left the secret island this morning. He felt differently about Maura, about Elysia… about all of it. He missed Maura, and he would love her always, but when he had agreed to keep his promise, to release her and try to open himself up to Elysia, he had felt himself let go of her in a way he couldn't quite explain. His heart was still tied to her, with love and memories, but the string between them felt gauzy and tenuous, like a spider's fragile webbing. The connection wasn't like it had once been when she lived on his side of the door. He had released her from his grasp, freeing her to her side in the Hereafter. And, amazingly, he felt okay with that.

His hands were empty, now, and that provided room to hold a new possibility. That possibility was walking in front of him, and she would marry him, in a few moments. He hadn't thought it possible, but, in truth, Kai found the idea thrilling.

He grinned after her as he stepped down the hall. For now, it was probably best if she thought him indifferent to her. They hadn't even made it to their wedding vows, and already they were fighting, again. The more contact they had, the more they would surely fight. There was no way they could keep up their act as the symbol of unity for the court that way. The clans were at each other's throats, as it was. If their seal of a marriage failed, what would that mean for the newly minted Court of the Sea?

CHAPTER 24

Elysia tipped her chin, studying the throne room from her place at the foot of the dais. She was amazed at the transformation. It had always been lovely, but tonight, the glass hall was overwhelmingly beautiful.

Delicate bouquets of night-blooming jasmine scented the air, while moonflowers, Evening Stars, and water orchids had been woven into a thick tapestry that spanned the room like a living ceiling. Glowing candles lit glass chandeliers and silver candelabras, while large arrangements of white roses entwined with silver water thistles adorned every available corner.

The wedding party was small and intimate. Only the councils, Lady Sirena, Ena, Seamus, and Elysia's mother and grandmother were in attendance. Their smiling faces gathered tightly around the dais, clearly thrilled for the heirs' forthcoming union. Ena nodded to each of them politely, but she couldn't say shared their enthusiasm.

Ena grinned at her from her spot beside Seamus on the front row, leaning her head tiredly against his shoulder. She was quite pale in her blue gown. Seamus smiled contentedly as he brushed his thumb lightly against over the back of her palm. Ena grinned up at him, and he kissed her forehead, then he bent to whisper in her ear. Ena covered her mouth, giggling weakly at their private joke.

Elysia's throat tightened at the scene. She was so thankful for her friend's recovery, and she was sure Ena and Seamus would make their own wedding announcement soon. They were a perfect match, and Elysia was happy for them. But, even so, she had to admit she was a little jealous. She watched as Seamus beamed down at Ena, and her heart sank. As much as she wished it, she knew Kai would never look at her that way. The only reason he was marrying her was for the good of their court. He loved Maura, and that was that.

Kai cleared his throat loudly, and Elysia jumped as the sound echoed off the glass walls. She flushed as she stared at him across the aisle, hoping he couldn't read what she had been thinking. A slow grin formed on his lips, and she pressed her own flat, looking to Lady Sirena.

The ruler was waiting patiently to begin. She was holding a three-fold silver cord in her hand. Elysia examined its shimmering fabric. It had been braided into a single, thick strand. Lady Sirena shifted, and Elysia met her gaze. The ruler raised her brows. "Are you ready?" she whispered.

Elysia nodded. She blew out a slow breath, trying to relax, but when she turned back to Kai, she stiffened. He was holding out his hand. Elysia stared down it uncertainly, then she flicked her eyes to his face. He shot her another smile, and she bit her lip, slipping him her palm.

Wordlessly, Kai slid a thin silver band onto her fourth finger. Elysia blinked down at it in surprise. She couldn't believe this was happening. Never in her life had she dreamed she would marry a silver-haired Merrow.

As she watched, Kai wrapped her hand into his own. His hand felt warm and sure. It was kind of nice, if she was being truthful, but her legs shook, and she stared hard at her thumb as Lady Sirena bound their hands with the silver cord.

She could feel Kai's blue eyes studying her curiously, but she refused to meet his gaze. She was afraid she wouldn't like what she saw there. Or maybe she would like it too much. Either way, it was too hard. She steadied herself, focusing on the silver strand winding around and around their joined fingers. It was best to ignore him—less painful.

When Lady Sirena finished, she lifted a crown of white roses from a small table behind her. It was interwoven with silver water thistles, and she sat it atop Elysia's head as Kai removed his silver sash. Lady Sirena replaced it with one of the same color, marked with the emblem of the Court of the Sea: A white rose encircled by a shimmering, silver water thistle.

Lady Sirena placed a hand on each of their shoulders, and Elysia frowned, flicking her eyes to the one on her own. Her palm was too warm and slightly damp. Worriedly, she lifted her eyes to the Lady Sirena's face. It was pale and drawn, and a tiny scale on the side of her brow had begun to peel, showing the tender pink flesh beneath it.

Elysia searched the rest of her features worriedly, and her heart dropped at what she saw. A pale blue hue circled her lips, and her forehead was beaded with sweat. Lady Sirena was clearly sick. Something was very wrong.

She watched as Lady Sirena pulled in a shallow breath, addressing the room.

"Tonight, it is my great honor to present to you, a living symbol of our unified courts."

She flicked her eyes to Kai and Elysia, smiling proudly. "May their days be long together."

All heads bowed as Lady Sirena began to recite the marriage vows, all but Kai and Elysia's. They were words that Elysia had heard countless times, ancient, ageless blessings that she had once glossed over. But tonight, at her own wedding, they seemed very sacred.

"With this three-fold, silver strand, I do bind thee, Kai Bennet and Elysia Bryn, for once and all Time. May you no longer be known as separate beings, but a single, unified force. May that force grow deeply, as your love for one another grows. May it bind you, like this silver cord, and never be released. And may it hold you to your vows, until you are old and grey, and have no life left, save that with the Source."

Lady Sirena lifted her head as she placed her hands on top of Kai and Elysia's bound ones. Then the whole room began to speak the final blessing.

"May your days be long together,
and bless-ed, may they be.
If the silver strand unravels,
hold its ends, and again, you'll meet.
And wind it all the tighter,
'round your hands, your vow to keep.
And so, bind you together,
In great love, with joy and peace."

Shyly, Elysia lifted her eyes. Two deep blue pools peered back at her from Kai's face. A tiny smile lit his features as he studied her own. He gave her hand a small squeeze, and she flushed, her stomach turning a little flip. His expression reminded her of how he had looked at her in the garden.

Elysia could see her mother and grandmother in their seats beyond Kai's shoulder. Lady Malca dabbed her eyes with a small handkerchief, and Elysia frowned as she studied her face. She looked pale, almost as sick as Lady Sirena, and her grandmother looked even worse. The bluish hue around her mouth was dark, and she sagged in her chair, sweating profusely.

Back at the dais, Lady Sirena braced heavily on her scepter, gripping tightly to the large orb at its hilt. She swayed, then righted herself, smiling weakly as she addressed the room.

"In the Selkie Court, it's tradition that the silver strand be unwound before the wedding party. Then, the couple seals their bond with a kiss. However, we merrows have a different tradition." She gestured to Kai, grinning. "Kai, if you would do the honors." Kai grinned down at Elysia mischievously. Then, without warning, he scooped her into his free arm. Elysia shrieked as he lifted her off her feet, and he gripped her to his chest, a low chuckle forming in his throat.

Elysia perched shyly in his arm. She tried to ignore his nearness, avoided his glittering blue gaze as she focused on their bound hands. Lady Sirena continued.

"In the Merrow tradition, the new couple will unwind their strand in a private ceremony; alone. Then, they will share a kiss to seal the promise they have made." She nodded once to Kai, grinning. "Kai, you may now take your leave."

With that, the room erupted in applause. Elysia could hear Seamus *whooping* from the front row, and Ena's voice calling "Congratulations!" above the fray. Her mother and grandmother clapped lightly, tears glittering in their eyes, and despite the strangeness of her situation, joy bubbled up in Elysia's throat. She let her head fall back, laughing out loud as Kai spun her in a circle.

He grinned down at her, eyes shining, as he pushed his back against the throne room doors. Then, swiftly, he moved into the garden.

CHAPTER 25

The garden was silent, except for their sounds. Kai paused at the far end. Quietly, he tucked inside a small alcove, placing Elysia gently onto her feet near the stone wall.

He stepped away, eyeing her as she pressed her back against it. The rock was cool against her palms, and Elysia focused on the solid feeling as she gulped down the fresh night air. The excitement in the throne room had been contagious. Her head was still spinning, and the way Kai was looking at her didn't help matters. His blue eyes glittered, and he grinned slightly, his expression causing Elysia to look shyly away.

Silently, he stepped closer. Elysia focused on their bound hands while he waited, and when she didn't raise her eyes, he took one more step.

"Look at me," he whispered gruffly.

Slowly, Elysia lifted her eyes to his face. He was so close to her, now. She could see every detail of his features. She worked to memorize them, because she was sure he would never be this close to her again.

Silently, she studied the moonbeams glinting on the tiny scales at his temple. She wondered how she hadn't noticed that their color faded to dark blue in the edges of his hair. She dropped her eyes. Or how he had a small dimple in the center of his chin. Silently, she let her eyes drift upward, following the line of his straight nose before allowing herself to study his gaze. His eyes were dark blue tonight. They hinted with chips of silver at their edges, like shards of glittering ice.

Kai's grin had long faded under her examination. His face was serious, his expression deep. Slowly, carefully, he reached towards the winding silver strand between them. It was wrapped around and around their joined palms and tied in a bow at the center. Wordlessly, Kai pulled the loose end of the bow on his side free.

Elysia dropped her eyes to it. She followed the braided strand as it lengthened behind his fingers. Then, quietly, she reached for her end of it. She flicked her eyes to his face, holding his gaze as she pulled her side of the bow loose.

Kai's eyes were blazing as he reached to unravel the wrapped strands from their palms. Their intensity made her stomach leap, and she flushed as his fingers brushed the back of her hand. He unwound the silver cord once, twice, three times.

Their hands were free, now. But neither of them moved to break their hold. They stood still, their hands clasped, the long, braided strand spanning between them.

Kai flexed his hand against her palm, causing her heart to do little flips. He studied her intently, and she peered back at him in anticipation. The evening light glowed across his silver hair, and she followed its trail to the three tiny slits just beneath his ear. They were the mark of all Merrows, but she had never noticed Kai's before. She smiled slightly, wondering how many more new things about him she had yet to discover. She hoped she would get the chance, hoped he would want the same.

All at once, Kai began rubbing a small circle with his thumb on the back of her palm. Her skin flamed with his movements, and she flicked her eyes to the spot, then slowly, she lifted them to his face. He took a step closer, then another, his chest nearly brushing her own. His eyes glowed down at her in the moonlight, and for a moment longer, he held her gaze, then he dropped his eyes to her shoulder.

Silently, he dipped his head, resting it in the crevice of her neck. Elysia was sure he could feel her hammering heart, and she swallowed, willing it to slow. He lifted his chin, grazing her collarbone. Then, gently, he pressed her skin with his lips.

She stiffened, and he pulled back, studying her eyes. "What's wrong," he murmured. Elysia shook her head. "It's nothing," she said quietly. Her chest flared with embarrassment, and she dropped her eyes to the silver cord.

Kai ducked his head, forcing her to meet his gaze.

"Tell me," he said softly.

Elysia opened her mouth. Then she hesitated, closing it again. She sighed.

"I've never been kissed," she whispered. She met Kai's face briefly, then looked away. "There was a moment, with Connor, in the gardens of the Selkie Court, but he never..." She shook her head at the memory. "I was glad."

For some reason, her throat was tightening. She swallowed around the lump.

"It's just that I...I don't want you to feel like...like you *have* to do this, just because of tradition." She shook her head, sniffing. She could feel Kai's piercing eyes assessing her, but she couldn't bring herself to meet his gaze.

"I'm under no illusions," she said quietly. "I know this isn't a *real* marriage. and I know you'd rather not."

Elysia bit the inside of her cheek, fighting back tears. She wanted to drop her end of the strand and flee to her rooms, but Kai was still holding her firmly with his hand. She took a deep breath, then slowly released it, watching as he continued to rub gentle circles across the back of her palm.

Kai shrugged. "It's more than just a tradition, Elysia. It's a seal. In fact, a merrow wedding isn't considered final until the couple shares a kiss."

He lowered his face towards her, breathing softly against her ear. "And how do you know what I'd rather do?"

He pulled back, gazing down at her curiously as Elysia blinked back at him. Her mind had gone hazy, and she was finding it hard to think. She frowned, trying to sort through her muddled thoughts. If what Kai had said about merrow weddings was true, then surely, he was just saying the other thing so she would allow him to kiss her. It was for the seal, for the good of the court. Of course, it was. She knew that. But the way he was looking at her made her wonder.

Slowly, Kai brought his hand behind her waist. He tugged slightly, pulling against the small of her back as he pressed her towards him. Then, carefully, he lowered his lips.

At first, his kiss was soft and gentle, but then, it became more insistent. A thousand emotions erupted inside of Elysia, and she gripped her end of the silver strand, winding it around the back of his neck as she returned his kiss with equal fervency.

Inside her chest, her feelings gathered themselves like tight coil of string, and a warm, burning feeling began to the left of her heart. Kai's kisses continued, and as she returned them, the string began to unravel.

Silently, it wove down the length of her arm. The skin on its path felt ablaze, and soon, so did her palm. But then the string stretched outward, moving from the tips of her fingers to travel along the braid of the silver cord. At last, it reached Kai's hand, and Elysia knew he felt its burn, because he inhaled sharply, then deepened his kiss even more.

Elysia was so absorbed with Kai's kisses that she hadn't noticed the silver strand between them had begun to glow. It grew brighter and brighter, until finally, it was too bright to ignore. Its light was like a second sun, and Kai broke their kiss as the two of them squinted against its blaze. For a moment, they stared at the glowing cord in silence, marveling at its glimmering, silver length. But then Elysia's ears pricked.

A whisper began at the spot near her fingers. Quietly, it wound itself along the strand, weaving in and out of the braided cord until it spanned its length. Words and phrases that Elysia could not name flowed from the strand into her fingers. They swirled up her arm before depositing in the left of her chest, and as the Voice continued to speak, a soft light glowed out from her Amloga. She dropped her eyes to examine it, then flicked her eyes to Kai. The same spot glowed beneath the fabric of his jacket. The whispers intensified, swirling about them in circles, then, slowly, the light of the strand dimmed, and the whispers became silent.

Kai blinked down at her in the quiet. He leaned towards her, and for a moment, Elysia thought he would kiss her again. But he didn't.

Wordlessly, he reached for her end of the cord. He slid it gently from beneath her palm as he held her gaze. Then, he wrapped it into a small bundle and stuck it inside his jacket.

He stepped backward as he cleared his throat. "The seal," he said quietly. "It's done."

Elysia gazed back at him mutely. The feel of their bond still lingered in her left chest. That and Kai's kisses had rendered her silent. Kai studied her a moment more, then he dropped his eyes.

"I'll…walk you to your rooms," he said gruffly. He extended his arm, and she took it mutely, still reeling as he led her swiftly behind the waterfall.

They didn't speak again, and soon, they arrived at the door of her rooms. Elysia stood before it uncertainly, biting the inside of her lip. She watched as Kai pulled it open. He stuffed a hand into his pocket as he stood aside, staring hard at the air to her left. "I'll, uh…I'll see you in the morning," he said quietly.

So, we're back here? Back to your refusing to look at me? Elysia's heart sank, and suddenly, her throat felt tight. Tears threatened, but she would've rather died than let him see her cry, again. She swallowed hard against the lump, gripping her hands to her sides. Then, without a word, she brushed past him. She didn't turn as she closed the door soundly behind her. Then she sank onto the floor, silent tears dripping off her chin. She fell asleep there, in a small, curled heap, her head resting against the cool floor.

Sometime later, deep in the night, she heard a door creak open. Her body tightened at the sound, and groggily, she sat up on one elbow, peering at the adjoining door. She expected Kai to appear from behind it, but silence bathed her in the darkness, and the adjoining door remained closed.

Elysia blew out a breath. She sank back to the floor, closing her eyes. Loneliness overwhelmed her, and she wished for all the known worlds that she had never come to the Court of Merrows, that she had never met Kai Bennet.

Moments later, familiar footsteps passed her in the hall. She opened her eyes. Quietly, she sat up onto her knees. She pulled the door to a crack, peeking out into the hallway. But even before she saw him, she already knew who she would see.

Kai's frame was moving silently away from her. She watched as his silver hair disappeared around the corner, willing him to turn. But he didn't, and her heart sank.

Her suspicions about their garden exchange were confirmed. The kiss had only been for the seal, for their court, and nothing more. She bit her lip, holding back tears as she tucked herself back into her room.

She closed the door, sinking silently to the floor as she stared blankly into the darkness. She knew where Kai was headed. He was going to see the one he truly loved. He was going to see Maura.

Chapter 26

Sometime later, Elysia woke again on the floor. Tiredly, she glared up at the connecting door. Someone was pounding on Kai's side of it. She groaned, then lifted onto her elbow, massaging her neck. Her muscles were stiff from leaning against the door all night. The pounding started again, and she squinted at the sound.

"Come in," she croaked.

Kai burst into the room, just as she sat upright. His eyes searched the bed, then he turned to the door where Elysia sat, frowning in confusion. She was still wearing her wedding gown, and he flicked his eyes over it as he sank down beside her. He was holding three large Tamarisk fronds in his hand.

"Why are you on the floor?" he asked, frowning. He put a hand to her brow, worry creasing his features.

"Are you feeling alright?"

He studied her face as Elysia flicked her eyes to the Tamarisk fronds. She pushed his hand away, scrambling to her feet as she smoothed the tangled mass of hair at the back of her head. "I'm fine," she said flatly.

Kai frowned at her anxiously, but she ignored him. She moved to the mirror as she unwound her rumpled braid, then grabbed a brush, working it silently through the stiff knots. He continued to stare, and she flicked her eyes to him, frowning. "Why are you staring at me like that?" she spat.

Kai didn't answer. He stared at her a moment more before he stood. Then, silently, he moved towards her. He stopped behind her in the mirror, studying her reflection, but Elysia ignored him, continuing to pull the brush roughly through her matted knots.

Kai brought his hand to her arm, stopping her movement. She glared at his reflection as she placed the brush on a small table, but Kai's expression was worrying her. She frowned, turning to peer up at his face. Something like grief tinged the edges of his features, and she swallowed hard as he grasped her hand, tugging her gently to sit beside him on the mattress. Something was very wrong.

Worry creased Elysia's features as she peered up at Kai's mournful expression.

"Kai, you're scaring me. What is it?" she prodded.

Kai blew out a breath. He reached for her palm. "I have news," he said quietly.

Elysia's heart was pounding in her ears. She felt oddly detached from her surroundings, and her throat constricted around her words. She swallowed tightly. "Tell me," she breathed.

Kai took a deep breath. "There were riots last night, after our wedding ceremony," he said quietly. "In both lands, Selkie and Merrow, the radicals took to the streets. Our Merrow Forces are doing what they can here to keep things subdued, but in the Selkie Isles." He swallowed. "They've looted and burned the palace." Elysia gasped, and he tightened his grip on her hand.

"It seems the courts are divided on the…unification of the clans."

"How bad is it?" Elysia asked.

Kai shook his head. "Bad. Some are already dead, and there are several injuries in the Forces and Guard."

Elysia searched his face. "What are we going to do?" she whispered.

Kai shook his head. "I don't know." He dropped his eyes. "But that's not all. Last night I went to the secret island," he said quietly.

Elysia flicked her eyes to her lap. She nodded stiffly as Kai continued.

"I don't know if you noticed, but you used all the Tamarisk to treat Ena after the attack with the ray's barb. So, I went to get more, just in case." He laid the Tamarisk fronds down beside her on the mattress, and Elysia flicked her eyes to them. She knew that wasn't all he had gone to do.

Kai sighed heavily. "And it's a good thing I got it when I did." He lifted his gaze, peering deeply at the side of her face.

"Elysia, there's sickness…in both courts. Lady Sirena is near death, and…so is your mother." Elysia's eyes flew to his, and he paused, searching for his words. "I…I'm so sorry, Elysia. But your grandmother left this life just before the sunrise." He hung his head. "Now, she's with the Source."

Elysia's mind reeled, and she blinked at Kai in confusion. "She's gone?" she said quietly. The words sounded strange to her own ears, distant and hollow. They left a bitter taste on her tongue.

Kai nodded. "Yes," he said solemnly. "I'm so sorry."

Tears sprang into Elysia's eyes, and she hung her head, sobbing quietly. They dripped from her chin, staining her skirt, but she didn't bother to dry them. Her grandmother was gone. The beautiful, wise woman with soft brown eyes had passed to the Hereafter. It would be a long while until Elysia could see her again. She would miss her more than she could explain.

Kai reached into his jacket. She sniffed, and Kai placed his handkerchief into her lap, Silently, she raised it with shaking hands, dabbing her cheeks. She had noticed her grandmother looked worse during the wedding ceremony, but other things, like Kai and his feelings—or lack of feelings—about her, had been occupying her mind.

Elysia cursed herself for being so selfish. She was the realm's healer, for the Source's sake. She should have realized her grandmother's condition was more serious.

Kai continued. "You and I, and Seamus and Ena are the only ones who aren't sick," he said quietly. "Seamus says it's because of the diving spider. He's been scouring the records in the palace library since Ena's attack, searching for a treatment. During his research, he found a selection that talked about using the blood of a diving spider as an antidote to various poisons. Seamus thinks that's what this is—poison. The four of us have been exposed to the diving spider blood, so that's why we're still well."

Elysia flipped back in her memory. She tried to recall the diving spider, but the only things she could remember were following Kai's tail through the tunnel and awakening in the abandoned house. The rest of it was blank. But the diving spider didn't sound like something she wanted to remember anyway, so it was probably for the best.

Kai frowned. "Seamus thinks someone poisoned the water surrounding the dome. But what he can't understand is, the people in the Selkie Court are sick, too. It started after the riots last night. And, since then, the sickness has spread. It's everywhere, now."

Elysia turned to the window. Outside, the water appeared much the same as it always did. It was scary to think that it was polluted with some invisible poison. Quickly, she stood, grabbing the Tamarisk from the mattress.

"I've got to help them," she whispered. "Take me to my mother and Lady Sirena."

CHAPTER 27

Lady Malca lay pale and still beneath her coverlet. Ena sat beside her. She dabbed softly at the ruler's damp brow, worry lining her face.

Elysia rushed to her side. She sank to the floor as she reached for her mother's hand, anxiously scanning her features. Her mother's fingertips were cool, and there was an ominous blue shade encircling her lips. It was damp with sweat.

Silently, Elysia moved to the bedside table. A small bowl and pitcher of water sat on it, and Elysia's fingers trembled as she picked several of pink blooms from the Tamarisk frond. As quickly as she could, she dropped them into the bowl. Then she filled it with water and sat down to wait.

In a moment, the water had taken on a faint pink hue. Ena

helped to raise her mother's weak head, and Elysia willed her hand not to shake as she lifted a spoonful of the mixture past her mother's pale lips. She watched silently as Ena settled her mother back onto the pillow, then wiped her mouth with the edge of the cloth. Elysia willed her mother to move, but she remained still and quiet. Her breathing was shallow, and Elysia wondered if the Tamarisk tea would do its work. She wished she could do more, but she had done all she could. There was nothing left to do but wait.

She brushed a damp lock from her mother's forehead as she bent to her ear. "Please, get well," she whispered. She kissed her cheek, breathing a silent prayer that she would. Then she sat upright, tucking the covers tighter under her mother's chin. She hated to leave her, but Lady Sirena needed treatment, too.

In the next room, Kai and Seamus sat silently beside the canopy bed. Beneath its gauzy silver curtains, Lady Sirena's pale frame lay limply under the covers. Her dark hair fanned across the pillow, exposing the glittering scales at her temple. More had peeled away since the wedding, and the skin beneath them looked raw and sore. The blue hue surrounding her lips was deeper than her mother's, and a dark spot of blood stained the pillow beneath her ear. Elysia frowned down at it as she waited for the Tamarisk tea to steep. Carefully, she turned Lady Sirena's chin.

The three small slits beneath her ear marking the entrance to her sea lungs were ragged at their edges. The skin around them held the same blue hue as her lips, and as Elysia watched, a dark line of blood trickled from the furthest one. Slowly, it trailed down her neck, then it dripped to join the stain below.

Elysia flattened her lips into a hard line. She wasn't sure Lady Sirena was going to make it, even with the Tamarisk. Silently, she lifted her eyes to Kai.

He looked as if he were reliving a nightmare. His face was a pale mask, and he barely moved as he stared down at Lady Sirena. The pain in his eyes was acute, and Elysia had the sudden urge to wrap him into her arms. But she knew she couldn't. He wouldn't like that.

She turned back to the Tamarisk. The water in the bowl had turned a pale pink, and she dipped some onto a spoon as Seamus lifted Lady Sirena's head. She coaxed it past her pale lips, making sure she swallowed. Then Seamus settled her back on to the pillow.

He dabbed her head with a cool cloth. "Sea Lily poison," he said quietly. His lips made a hard line, and he flicked his eyes worriedly to Kai.

"We've seen it before. Haven't we, Kai?"

Elysia flicked her eyes to Kai in confusion. What did Seamus mean? She searched Kai's face, watching as grief, fear, and worry skittered rapidly across it. And then, it dawned on her. Sea Lily poison was what had taken Maura.

No wonder Kai looked like he was reliving a nightmare. He really was. Silently, she reached across the mattress, slipping his palm into her own. A muscle feathered in his jaw, and she squeezed, but he never lifted his eyes.

"I'm so sorry, Kai," she whispered.

Hearing his name, he flicked his eyes to her face, and what she saw there broke her heart. His eyes were two deep, swirling pools of grief. Tears glittered at their edges, and as one slipped past the lid, he swiped it, dropping his eyes.

Elysia coaxed one more spoonful of Tamarisk tea past Lady Sirena's lips. Then she stood, watching as Seamus dabbed the excess from her chin. "I've done all I can," she said quietly.

"I'm going to go see who else needs my help."

She turned for the door as a chair scraped against the floor. "I'm coming with you," Kai said gruffly. Elysia spun. Kai was standing by the bed, his hands gripped into fists.

"There's no need," she said quietly. "Stay with Lady Sirena. I'll be alright."

Just then, a strange, strangled gurgle emitted from the mattress. Elysia's heart leapt into her throat as her eyes flew to Lady Sirena. She coughed, and dark red blood spurted past her lips. It landed on the pale coverlet in a wide spray.

Kai dropped to his knees, and Elysia rushed to her side as the ruler began to shake. She convulsed violently, and blood flowed freely from the corners of her lips and the slits on her neck. Elysia braced her arms, watching in horror as Lady Sirena sputtered.

All at once, her neck strained upward. She heaved once, and then her head fell to the side. She exhaled deeply, and then her body went slack as the strain on her beautiful face melted into an expression of peace. Then, her breath was still, and she was silent.

Kai stared down at her still face in horror. Abruptly, he dropped her hand, pushing off the mattress. Elysia watched as he paced the room. He covered his eyes with his forearm, and a deep groan of grief slipped past his lips. Then he looked towards the ceiling, tears streaking his cheeks as he braced a hand on his waist, blowing out a breath.

Elysia swiped a silent tear as she looked away. Silently, she pressed her ear to Lady Sirena's chest. She closed her eyes, listening. Her breath was as still as her heart, and the tiny whir of her Amloga was silent. She pulled away, a deep fear swirling in her belly. The Tamarisk had failed. Lady Sirena was gone.

Reverently, Seamus tucked the linen coverlet over Lady Sirena's still features. He stood, then, bowing deeply from his waist. Elysia frowned gently down at the linen cover. She didn't understand it. If the Tamarisk had worked for Ena, then why wasn't it working now? She flipped through her memory, searching for an answer, and suddenly, a story about the realm's former healer, Ita, came to mind.

It was a story she had studied in the Histories, several cycles ago. Apparently, there had been a failed attempt to heal the Court of Merrows with Tamarisk after an algae bloom has poisoned the waters around the dome. Elysia's current dilemma seemed similar. It was Sea Lily poison, now, but still, there had to be something about both scenarios that made the Tamarisk ineffective. But what was it?

Quietly, Elysia closed her eyes. She stilled her mind, focusing, until the wide, blank pool appeared in her head. She sank into it to wait. Moments passed, and nothing happened, so, she cast a stone into the deep water. Ripples spanned out from the spot, and in a moment, faint whispers began.

Elysia frowned as the images the Voice created came into view. They seemed unrelated to her current problems, but all she could see in her mind's eye was an image of her standing in the shallow waves, collecting her water weaving.

She watched as her empty hand pulled the tiny droplets from the air. She laid them flat against her body, and suddenly, her eyes popped open. The *air* inside the dome was full of water droplets, too.

That was it. If the water surrounding the dome was poisoned, then that poison was being filtered through. That would mean the people breathing the air inside the dome were continuously exposed. If that was the case, it would be almost impossible for the Tamarisk to counteract the poison. Every time they breathed, the people inside of it were constantly taking in contaminated water droplets. They were constantly passing them from person to person. The Tamarisk could never work like that. The moment she treated the sick, they would simply take a breath and be infected again.

It had been the same for Ita, too. The algae bloom's poison had filtered in, creating a continuous exposure. The Tamarisk hadn't had any hope of doing its healing work.

The reason the Tamarisk hadn't worked made sense, but there were still parts of the situation that didn't—like why people were sick in the Selkie Court. Elysia twisted her lips, thinking. It was possible that an angry merrow had broadly seeded the air on the island and somehow managed to bring the poison home, but that seemed unlikely. If that wasn't the case, then the only possible scenario was that the poison was planted in the Court of Merrows by someone from the islands. And she had a pretty good idea who that someone might be.

She thought back to Connor's threats in the garden with her mother and Ciar's glaring face at the dinner table on the night of the urgent meeting. Both were angry enough to have done something like this, and after, they would've carried the poison back to the Selkie Court in their breath, unaware. If they so much as breathed near another Selkie, that was all it would take. That one would pass the poison to another, and then another, until finally, everyone would be infected. And it could happen fast. Especially if everyone was close—like they would be in a riot.

Regardless of who had planted the poison, the Tamarisk wouldn't work. She needed to find another way. She bit her cheek, thinking hard as she and Kai moved back to their rooms.

The people needed another place to go, a place where the air was clean and safe. Poisons from the sea tended to linger, whether inside the dome or on the islands. So, right now, neither place was an option. In fact, it had taken a long while for the Court of

Merrows to be clear after the algae bloom incident. So, there was no chance of simply waiting it out. The longer they did, the more risk there was for people to die.

Elysia sighed. It seemed an impossible dilemma; one to which she wasn't sure she could find the answers. In the meantime, though, she needed to do what she could to stop the spread. She turned to Kai.

"Send Seamus to the Selkie Court. If the palace is still standing, ask him to gather the sick there. Maybe if we isolate them, we can slow the spread. Then find any members of the Forces that are still well. Have them bring the sick Merrows to Lady Sirena's throne room."

Kai nodded. Wordlessly, he hurried into the hall. Elysia watched her door close as she sat heavily onto her mattress. Her thoughts and feelings swirled, and she put her hands to her head. There were too many things happening at once, too many questions and problems for her to solve on her own. Anxiety overwhelmed her. She was in over her head, and she couldn't think.

Quietly, she braced her elbows on her knees. She tucked her forehead into her hands and closed her eyes, breathing deeply as she cleared her mind into a blank pool. She let herself drift above its smooth, silent surface, focusing on the air coming in and out of her lungs.

Soon, she had drifted back to the reef. In her head, she settled down behind the crisp orange coral, watching as it swayed back and forth in the current. The first time she had come here, she hadn't known what direction to take, and her gift had guided her to the right path. It had led her right to Nathair's lair, and she had saved Kai from certain death. Maybe now, her gift would guide her to the right place, again.

Carefully, she turned down the sounds of her own mind. She watched the coral fan to and fro, and she forced her body to relax, imagining herself floating peacefully with it in the tides. Silently, she rested there, allowing the arms of her thoughts to fold slowly in on themselves, until, at last, they reached a single, pinpoint spot. Then she focused on that spot, making it smaller and smaller, until her thoughts disappeared entirely. All that was left was a quiet relief, herself in the reef with the coral, and Elysia sank into it, her hair fanning above her head as she basked in the silence of the space.

As she became one with the tide's ebb and flow, a deep, knowing comfort enveloped her body, until all at once, the reef faded, and she was back again in the blank pool. She rested there, waiting, expecting, until, at last, she felt a stone resting in her hand. She skipped it, and a soft splash sounded in the distance. Elysia lifted her head, focusing on the sound.

A tiny point of colorful light bobbed there in the pool, and she watched as a ripple spread out from it. Like before, it widened in concentric circles, just like she had tossed a stone into the sea. The Voice hovered lightly above the small waves, whispering and weaving as the ripple continued to spread. The Voice rose, louder as the small wave moved towards her.

As it approached, she realized it was much larger than it had first appeared. It picked up speed, gathering the whole of the water in the pool, and as the crest of it advanced, a glimmering rainbow arced with the water over her head. The Voice filled her mind, and the colors rose with the sound, until, at last, the space behind her eyes was nothing but a kaleidoscope of color and ethereal sound.

The water arced above her, and she sat still, listening, watching in rapture at the display, as the wave lifted high. It paused above her, and then all at once, the water began to weave itself into a long strand. The strand glimmered above her with internal light, and Elysia smiled as it rose. It reminded her very much of the silver strand from her wedding ceremony.

The Voice whispered along its length, just like the strand in the garden, and then, all at once, the strand shrunk in on itself. It became thin and long, like a sparkling silver ribbon. Suddenly, a dark blue, velvet wrapper appeared beneath it. The ribbon floated to the wrapper's middle. It wrapped itself around it, cinching in a neat bow.

Elysia's eyes snapped open. That was it. Her father's wedding present. That's where the answers would be.

Quickly, she hurried to the jewelry box on her nightstand. She fumbled through the contents, tossing a mound of jewelry and tiaras on her bed, until, at last, she produced the blue velvet wrapper. She sat on the bed, running her hands lovingly over the soft fabric. Then, carefully, she pulled the silver ribbon. She was certain. This was the right moment to open it. The Voice had spoken. Slowly, she unrolled the velvet.

She only vaguely heard Kai shut the door as an aged, cream parchment crinkled beneath her fingers. He sat down on the bed beside her, peering over her shoulder. "What's that?" he asked her.

Elysia frowned down at the parchment, but as she scanned the words, a slow smile spread across her face. She turned towards him. "It's a wedding gift, from my father," she said quietly. She passed it to him, watching as Kai studied its contents. "It's a letter, and a map" she said, excitedly. "To the Lost Lands."

Kai peered at her in confusion as he passed the parchment back to her.

"The Lost Lands?"

Elysia shook her head in wonder. "I thought they were a legend," she murmured, smiling down at the parchment. "They're the lands that were stolen from the Selkie people, by Lord Dolion, all those cycles ago. It says here that the doors were sealed by my father. They were hidden, from thought and mind. The only way to open them is to sing the Selkie's Song."

She scanned the parchment as Kai read over her shoulder.

Dearest Elysia,
If you are reading this, then I am long passed into the Hereafter.

I am giving this letter along with my map to your grandmother for safekeeping. She will know it's for you when the day comes. And you will open it when the moment is right.

At the moment you read this, I feel you will have need to access the lands of our forefathers. These lands were part of the Court of the Sea, so long ago, before the exile. We lived there in harmony with our Merrow neighbors, but of course, the peace of these lands was lost.

You must know that things are not always as they appear. By now, our lands will have become legend, or a daydream, rarely relived, just as the peace the clans knew there is so long forgotten. It is because of the seal I have placed on the doors. I did so to keep our lands safe. I couldn't bear the corruption of Lord Dolion to darken our silver shores.

But you must know, my darling Elysia, that those lands are real. I have hidden them, in plain sight, all these cycles. No one can enter there again but by the Selkie's Song.

And only the Voice knows the way.

All my love until I see you again,

—Father

Kai frowned. "Okay, so there's something called the Lost Lands. That's great and all, but what good does that do us, now? The doors are hidden, and if we manage to find them, we're not even sure we can open them."

Elysia stood, pacing the floor. "I know, but we *need* to find them. We've got to. The clans need a safe place to go, while the air clears." She studied the page further. "My father says no one can enter without the Selkie's Song." She frowned at the parchment, then lifted her gaze. Kai raised his brows.

"Don't you know it?" Elysia shrugged. "I'm not sure," she said uncertainly.

Kai stood. He folded his arms, watching as she paced the floor. Then he held out his hand, stopping her rapid steps as he peered into her eyes. "Of course you do. You heard it with me on the secret island, remember? You spoke the words—the words of the Voice. They were exactly what I needed to hear."

Elysia bit her lip. She thought about how her gift had expanded since that first night with Kai. Her ability to listen to the words of the Source had already developed more than she could have imagined. Now, she heard the Voice in everything. It had led her to Kai in Nathair's dark canyon, and it had led her to her father's parchment, but the task of finding the Lost Lands, of opening the ancient doors sealed by her father still seemed daunting.

Everything depended on her. If she failed to hear the Voice, if she failed to sing the words of the Selkie's Song, then more people would die. It was terrifying—more terrifying than anything she had experienced in her adventure beneath the sea.

"I guess," she said doubtfully.

Kai grinned. He gave her arm a little shake. "I *know*. Your gift doesn't just depend on you, Elysia. It's from the Source. You have to trust that. The words will come to you when the moment is right, just like they have before."

Elysia pressed her lips uncertainly as she lifted the Tamarisk from the mattress.

"I hope you're right," she said quietly.

Kai rolled his eyes as she tucked the fronds into a small bag and slung it across her shoulder. He put his hands to his hips, broadening his chest proudly. "Of course, I'm right," he said teasingly. "I always am." He shot her a small smile, and Elysia gave his arm a little punch.

"Now, where do we start looking?"

Elysia looked past him to stare out the window. The open sea looked vast and endless beyond the dome, and her heart shrank a bit at the enormity of the task ahead.

"I have no idea," she whispered. "But we'd better start now."

Chapter 28

Elysia and Kai stood in their water weaving on a high, stone platform on the outside of the fortress wall. Before them, streams of sunlight danced through the glittering dome. Elysia clenched her hands at her sides as she stared through the dome's transparent surface. Beyond it, the vast sea loomed endlessly, and her task to find the Lost Lands and open their sealed doors swelled impossibly in her mind.

When she had wished for an adventure in the open sea, she had never dreamed it would be like this. The fate of the clans rested squarely on her shoulders. Though she knew her gift was from the Source, she felt the power of life and death was solely in her hands. If she didn't find the Lost Lands, there was a real danger that their court would be wiped out. Then there wouldn't even be a Court of the Sea anymore.

Silently, she closed her eyes. She inhaled, then she released her breath, and with it, she released her thoughts. She exhaled her fears, worries, and doubts about her abilities and the risk the Sea Lily poison posed to their court. She took another breath, relaxing her hands, then she exhaled, pushing away shame and embarrassment, and a few other feelings about her relationship with Kai that she wasn't ready to name. Then she opened herself up to the Source, attempting to do what Kai had suggested—attempting to trust.

When her mind was a smooth, blank pool, she skipped a stone across its silent surface. The stone bounced swiftly across the water, creating a rippling, silver strand behind it. The strand extended far into the distance, further than Elysia could see. And then, the strand's threads unraveled.

Rippling, whispering echoes, a rainbow of color and light, spread out from the strand in all directions. They filled the edges of her mind. Quietly Elysia waited, watching the echoes travel.

All at once, the strand collected itself into a single, uniform line. The Voice vibrated down the length of it, and in her mind's eye, Elysia reached for its edge. She grasped one end and held it fast, like she was holding the end of a long, silver string. The Voice moved along its threads, weaving in and out of them like the rhythm of the tides, and Elysia allowed herself to sink into its flow. She swayed with the sound, as whispering echoes floated from the strand to her ears. Then, slowly, the Voice receded. It traveled backwards along the strand, moving out past the dome. It wove out with the tides, reaching far into the open water, until, at last it rested. The Voice hovered there, unmoving, an invisible tether holding the other end of the string.

Elysia could barely see the other end of the strand behind her eyes, but she focused hard on the spot, committing it to memory as she opened them. She pointed past the dome, to a blank patch of open sea far beyond it.

"There," she whispered.

Kai narrowed his eyes at the spot, where the sunlight danced on the open sea floor. Nothing was there but a small, stony reef and open water. He peered down at Elysia uncertainly. "You're sure?" he said.

She nodded. "I'm sure."

Kai turned back to the empty patch of sea. He studied it thoughtfully, then he grinned down at Elysia. "Alright, then, are you ready for this?" he said mischievously.

Elysia frowned up at him. "Ready for what?" she asked.

Kai didn't answer. Wordlessly, he stepped to the platform's edge. He shot her a grin over his shoulder, then he gave a low whistle before stepping swiftly back beside her.

All at once, two large, grey seahorses emerged from a low opening near the base of the stone fortress. They tossed their high necks, rearing and chuffing with excitement as they thundered up towards the platform on the open air. Elysia's eyes widened as they skidded to a stop before her on the stone.

Kai stepped into their path, holding up his arms. "Whoa," he said softly. He reached carefully to the seahorse closest to him, and the large grey horse tucked its chin, allowing Kai to swirl soft circles across its dark forehead with his fingers. He waited until the horse's clouded, stormy eye softened under his hand. Then he grasped its grey, seaweed-streaked mane and hoisted himself onto its back.

Elysia stared up at him open-mouthed, watching as Kai grinned down at her shocked expression. Just like all the selkies, she had heard the horrifying stories about seahorses. The famed guardians of the Court of Merrows had been known to appear to land-dwellers, charming the unsuspecting passer-by into climbing onto their backs, after which the rider was dragged to their death in the depths of the sea.

"Sea folk are the only ones who can ride them," Kai explained. "Don't worry. Selkies count. You'll be safe."

Elysia bit her lip, watching the horse nearest her stare with his great clouded eye. She flicked her gaze to Kai uncertainly, and he chuckled low. "Trust me. Just give him a pat and jump astride."

Elysia blinked at the horse's strange gaze. "You're a good boy," she said shakily. Then she tucked her trembling fingers to his neck. His dark grey hair was coarse, slick, like it would keep the water out. The horse reared its neck, and she recoiled, giggling at her own jumpiness. She watched as her mount tossed his head towards his back. He gave an echoing nicker, inviting her to jump astride.

She grinned at the gesture, and despite her fear, she gripped the seahorse's mane and jumped.

As soon as she had her seat, Kai whistled, and the seahorses lunged from the platform and galloped towards the dome through the open air. They passed easily through the dome and continued their race through the open sea.

Elysia held her mount's mane fast as they hit the water. The familiar tingle blazed over her lower limbs as her silver tail formed over her skin, and she fanned it out behind her, just above the seahorse's back.

At first, she was tense, jerking with the horse's every move, but as she rode, she relaxed, allowing the gentle gallop of the seahorse to lull her into a place of concentration. Kai allowed her horse to take the lead, and Elysia closed her eyes. Once more, she pulled up the threads of the skipped stone inside her mind. The Voice still vibrated along its length, and she followed its resonance, gently tugging the seahorse's mane in the right direction.

Their mounts flew, and soon, they arrived in the spot where the strand had been tethered. Elysia released her hands, allowing the seahorse to go free in the open water. Kai did the same, and the two galloped back towards the dome.

Elysia watched them go in amazement. Seahorses were wild creatures, dangerous—or so she'd heard. But these two didn't seem to be.

"Misunderstood beasts, the seahorses," Kai said quietly.

"They're dangerous, to be sure, but only if your home doesn't lie beneath the water. They're protective of the sea and its occupants and mistrusting of outsiders. That's why so many are pulled to their death, if they climb aboard at the shoreline."

He smiled sadly. "Lady Sirena called them the *first sentries of the Court of Merrows*." His jaw flexed, and he hung his head.

Elysia understood his pain. She missed her grandmother more than she could explain, and she was sure he felt the same about Lady Sirena. Silently, she moved her hand to his. She squeezed, and he quickly laced his fingers into her palm.

Elysia gazed down at their twined fingers. Her skin burned where his hand touched, and little tingling sensations zinged up her arm into her chest from his palm. It felt something like when they had held the ends of the silver strand between them in the garden.

Kai cleared his throat. He didn't bother to drop her hand as he lifted his chin, gesturing before them to the open water.

"Alright, what do we do, now?" he asked her.

Elysia peered hesitantly at the open sea. She reached her free hand into her bag, pulling out the small parchment. Then she frowned down at the letter and the map uncertainly.

She shook her head. "It doesn't say. This map doesn't make any sense. It didn't tell me how to get here, and it doesn't tell me where to go now. It just shows the layout of a city on a hill. According to this, the city lies above a wide strand by the sea." She lifted her eyes, scanning the water. "And I certainly don't see a city. Or a hill, for that matter."

Kai blinked in confusion. To his left, a small pile of stones rested on the sea floor. Colorful coral and sea grasses grew from its crevices. They waved in the current, and little fish swam in and out of the rocks. He leaned against it with his shoulder, studying the water ahead of them.

"How did you get to this spot in the first place?" he asked her.

Elysia pressed her lips uncertainly. She shrugged. "I just… listened," she said quietly.

Kai nodded. "Maybe just try the listening thing, again, then. If it led you here, then surely it will lead you on, right?"

Elysia frowned. She wasn't sure about any of it, really, but she figured it was worth a try. She nodded, closing her eyes as she pressed out any personal thoughts. Then, she skipped another stone along the surface of her mind.

Like before, a silver line followed the stone. Rainbows of ripples spread out from it, and whispers again spoke along its length. Then the ripples collected themselves. The Voice receded down the strand, but this time, it tethered a short distance before her. It halted rapidly, banging against a large, blunt object, with a loud, metallic clang.

Elysia studied the object behind her eyelids, feeling its surface, size, and shape. It was massive, heavy, and it deflected all sound. She listened harder, focusing on the movement of the sea. In the world outside her mind, the current moved steadily around the invisible object. It was so large that it had created a bend in the current.

Silently, Elysia stuck out her hand. She could feel the current bending around her fingers.

It swirled sideways, but still, the invisible object was just out of her grasp. The bend in the current whispered with the Voice, and, instinctively, Elysia stepped forward, allowing the sound to envelope her body as well as her mind.

As she listened, the Voice began a hum. It swirled past her ears, coiling into her left chest. Elysia matched its tune. Quietly, she pushed her own voice out through the open water. She hummed softly, then she paused, listening, waiting.

For a moment, all she could hear was the bend in the current's flow. Panic rose in her chest as she stood still, straining to hear the least sound. But she couldn't hear anything. She couldn't see anything in her mind's eye. No Voice, no landscape, nothing.

Elysia's breathing became hard and fast as her heartbeat thumped in her ears. It all depended on her. Every bit of it. If she couldn't hear the Voice, she wouldn't be able to find the doors. And even if she somehow did find them, she wouldn't be able open them unless she was able to sing the Selkie's Song.

There was no hope without the swords of the Source. The rest of their clan was going to die. She wasn't going to be able to save them—just like she hadn't been able to save her grandmother or

Lady Sirena. She closed her eyes, breathing a prayer. "Please, help me," she whispered.

Anxiously, she sloshed through the blank pool of her mind. She fought panic, straining to listen as a muffled whisper lifted from the water. Then, all at once, a deep, heavy feeling blanketed her body, and she felt strangely at peace. Kai squeezed her palm, and she relaxed in his grip, allowing her panic to drift away with the tides. Only then did the words of the Voice become clear. Silver flames lit inside of Elysia's chest, and she opened her mouth to sing.

Hiraeth, Hiraeth,
My homeland I see.
Long it's been hidden,
In the heart of the sea.
No shadow of darkness,
No scheme of the night,
Can shadow the Lost Lands,
From soon coming light.
Hiraeth, Hiraeth,
A great golden door.
And past it a sea,
With a smooth, silver shore.
I'll meet you there,
Past the golden bowl.

To the silver strand,
Is where I'll go.

As Kai held Elysia's hand, the Voice whispered in a soft, soothing tone. Slowly, it moved down her arm and into her palm. There, it rested, like a coil of string, then it wound itself outward, like a long strand of silver moving past her fingers.

Kai's hand was on fire as the strand swirled into his palm. It moved upward, lighting flames with its words as the Voice carried into his chest. There, it rested, hovering as it curled inside his Amloga. Though he had never heard it before, the Voice sounded oddly familiar to Kai. It was one he somehow knew. And as he listened, the Voice became even more familiar.

He stood slack, and tears streamed down his face, as the Voice transformed into a sound that was very dear, one he had held close for most of his life. It was the voice of Maura. She sang softly, and her voice was sweet in his ears.

Hiraeth, Hiraeth
My homeland I see.
Long I've been buried,
And hidden from thee.
In grief, I departed,
But love, shall provide,
A way out of sorrow,

And hope none deny.

Elysia smiled as she sang the words to the Selkie's Song. Before, the Voice she had heard had been nameless; a strange, yet familiar sound. But as she stood singing before the golden door of the Lost Lands, the Voice she heard was that of her grandmother, Ríona, and her father, Lord Ríonan.

Though their familiar tones had come from a far-off distance, they melded with the the Voice in such a way that Elysia knew they were singing to her from just beyond—from their side of the door, in the Hereafter, with the Source.

Hiraeth, Hiraeth,
My homeland I see.
Long have I waited,
To be here, with thee.
And though you can't travel,
To visit my home,
I've led you to yours,
In the sea, by the stones.

Elysia opened her eyes. Before their joined hands was a large golden door. A bright stream of sunlight glinted against its ancient surface, and a small rose intertwined with a water thistle was carved into its center. Elysia smiled at the insignia, and Kai squeezed her hand. Their likeness was mirrored back to them in the door's golden surface, and they paused for a moment, studying their reflection.

Elysia touched the center of the rose with the flat of her palm and Kai placed his hand across it. Within moments, a quiet hum emitted from beneath their hands, and the insignia glowed brightly—as bright as the sun. Then the golden door cracked open.

A rush of fresh, dry air lifted towards them from the opening, and together, they pushed the door inward. A glimmering, transparent surface, much like the dome, lined the entrance, and Elysia gasped as she passed through it. She was standing in a large courtyard, beneath a wide, blue sky. Ancient, moss-laden columns lined the courtyard, and a still, quiet pool of water was set in the center of the stone platform between them. Beyond, the stone structures of a vast city towered on a high hill, cascading down towards a wide silver shore at the edge of a crystal sea.

Elysia lifted to the platform's steps as Kai shut the door behind them, climbing up to the edge of the still pool. At the pool's far end, a golden bowl hovered above a set of large hands carved from white marble. The bowl was tipped onto its side, and a stream of clear water ran from its edge into the pool beneath. There was no source of the water in the bowl that Elysia could see. It appeared to regenerate endlessly from the center of the bowl. She studied the place where the stream hit the water. It bubbled and frothed where the two waters met, but strangely, the pool wasn't disturbed beneath it.

Elysia knelt beside the bowl and cupped her hand beneath the stream. She watched in amazement as the water collected itself into her palm. It coiled there, like a long, silver ribbon, and when she pulled her hand away, it dissolved into a clear liquid.

The water looked cool and refreshing, and Elysia found she was thirsty. She lifted her hands to her lips, drinking deeply. The water was sweet, and as she drank, she felt new strength come into her body. In fact, she felt stronger than she ever had in her life.

She turned to Kai, grinning as she gestured towards the water. "It's good," she said excitedly. "Come have some."

Kai knelt beside her. He collected a stream into his palm, frowning as the silver strand formed and dissolved into a liquid. Then, he lifted it to his lips. He drank it all, tipping his head back until the water dripped off his chin. Then he grinned down at her, wiping his chin with the back of his arm. "It is good. And I feel even better."

Elysia smiled as she studied the water. She thought about the Sea Lily poison, how it polluted the waters around the Court of Merrows and the air in the Selkie Court. Now, every breath the people breathed was full of toxic water droplets. She thought about the strange strength that had infused her from head to foot since she had drunk from the golden bowl.

"It's perfect!" she said excitedly. "We can bring everyone here, to the Lost Lands. The Tamarisk needs clean air to be effective against the Sea Lily poison. It won't work right now, because the air in the courts is infested with poison water droplets. They get reinfected with every breath.

The air here is clean and fresh. Once we bring the people here, I'm almost sure the Tamarisk will work. Once we treat them and the people recover, everyone can live here, together, while the poison clears from their homes."

Kai grinned back at her, then he stared down at the bowl, frowning. "But how will we get the sick people here? They'll be too weak to make the trip."

Elysia gestured to the golden bowl. "We'll carry the water back to them." She gripped Kai's arm. "Now that you've drunk it, don't you feel a strength unlike any you've ever known? One or two drops per person will be enough to strengthen their bodies for the journey. And if some are still too weak to swim, the seahorses can carry them here or we can use Lady Sirena's glass carriage. Seamus and Ena can help us."

Elysia stood, searching their surroundings. "Now all we need is something to carry the water," she murmured.

On the hillside beyond the courtyard, stood a sprawling, stone palace. Elysia flicked her eyes to it. "Maybe we can find something inside."

The entry hall of the palace was dark. Dust lay on every surface, and the air was thick with disuse. Elysia squinted through the front room, searching for the kitchen as Kai trailed behind her. She poked her head inside several doors before finding it, at the back of the right hall.

She fumbled through several cabinets before she came upon a collection of small glass bottles. Tiny stoppers closed the lids, and most were filled with various tinctures and spices. But, near the back, some of the bottles were empty. Elysia swiped four of them. She tucked them into her bag, hopeful for the first time in days.

As quickly as they could, she and Kai filled the bottles to the brim with the water from the golden bowl. Then, they hurried from the courtyard, shutting the large golden door soundly behind them.

Kai whistled low, and soon, the thundering grey sea horses appeared from behind the dome. They galloped swiftly through the open water, barely slowing as Kai and Elysia swung onto their backs.

Soon, they were back in the Court of Merrows. The horses thundered onto the platform, and Kai dismounted, staring past the dome at the golden door in the open water. Despite its large size, it was a tiny dot on the sea floor in the distance.

"I can't believe it's been there all along," he said quietly.

Elysia nodded. She stared out at the door, then she peered sadly at his profile. "Sometimes you can't see the things that are standing right in front of you, until you are ready to see."

He flicked his eyes to her, but she quickly looked away, staring past him towards the golden door. Kai continued to stare, and she swallowed, dropping her eyes.

"Wait here," she murmured. "If these healing waters work, Ena will bring my mother to you shortly."

Abruptly, she turned, and with quick steps, she disappeared into the fortress.

Kai stared after, flexing his palm. He stood still, but his heart trailed after her, as if they were connected by a long string. He swallowed quietly. "I see you," he said softly. "I see."

Elysia worked to avoid her thoughts of Kai as she hurried to her mother's rooms. Quickly, she knelt by the bed, scanning her eyes over the coverlet. Ena and Seamus sat silently by the mattress, their eyes fixed on the ruler's face. Her mother was much worse. Her breathing was wet and ragged, and the bluish tinge around her lips had darkened to an ominous indigo.

As quickly as she could, Elysia lifted one of the small bottles. Silently, she lifted the stopper. She dropped two drops of the healing water past her mother's lips, then she knelt on the floor beside Ena and Seamus to wait.

Time passed like an eternity. What were mere moments seemed to Elysia to stretch on endlessly. The waiting had no end. She braced her forehead on the coverlet, breathing a prayer, and holding on to hope.

She almost gave up, certain her plan had failed. But, soon, the bluish color around her mother's mouth lightened. She coughed slightly, then she took a deep breath, fluttering her eyes open.

Elysia grasped her mother's palm. Her fingers were warm, and the color was returning to her cheeks, but she was still very weak. "Water," she whispered.

Elysia hurried to drip several more drops of the healing water onto her mother's tongue. She was careful to save enough for the rest. There were so many others she needed to treat, and she knew her mother would be fine, now. She turned to Ena.

"As soon as she's able to stand, take her to meet Kai on the platform." Ena frowned in confusion, but Elysia shook her head. "I can't explain. You wouldn't believe it if I told you. Just know she's going to a safe place. Once you've taken her to Kai, meet me at the palace."

She turned to Seamus, handing him a small glass bottle of the precious healing water. "Seamus, take this. I've instructed the well members of the Merrow Forces to bring the sick into the throne room. Now that they've been exposed, it's likely that they're lying sick there, too. Give them each a drop or two of this water. It should temporarily restore their strength. Then, take them to meet Kai on the platform outside the fortress."

Seamus nodded as she passed him the small bottle. "What about you?" he asked. "Where are you going?"

"To the Selkie Court," Elysia said grimly. "I think I already know who it was, but once I treat the sick, I'm going to find out who did this to us all."

Chapter 29

Elysia sped through the abandoned tunnel at top speed. The healing water had made her fast, faster than she had ever been. She grinned, wishing Kai could see her now. She was probably even faster than he was. She glided seamlessly, one with the water, until suddenly, her path was cut short.

Elysia yelped as a thick, crusty claw clamped around her waist. It lifted her out of the water, and Elysia stared in horror at the large cave creature below it. He brought her close, picking at her hair with the ends of his second arms. Then he fluttered his papery wings, and she held her breath as he opened his fangs near her head. There was a terrible stench coming from behind his teeth.

All at once, he lowered her, smacking her back flat against a large stone. He held her fast with his claw as he reached behind it, emerging with a thin, papery material. Much to Elysia's horror, he began strapping her to the stone with it. It was slick against her skin, and it smelled like gore.

Elysia's stomach turned at the stench. She thought she might vomit, but that might anger whatever beast this was she had encountered. Silently, she swallowed against the sick feeling and squeezed her eyes shut.

The creature feathered its wings once more as it settled down beside her, and Elysia turned her head, gagging. He smelled like dead flesh.

Strangely, the creature produced a small stringed instrument from behind his rock. Elysia stared down at it in surprise, and he plucked at a string with his second arms, causing a sharp note to reverberate off the cavernous ceiling. She sat silent, listening to its echoes while the creature glared at her expectantly with his eyeless face.

Elysia blinked blankly down at the instrument, then back at him. She didn't understand what he wanted from her. She watched as he made a menacing gesture with his front claw, then he plucked at another string.

Suddenly, Elysia realized what he wanted. The creature wanted her to sing. Her heart was tripping in her chest, but she opened her mouth, matching the note with a terrified quaver in her voice.

The creature chittered in delight, and Elysia smiled at him uncertainly as he plucked another note. She matched the instrument's sharp twang, wishing that Kai had told her to beware of a large, cave-dwelling trow that enjoyed musical games. Then again, they had spent nearly every moment fighting or trying to save their people from imminent death, so he probably hadn't had the chance.

They continued like this endlessly, with the terrifying creature plucking a single note, and Elysia attempting to match it, until, at last, she was completely spent. Her voice was nearly gone, and it was obvious the creature was upset. He plucked the instrument hard, and she rasped a final note. Then, her head lolled forward in exhaustion.

Elysia closed her eyes as the stinking trow released a chittering roar. The sound was terrifying, and she whipped her head up hard and fast, striking the back of it hard against the rock.

Crack. The sound of her head hitting stone split her ears as a dark, wet feeling seeped down her neck. Her vision went hazy as the creature bared his fangs. He lunged, and her eyes went dark, but not before she caught the flash of silver hair and the squish of a spear sticking through the center of the creature's chest.

Sometime later, her chin bobbed against Kai's chest as he swam hard through the tunnel.

She opened her eyes to slits, peering up at his jaw. The back of her head throbbed, and she moved her hand towards it, but Kai gently stayed her arm with his palm.

"You hit your head pretty hard back there," he said gruffly. "It's cut and bleeding." He gestured to a bag strapped across his back.

"I brought some Tamarisk with me, but I'm stopping to get more, when we reach the secret island. You can use some of what I have here to heal the wound."

Elysia nodded mutely. She flicked her eyes to his neck. The chain with Maura's golden ring floated lightly above it in the water. She stared at it thoughtfully but said nothing about it.

Soon, they arrived at the Selkie shore. Kai bent to a flat rock, sprinkling several Tamarisk blooms on it as she collected her water weaving. Then, he began grinding them into a fine paste.

The world had begun to spin as Elysia stepped onto the shore. Her head throbbed, and she stumbled, but Kai caught her in his arms. Carefully, he guided her down onto the rocks. "Lie still," he said quietly.

Elysia obeyed. She was too dizzy not to.

Gingerly, he turned her head. Then, carefully, he dabbed the paste onto her wound. It burned slightly, and Elysia hissed as his fingers patted the torn flesh. Then he scooted behind her, bracing her back against his chest.

Elysia closed her eyes. The burn felt better. In fact, she could feel the Tamarisk doing its work. The throbbing ache was gone, and she could feel the edges of the wound moving together.

In a few moments, her head stopped swimming entirely, and she sat up onto her palms.

Kai peered around her shoulder. "Okay?" he asked her.

Carefully, she touched the back of her head. The wound was

nearly closed. "Yes," she croaked.

Slowly, Kai helped her to her feet, gently bracing her upper arm. He handed her the bag full of Tamarisk. "I'm headed to the secret island, but I'll meet you back at the palace," he said quietly.

Elysia's heart sank. She was sure he was going to the treehouse again. She nodded mutely, struggling to smile as Kai grinned at her. "See you soon," he said quickly. Then he turned and jogged towards the woods.

Elysia pushed her feelings down a she hurried towards the palace. She didn't have a spare moment to wallow in self-pity. What did it matter if Kai went to the treehouse? It wasn't like they had a real marriage anyway.

It was his own business what he did, not hers. Anyway, she knew he was still in love with Maura. That was just the way things were.

And as much as she wished they were different, there was nothing she could do about that.

Chapter 30

The gardens were decimated, and the palace was charred at the edges, but to Elysia's relief, it was still standing. Silently, she crept through the back doors. Most of the furniture was broken or missing, but otherwise, the space was useable.

The throne room was the most gruesome sight. Elysia pushed past the doors, gasping as the nightmare scene came into view. Sick Selkies lay on pallets from the door to the dais. By the looks of it, nearly the whole of the islands was sick. Only a few in the clan and two Guards remained standing.

Elysia knelt beside the first pallet and put her hand to the damp forehead, watching as the little girl fluttered her eyes open. She peered briefly up into Elysia's face, then closed her eyes again. Her breathing was ragged, and she was very pale. The color around her mouth was deep blue. Elysia knew she was nearly gone.

Quickly, Elysia thrust her arm into her bag. She hurried to open the bottle of healing water, but before she could drop it onto the child's tongue, the child's breathing went quiet and the tension on her brow released.

Tears sprang into Elysia's eyes, and she bowed her head. Reverently, she pulled the linen sheet over the child's quiet face. She closed her eyes, placing her hand over the left of the girl's still chest.

All at once, strange words whispered inside of her own. They rose to her tongue, and Elysia opened her mouth, repeating what the Voice had said.

"I'll meet you past the golden bowl, by the sea with the silver strand."

There wasn't a moment to linger. Hurriedly, Elysia dried her eyes. Then she moved to the next pallet. She dropped the healing water onto the sick Selkie's tongue, and she continued in this fashion, moving from one pallet to another, until she was nearing the end of the room.

Elysia sat back onto her heels, sighing. Behind her, the treated patients were beginning to stand. She wiped the sweat from her brow, then put a hand to the back of her head, frowning. The wound from the rock was closed, but she was beginning to feel a bit woozy. She blinked past her fuzzy vision, attempting to focus on he pallet in front of her. Lord Ciar lay on it, but his body was still and silent. He was already gone. She flicked her eyes to the next pallet.

Connor lay there, nearly lifeless on his pallet next to Delia. Elysia moved towards him on wobbly legs. She knelt beside his frame, eyeing Connor's grim state. The blue color around his mouth was dark, and at first, she thought he was already gone, but as she watched, his chest rose slightly. Carefully, she parted his lips, dropping two drops of the healing water onto his tongue. Then she sat back on her heels to wait.

In moments, Connor inhaled deeply. The blue tinge lightened around his lips, and then he fluttered his eyes open. Connor blinked up at Elysia in confusion. She studied his gaze, watching as recognition registered in his eyes, and then he scrambled backward on his palms. He backed into the wall, tucking his knees to his chest.

He wrapped his arms around them, sobbing. "It was me," he croaked. "I was the one who poisoned the Court of Merrows." He shook his head rapidly back and forth. "You have to understand. I never meant for it to go this far."

Connor swallowed convulsively, swiping at his eyes. He gestured to the room.

"I never meant for all this to happen. After that day, in the garden, I was blinded by rage. And so was my father. Later that night, I hatched a plan. He would come to the meeting in the Court of Merrows with a Sea Lily bloom. He would poison your cups. But in the process, he poisoned himself and everyone else."

Tears ran freely down his face, and he swiped them with

the back of his arm. "I just…wanted to get back at you and your mother for the day in the garden. I didn't know it would do all this. Now, my father is gone…and Delia." He sobbed, moving towards Delia's limp frame to kneel beside her. "I'm so sorry…please…" He stared down at Delia anxiously, placing a hand to her pale cheek before lifting his pleading eyes to Elysia.

"Help her," he pleaded.

Delia's golden hair lay limply against her damp forehead. The skin around her lips was dark, and her breathing was shallow. Quickly, Elysia coaxed her mouth open and dropped two drops of the healing water onto her tongue. In moments, Delia's color returned, and she fluttered her eyes open.

Immediately, she searched for Connor's face. "Connor?" she rasped. Connor laughed in relief as he lifted Delia's head onto his lap. He swiped a lock of hair from her damp cheek.

"I'm here, my love, I'm here," he said in relief.

He flicked his eyes up to Elysia, and she smiled at him quietly.

"I forgive you," she said softly.

Connor blinked at her in surprise. "Thank you," he murmured. He turned his gaze back to Delia. "For all of it."

Seamus was waiting for her at the shoreline. In turn, he led each Selkie who was able to walk into the shallow water. There, he lifted them, one by one, onto the backs of large, spotted rays.

Elysia shielded her eyes, watching as he slung himself onto one. He grinned sideways, and she raised her brows in surprise.

"Rays?" she asked, grinning back at him.

"Ena's idea," he called. "She's been obsessed with them since her attack with the barb." He brushed a hand down the ray's spotted wing. "Seems that now she has the ray venom in her blood, she can coax these beauties to do anything she wishes."

Elysia giggled, and he shrugged. "She's amazing, right?!" he called brightly

Seamus didn't wait for her to answer. He held tight as the ray dove beneath the water, and Elysia laughed after him. "Amazing!" she called.

When the last Selkie had gone into the water, Kai stepped up behind her. His bag was full of Tamarisk fronds. "Ready?" he asked her.

Elysia turned. Kai was hazy in her vision, and she stumbled into him, falling into his chest as her knees buckled.

Kai grunted as she smacked into him. He caught her before she fell, then wordlessly, he swept her into his arms. He studied her face worriedly.

"Let's get you back," he said quickly. "You need to rest."

Gingerly, he lifted her onto the last ray's back, holding fast to its wing as the giant creature dove beneath the water.

Elysia felt herself growing weaker by the moment. Her head bobbed limply as the ray glided through the surf, and she drifted in a dreamlike state. Vaguely, it occurred to her that something was wrong, but she was too tired to worry much about it.

At last, they arrive at the golden door, and Kai slid her carefully from the ray's back. He cradled her in his arms as he pushed past its glittering surface. Elysia was barely conscious as he knelt before the golden bowl. Silently, he tucked his hand beneath it, gathering the silver liquid. Then he lifted his palm to her lips.

All around them, selkies and merrows sat side by side around the pool, lifting cups of the healing water in their hands.

"Drink," he commanded. Elysia obeyed, pulling down gulps of the cool, sweet liquid.

In a moment, a small amount of her strength returned, and she sat up in his arms.

"We need to prepare the Tamarisk tea," she said groggily. "The people still need it."

Kai nodded. "I'll help you," he said. Then he lifted her in his arms and headed for the palace.

Once inside, he headed for the kitchens. He sat her carefully on the countertop, then he moved towards the cupboard, rummaging through the cabinets. In a few moments, he produced a small cup. He filled it with the healing water, then dropped some blossoms into it.

Elysia watched him work from her perch. His square jaw was set in a hard line, and his brow was furrowed deeply in concentration. She giggled quietly, and Kai turned, peering at her with his too-blue eyes. He smiled.

"What's so funny?" he asked.

Elysia shook her head. "It's nothing. Just…" She bit her lip. "You make this face when you concentrate. It's, um…" She tried to mimic the set of his jaw, then she giggled, dropping her eyes. "It's nice."

He grinned back at her, raising his brows. "Compliments, huh? You really are out of it," he teased. The tea was already pink, and he handed her the cup, watching as she downed it in one gulp.

In moments, the strength returned to her face, and Kai moved in front of her, penning her in with his arms. He studied her face thoughtfully for a moment, then lifted his fingers to tuck a lock of hair behind her ear. She tried to pull away, but he stilled her with his free hand, allowing his lifted fingers to graze the back of her neck.

Elysia watched him warily as he leaned towards her. He placed a feathery kiss on her cheek, and when she didn't pull away, he grasped the back of her neck, pressing kisses down towards her chin. Elysia closed her eyes. Silently, she wrapped her hands around the back of his neck, holding him to her.

All at once, her fingers brushed against the golden chain, and her eyes popped open. She stiffened, and Kai stilled. He pulled away, frowning slightly. "What's the matter?" he said gruffly.

She swallowed convulsively, flicking her eyes to the ring as she slid off the countertop.

"The Tamarisk tea." she said quietly. "The people need it."

Then without another word, she grabbed her cup, brushing past him.

Kai sagged against the countertop, frowning after her. He didn't know what he had done wrong, but obviously, it was something. Elysia was clearly upset.

He studied her back as she turned the corner. Maybe she had been serious about their marriage being a show for the court. Maybe she didn't want him to kiss her. He narrowed his eyes. Or maybe that wasn't it at all. Maybe it was something else. Quickly, he lifted a few more cups into his arms and followed after her. He wasn't sure what was the matter, but whatever it was, he wanted to find out.

Outside, Kai, Elysia, and Seamus worked tirelessly to administer the Tamarisk tea. Through the rest of the afternoon and into the early hours of twilight, they watched the strength return to each person's ill body. Meanwhile Ena and Lady Malca, who was now more than recovered, prepared rooms in which the newly treated people could convalesce.

The Lost Lands had no shortage of space. Their new home was a large island, surrounded by a sparkling crystal sea. Ancient stone buildings cascaded down the hillside from beyond the palace and the front courtyard, spilling down towards a winding shore of silver sand. Above them, fresh air and blue sky surrounded, illuminated in the day by two bright suns and at night by a single, full moon.

Elysia stared up at the wide sky, smiling. The suns were setting on the horizon, and the large, glowing moon was starting to rise.

It was so beautiful—more beautiful than she could have imagined. She understood why her father had sealed the door. It was too precious a place to risk.

Suddenly, the sky blurred. Elysia swayed, and she braced herself on a large column. Silently, she put a hand to her forehead. Despite having drunk the Tamarisk tea, her body felt drained, weaker than it had been even a few moments ago. Slowly, she moved towards the palace, climbing the steps to the door with heavy feet.

Kai studied her back. He frowned at her stumbling steps as she climbed, then he moved to follow her. Something was wrong.

He met her on the steps, turning her to face him. Her face was slightly pale and damp with a sheen of sweat. Kai placed a worried palm to her brow, but she brushed him off.

"I'm fine," she said groggily. "Just worn out." She took a deep breath, trying to stand. It sounded ragged.

"This adventure has been…a *lot*."

Kai frowned down at her. He put a firm hand to her back, leading her gently up the steps. "Come on. You don't look good," he said gruffly.

Ena had already made up their rooms. They were similar to the ones they had occupied at the Court of Merrows. Two large bedrooms were adjoined in the middle by a connecting door.

Kai led Elysia to her mattress. Wordlessly, he scooped her into his arms and laid her gently across it. She didn't protest as he pulled the covers under her chin. "Rest, now," he whispered. "I'll be back to check on you before dawn."

Elysia nodded weakly, watching his back as he moved through their adjoining door.

Her body felt heavy, like it was made of stone. She could feel she was too warm, but a cold sweat prickled at her arms and neck. She could barely keep her eyes open. Silently, she closed them, allowing sleep to pull her under.

Sometime in the night, she awoke in a sweat. In her half-delirious state, she thought she heard Kai moving on his side of the door. She peeked one eye open, listening as he stepped out into the hallway, but even that small movement made her head throb, and she closed her eyes again.

At daylight, Kai pushed silently past their connecting door. Elysia was still beneath the coverlet, and he crept carefully to the bedside. Her brow was damp with sweat, and tiny curls stuck to the space in front of her ears. Kai knelt beside her, swiping them away with his fingers. Then, he put a cool hand to her forehead.

Kai's heart leapt into his throat. Elysia was burning. Fear pricked the back of his neck, and his mind raced with worry.

Despite her exposure to the diving spider blood, Elysia was sick. She was sick—just like Maura had been. In fact, Elysia looked almost as weak as Maura had looked the day before she died. Kai gazed down at her helplessly. Her skin was a deathly pale shade, and the skin around her mouth was tinged dark blue.

Chapter 31

Elysia's mind was clear and white, and the center of it shimmered like a wide, crystal sea. Her body floated there, weightless, and she allowed herself to relax, bathing in the cool, clear water. The waves rocked her gently, and she stretched her arms, flicking her silver tail lightly in the surf. She let her head lie back, fanning her hair above her in the water. It was night, and the moonlight bathed her in a clean, silver glow.

Distantly, she could hear a voice. It was calling to her. She lifted her head, squinting in the voice's direction. Someone was calling to her from the shore. Their outline was hazy, but something about them was familiar. The hazy outline waved, and Elysia smiled. She lifted her hand, then dove under, cutting swiftly through the water.

As she made her way towards the shore, the hazy outline was joined by two others. The third was much smaller than the other two, a child, by the looks of it. Elysia moved closer, squinting as the outlines came into sharp relief. Then she stood in the shallow water, staring in disbelief. Her grandmother, Lady Sirena, and the young child stood on the winding silver seashore, beckoning to her.

Elysia studied the small child curiously. Something about her was very familiar. The little girl giggled, splashing towards her in the water. "It's you!" she said happily.

She reached for Elysia's hand, and Elysia took it, smiling softly as the child tugged her down to whisper in her ear.

"I've been waiting for you, past the golden bowl, by the sea with the silver strand," she whispered.

Elysia's heart squeezed at the words. She remembered her now. The girl was the first one she had treated on the Selkie Islands. But she wasn't sick any longer. She was well, and happy, and strong. Elysia smiled down at her and the girl tugged her hand, pulling her onto the winding silver sand at the shore.

Suddenly Elysia remembered her water weaving. She reached out a hand to collect it, but then she realized there was no need. A long, white linen garment hung loosely from her shoulders to her feet. She studied it in surprise, then flicked her eyes to the group. They were each wearing something similar.

Her grandmother was the first to meet her. She tugged Elysia into a tight hug. "Hello, sweet 'Lysia," she whispered.

Elysia squeezed her arms tightly around her grandmother's plump shoulders. She buried her face against her warm neck. "I've missed you," Elysia whispered.

"I know. I've missed you, too," her grandmother said softly.

Just then, Elysia felt a gentle hand on her shoulder. She pulled back, watching her grandmother smile proudly at whoever was behind her. Then Elysia turned.

Instantly, tears sprang into her eyes. She squealed in delight, jumping into his arms. Her father chuckled warmly, as he hugged her close. He spun her around in a circle, then sat her onto her feet, kissing the top of her head.

"I'm so glad you're here, my darling girl. I've missed you," he murmured into her hair. "I've been waiting."

Elysia smiled into his chest. She inhaled deeply. His scent was the same. She had forgotten it, but she remembered now, and it made her heart soar.

"I've missed you, too, Father," she whispered. "So much."

Lord Ríonan pulled back slightly, grinning as Elysia studied the lines of his face. He looked younger than she remembered. He braced his palms on her shoulders, peering deeply into her eyes, his own brown ones full of love and light. "I wish you could stay," he murmured. "But you must return, soon."

Elysia shook her head. There was nothing in the world that could make her want to leave. She studied her father's kind face and her throat constricted. "No. I want to stay," she pleaded.

He pulled her against him, whispering into her hair. "I know you do. But he needs you, my love. They all do."

CHAPTER 32

Kai flung himself to work, wetting a cloth and laying it across Elysia's burning forehead. He didn't understand it. She'd been fine, before. She'd been exposed to the diving spider blood, and besides, everyone else had been healed by the Tamarisk tea. It didn't make sense. Why was she still so sick? His heart squeezed, and he pressed his eyes shut. How could this be happening again? How could he survive without her?

Later that evening, Kai stood on the winding silver shore of the Lost Lands, staring dejectedly down at two narrow cypress boats floating in the water. Lady Sirena and Mother Ríona lay still inside of them, each wrapped in a linen sheet. Their hands were clasped at their chests, and a single Evening Star rested in each of their palms. Its blue light illuminated their faces in an ethereal glow.

Ena and Seamus stood just to his left. Ena still wore her wedding gown, and their hands were still clasped with the braided strand of silver from their wedding ceremony. Kai studied it dejectedly. He was happy for them, but his heart was heavy. Elysia was still so sick, and as he stared at the narrow boats, he wasn't at all sure she wouldn't soon be in one of them.

Silently, he released the small cypress boats from their anchor. He watched them as they floated out on the sea, and soon, they were small dots on the horizon. Kai followed them with his eyes, focusing on the bobbing dots until they disappeared out of sight. He knew it wouldn't be long until the sea reclaimed them. Soon, a wave would topple the narrow boats in the surf and the bodies inside of them would settle to rest in the depths.

For Kai, the next days passed in a haze. Though Elysia did not improve, and his fear and grief did not relent, he assumed the throne of the Court of the Sea with flourish. He ruled the people with fairness and honesty, leaning heavily on the support of Seamus and Ena, as well as the newly combined councils.

In the weeks that followed Kai's ascension, the community behind the golden door thrived. Though meant for harm, the Sea Lily poison had worked for the good of the Court of Sea. Selkie and Merrow lived side by side in the Lost Lands, enjoying a peace and harmony that many had never known. Long after it was safe to return, the people chose to stay behind the golden door, and Kai knew Lady Sirena would be pleased if she could see the clans, now, from her side of the Hereafter. He often hoped she could.

When he wasn't by Elysia's bedside, Kai would often sit on the winding silver strand by the sea. He would gaze out over the water, hoping for solace, but everywhere he looked, he was reminded of Elysia and the love he might've lost. So, in his own way, he tried his best to prepare for her death.

After Elysia had fallen ill, he had begun to think heavily on his past, as well as his future. It had been on his mind for a while, especially after his and Elysia's marriage vows, that he should let go of Maura's ring. So, one day, he did just that. He took it from his neck, and he tossed it into the sea, watching as a silver line followed its skipping path in the surf.

The line dissolved as the ring sank softly to the bottom, and to his surprise, Kai felt strangely lighter. He wished it hadn't taken him so long. Maura had asked him to release her, and he had partially done so, but if he was being honest, he hadn't really moved on. Not until now.

Now that he had let go of the ring, he felt completely free—ready to move on with his life. But he wasn't sure he would get the chance. He wouldn't unless Elysia recovered. He hoped to the Source she would, because Kai didn't think he could bear the alternative.

He had thought that nothing could hurt him more than Maura's death. After he lost her, he was convinced he would never recover. But his marriage seal with Elysia had awakened feelings in him he had never known. It was an even deeper bond than he had shared with Maura. If he were to lose her, he knew he would never get past it.

Back in her rooms, Kai stared anxiously at Elysia's still frame. He dabbed her brow, then placed the Tamarisk poultice across it.

"Ena and Seamus are having a baby," he said quietly. Elysia didn't move, and he swallowed past the lump in his throat, wishing the good news could've been their own.

Later that evening, he sat down on a flat rock at the shore. Silently, he twirled a pink Tamarisk frond in his palm. As usual, his chest ached to the left of his heart. He rubbed at the spot and peered down at the Tamarisk blossom, then gazed out over the water. He had no words for the depths of his sorrow, and the sea, in return, echoed his silence. He hung his head, running his fingers through his silver hair.

All at once, an idea formed in the corner of his mind. Kai stood, staring thoughtfully down at the Tamarisk blossom. Then he turned and strode up the hillside, stopping at the highest point to stare down on the winding silver strand of sand below. He knelt there, scraping his fingers into the dirt, until a shallow hole had formed in the ground in front of him. Then, carefully, he placed the Tamarisk frond inside of it. He covered it with the dark soil, then sat back on his knees, smiling down at it.

In the morning, he returned to the hillside, and his heart leapt with excitement. The Tamarisk tree had grown to his knees. After that, each evening, when the moon was high, and it shone brightly on the silver sands of the shore below, he would return to the Tamarisk tree. Within days, it was taller than his head, and soon, several other small shoots had erupted from the ground around it. By the span of some weeks, an entire grove of Tamarisk trees circled the hill like a crown.

One evening, Kai sat beneath the Tamarisk tree closest to the water. In deep thought, he peered out from the low hanging limbs, across the sea. In his mind, the memory of Elysia dancing in the grove of the secret island played before his eyes. He could almost see her, baring her slim shoulder before she dove into the water.

In that moment, something moved in the grove behind him. Kai turned his head, peering beneath the low branches. For a moment, there was no sound. Then, all at once, Connor stalked into the grove with his spear drawn.

A deep fear twisted in Kai's belly as he watched Connor turn in a circle. He watched as his dark eyes peered hard beneath the Tamarisk branches.

"I know you're in here, Kai," he sneered. "Might as well come on out."

Kai waited for a moment, frozen in place. He'd left his spear back at the palace. There hadn't been much need of it since coming to the Lost Lands. There was peace, and though he still kept a small Force and Guard, he'd all but abandoned carrying his own spear. He studied Connor's weapon and ground his teeth, wishing he had brought it.

Silently, he reached for a small rock, then he emerged from beneath the low hanging branches. Connor spun towards him, and before Kai could speak, he held the spear up to his throat. Kai swallowed hard against the cold spear's blade. He dropped the rock, holding his arms up in surrender.

Connor's eyes were a strange mixture of hatred and sorrow. He pushed the spear harder against Kai's neck, drawing a thin line of blood. "You don't have to do this, Connor," Kai breathed.

CHAPTER 33

Lord Ríonan smiled as he gestured towards the crystal water.

"There's someone out there waiting for you," he said quietly.

Elysia turned her head. In the shallow waves, a young merrow woman with dark reddish-brown hair beckoned to her.

"She's come to take you home," Lord Ríonan said solemnly.

Elysia studied the young woman silently as her golden eyes danced above the surf. There was something about her that was vaguely familiar. The woman smiled and Elysia returned the gesture, studying her lovely face. She felt like she knew her, though she knew she had never met her before.

Uncertainly, she turned back to her father. He smiled encouragingly, and she flung herself into his arms, squeezing. "I'll see you soon," he said softly.

Elysia nodded. "I'll miss you 'til then," she said quietly. Then, she pulled away and turned towards Lady Sirena.

The merrow pulled her close. "Take care of him, Elysia," she said softly. "He loves you. I am sure of it." Elysia's heart swelled, and she hugged the ruler's slim frame tightly before turning to her grandmother.

Mother Ríona was younger than Elysia had ever seen her. Her face glowed brightly as she squeezed Elysia's palms.

"Hold to the promise, dear 'Lysia. Listen to the Voice. It has led you here, and it will lead you on, and when the day comes, it will lead you beyond."

Elysia nodded. She bent to kiss her grandmother's cheek. Then, she turned towards the water.

The dark-haired merrow woman was still waiting patiently in the shallow waves. Elysia took one last look at the winding silver shore, where its occupants gathered in a small cluster. They raised their hands to wave at her, and she lifted her hand before diving into the water. She would miss them all, but she knew, someday she would meet them here again.

She surfaced next to the merrow woman, who grinned at her, then clasped Elysia's hand in her palm. At her touch, Elysia gasped as a silver shock bolted up through her arm. With it, a cascade of memories played rapidly inside her mind. Some of the memories were distant and some were very close.

At first, the young woman was a girl. She played in the gardens of the Merrow palace with a young boy. A shock of silver hair fell over his forehead. He broke into a run, chasing her, and the girl shrieked as the image swirled. Now, she and the young boy were older. He grabbed her hand and whispered something into her ear, and the young woman giggled with delight.

Faster and faster the images flew, until the young woman was nearing Elysia's age. She sat on a set of wooden steps, leading up to a treehouse. Kai held out a golden ring, and she put it onto her finger.

The image spun, and then, the woman was diving into a Sea Lily grove. Elysia watched as the woman fell heavily to the sea floor. Kai's face was a mask of horror. "Maura!" he screamed.

But it was too late. The ring slipped off her finger from the bed where she laid, and she was gone.

Maura released Elysia's hand, peering at her with sparkling gold eyes. Elysia gazed into her face in wonder. "Maura," she said quietly. "It's a pleasure to meet you. I've heard so many wonderful things."

Maura giggled. It was a tinkling sound. "As have I," she said kindly.

"But we must not linger. Kai needs you. Take my hand. He's in the Tamarisk grove."

CHAPTER 34

Connor's hands gripped white against the spear, and he swallowed convulsively. "Yes, Kai, I do. I know I told Elysia I was sorry, but I promised my father, no matter what, I would take the throne.

Once you're gone, there will be nothing else standing in my way." He ground his teeth in anguish. "The selkie throne was my destiny, and you've taken that from me." He shrugged. Murder was in his eyes. "But I suppose this is even better. Now, I'll have the Lost Lands, too.

After I kill you, I'll make sure Elysia is dead. Then, I'll put Delia on the throne beside me. Once I get rid of your friends and the council, we'll reverse the treaty, and I'll exile the Merrows from the Lost Lands. The lands behind the golden door will be Selkie, as they were always meant to be."

Kai stood silent for a moment. He peered quietly at the emotions playing across Connor's face. He was gripping his spear too lightly. With the right push, it would be easy to knock him off balance.

With that in mind, he brought his arm swiftly up against the shaft of the spear, knocking it to the side. Connor stumbled, and Kai reach for the rock, but Connor was faster. He recovered quickly, lunged towards Kai as he swiped him off his feet with his spear.

Kai groaned as he landed on his stomach with a thud. The rock tumbled from his fingers, but he scrambled to grab it as he jumped to his feet. Then he spun, swinging the rock hard towards the side of Connor's head.

Kai lost his balance as Connor dodged his hit. The Selkie quickly righted himself, but Kai was not so fast to recover. Before he could get his feet, Connor lunged towards him, lodging the spear just beneath his right shoulder.

Kai shuddered as the spear squished into his flesh. Blood poured from the wound, and he grasped the shaft in shock, then he fell onto his back beneath the low limbs of the tree behind him. Connor stared down at Kai with a mix of hate and horror. Then he pulled the blade free and turned, fleeing from the hillside.

Connor ran as fast as he could, out of the grove and into a valley below. A stream wound through the narrow valley, and in his haste to flee over it, his foot slipped on a moss-covered rock. He yelped loudly as his feet flew out from under him. And then he fell backward, striking his head on the sharp corner of the rock's edge.

Blood flowed freely from the deep wound, darkening the path of the crystal stream. Connor tried to reach a hand to the back of his head, but he couldn't feel anything from the neck down. For a moment, he lay there in disbelief. Then, his eyes went dark, and he exhaled his last breath.

Dark blood poured from Kai's wound, wetting his shirt. It pooled in a large puddle on the ground beneath him, and it occurred to him, in that moment, that he was going to die. He relaxed against the soft earth and allowed his head to fall to the side. Below him, the silver strand of sand glowed in the moonlight, and the waves of the wide sea lapped gently against its shore. As he lay there, a strange peace enveloped his mind, and he closed his eyes, imaging himself drifting away on the water.

In moments, he floated in a white, crystal sea. The moonlight shone softly on his face, and he flicked his tail, allowing the cool water to slide gently over his body. Somewhere to his side, a woman was singing. He lifted his head and listened to the sound.

High on the hillside, above the winding silver strand, was a lovely Tamarisk grove. He peered up at it as he lifted himself from the water. The woman was singing from the midst of the grove, and it was a lovely sound.

Silently, Kai climbed the hillside. He wove between the low hanging branches, listening to the woman sing. At last, he came to her—a dark-haired woman standing in the midst of the grove. It was she who was singing the song. She was facing away from him, and she held a strand of braided silver ribbon in her hand.

> The silver strand,
> It binds our love,
> It binds my heart to thee,
> The silver strand,
> Glows bright and clear,
> It leads you back to me.
> I'll meet you there,
> My soul's own love,
> On the hill by the silver strand.
> I'll hold my end,
> My soul's own love,
> I'll hold fast to the silver strand.

Kai moved towards her. He stood just behind her, his heart beating out of his chest as he placed a hand on her shoulder. She spun…

CHAPTER 35

Elysia shook Kai's shoulders violently. "Wake up, Kai!" she shouted. Dark blood spurted from the wound on his shoulder, and she pressed the hem of her dress on top of it, hissing.

Quickly, she reached her free hand into her bag and lifted a bottle of Tamarisk tea from it. She opened Kai's mouth and dropped some onto his tongue. She waited, watching as Kai laid still, until all at once, he sputtered and choked. Then he fluttered his eyes open.

Elysia hovered above him. She was crying. A tear dripped onto his cheek, and she swiped it with her thumb.

"Elysia?" he said groggily. "Yes, it's me, Kai!" she cried. "I came back to you, and now, you've come back to me." She bent, raining kisses onto his cheek, and he wrapped his arms across her back, grinning.

She pulled away to wipe her eyes, and Kai sat up onto his palms, wincing. Elysia braced his shoulder, watching as he reached into his pocket. She sat back onto her knees as Kai lifted the silver strand from their wedding ceremony.

He peered at her lovingly as he held tightly to his end, and Elysia's tears began anew. Slowly, she reached to grasp her own end of the strand. Kai smiled at her, then pulled the cord gently, tugging her into a kiss.

As they held each other, the braid of the silver strand glowed between their palms, and below them, the silver strand of sand glowed beneath the light of the bright moon. It wound softly along the shores of the crystal sea, its never-ending path infinite and eternal.

Keep reading for a bonus epilogue!

EPILOGUE

A few days later, in the palace of the Lost Lands, Kai sat beside Elysia on their newly acquired thrones. He squeezed her palm and stood, addressing the Court of the Sea. In his hands he held one end of the silver strand from their wedding ceremony. The three-fold cord wound down from his palm, gently brushing the floor of the dais.

"Today, we honor those who have given their lives in pursuit of the peace and the place in which we now live. The Source has, in great mercy, led us to the Lost Lands, a home we have longed to know.

While we, here, in the Lost Lands, are thankful for great healing and great peace, we know that, beyond us, there is a greater healing and greater peace we have yet to see, in a home we have yet to know.

While we grieve those who have passed on before us, it is this we know: It's to the silver strand they have gone."

He lifted the braid of the silver strand in his palm and Elysia stood, grasping the other end.

"And it's the silver strand that binds us. Though the cord of this life has broken for those who have passed before us, the silver strand yet remains; renewed, strengthened, and alive. The three-fold cord holds us to one another, to those who have gone before, and to the Source.

So let us have peace in the knowing, we will meet them there, one day soon. When the day has come, we who remain will pass beyond. We will step through the door into the Hereafter. We will meet them there, past the golden bowl, by the sea with the silver strand."

Read on for an exclusive first look at book 3
in The Chronicles of Caelium series!

THE OPEN DOOR

CHARLEMAYNE REEVES

Chapter 1

BEN

Benjamin frowned as he bent to eye level with the wooden beams of his latest project. The right corner slat just wasn't fitting the way he wanted. It was slightly off-center. He scanned the slat for the umpteenth time, then shook his head, frustration creasing his brow. He couldn't see anything amiss. Sighing, he moved his eyes back over the wooden bars. He'd been working on this project for weeks, now. The Castle Ball was fast-approaching, and if he didn't find the problem soon his gift wasn't going to be ready in time.

At last, he spied it. There was a tiny bend in the wood at the edge of the longer beam where it slid in place with the crossbar.

"Ah, there you are," he whispered. Grinning, he pulled it free.

He moved to the lathe, working to smooth the bend into submission. He had done the same maneuver more times today than he could count. The muscles in his back and arms ached with fatigue. They strained with his effort, and a line of sweat ran through his brow towards his right eye. He paused to swipe it with the back of his sleeve.

A few more passes, and he held up the beam again. The bend looked smooth, but looks could be deceiving. He'd been fooled before. This time, though, the beam fit just right. To Ben's relief, it slid right into place. He blew out a breath, slipping a wooden peg through the slot. "Finally," he breathed.

He tapped the peg gently with his mallet, then he stepped back and admired the new piece. For all his smoothing and re-smoothing, Ben was satisfied. It looked great. All it needed now was a nice stain, then the crib would be ready for its tiny, new occupant.

Exhausted, Ben collapsed into a worn leather chair in the corner and laid his head back against the seat. He had converted the back room at the Timekeeper's Court into his workshop after the fall of the Court of Orm. Peace had blanketed the land in sleepy silence for several cycles, now, and Benjamin enjoyed the quiet solace of his West Mountains home and the workshop where he spent many of his afternoons. Sunlight streamed through the open window, and dust motes floated peacefully in its rays towards the wood shavings littering the floor. His well-used lathe sat atop them in the center of the room, along with the new piece and several stacks of wood of various shapes and sizes. Pots of stain and paint sat in shelving along the walls, and his tools hung from pegs and sat in boxes beneath them on the floor.

A narrow cot perched in the corner. Rumpled blankets were strewn across it. He slept there often when he had worked well past dinner, and he was too exhausted to climb the steps to his room. Last night had been one of those nights. So had a lot of others recently. Benjamin had been working endlessly on the new piece. He was trying to have it ready before for the Castle Ball, but with all the other responsibilities of his role as steward of the Timekeeper's Court, the extra work had exhausted him. Even though his woodworking added to his load, he enjoyed the silence of the shop. Working with his hands eased his burdens somehow.

He sighed as he ran a hand through his too-long hair. The thick golden strands curled on their ends and reached well past the pointed tips of his ears. He was going to need a haircut, soon. He scratched absently at the edge of his jaw, where a thick patch of stubble was growing over his chin. That, and a shave. It was probably best if he did it before tonight's dinner, too. That was, if he could manage to drag his tired frame up the steps to his room.

The muscles in his temples ached, and he gazed longingly at the cot in the corner. Just a short rest before dinner, that was all he needed. He closed his eyes, too tired to move from his seat.

He was just drifting off when a loud rap sounded on the window in front of him. A small smile formed on his lips at the sound. He already knew who it would be. He sighed, opening one eye to a slit and gazing groggily through the glass pane at the far end of the room.

Reina's wavy, red hair fanned out from her face like a wide halo. Her hands were cupped to the glass, and her bright green eyes peered in at him through the pane. Her bare forearms were stained with dirt, and the knees of her linen pants were muddy from working in the garden. She was always there after training. It was her special place, just like the workshop was Ben's.

"Get up, sleepyhead!" she shouted. Her voice sounded muffled through the windowpane. "It's almost time for dinner!"

Benjamin closed his eye. Pretending to ignore her, he threw an arm over his face, settling further into the chair as he tried to hide his grin. He knew the action would irritate her, and irritating Reina was one of his favorite things to do. He pressed his lips together, stifling a laugh as her growl of annoyance sounded through the glass. She waited a moment more. Ben didn't move.

"Ben! Seriously! Don't make me come in there!"

Ben dropped his arm, chuckling as he gazed through the window at her. Reina smirked. "Very funny." She made a rolling gesture with her hand, as if to say, 'get a move on.' Her look was enough to make him know she meant business.

Ben held up his hands. "Alright, alright, no need to get huffy," he teased.

Slowly, Benjamin pulled himself to stand. He made an

exaggerated display of moving at a creeping pace as he stretched his arms, yawning. He ruffled his hands through his messy hair, making it stand on end as he eyed the cot in the corner. "Maybe just a short nap before dinner?" He slid his eyes to Reina, watching her warning glare intensify. Her green eyes smoldered, and he flashed her another grin, holding up his hands. "Alright. I'm coming."

Reina narrowed her eyes. "You better be," she said quietly. Then she disappeared from the glass.

Ben turned back to the workshop, another chuckle rumbling in his chest. A pile of wood was stacked on the floor at his feet. He didn't see the end of one long beam sticking out in his path, and he hung it with his smallest toe as he turned. A jolt of sharp pain shot up from his foot as his toe turned at a wrong angle. "Ah!" Ben hopped to the cot on his good foot, pressing his mouth together as his toe throbbed. He sat, tucking his knee to his chest and holding his foot in his palms. He pressed his hurt toe with his fingers, glad Reina hadn't seen it. He knew what she would say. "Serves you right for not covering those feet! Who works without shoes anyway, Ben?!" Ben smirked at her imaginary words. Reina was always on him about wearing shoes.

Silently, he scanned the room. The floor and the work bench were littered with supplies, wood chips, and shavings. He should really pick up before dinner, but it was already so late. He thought of Reina's sharp green eyes peering through the window. She wouldn't stand for him being late, again. Especially not after last time. Ben had barely made it to dinner before dessert and coffee were served. He'd come barefoot and still dressed in his work clothes. Reina had been furious.

He grinned. Her face was almost worth repeating his infraction, but he wouldn't irritate her further. Not tonight, anyway. Cleanup would have to wait. Besides, he was too tired to do it right now.

So many of his responsibilities felt like that lately—too much work for a too tired Ben. Most days, he was stretched beyond capacity. But it couldn't be helped. There was just so much to do as steward of The Timekeeper's Court. Ben worried things would fall through the cracks.

Johann and Henri had helped him with the fleet of griffins for several cycles, and they mostly had it in hand. But other things weren't so easy to delegate—like the Mortal Timekeepers. Most of them were well-acclimated to life in Caelium after leaving their Mortal homes to battle the Court of Orm with the king's army. Some had elected to leave Caelium after Orm's defeat and return through the gate, but the ones who had stayed still needed training and skills practice. They needed to stay sharp. Who knew when they would need to stand and fight again?

At first, Ben had felt inadequate to the task. It was terrifying to think that it was mostly up to him to train the Timekeepers. He wasn't even a Timekeeper in his own right, so how could he train those who were? As a Mountain Fairy, he had no special skills. He couldn't control the elements like the Timekeepers could, and he had never trained anyone outside of the griffin's stable yard.

It was Arto and Lina who had convinced him. For some reason, they believed in him. The Master Timekeeper to the king and his mate, the Princess, had seen something in him he still could not see in himself. Arto had said he had a "leadership quality that people responded to," or something like that. Ben didn't quite believe him, but according to Master Arto, this quality was what made him the "obvious choice" for stewarding the Mortal Timekeepers and the Timekeeper's Court after he left to live with his Royal wife in Leyth Castle.

It probably had something to do with his heritage. Ben had, at one time, been the heir to the Court of Mountain Fairies. But that was before. Before Orm stole the throne from King Ard-Mathan, and before his parents, and nearly everyone he knew had been killed and his court had been destroyed by the giants and the fires of the drake. Now, the Court of Mountain Fairies lay as a pile of rubble in a valley further south. Ben's heart still ached with the memory. His true home was gone forever.

After their court was destroyed, Ben and the few others who had survived had taken up residence at the Timekeeper's Court with Benjamin's grandmother Ita, where they'd lived for many cycles. But his grandmother was gone, now. She had been killed in an attack by the Court of Orm—the last of his family.

Since her death, the Timekeeper's Court had felt even less like home. Of course, Ben was grateful that Master Arto had opened his court to them, but Ben had to admit that he spent most of his days there feeling overwhelmed and out of place.

When Ben had first come to the Timekeeper's Court, Master Arto had placed him in charge of the griffins. Ben had gladly spent his days in the stable yard with Johann and Henri, and he had come to love caring for the large, flying animals that lived there. When Arto was home, he had personally seen that Ben was taught the Histories and well-trained for combat. His lessons had served him well in the battle with the Court of Orm, and now, he felt well-equipped to pass on those skills to the Timekeepers. Combat wasn't the problem. Thanks to Arto, Ben could teach those skills in his sleep. But the Timekeepers had special skills of their own, and Ben was at a loss when it came to their powers. *That* was the problem. The powers.

Each Timekeeper had developed a gifting since passing through the gate into Caelium. Ben was hopeless when it came to that side of their training. He was mystified by their abilities to manipulate water, earth, air, and fire. Thankfully, he had Reina. Almost immediately, she had taken the helm on that side of the training. Ben didn't know what he would do without her.

Reina was a Timekeeper herself and natural leader. The group responded well to her. Ben did, too. In fact, she had helped him understand, as best he could without performing the skills himself, the Timekeepers' abilities. Because of her, he'd learned to incorporate their skills into their daily training. He, in turn, had taught Reina to fly on a griffin's back and had helped her with the more physical battle maneuvers. He also taught her the Histories and incorporated the same lessons into the Timekeeper's training.

Reina was often bored with the Histories, and she would grumble and squirm in her seat in the library alcove when he brought out the large book-a copy lent to him by the Princess Lina herself. But the Histories were a necessity. Ben ignored her, no matter how much she protested. Often, he found himself repeating Arto's words. "You must understand Caelium's past in order to prepare for its future."

Ben understood that wisdom, but after Orm's deafeat, he hoped they'd never need to fight again. So far they hadn't, but evil would always lurk in the deep and dark corners of the realm. So, Ben vowed to keep his corner of the West Mountains ready. And, despite her protests at the Histories' lessons, Reina was helping him to do just that.

Reina was like Ben's right hand. In many ways, he felt as if she had always been with him. They were so close that Ben sometimes wondered if they could read each other's minds. The two of them were a 'great pair.' At least, that's what Amelie always said. Ben knew she was hinting at more than friendship, but he shrugged off her words every time she said them. He and Reina were best friends. Nothing more. Why couldn't everyone just accept that fact?

It was funny. Before Reina had come through the gate, he had always been more of a solitary creature. He preferred to spend his days in the stables with the griffins. Master Arto had somehow sensed his need to be alone when he'd first come to the Timekeeper's Court, and Ben would always be grateful that he was allowed those early cycles after his parents' death and the destruction of his court to grieve with only the griffins to see. But now? Now, he'd hardly make it through his early morning before he would be off in search of Reina.

Most people made him feel self-conscious, and he felt drained if he was around anyone for too long. Every day after Timekeeper training, he would retreat to his workshop or hop on the back of a griffin and take to the skies, craving the restorative solitude of the open air. His favorite spot was just south of the Timekeeper's Court, where he would hide out beneath the falls of a wide pool, finally able to release his breath. But Reina didn't make him feel that way at all. He didn't feel drained after being with her. Not even if he was with her for the whole day. Not even a little bit.

Wearily, he stepped into the hall and shut the door of his workshop. He moved through the house, ignoring the ache of his limbs as he trudged up the entry hall steps to the second floor. At the top, he turned right. Ben nearly always went barefoot, and he savored the feeling of the plush carpet of the upper hall beneath his tired feet. Once behind his door, he flopped onto his mattress and stared up at the ceiling. Green vines curled across the exposed beams. They had just begun to bloom, and the delicate white moonflowers gave the room a heady scent. He inhaled, struggling to lift his heavy eyelids. If he wasn't careful, he would be lulled to sleep under their thick canopy.

Sighing, he hauled himself upright and scratched his head, causing a wood shaving to fall from his hair to his lap. He watched it as it tumbled onto his work pants, then flicked it to the floor with his thumb. Its tip was tinged dark with wood stain. Slowly, he stood and lifted his arms in a stretch, his shirt crinkling with the movement. It was stiff with dried sweat. He sniffed the crook of his arm. "Ech." There was no doubt about it. He would have to bathe before dinner. If he showed up like this, Reina's angry face would be nearly as red as her hair.

He chuckled, imagining her temper flaring out of control at his appearance and her fingers igniting with flames. Her fiery temper matched her curly locks, that was for sure. And both certainly went well with her fire skill. He could see her pointed green eyes now, glaring at him across the table, struggling to keep her heating fingers in check. It was a tempting idea, but he thought better of his prank and lifted the stiff shirt over his head as he padded to the bathing room. It was her special night, after all. He couldn't tease her too much.

The hot water had made him feel better. It had infused him with energy and loosened his tired muscles. His arms and shoulders barely ached as he pulled a clean dinner shirt over his head. He moved to the mirror, checking his appearance. The gold of his curls was tinged dark with water and the stubble still grew on the square turn of his jaw, but at least he was clean. "Good enough," he muttered. He tucked the tail of his shirt into his good slacks, grinning at the dark leather on his feet. He'd even worn shoes for the occasion. Reina couldn't balk at such an effort, even if he was going to be a *tiny* bit late.

Mountain Fairies almost never wore shoes, and Ben was no different. It was the one holdover from his former life that he refused to relinquish. His grandmother, Ita, had always worn them, but then again, she'd been…domesticated. Her days at Leyth Castle and the Timekeeper's Court had seen to that. Besides, she had been the realm's healer. Shoes were a necessity if you were going to travel all over the realm. Ben grinned at her memory, his heart giving a squeeze. He still missed her more than words could say.

Benjamin had never seen Johann or Henri wear shoes. Granted, his friends spent more time in the stable yard with the griffins than they did with anyone else, and shoes weren't a requirement for riding griffins.

Unlike her constant pestering of Ben, Reina had never mentioned Johann or Henri's lack of footwear. At first, Ben had balked when she insisted that he wear shoes to dinner. But still, she had insisted. She said it was only proper that the steward of the Timekeeper's Court wore them. Ben didn't understand why she thought it was 'proper', but he guessed it had something to do with her being from the Mortal Realm. Rules were different there, or so he guessed.

Eventually, like most things she asked, he'd given in. Ben had pretended he hadn't seen her small smile when he showed up to dinner that first night with shoes on. But of course, he had noticed. He noticed everything about Reina.

He grinned as he flipped down his collar, smoothing its edge. If he didn't have time to shave, at least his shirt could look presentable. After all, tonight was Reina's 21st birthday. Marking her Mortal birthdays had given Ben great enjoyment since she'd passed through the gate. He always made time to carve her some trinket or another to add to her collection, and this Mortal year had been no different. He grinned as he imagined the look on her face when she opened his gift. He was pretty sure she was going to love it.

A towering load of lumber from the Eiks in the North Forest had appeared at his door two weeks prior, with a note from Willow, the dryad leader. At the center of the forest was the Grove of Eiks, where Willow and the other dryads made their home. The Eiks were the messengers of the Four Winds, and their wood was very sacred.

Dear Benjamin,
A gift for your Reina, on her 18th birthday, from the Four Winds.
Or perhaps…it is a gift for them all.
-Willow

Benjamin had frowned down Willow's scripted scrawl. He hadn't known what she meant by "a gift for them all." In fact, the note still puzzled him. Still, he had used a small piece of the beautiful, stripped wood from a fallen Eik to craft Reina's gift.

Grinning, Ben stopped at his desk to scrawl his own quick note. Swiftly, he rifled through the stack of parchments until he found a clean scrap. Then he dipped his quill, hurrying to write his words. When he finished, he folded the note into fourths and carefully tucked it into his pocket for later. Then he swiped Reina's small gift from the shelf above the desk and headed towards the dining hall.

He thought about Reina as he moved down the steps. In the past, she'd been excited for her birthday dinner. She'd spent days planning the menu and talked endlessly to Ben of flower choices and her own attire. He frowned. This year, she didn't seem to be looking forward to it. She and Amelie had planned for the event as they normally did, but according to Amelie, Reina had allowed her to make most of the choices. Reina barely talked about the dinner, and when she did, Ben thought there was something…*off* in her voice. Even when she had babbled on about flower choices with him, there was a sadness in her eyes that he didn't quite understand.

Reina loved flowers. The courtyard gardens where Benjamin's grandmother had often worked were a testament to that fact. The central space of the Timekeeper's Court was overflowing with hanging vines, tall green plants, and heaps upon heaps of flowers from all across the realm. Every possible bloom from the four corners of Caelium had been propagated in the West Mountain dirt. There were tall larkspurs from the North Forest, squat water thistles from beneath the Southern Sea, wild mountain aster from their own West Mountains, desert lilies from the East, night-blooming jasmine, primrose, Evening Stars from the Selkie Isles, and so many more. Reina had spent every afternoon that Ben could remember on her hands and knees, turning over soil and clipping away wilted buds until the courtyard was nothing short of artistic beauty in living display.

It was twilight when Ben stepped into the entry hall, the heady scent of Reina's blooms lifting to his nose as he rounded the stairs. In front of him, the doors to the back courtyard were flung open, and gauzy curtains billowed inward from their high frames. The petals of the towering Evening Stars Reina had planted along the walkway lit the path to the pavilion in a calming blue glow. Their bell-shaped blossoms swayed gently in the warm evening breeze.

Ben scanned the entry hall. When no one appeared, he tucked himself beneath the stairs, hiding between two tall columns to wait for Reina. The narrow space beneath the stairs was one of his and Reina's secret spots. They always met here before dinner to have a moment alone before going in to the dining hall with the rest of the group.

Tonight, though, Ben had another motive. He wanted to give

her his gift without the prying eyes of Johann and Henri. He knew the two of them would poke fun at him for it anyway, but at least he could have a moment alone with her while she opened it.

His two friends always seemed to get a good laugh from joking about his and Reina's close friendship. Benjamin had no idea why. He and Reina were just that—close friends. Amelie was no better. He remembered her grey eyes twinkling over a note he had written to Reina earlier in the week. He certainly didn't want to be pinned under her knowing grey gaze while he gave Reina her gift at the dinner table. So, he would do it here. All three of them would be with the others in the dining hall, by now. He would be safe to give Reina her present, tucked beneath the stairs and out of sight.

In a moment, he heard Reina's familiar footfalls descending the steps. He narrowed his eyes. Another set of footfalls matched her pace. Ben's heart sank. *Blast.* There was someone with her.

He grimaced, tucking himself further beneath the stairs as Amelie's eager voice carried to his ears. She was ticking off the boxes for Reina's dinner tonight. Amelie's long, golden hair swished as she and Reina came around the corner, and Ben stood stock still in his hiding place, waiting for the two to pass him. Reina pretended not to notice him, but he knew she would circle back once Amelie was gone.

At last, he heard Amelie's heels clacking away from him against the marble hallway. He heard Reina give her some excuse about a forgotten scarf, then he heard her soft flats padding towards him. In a moment, she slipped in beside him, smiling sheepishly. "Hi," she whispered.

Ben didn't answer. He couldn't. Not when she looked like… like *that*. He scanned her slowly from head to foot, hoping his thoughts didn't read on his face. She looked unbelievable. He wasn't used to it, and for some reason it was making him nervous. His heart skipped as she readjusted her position, brushing his arm in their narrow hiding place.

Ben cleared his throat too loudly. "Hi," he answered. His voice reverberated off the stone of the entry hall, and he nervously stepped backward, forgetting to tuck himself into their hiding place. He was nearly standing out in the hall.

Reina jerked his arm, pulling him back in beside her. "Shh, Ben! Someone will hear!" she hissed. She searched his face, her green eyes glittering in the dim light. Ben stared down at her blankly, and she frowned.

"What's wrong with you? Why are you staring at me like that?"

Ben opened his mouth, then closed it again. He didn't know how to answer. Instead, he let his eyes drift. Reina's long red curls were pinned back from her face. Tiny coils trickled down beside her cheeks and the tip of her thick locks curved down her back. Her floor-length dress was deep blue and strapless, and she wore dangling, blue sea glass earrings. He assumed they were a gift from Lady Elysia in the Court of the Sea. Delicate sandal straps peeked out from the hem of her dress. They were sewn together with silver thread. Amelie's handiwork, no doubt. He swallowed, lifting his eyes again to her face.

She frowned up at him, then glanced down at her dress, smoothing her hands across her midsection.

"Is there something on my dress?" She swished her skirt left and right, looking for an imaginary stain. Ben shook his head. "N-no," he stammered. "You look…" He gestured weakly with his hand. "You look fine."

Reina's face relaxed, and Ben smiled what he hoped was a normal smile, then reached into the pocket of his shirt, producing the note. He held it out to her, and she took it, smiling softly. "For later?" she whispered. Ben wet his lips. "Y-yes. Later," he stammered. He didn't know why, but he was still having trouble speaking. His head felt all muddled.

Reina swiped a long curl behind her neck as she studied the folded parchment, and his eyes flew to the spot, transfixed. Ben ground his teeth, gripping his fists into tight balls as he fought to ignore the sudden flurry of feeling. What was wrong with him? This was Reina he was talking to. Usually, he said what he wanted. Jokes, teasing. But right now, the curve of her neck was distracting him. He blinked at it, frowning. His throat felt sort of dry, and he pulled on the edge of his collar, clearing his throat.

Reina flicked her green eyes up to him at the sound. They crinkled at the edges with her smile, and his heart did a little flip.

He dropped his eyes to her mouth, and suddenly, there was a tinny sound in his ears. He could see her lips moving, but he couldn't hear the sound. His head felt fuzzy, and he braced an arm on the wall in front of him, leaning towards her instinctively. He was so focused on her moving mouth that it startled him when Reina nudged his shoulder. She arched one brow. "Ben? Did you hear me?"

Ben tore his eyes from her lips, dropping his arm as he stood abruptly upright. He had heard her that time. "Um, yes." He shook his head. "I mean, what did you say?" Reina grinned again, and he flicked his eyes back to her mouth. She had put something on her lips to make them slightly darker. They shimmered in the soft light. "Intoxicating," he whispered. Reina frowned. "What did you say?" Benjamin tugged on his collar. *Intoxicating??* He shook his head. "Um, nothing. I just..I think I need to eat. My head feels a little fuzzy."

He brushed his forehead lightly as Reina studied him curiously. He ignored her stare until she looked back at the parchment, and he finally released his breath. What in the name of the realm was wrong with him?! Wasn't she the same girl he'd chased through the valley on a griffin's back yesterday?

He had come to see her in the garden, to pass a note. As usual, she'd been digging in a dirt patch. This was a particularly muddy patch right beside a small stream. When she'd turned, she'd lobbed a fat mound of mud right at his face. It had hit him square in the jaw. *Thwack!* "Ha! Take that!" she had shouted. She had jumped up and run, cackling as Ben scooped up a mound of mud, taking off after her. He'd chased her all the way to the stable yard, where she'd mounted the closest griffin. He'd swung astride Jade, chasing her into the sky. Ben had followed her in the air all across the valley until he'd finally controlled his laughter enough to whistle low, signaling both griffins to return to the earth. When they touched the ground, Reina had taken off again at a run, but he'd tackled her and held her still beneath him while he smooshed the mound of mud into her cheek. His hand had been so slick that it had slid across her teeth, swiping them with gritty, dark brown sludge. "Ha! Take *that*!" he had shouted. But Reina had not been amused. She had sat silent beneath him with mud on her teeth, her shoulders heaving. Peals of laughter had rolled out of Ben's chest.

Suddenly, she'd let out a battle cry, scrambling from beneath his hold to pin him to the ground. Then she wiped her muddy cheek all over his face. He had let her. He hadn't wanted to stop her. Not even a little bit. Besides, he was laughing too hard to fight her off. That-his laughter-had only succeeded in making her madder. She'd growled loudly as her cheeks flamed red, and then she had stalked away from him, fingers flaming.

He grinned at the memory and let his eyes drift to the freckled spot on her cheek where the dark mud had been. Her skin was luminous in the evening lantern light. It looked soft. Ben wanted to brush it with his fingers. He started to reach to do just that, but he stopped himself, sticking his hand in his pocket instead. He glanced up, hoped she couldn't read his thoughts in his expression. If she could, she'd probably laugh in his face. He gripped her gift tightly in his other palm. What was he thinking?

Reina raised her slim brow. She pointed to the small package in Ben's hand, the one he was holding in a death-grip. "Is that for me?" she said quietly. Ben's eyes flicked to her mouth. *Blast.* He hadn't heard her again. "What did you say?" Reina rolled her eyes and swiped the small package from his palm. "Never mind." She lifted the package to her ear and shook it gently, then frowned over at him. "What's with you tonight, anyway? You seem…distracted."

Ben didn't answer her immediately. The candlelight from the entry hall was striking her hair in such an interesting way. It was distracting. There were tiny threads of gold in it that he hadn't noticed before. It made her look like her hair was on fire. The muscle in his jaw flexed lightly, and he stuffed his other hand into his pocket, leaning casually against the wall. He shrugged, forcing himself to look back at her face.

"It's nothing. Just got a lot going on."

Reina pressed her lips together, but she didn't question him further. Instead, she flicked her eyes back to her present and began ripping the paper off it. She stopped mid-rip and grinned. "May I?" she asked. Ben grinned, relieved to have something to focus on besides Reina. "Of course. Be my guest," he teased.

Reina pulled the rest of the paper away, revealing a small wooden box. Its top was carved to resemble a pair of wings. She grinned down at them, brushing her fingers over the carved feathers. "Lovely," she murmured. Ben smiled at her profile. "Griffin's wings," he said lightly. He studied her face, watching delight skitter across her features. "Look inside."

Reina lifted the lid. There, a satin strip of cloth cradled a small wooden bracelet. Reina gasped as she lifted it. She held it to the light, examining the details. Two delicate strands of wooden leaves were strung together with a small wire, and in the center, a perfect, star-shaped mountain aster hovered between the strands. Ben had fitted its petals with small, lavender gems, Reina's favorite color.

ABOUT THE AUTHOR

Charlemayne Reeves has been writing stories since she can remember. She comes from a family of storytellers, so it's kind of in her blood. Charlemayne is a Christian wife and mom, who enjoys telling epic tales of truth and light. She holds a master's degree from Belmont University and enjoyed a long career in healthcare prior to becoming a writer. Since, she has retreated to the hills of Tennessee with her husband, two children, and their beloved cat, Captain Meow.